CW00763114

THE

COLLECTED

SHORT

STORIES

Volume 5

Fiction Titles by P. C. Wren

Dew and Mildew. 1912
Father Gregory. 1913
The Snake and Sword. 1914.
Driftwood Spars. 1916
The Wages of Virtue. 1916
The Young Stagers. 1917
Stepsons of France. 1917
Cupid in Africa. 1920
Beau Geste. 1924
Beau Sabreur. 1926
Beau Ideal. 1928
Good Gestes. 1929
Soldiers of Misfortune. 1929
The Mammon of Righteousness. 1930 (U.S. title: Mammon)
Mysterious Waye. 1930
Sowing Glory. 1931
Valiant Dust. 1932
Flawed Blades. 1933
Action and Passion. 1933
Port o' Missing Men. 1934
Beggars' Horses. 1934 (U.S. title: The Dark Woman)
Sinbad the Soldier. 1935
Explosion. 1935
Spanish Maine. 1935 (U.S. title: The Desert Heritage)
Bubble Reputation. 1936 (U.S. title: The Cortenay Treasure)
Fort in the Jungle. 1936
The Man of a Ghost. 1937 (U.S. title: The Spur of Pride)
Worth Wile. 1937 (U.S. title: To the Hilt)
Cardboard Castle. 1938
Rough Shooting. 1938
Paper Prison. 1939 (U.S. Title: The Man the Devil Didn't Want)
The Disappearance of General Jason. 1940
Two Feet From Heaven. 1940
The Uniform of Glory. 1941
Odd—But Even So. 1941

The

Collected

Short Stories

of

Percival Christopher Wren

Volume 5

Edited

by

John L. Espley

Riner Publishing Company
Riner Virginia
2012

ISBN
978-0-9850326-4-7

Introduction and
Introductory Material
Copyright 2012
John L. Espley
espleyj@vtls.com

Contents

"Soldats de la Légion,
  De la Légion Étrangère,
  N'ayant pas de nation,
  La France est votre Mère." . . .

PREFACE

The Collected Short Stories of Percival Christopher Wren (hereafter *The Collected Short Stories*) began as a desire on my part to make the short stories and articles written by P. C. Wren more available to the reading public. His novel, *Beau Geste*, is usually recognized by most of the book dealers I have met over the years, but his other works are not so easily remembered. In my opinion, his short stories are some of his best work and worthy of greater recognition.

I have been collecting P. C. Wren for almost fifty years now, and have been working on a comprehensive bibliography for almost as long. Hopefully, the bibliography will be published later this year (2012), which is the 100th anniversary of Wren's first published work of fiction, *Dew and Mildew*.

The text of the 116 short stories published in the seven Wren collections, *Stepsons of France*, *The Young Stagers*, *Good Gestes*, *Flawed Blades*, *Port o' Missing Men*, *Rough Shooting*, and *Odd—But Even So* were easily obtained from copies in my own collection. For that collection, I certainly need to thank the hundreds of used book dealers I have purchased items from, but I need to thank by name, Steven Temple, David Mason, Walt Barrie and, especially, the late Denis McDonnell for the advice and help they have provided over the years.

For helping me obtain the text of the remaining items in *The Collected Short Stories*, I need to acknowledge the assistance and guidance of the "chums" of the Fictionmags listserv and specifically Mike Ashley. My friend, Lane Rasmussen, was able to obtain a copy of the article, "Wonderful Egypt", through the Inter-Library Loan department of our local university. My friend, Robert Maxwell, from Brigham Young University went beyond the "call of duty" when over one weekend he was able to find (after a search in the stacks for a potentially lost item) a copy of the rare periodical *Prediction*, in which the article "I Saw a Vision" appeared. The book dealer, Bevis Clarke, of Clearwater Books, is owed a great deal of thanks for making the manuscript available of the unpublished short story "Broken Glass".

Mr. John Venmore and Mr. Philip Fairweather, both descendants of the late Mr. Richard Alan Graham-Smith, Wren's stepson, and the executor of Wren's estate, have both been very helpful in providing information about Wren. Based on information provided by Mr. Venmore and Mr. Fairweather attempts have been made to contact their relative, Elizabeth Jane Ellen, the person last known to own the works of P. C. Wren. It is presumed that Ms. Ellen is deceased, but I have been unable to verify that. It has been over seventy years since the death of P. C. Wren (November 21, 1941), and it is assumed that his works have passed into the public domain.

I also need to acknowledge the help and guidance of the members of my family: my daughter and son-in-law, Dawn and Andrew; my son and daughter-in-law, Jared and Claudia; and my long-suffering wife, Cathy. Thank you.

In conclusion, I need to thank Percival Christopher Wren for the many years of great enjoyment that his stories have provided. I know that Wren is not a literary or critical success, but, at least for me, he is one of the great storytellers of the early twentieth century.

John L. Espley
Riner, Virginia
July 4, 2012

INTRODUCTION

Percival Christopher Wren is best known as a novelist, publishing twenty-eight novels from 1912 to 1941, the most famous of which being *Beau Geste* (1924). Wren also published seven short story collections: *Stepsons of France* (1917), *The Young Stagers* (1917), *Good Gestes* (1929), *Flawed Blades* (1933), *Port o' Missing Men* (1934), *Rough Shooting* (1938), and *Odd—But Even So* (1941). These short story collections contained a total of 116 stories. There were also two omnibus collections published, *Stories of the Foreign Legion* (1947) and *Dead Men's Boots* (1949), containing stories taken from *Stepsons of France*, *Good Gestes*, *Flawed Blades*, and *Port o' Missing Men*.

Wren was a man of mystery in that the more popular biographical statements about him seemed to be more fiction than fact. A typical biography has him born in Devon in 1885, educated at Oxford, and having a career of world traveler, hunter, journalist, tramp, British cavalry trooper, legionary in the French Foreign Legion, assistant director of education in Bombay, and a Justice of the Peace. Most of the above biography, however, has not been verified. Wren was born Percy Wren November 1, 1875 in Deptford, a district of South London on the banks of the Thames. He did attend Oxford University, graduating in 1898 with a 3rd class honours in History leading to a Bachelor of Arts degree. He attained his "M.A." in 1901. In those days, a person acquired a "M.A." after a certain number of years (three in Wren's case) and purchasing it.

After leaving Oxford he was a teacher at various commercial schools until 1903 when he and his family left England for India. He married Alice Lucie Shovelier in December 1899 with whom he had a daughter, Estelle Lenore Wren, born in February 1901. From 1903 to approximately 1919 Wren was employed as an educator by the Indian Educational Service (I.E.S.). During that time he published a number of educational textbooks, some of which are still in use in Indian schools today. It was at this time that he started using the name Percival C. and Percival

Christopher on the textbooks. From 1905 to 1915, he also served in the Volunteer Corps (Sind and Poona) in India (see the novel *Driftwood Spars*), and was appointed a Captain in the Indian Army Reserve of Officers, the 101st Grenadiers of the Indian Infantry, in November 1914. He probably saw action in the East African campaign of World War I (see the novel *Cupid in Africa*), and resigned from the Indian Army Reserve of Officers in November 1915.

Wren's first novel, *Dew and Mildew*, was published by Longmans, Green in 1912. His first novel of the French Foreign Legion, *The Wages of Virtue*, was published by John Murray in 1916 (written in 1913). One of the many questions about Wren, is whether he actually did serve in the French Foreign Legion. Given the chronology of his documented biography it is hard to see where he had time to actually serve in the Legion. Wren himself always maintained that he had served, and his stepson, Richard Alan Graham-Smith, who died in 2006, "strongly maintained that Wren had indeed served in the French Foreign Legion and was always quick to refute those who said otherwise."[1]

The Collected Short Stories is an attempt to bring Wren's shorter fiction back into print. Twenty-six of the 116 stories published in the seven collections have been identified as being first published in the newspapers and fiction magazines of the early twentieth century. Many of the other stories were probably published in the newspapers and fiction magazines but information about these appearances is limited since the indexing of the fiction in the newspapers and magazines of the early twentieth century is incomplete. A bibliographical history (as known as of 2012) is included in each introductory commentary to each story.

The order that the stories are presented is primarily chronological, but there are some discrepancies in order to keep some stories that were presented within a frame together. The original spelling, punctuation, and grammar have been preserved as found in the latest editions/printings of the stories during Wren's lifetime (1875-1941). The footnotes within the individual

---

[1] http://en.wikipedia.org/wiki/P._C._Wren

stories are also found in the original source material.

In addition to the 116 stories published in Wren's short story collections there are some additional items. "At Oxford: Innocent Ernest and Artful Eintz" is a short story originally published in 1919 in an obscure fiction magazine. "The Romantic Regiment" and "Twenty-Four Hours in the Foreign Legion" are "factual" articles originally published in magazines. "Wonderful Egypt" is an article (more a photographic essay) originally published in *The Strand Magazine*. The article "I Saw a Vision!" originally appeared in a rare psychic magazine, *Prediction*. There is also an interesting article found in an Australian newspaper, "Meaning of Dreams", where Wren relates a couple of dreams he had experienced. Finally there is "Broken Glass", an unpublished short story.

Volume Five

Volume five of *The Collected Short Stories* has a total of twenty seven items: nine stories from *Rough Shooting* (1938), fifteen stories from *Odd—But Even So* (1941), one previously unpublished story, one article from an Australian newspaper, and another article from a psychic magazine.

The nine stories from *Rough Shooting* utilize a framing device drawn from the novel, *Fort in the Jungle* (1936), where legionnaires, on their last night before being overrun by the Black Flags, tell each other their "dirtiest" deeds. The fifteen stories from *Odd—But Even So* include some of Wren's strongest and most interesting stories (see "Called", "The Pahwang", "Ordeal by Water", "A Fool and His Money", and the political "White Ants"). One article, "Meaning of Dreams, is where Wren relates, in some detail, a couple of his dreams, one of which he wrote into the story "As in a Glass Clearly." The other article, "I Saw a Vision!" from the psychic magazine, *Prediction*, is concerned with a day-dream he had as a young boy. The unpublished story, "Broken Glass", is attributed to Wren, but complete provenance is not available.

A DOZEN OF ALE

As noted in the very first sentence, "A Dozen of Ale" has a connection with the novel Fort in the Jungle *(1936). Part I of the novel tells the same story as the frame for Part II, "Dirty Dogs of War", of* Rough Shooting *(1938), where "A Dozen of Ale" is the first of nine stories. In "A Dozen of Ale", legionnaire Blanke tells what he is the most ashamed of. It is the story, while on safari in Africa, of sending twelve exceptional natives to run a hundred miles through the jungle to fetch twelve bottles of beer. All so Blanke could impress another white man that he met in the jungle. "A Dozen of Ale" has previously only been published in* Rough Shooting. *There is a slight discrepancy between the British title* Fort in the Jungle, *and in the footnoted title in the first line of the story below.* The Fort in the Jungle *is the U.S. title, and it is unknown, at this time, why a British edition of* Rough Shooting *would use the U.S. title and not the British title of* Fort in the Jungle.

As has been told elsewhere,[2] the Annam jungle fort of Houi-Ninh stood deep in the heart of the Annamese jungle which surrounded and almost submerged it, as does the deep green sea a little rock.

Between it and the far far distant Base was a mighty river, an almost impenetrable swamp and a vast trackless forest.

The little fort was besieged, and great hordes of flat-faced, slant-eyed fighting-men, partly brigand, partly dacoit, partly Chinese Mandarin's irregular soldiers, swarmed about it. In the gloom of the jungle, from the tall iron-wood trees, a heavy fire had been kept up for days by the Chinese, Muong, Tho, Lolo and other Annamite warriors, until more than half the garrison had fallen, the dead including the Commandant and a half-dozen non-commissioned officers.

The remainder of the garrison was now commanded by an ordinary soldier, *première classe*, the *légionnaire* Paladino, senior man present and readily accepted leader.

Had Paladino been the junior man of the survivors, he would

---

[2] *"The Fort in the Jungle."*

still have been the readily accepted leader of this handful of assorted soldiers of the French Foreign Legion, men gathered from the ends of the earth, representing a score of nationalities, and differing widely in creed and breed, in education, birth, and social experience.

And these men knew that no power on earth could save them, that no power in heaven would save them, that this was as certainly the last night of their lives as it would have been had they each been seated alone in the condemned cell, doomed by law to meet at dawn the guillotine, the hangman or the firing-party. They knew that to-morrow's dawn was inevitably the last that they would ever see; that they were face to face with death inexorable, ineluctable, death now certain as—Death.

For the victorious and triumphant army of the *pavillons noirs*, the Black Flags, jungle savages and river pirates, Tonkinese dacoits and bandits, with a large and powerful force of Chinese regulars disguised to resemble their savage allies, was bearing down upon them, to join their besiegers and to outnumber them by a hundred to one. It could and would, by weight of numbers alone, overwhelm them. Against it, they had precisely as much chance as has a snail against a steam-roller.

They could overwhelm and obliterate the little *poste* or ring it about, and with the heavy fire of their rifles alone, almost blast into dust its mud walls.

And well these doomed men knew that they had been, of necessity, abandoned to their fate, since to have saved them would have cost the lives of a hundred times their number; to have saved the little fort, a hundred times what it was worth.

This was their last night. How should it be spent? Had these men been of a homogeneous regiment whether English, Scottish, Irish, Welsh, French, German, Italian, Turkish, Serbian, Bulgarian, Swiss, Portuguese, Dutch, Greek or Spanish, their general reaction to such a situation would be to some extent predictable. Condemned to death without the possibility or faintest hope of reprieve; doomed to die at dawn without the slightest chance of escape, the men of one of those nations would have spent the night in grim jest; of a second, in dour resigned solemnity; of a third, in hectic nervous gaiety; of another, in bitter recriminations against those by whom they had been "betrayed"; of another, perhaps, in quiet prayer and pious exercises; of another, in a drunken orgy and a stout effort at the consumption of all the food and drink; of another, in the singing of national and sanctimonious songs; and of yet another, in carrying on precisely as usual.

But, of these particular men, not more than two or three were of the same nationality, and they represented most of the countries of Europe. And now they had no nation. They were soldiers of the French Foreign Legion.

> "*Soldats de la Légion*
> *De la Legion Étrangère,*
> *N'ayant pas de nation,*
> *La France est votre Mère.*"

And as General Négrier had once asked the Legion, what were they there for but to die? They were hired to die. It was simply their business.

And so on that last night they sat about a fire, a wasteful plethora of tins of "monkey meat," black issue bread, *bidons* of wine and packets of cigarettes beside them, talked and played *mini-dini* and ate and drank, and made reasonably merry with wine and song and unwonted luxury.

It was their leader, the suave cynical Paladino, a forceful yet baffling and enigmatical man, who made the suggestion as they sat about the glowing embers of the fire, drinking and smoking and waiting for death, matter-of-fact, business-like, each man *bon camarade* and *bon légionnaire*.

Although it was quite literally a case of "eat, drink, and be merry, for to-morrow we die," they maintained, from force of habit, all correct military procedure, and a sentry paced the cat-walk, a long narrow platform that lay inside the fort, four feet below the top of the wall.

"Hell!" yawned Paladino lazily, and stretched himself. "And we shall soon be there, too.

"I wonder whether *le bon Dieu* tries us one by one, or in batches, or the whole of us in a bunch," he added, as he lay back against a box of ammunition, settled himself comfortably and lit a cigarette.

"What, us? Us old *légionnaires*? Oh, one by one, of course," asserted Lemoine. "And in camera too."

"In camera? The Court cleared, and behind closed doors? Oh, too bad," grinned Borodoff. "We should have liked to hear the worst about one another."

"True," agreed Paladino. "Very true."

"Well, why not have it now?" he added, a moment later.

"Afraid we haven't quite time enough," smiled old Bethune. "My own sins alone would take . . ."

"Of course they would, *mon vieux*," agreed Paladino. "Take a month at least. I wasn't so optimistic as to imagine that we were going to have time to hear it all. Not even all yours. What I suggested was the worst. Let us each confess, fully and faithfully, truly and honestly, our own worst, blackest, beastliest deed, the act, of which, in our heart of hearts, we are most ashamed."

"Yes," agreed Lemoine. "Good. Let's do it. And no boasting."

"*Mon Dieu*, yes," chimed in O'Halloran. "Let's form a Dirty Dogs' Club, and decide who, on his own confession, is the dirtiest dog. He shall be proclaimed President, first and last President of the most short-lived Club on earth."

Paladino rose to his feet.

"Listen," he said solemnly. "I hereby declare the Dirty Dogs' Club of Houi-Ninh to be in being, or to be about to be in being. We are the original and only candidates for membership. O'Halloran is the founder. Our friends the Black Flags will be the un-founders. Let none of your confessions be unfounded, though."

Paladino turned first to Blanke, who was sitting beside him, a tall lean fair man, whose handsome and aristocratic face was far older than his years.

"Well Blanke, anything on that tender conscience of yours?"

"Plenty," smiled Blanke.

"Anything qualifying you for admission to the Dirty Dogs' Club?"

"Undoubtedly."

"Out with it, then. The worst of all the horrible things you've ever done."

"Not easy. The thing I am most ashamed of is . . . a dozen of ale."

"*Per Dio!* That sounds bad. Don't say you sat and drank the lot before your comrades arrived."

"No, I didn't drink any of it, as a matter of fact. A case of '*It is as the blood of my young men.*'"

"Drinking beer? . . . Drinking blood?" murmured Van Demon.

"You may have heard of one, David, of Jerusalem. Quite a good soldier in his day. Would have been *bon légionnaire* and *bon camarade* too. A lad who could fight, love and drink.

"As you may remember, he was in a tight place once, scrapping with the Arabs, and he and his escouade had emptied their bidons; not a drop in the whole outfit, and their tongues gone dry and hanging out. We used to know the feeling in the Sahara.

"Well, in case you've forgotten, a couple of his stout lads with an eye on the *croix de guerre* took a chance—apparently a chance in ten thousand—got among the *Arbis* and brought their officer, this David, some water. They must have had charmed lives. When they brought the water to David, he wouldn't drink it. Poured it on the ground, and said, '*It is as of the blood of my young men*' . . . Fine fellow, David."

"I remember him well," averred old Pere Pierre. "Yes, Abraham, Isaac, Jacob and their son David. Went down to Egypt and became Pharaoh or something. Got into trouble with a lady from Sheba or somewhere. Name of Madame Potiphar. Yes . . . It wasn't his beer you drank, was it?"

"I told you I didn't drink it," explained Blanke patiently.

"Then why drag him in?"

"True . . . It was in Africa. I was on *safari*, and, by bad luck, heard that there was a white man camped a few miles beyond where I was going to halt for a week or two.

"As I hadn't seen a white man or spoken a word of my own language for months, I pushed on till I came to the camp of the weirdest specimen of European humanity I ever met. If I told you all the truth about him and his outfit, you wouldn't believe me. So I'll just say he was something very unusual in the way of travellers, explorers, prospectors and big-game hunters. To begin with, although he was the goods, the genuine article, and a man with a very fine record, he was flashy, a boaster, a person of overbearing manner and overpowering swagger.

"He had an extremely bad effect on me, and brought out all the worst traits of my nature, which is saying something.

"Having invited me to chop, he actually asked me if I would care for a glass of champagne! Sounds hospitable, I know; but it wasn't. It was the purest swank and ostentation. I said I detested champagne. Greatly preferred beer.

"That took him aback a little, and he remarked that, in that case, I had better send out for some.

"As we were hundreds of miles from the nearest beer, the remark was a safe one; but as almost everything he had said and done had put my hackles up, I thought it was time I got a little of my own back, and I had an idea—unfortunately.

"Now a very curious bird had attached himself to my *safari*, in the way that wandering natives often will. You don't know when they come, but one day you are quite conscious of the fact that you have, for some time, been faintly conscious of the fact that you've seen that face before. It has been hanging around. Then you come to expect it, and more or less to look for it when you break or pitch camp; on the march; or when you go out shooting for the pot, or after lions or other big game.

"It was so with M'Pugu. He gradually happened, and then— there he was. Minister without Portfolio; servant without wages; follower without orders. Only there was a dozen of him. Either he had begun life early and worked hard, and they were his eleven sons; or else they were just a bunch of brothers, sons and nephews.

"I know I used to refer to the gang mentally as Messrs. M'Pugu and Sons; sometimes as M'Pugu Brothers, Sons and Co.; and sometimes, when I was a bit sun-dazed, as M'Pugu, M'Pugu, M'Pugu, M'Pugu, M'Pugu and M'Pugu. When I couldn't hit off the eleven before the 'and,' I just dismissed them as M'Pugu Un-Ltd.

"And they were stout lads. The sort of chaps who stand up to a lion with a spear. And when it's a case of man with spear *versus* lion with ten claws and a mouthful of teeth, the odds are heavily on the lion.

"Whether they were an outcast family of Masai, I don't know; but for pluck and endurance they might have been Zulus. Broad-chested, upstanding, straight-eyed men who ought to have been in the King's African Rifles, or trained as gun-boys, instead of being just *shenzis*.[3]

"And in an evil moment, annoyed because a fellow White Man threw his weight about, carried too much side, swaggered and boasted, I sent my personal boy for M'Pugu, knowing that he and his Eleven would be squatting round their fire, gorging the meat I had shot that day.

"M'Pugu stalked up to where I was sitting in a roorkie chair, in front of my host's grand tent—the fellow had actually got a *dhurrie* and a folding-table with a cloth on it—and I told M'Pugu to run out and fetch me a dozen of ale.

"I then proceeded to make myself a little clearer, explaining carefully to my boy, in Swahili, that M'Pugu and his band were to set off immediately for Nairassa, and there get the beer. Each one was to carry a bottle; defend it with his life; treasure it as though it were his first-born; and deliver it, with the label intact, in record time and perfect condition.

"To enable M'Pugu to get it, I scribbled a chit to the manager of Machado's Nairassa Stores, a man who knew me well, and would have sent anything for which I asked.

"I did it all with an air, in order to impress my flamboyant and pretentious host. Whether I succeeded in that high ambition I don't know, but my attempt to achieve it cost a dozen lives.

"M'Pugu and his family took me at my word.

"He and one other completed the journey—at record speed, and surely in record time.

"Ten fell and died by the wayside. Two arrived, each clasping a bottle of beer, and died at the winning-post. I don't mean fell down dead like a race-horse that some inhuman devil flogs to its death, but just died quietly and comfortably of wounds, starvation and exhaustion, after telling the tale.

"No, I didn't drink the beer."

"What exactly did you do?" enquired Paladino.

---

[3] *Simple savages.*

"Soaked the labels off the bottles and stuck them on the chests of M'Pugu and the other. Decorations—in a double sense. Victoria Crosses. And they died happy.

"Then I stuck the bottles up and shot 'em. And contemplated shooting myself. Unfortunately I didn't.

"M'Pugu lasted some hours, his follower some minutes. They had lost too much blood ever to recover. . . .

"The band had set off at a trot, proposing to run all day and all night until the weakest fell down, when they would halt until he could get up again.

"As M'Pugu said, they wanted all twelve to arrive safely. Twelve left hands for a dozen of ale, twelve right hands for the big heavy stabbing spears wherewith to protect them.

"N'Sulu had died first; because he was the last. A leopard, letting the others pass, had dropped on him from a tree, breaking his neck and tearing out his throat. They had stopped just long enough to spear the leopard and for Tsamba to get a claw-flick across the abdomen, which had done him no good. It had been a nuisance, of course, as a little piece of bowel would keep on protruding. But that didn't matter much until, on the return journey, he had to carry a bottle of beer in his left hand and could no longer use it for the purposes of compression.

"That evening, because they were travelling absolutely straight for Nairassa, making a bee-line through jungle and swamp and river, over desert and mountain, they had to swim the Umbulu river. Here they lost Koto, not so good a swimmer and lagging behind the rest. A big crocodile took him and they could do nothing about it.

"On ran the ten, and maintained their steady unchanging jog-trot until M'Sofo fell dead. He had never been quite right since an arrow had gone through him and been pulled out between his shoulder-blades. It had affected his lungs a little. Round him the rest lay for a brief space, dropping instantly asleep, as dogs do; and, on M'Pugu's order, rose as one man, and ran on until Fukolini, weary, and running carelessly, trod upon a snake which, like lightning, coiled and struck him. They rested while he died, a matter of some twenty minutes.

"And then, as M'Pugu said, their luck changed, and things

went badly. They ran into some thoroughly nasty people, gathered about a water-hole. It was absolutely essential that the runners, their tongues hanging out with thirst, should drink, for it was not merely a case of drink or die, but positively a case of drink or fail to get the beer.

"The bad people waved them away from the water-hole, using threatening gestures and evil words, so M'Pugu and his seven formed line and charged with raised spears. Most swift and fierce was their on-set, and the inhospitable bad people broke and fled, but Wolofobo, alas, took a spear-thrust in the chest. Nor, although he drank plenty of water and put his best foot foremost, could he run well or long, for the air whistled in and out through the wound, blowing little bubbles of blood. So in time, he fell, regretting and regretted, and M'Pugu put him out of his misery.

"Seven ran on and, although there were certain narrow escapes from man and beast and reptile, M'Pugu led his six into Nairassa, received the dozen of ale, turned about and, still at a fast jog trot, led them out again, himself carrying two bottles, K'Nouma carrying two, M'Sedu carrying two, Dinidini carrying two, M'Dabalaka carrying two, T'Samba carrying one and Lobi carrying one.

"To K'Nouma, M'Sedu, Dinidini and M'Dabalaka, M'Pugu entrusted two bottles each, because they were lion-men, each having killed a full-grown black-maned lion with one spear; were champion runners; and were faithful unto death.

"Swift and untiring, they ran back; and all went well with them until they ran into a fog—bad *juju* of inimical gods indeed; for how shall man run his fastest through a forest in a fog, and how shall he see the enemy who comes upon him suddenly?

"Oh yes, there are fogs in Africa. Pretty dense ones too. Quite common phenomena where a sun-blistered plain turns to swamp, or borders a big expanse of water.

"Into this fog they plunged, M'Pugu leading, his hands stretched out before him, running blindly.

"Suddenly, straight in front of him something moved. A man sprang up from behind a great tuft of high reeds. M'Pugu saw the arm swing back, the spear-blade flash, and instinctively ducked as the spear, whizzing past his head, thudded into the broad chest of K'Nouma behind him.

"With a yell, a leap, and a bound, M'Pugu drove his spear up, in a haymaker's swing, into the abdomen of this sudden assailant, and, wheeling about, found tragedy indeed, for K'Nouma, the spear transfixing his heart, had fallen, and broken both bottles in falling.

"As M'Pugu explained, had K'Nouma been but a one-bottle man, all might have been well; but one of the bottles must have struck the other as he fell, and glass is fragile and brittle, so different from iron.

"Well, there it was, and no good crying over spilt beer. And it was but poor consolation for each of the six to give the dying foeman a prod with his spear as he passed.

"That fog was a nuisance, its coming a piece of real bad luck. For it slowed the pace and caused another catastrophe.

"M'Pugu still leading, but unable to see well, suddenly felt the ground give way beneath his feet, or rather, one foot. With the other still on *terra firma*, he made a mighty effort, a spring, a wriggle, a twist, threw himself sideways, and, with a mighty scramble and roll, fell clear of the game-pit, his precious bottles held high and safe. But M'Sedu, behind him, was less agile, less lucky, and still less able to see where he was going, by reason of his leader's broad back. He fell into the game-trap and was staked; a sharp pointed bamboo clean through him, his precious burden destroyed.

"Him also M'Pugu put out of his misery.

"But this was terrible. Four bottles out of the dozen gone! Count as he might, figure it out with scratches of his spear-point on the ground as he could, M'Pugu could think of no way by which he could do other than have two of his party carry two bottles. He took Dinidini and M'Dabalaka aside and, appealing to their higher natures, their best traditions, and all the manhood that was in them, bade them not to die with their sacred charges in their hands. Carefully he wrapped the bottles in leaves that they might not knock together, and besought Dinidini and M'Dabalaka to drop them gently, nay, lay them reverently down, should catastrophe or death overtake them.

"Dinidini and M'Dabalaka promised to do their best, observing that no man can do more.

"On the party ran.

"When the fog lifted, or they ran out of it, M'Pugu fell behind and brought up the rear, that he might watch his young relatives, see all that befell, and urge them to their top speed.

"Thus it was that Dinidini and not M'Pugu received in his ear the little dart—that seemed to come from nowhere, but probably came from behind a bush not more than ten feet away—pitched on his face, broke the bottles he was carrying, was paralysed in two minutes and dead in five. The sticky stuff smeared behind the barb of the dart must have been a very powerful poison, probably of the *stropanthus* order.

"When the others would have gone bush-whacking for the pigmy archer, M'Pugu cursed them and bade them run, not for their lives but for the Beer.

"This was terrible. Half the bottles gone. Was this the way to repay the White Master's noble trust in them?

"'On, on, damn your souls and hides, you worthless sons of black bitches,' he cheerily urged the three.

"And on ran the Bearers of the Beer.

"Suddenly T'Samba collapsed. He had been doing his best about the little hole in his side, by holding the bottom of the beer-bottle against it, and had got on very nicely. But now the end of the bottle had gone right in. And what with flies and one thing and another, T'Samba was in a bad way.

"Him also M'Pugu put out of his misery, and entrusted his bottle to Lobi, young and inexperienced, but anxious to improve.

"And on ran the three bearing the six bottles.

"And when young Lobi could run no longer and began to sway, to stagger, and to hold his bottles aloft that they might not touch earth when he sprawled, M'Pugu called a halt, bade them sleep and then eat of the last of their provender, some nice entrails, a handful of excellent beetles each, and the remainder of the curd, black but comely.

"And as they lay sleeping, Simba the Lion found them at dawn, sprang, clawed M'Dabalaka's face nearly off and so startled Lobi, that losing his head completely, the clumsy youth used one of his bottles of beer as a club—and smashed it between the lion's eyes.

Certainly this gave M'Pugu a fine chance to drive his spear in behind the lion's left shoulder, but it did not excuse the wretched youth's dreadful act; and although the spear sliced the lion's heart, it still had time and strength to make quite a mess of the front of M'Pugu and the back of M'Dabalaka across whom it rolled, clawing hard.

"So that when M'Pugu had pulled himself together, picked himself up, and stopped his wounds with clay, he found that only he and the miserable Lobi remained.

"That was a small matter, but what of the bottles?

"But four remained, for this accursed lion, this beast of ill-omen, when swiping at M'Dabalaka had not only taken most of his face off, but his other paw had smashed one of the bottles that M'Dabalaka hugged faithfully to his bosom.

"Very bad indeed, for the bottle beneath M'Dabalaka's arm was literally crushed into his ribs, and his side was full of glass.

"That was a small matter however, as poor M'Dabalaka had lost both his eyes with the rest of his face, and was no further use as a Beer-bearer. Very bad *juju* indeed.

"Him also M'Pugu put out of his misery.

"And again consigning two of the bottles to young Lobi's care, with heartening promises of incredible rewards, shattering threats of unbelievable punishments, and a reasonably gentle prod in the back with his spear, M'Pugu drove the young Lobi on before him.

"So two men ran, each with two bottles of beer and the hope of keeping clear and clean their record for reliability, sobriety, honesty and respectability.

"Unfortunately the shortest line between that spot and the place where their Beer-demanding Bwana was, took them past the temporary but unsavoury camp of some gentlemen who dealt in such black cattle as themselves.

"There are, of course, no such things to-day as slavers, slave-traders and slave-markets, but there is quite a considerable number of these hawk-faced Allah-worshipping merchants who do gather to themselves, by various means, quite a following of unintelligent and inconsiderable people, men, women and children, and take them on personally-conducted tours from various portions of the interior of Africa to a place on the Eastern coast of that Continent, and thence give them Sunshine Cruises on the Red Sea, letting them go ashore to see the wonders of foreign parts, accessible through such ports as Jiddah.

"From these Pleasure Cruises they do not return.

"And it was a couple of members of this particular merchant-guild who, about their lawful, though in some parts, un-lawful, occasions, beheld two black men running for dear life.

"Said Sayed Ali Burgash to Marbrouk ben Hassan:

"'Bet you can't hit the man in front before I do the man behind,' or words to that effect.

"Both slavers raised the rifles that never left their hands, and fired at the two negroes running across the wide clearing, a quarter of a mile away.

"A sporting challenge is a challenge; a running negro had better be stopped from running; and the disappearing man is always a popular target.

"Sayed Ali Burgash shot very well indeed, taking the foolish Lobi through the elbow with a bullet that not only broke his arm but ploughed across the edge of his diaphragm; while Marbrouk ben Hassan, in a way, fired better, for though he did not really wound M'Pugu, the bullet creased him, crossing the back of his neck and grazing the spinal column without breaking it.

"Both runners fell and there was a hideous crash—of glass—as M'Pugu's bottles struck the boulder against which they were hurled when he collapsed unconscious.

"Both Arab gentlemen roared with laughter, clapped each other on the shoulder, and began to wrangle as to the amount that Sayed Ali Burgash had betted Marbrouk ben Hassan that he wouldn't shoot the first man before he, Sayed Ah Burgash, shot the second.

"M'Pugu recovered first, came back to life as does a man who has received an inadequate blow upon the head, took stock of the situation, and perpended.

"Should he, best man of the lot, arrive alone, bearing two bottles—and thus not exactly cover himself with glory, but wear a small rag of it, sufficient for decency—or should he, less selfishly, give one bottle to Lobi so that at least one would arrive if the other should meet with an accident?

"Of course it was not likely that accidents would happen. None had ever happened to M'Pugu, but one never knew. And, as an honest man, he had to admit that it was better that Lobi should continue the journey, if possible, since two heads are better than one, four hands and feet better than two.

"So he kicked Lobi up, tied the hand of the wounded arm to Lobi's neck, plastered his shattered elbow well with clay, took his spear, put one of the bottles in his good hand, and bade him run.

"On the two ran. . . .

"And shortly thereafter M'Pugu got a fright, realized that an accident might happen, after all, and that, say what you may, there *are* dangers attendant upon African travel.

"For a dog, lying asleep under a tree, raised its head and looked at them, arose, shook itself, and barked. Not a village dog but a jungle dog, a wild dog; and to M'Pugu, who knew his way about, this meant death.

"A lion, a man can deal with; a charging buffalo a good man can deal with; but who can withstand the attack of a pack of jungle dogs? Not Simba the Lion, himself; not Tembo the Elephant; not M'Bogo the Buffalo. For, when the pack has marked its prey, it will follow it until it has pulled it down and got it, be it what it may.

"'Run, Lobi,' he shouted, 'run, thou beautiful gazelle. Run like the devil, thou wart-hog.'

"And on M'Pugu and the worthless Lobi ran, while the dog-pack gathered and took up the trail . . . ran and ran until with aching lungs and bursting heart and reeling brain, the two sighted the good White Bwana's camp, put on a last spurt, stood each his bottle of beer before the Bwana's tent, and lay down in peace to die.

"Lobi, who had lost a lot of blood, died quickly, but M'Pugu lasted long enough to tell his artless tale."

There was a brief silence.

"No-o-o-o. I'm afraid you can't get by, on that," said Paladino at length. "If that is the worst thing you ever did, I'm afraid you can't join the Dirty Dogs' Club. . . . You see, it's not as though they had all come back with only two bottles among them and you had shot some of them, after they had done their best. You could have been admitted on that, I think. But as it is . . . No. You must think of something else."

"Well, as I said, I regret that more than anything I have ever done," replied Blanke.

"Would you care to come into the Club as a servant and wait upon your betters, the Members?" asked Paladino.

And before Blanke could reply, Paladino solved the problem.

"I know," he said, "you shall join as a Dishonorary Member, as soon as the Club is complete."

A FRANC'S WORTH OF GAS

"A Franc's Worth of Gas" is the second story of Part II, "Dirty Dogs of War", found in Rough Shooting *(1938). In this story, Mertin confesses that he attempted to murder the woman he loved, but was unsuccessful due to a ghost and "a franc's worth of gas." The story was published earlier under a different title, "The Ghost at the Window", and with a different frame (in the desert and not under siege), in at least three Australian newspapers:* The Courier-Mail Brisbane *(November 23, 1935),* The Argus *(December 28, 1935), and* The Mail Adelaide *(April 11, 1936). The story was also reprinted, in an abridged form but using the frame of the siege in the jungle, under the title "The Dirty Dogs' Club" in* Ellery Queen's Mystery Magazine *(July 1943).*

Paladino turned to Mertin.

"Well, Mertin, have you decided which is your worst effort?"

All turned and looked at Mertin whom Paladino then addressed.

And Mertin, a sad and usually silent man, suddenly found his tongue, and burst into a spate of speech that surprised his comrades. Undoubtedly wine had loosened his tongue, and perhaps he was a little drunk.

"I have no difficulty," he said thickly. "I am a murderer. That's what I am."

"Well, that may or may not qualify you for membership," smiled Paladino. "Don't you think that because you've committed a mere murder, you are *ipso facto* a genuine dirty dog. Murders may be very meritorious acts, let me tell you. In point of fact, most of mine were. Well?"

"A murderer in heart, a murderer in intent," went on Mertin, ignoring Paladino, and glancing appealingly from face to face of his listeners. "I meant to do it. I tried to do it; and what kept me from being a murderer, in fact, was a ghost."

"There are no such things as ghosts," interrupted young Henschel.

"No, there are no ghosts," agreed Mertin, "save of our pasts; save of our dead selves. Yet surely it was a ghost that kept me from murder, and rescued the woman whom I loved from death. It was the ghost of her husband, a good soldier, killed in Maroc.

"I had known Jules and his Juliette for many a long year before I murdered her. For that is what it amounted to. I am a murderer, I say, since I did my best to kill her, and actually believed I had succeeded.

"And yet I had loved her desperately the whole time. Yes, from the first day. But when I came back to the village, they had only been married a week, and she had neither eyes nor ears for any living man but Jules Despard. And yet I had only missed her by a few days. She had not known Jules three months before they were married, and it might just as well have been me. I mean, she was ripe for marriage. She wanted to marry. And Jules's battalion was transferred there.

"They met; and there it was. I should have done just as well, of course. She'd have loved me just as much, and she'd have been every bit as faithful to me as she was to Jules.

"For women are like that, *mes amis*. They are like the butterflies—some of them. And the rest are like the bees. Both hover across the field of life. The flower invites in flower language. The butterfly alights on one of all the hundreds of flowers that are within its sight, and that is her flower, her very own.

"She settles on that particular one, and unlike the bee, she is settled for life. The other flowers do not matter in the least.

"But, mark you, it might just as well have been any other flower in the field, for really they are all very much alike.

"And so it was with Juliette. Had I met her as and when and where she met Jules Despard, I could have made her fall in love with me, just as Jules made her fall in love with him, for I had everything to offer a woman that Jules had, and a good deal more."

Mertin reached for his *quart* and drained it thirstily.

"Huh! If only I had gone to Pirvyse a few days earlier! Look you, I shot a fellow out of a tree-top yesterday. A marvellous long shot—a fluke, of course. Had I gone to Pirvyse a week earlier, that Chinese would be alive, for I should never have joined the French Foreign Legion, never have come to this corner of Hell and killed him.

"Well, well. That's how life goes.

"Anyway, Jules got to Pirvyse before I returned. He was the flower and invited the butterfly to go to him. The butterfly hovered and settled, and the flower intoxicated her senses and made her drunk for her whole life, not merely for his.

"For, believe it or not, she loved the memory of Jules Despard as dearly as she had loved the man himself, and when I went to her three months after the news of his death, she repulsed me as angrily as she had done while he was alive. Yes, I had been fool enough to make love to Juliette Despard while Jules was abroad, and—well, I shall never forget it.

"And now that he was dead, she seemed to be as much insulted by my advances as she had been before. And yet, mind you, she was desperately poor, whereas I was very well off indeed and could give her all the things that a woman wants. All except one, that is to say.

"I took it badly. You see, she had been an obsession with me from the first time I saw her; an *idée fixe*; a sort of mania.

"Yes, positively, she was a madness in the blood. It had been pretty painful when she scourged and flayed me for trying to persuade her when the absent Jules was alive. But this was unbearable, that she should be just as fiercely contemptuous now that he was dead. It was an insult. And the more so that she seemed to think my proposal of honourable marriage was something disgraceful and injurious, a sacrilege to the holy memory of her noble Jules, who had been, in point of fact, a remarkably ordinary fellow.

"You can understand that I was nearly as insane with angry jealousy and wounded vanity as I was with love; anger at this poverty-stricken widow's contempt of me; jealousy of the dead man, a stupid lump of a fellow; wounded vanity at her comparing me with him, and greatly to my disadvantage.

"Let me be frank and admit that it was conceit, base pride and injured vanity that poisoned my mind, already unhinged by the consuming passion that had fed upon itself and yet had increased with each day that passed.

"With the utmost difficulty I bided my time, telling myself that the image of Jules would fade, the impression of him stamped upon her heart would grow faint, the realities of loneliness and grinding poverty would obscure the phantasies of memory. I would wait awhile and I would try again. I would show her that a live civilian is better than a dead soldier, a warm and living man better than a cold and decaying corpse. I would urge the fact of my long and unswerving devotion, and show her that always the man who comes is better than the man who goes, and who has gone for ever.

"Yes, but Jules Despard had not gone for ever. Dead he was, but though he was dead, he returned and saved the life of his adored wife. Didn't he, *mes amis*? Did he? I don't know. Listen.

"One lovely evening I went to her again, when I could keep away from her no longer, and begged her, with all the eloquence of love, to let me take her from that poor room, clothe her in silk and bedeck her with jewels, and install her as my worshipped wife in my fine house in the country near Pirvyse.

"And in return she insulted me unforgettably. She spoke as though I had offered her the deadliest insult. She drove me mad with her beauty and her contempt. Mad. So insane that I suspected her.

"'There's someone else,' I shouted, my tense hands flexing, clutching, as though they would seize her by the throat.

"'Yes,' she smiled. 'There's my Jules, whom I shall some day join.'

"'Join him now, you besotted fool,' I shouted, seized her by the throat, shook her, and flung her down.

"I did. Would not that alone have been enough to rank me with the dirtiest pariah dog that ever slunk about a gutter?"

"Yes," agreed Paladino unhesitatingly.

"There she lay, cowering, terrified, and there I stood, mad, triumphant, my burning love turned to searing hate.

"Let her join her accursed Jules; since she was so faithful to him, let her go to him, and let me be rid of her for ever.

"How should I do it?

"The sight of blood I could not bear. I wasn't a *légionnaire* in those days, *mes amis*. I was a white-handed pampered soft-living man of fashion. No, there must be no blood, no horrible mess. At that time it would have made me sick. That seems hardly possible now, does it? But for the blood that would follow, I could have stabbed her and been thrilled to the depths of my soul. I told you I was mad, didn't I? I could have closed my eyes, held a pistol to her head, and shot her and rushed away, but I had no pistol.

"I could have struck her on the head with something heavy, but—blood again. No.

"And besides, why should I die too? Why should I go to the guillotine because she was a besotted fool clinging to the dead love of a dead man? Let it be a case of suicide.

"Yes, let her put her head into the gas-oven and die. Obvious suicide. A poor widow who had found the struggle of life too hard; poverty, bereavement, loneliness, temporary insanity, suicide.

"Very sad, but such cases are common.

"'Go and join your Jules,' I shouted, half-raised her from the floor, dragged her across the room and flung open the door of the gas oven in which she did her poor cooking—when she had anything to cook.

"Wasn't that a brilliant idea? Who, then, could doubt for one moment that the unhappy, lonely, starving widow had taken her own life? For what murderer would ever dream of using such a means to kill his victim? It was an inspiration, a stroke of genius. One has heard of the perfect murder. This would be it; the utterly undetectable murder; and it would be perfectly simple because the word 'murder,' that ghastliest of all words, would never be uttered. From first to last, from the first discovery of the body to the last line of the burial service, it would never be used or thought of. No bruises; no marks on the face or neck; no signs of violence; no suggestion of any kind of assault.

"Luckily, when I had thrown her to the floor, I had not struck her in the face. So far, all was well, and if only I were careful and patient, I should escape all punishment. That would be splendid, soul-satisfying; to have revenge with impunity, to punish her for all my years of suffering, and to pay no penalty myself.

"Yes, let me only have patience, and I could commit a perfect murder.

"She struggled hard; she tried to scream; tried to bite my hand; but I was, of course, far stronger than she, and very much heavier. With my weight I kept her down. With my hands I covered her mouth and nose that she might not breathe, and with my great patience I kept myself from anger, from violence, from the use of that unnecessary force and roughness that would cause bruises and leave marks. I would tire her down, wear her out, exhaust her thoroughly, suffocate her, and when she could resist no more I would get her head into the oven and turn on the gas. She would never recover consciousness, and I would slip quietly away into the night.

"And for the first time since I had fallen in love with her, I was happy, insanely joyous. Every nerve in my body thrilled. I was expressing my repressed self at last, and casting off the incubus that had crushed joy out of my life, this hopeless love, this cancer of love that, eating out my heart, had turned to hate. Yes, I was getting my revenge for all that I had suffered.

"I remember that I was almost deafened by the loud singing in my ears, the singing of my heart, as I thought, for it was now so happy.

"I was mad, of course. I tell you, I was mad.

"And at length she ceased to struggle. The muscles of her face became still, her lips opened, and though her eyes were gazing wildly into mine, they were becoming glazed, and I could see that she was fainting.

"Patience a little longer. Care and patience—and the perfect murder.

"And soon her eyes closed and she lay as though dead. Uncovering her mouth, I was free to use both hands to raise her a little from the floor, to lift her forward and lay her down again in such position that her head was well inside the gas oven.

"There. Now all I had to do was to turn on the gas and the undiscoverable murder would be complete, the compulsory suicide accomplished.

"I turned on the gas and when I held her there, I laughed aloud. Never again would the contemptuous fool spurn a good man's love, return insults for compliments, repay adoration with hatred. No.

"But quickly I discovered that there was one small matter that I had overlooked.

"While the gas was killing her, it was inconveniencing me in a most objectionable manner. I didn't like the smell of coal-gas at all, and naturally it was very strong there, so close to the oven-door which of course I could not so much as half-shut.

"On the other hand, I didn't wish to leave go of her and move farther away from the oven, because she was not yet absolutely unconscious. If I released my hold, relieved her body of my weight, rose up and went to the door for air, she might, before the gas completely suffocated her, have the strength to crawl away from the oven, and I should have to return and struggle with her again. There might be marks, her clothing might get torn, the perfect murder might be spoilt through the prying police doubting whether it were a certain case of suicide.

"No. There must be no more violence.

"Could I hold on a little longer and then leave her for a few seconds while I went and opened the window and let in sufficient air to enable me to breathe, while she, with her head in the oven, suffocated?

"Measuring the distance that I should have to move and the time it would take me to open it, I glanced towards the window, and there in the very middle of it, was—*the face of her husband, Jules Despard.*

"It was a marvel that I did not die then and there. My heart literally stood still, and I felt desperately faint with fear, for there was not the slightest possibility of any shadow of doubt. There he was, plain and clear as in life, although the face was ghostly and framed, as it were, in whiteness—the face of a dead man.

"Yes, the face of a dead man was there at the window. The face of the dead Jules Despard.

"For one second I thought, 'He is not dead, though before long, I shall be.'

"And then I realized that it could not be the man himself watching me so intently, for the window was a dozen feet from the ground, the face was in the middle of it, and there was no body. The face was framed, I say, in whiteness, and it was the face of Jules Despard himself. There was the great curl of black hair across the forehead, coming almost down to the nose, and rising up again above the ear. There was the huge moustache drooping almost to the chin and curving upward and outward like the horns of a buffalo. There were those heavy beetling black eyebrows beneath which the eyes watched me . . . watched . . . watched.

"Suddenly I screamed like a hare, or a child, or a woman. And leaving Juliette there, with her head inside the oven and the gas turned on, I sprang to my feet, rushed from the house by the back way, and fled for my life from the watching face of the ghost of Jules Despard.

"I ran far into the forest of Pirvyse, stumbling over bushes and rocks, running against trees, scrambling over deep ditches, and through brooks.

"At length, exhausted, I flung myself down, and I believe I slept.

"I was awakened by the rays of the sun shining full upon my face. And as soon as I was fully alert and could remember, I felt that I must go back. I must go back to that room, even if I knew that the police were there awaiting me. It was quite possible that someone had seen me go in; possible that I had been seen to leave the house, and that the police had been informed of the fact. Whether they had or not, how should I explain my going to the house at that time in the morning and in the condition in which I was—hatless, dishevelled, muddy.

"Hatless! And suddenly I remembered that I had left my hat there; my hat in which were my initials. In my terror at the sight of the apparition at the window, I had fled, with no other thought but that of escape.

"I must go back. I could not keep away. I could not help myself. I must go and look at the body. And if the police were there, and had found my hat where I had thrust it, on a table or a chair, they would arrest me, and I would make full confession.

"And if they had not arrived, if no one passing had seen the open door and gone in, smelt gas, discovered her body and notified the police—if no one had done that, and if the crime had not been discovered, I would recover my hat and escape. I would recover my hat and . . . ? And do that which I knew I had to do.

"The perfect murder—with my hat, my name, there beside her! I might as well have left a signed confession.

"I told myself I was going back to remove this all-sufficient piece of evidence, but I knew that I was going back because I must.

"But there was something else.

"What I refused to admit, the thought that subconsciously I strove to prevent from entering my mind, was that there, in that room, I must take my own life too, or the ghost of Jules Despard would haunt me for ever.

"For ever. For every hour of the day and night, until I died. Like a drunken man or a man wounded almost to death, I rose to my feet, and staggered back along the way that I had come.

"I reached the road. I dragged myself along it. I reached the house.

"The front door of the house was open.

"Heavily dragging myself up the short flight of steps that led to the room in which I had committed the murder, I opened the door.

"Juliette Despard met me face to face. And glancing at the window, I half expected to see that other face, that dreadful ghost-visage of the dead man who had come to save her.

"She, on the other hand, glanced from me to the wall as though looking to someone for help, and there, mounted, glazed and framed, was the life-size photograph of her husband, the picture on which the moon had shone last night, illuminating it so that it had been perfectly reflected in the window.

"Yes, what I had seen in the window was the ghost, or rather the reflection, of Jules Despard's portrait.

"But why was Juliette alive?

"Because at the moment that I rose to my feet and fled, the gas had run out from the almost empty metre, the franc's-worth finished.

"That, *mes amis*, was my perfect murder!"

"I propose Pierre Mertin for membership of the Dirty Dogs' Club," said Paladino, breaking the silence which followed the cessation of Mertin's voice. "I declare him well qualified for membership. Those in favour, raise hands."

And all hands were raised.

A POISONOUS FELLOW

While "A Poisonous Fellow" is the third story of Part II, "Dirty Dogs of War", in Rough Shooting *(1938), Nul de Nullepart, the narrator, was the first person Paladino asked in* Fort in the Jungle *(1936) to tell his story. Nul de Nullepart's "dirtiest deed" occurred when, under the orders of his overbearing father, he broke up with the girl he loved, resulting in tragic consequences. This is the only known reprinting of "A Poisonous Fellow."*

"Well, Nul de Nullepart, what's your best effort?" said Paladino.

"M-mine?" stammered the man who called himself Nul de Nullepart. "The dirtiest deed I ever did? Merciful God, what a task! Well, well . . ."

And he lay back, clasping his hands behind his head.

Not very much was to be hoped from this Nul de Nullepart. Nothing very lurid, for he was a quiet, well-behaved and gentlemanly person, only just sufficiently riotous, tough, and insubordinate to be *bon légionnaire*; only just sufficiently drunken, rowdy and spendthrift to be *bon camarade*.

"H'm. Worst deed I ever did, eh? All a matter of opinion, really."

"Well, let's have your opinion," urged Paladino. "Tell us what you think was the dirtiest thing you ever did. And don't forget we haven't got all the time there is."

"It is selection that is so difficult," murmured de Nullepart. "Selection . . . The worst . . . ? I don't know. Well, yes, perhaps I do, though. I, too, murdered a woman once."

"It's bad deeds we're asking for," growled old Schenko.

"Silence in the gallery," ordered Paladino. "It is quite conceivable that our comrade did wrong in killing the woman, but if *that* is the worst . . ."

"Oh, I did wrong all right," interrupted de Nullepart. "Quite wrong. For she was a kind, delightful and beautiful girl, and she loved me with all her heart and soul."

"A little mad, obviously," observed Van Demon, as his comrades called the Dutchman.

"Surely, or she wouldn't have done what she did," agreed de Nullepart. "And I . . . I must have been more than a little mad or I should have known what such love as hers was worth. My sole excuse . . . But no, I have no excuse. Not a shadow of one. Only an explanation. And my sole explanation is that I was young. Too young to have proper knowledge of real values. Too young to set my weak and unformed will against the relentless iron will of my father, the joint communal will of my whole family. They said I was to marry money because the money was needed for the family business. And they had found the money already. All I had to do was to marry the plain female who went with it . . . Why are they always plain?"

"Law of compensations," replied Paladino promptly. "Lovely women have no brains; rich women have no beauty; clever women have no heart; fascinating women have no . . ."

"Character," supplied Schenko. "But neither has any other kind of woman. I . . ."

"Who asked you to wave your mouth?" enquired Paladino. "Go on, de Nullepart."

"Yes. They had found the girl with the necessary money, and they soon arranged the matter. And all the while I loved Thérèse.

"There had been a time when I was most desperately in love with her. But that was over, and now I merely loved her. There's a difference, of course, between loving a woman and being in love with a woman."

"Quite so. Assuredly," agreed Lemoine. "One loves one's wife, and is 'in love' with one's neighbour's wife."

"Yes, I still loved her," continued de Nullepart. "But I loved myself better. Loved some of my other pleasures better. Not to mention my peace of mind, my peace at home, and the comfortable soft job that was mine for life—provided I remained my harsh father's obedient son and heir.

"He was a terror, *le bon papa*. Powerful, ruthless, a driver. No, not a strong silent man—a strong noisy one. And how he could terrify me with his noise.

"And doubtless I was just at that moment a little tired of poor Thérèse, though all I really wanted was a little holiday from her.

So I broke it off.

"As weak men love to do, I took what I called a strong line; firm, ruthless, cruel-to-be-kind sort of thing.

"I wrote and told her that our affair was at an end; that I should never see her again; that I should always think kindly of her; that she could rely upon me to do the right thing financially, so far as lay in my power; and that this was absolutely final.

"It was final—until I got her answer.

"Then, after some very painful correspondence, I again informed her that it was final. Absolutely final this time. So it was, from my point of view, and until she wrote saying that unless I visited her at the cottage on Saturday night, she would visit me and my family at our house.

"That frightened me; terrified me.

"How much it terrified me nobody could understand who did not know my father.

"Although I had arrived at man's estate, I was literally afraid of him. I was as much afraid of him as anybody was ever afraid of anything. From babyhood he had crushed me, daunted my spirit, tyrannized my being. I had never once disobeyed him openly, defied him, or even contradicted him. Understand that I was far more afraid of him than I was of God or the Devil.

"Also I was afraid of poverty, hunger, shabbiness; afraid of the loss of everything that made life easy, comfortable and delightful. And although I was very afraid of losing the luxury I so enjoyed, knowing perfectly well that the old man would kick me out as soon as look at me, cut me off without a shilling if I gave him what he considered just cause, I feared him personally even more than I feared social and financial ruin.

"And it would be ruin too, for, as my father was at some pains frequently to assure me, I really was of less value in the employment-market than the cheapest clerk he had got.

"No. Thérèse must not pay him a visit. Must not go to him armed with my letters and a lovely old family ring that I had given her when first we became engaged; must not give him evidence of the strength of her position and the weakness of ours.

"I trembled in a cold sweat of fear as I thought of a breach of promise action, scandal, blackmail, and of the wrath of my terrible father, so austere, harsh and merciless.

"So, in spite of all that I had written, I decided to go and see Thérèse—once again—and of course this should really be final.

"It was.

"Even I, weak, cowardly, selfish, mean as I was, was shocked at the sight of her face.

"Even I, far too self-centred to have given much thought to what this must mean to the girl who adored me, and whom I had loved so madly, was disturbed to my shallow depths at the change in her.

"Her face had lost its colour, her bright eyes their light. She looked a different girl.

"Almost I flung prudence to the winds and my arms about her lovely body once again. For one moment my fate hung in the balance. In that moment I had my chance—of becoming a man, of possessing my own soul. Perfect love casteth out fear. My love was not perfect. It was marred by prudence, selfishness, the yellow streak . . . of gold and greed.

"Sick, sorry and ashamed, I blustered, stretched out a hand to hold her off. Had I but stretched out two to crush her to my breast . . . I should not be here now.

"I really don't know how I could have behaved as I did, for I was not really wicked, base, evil. I was weak, I was cowardly and, thanks to my father, I had no will of my own: none whatever.

"No, I don't know how I did it, but even then I realized that my 'better' self was standing on one side and watching what my worse self was doing.

"A pity my 'worse' self didn't interfere, you think. Quite so. But what stood between the two selves? My father. And here I am, blaming him for what I did. Well, why shouldn't I? Any father is to blame who makes his son a servile cur, a slave, and deliberately sets to work to crush the mind and will and soul out of him until literally he cannot call his soul his own, because he hasn't got one.

"Anyway, I let the absent father, whom I hated, defeat the present woman, whom I loved. She begged; she implored; she told me what I knew was true, that really I loved her almost as much as she loved me.

"She begged me to come right away from my horrible home,

and she would work her fingers to the bone for me. She would support me. I need have no fear on that score. She would take a house and let lodgings, and I should be not only her husband but her most honoured and valued and cherished lodger. Life should cost me nothing.

"And when I laughed scornfully and shook my head without troubling to give other answer than a sneering smile of contempt at such a picture, she put false modesty and shame aside, put her arms about my neck and endeavoured to draw my head to her breast, where so often it had lain, and said I need not marry her. All she begged was that I should let her work for me during the rest of our lives.

"Coldly I thrust her away, told her to stop talking nonsense, and to make a sensible and reasonable proposal for her own future. Married and wealthy, I should be able to make her a sufficient allowance.

"Suddenly she fell silent, drew away from me, and gave me a long look that I have never forgotten.

"'You really mean this?' said she.

"Her face seemed to me to age as she spoke, so pinched and drawn it was.

"'You are sure, Sweetheart?' she continued. 'You are perfectly certain? You are not joking nor . . .'

"'*Joking!*' I exclaimed.

"'. . . nor making a mistake? Because it is very very important. To me—very serious. You really mean this? It is absolutely true and . . . final?'

"'Absolutely true and absolutely final,' I replied.

"'Will you excuse me for one moment,' she said, putting her handkerchief to her lips. 'I shan't be a moment. Then I'll come and say good-bye.'

"She went from the room.

"And I knew. I knew.

"And I did nothing.

"A minute later she returned.

"'Say good-bye to me, darling—and quickly. Sit beside me once more on our little couch. Kiss me once more. Take me in your arms once more. Be quick, Sweetheart. Oh, be quick. And then go . . . Go, my darling, at once; and swear that you have not been here for days.'

"Almost she suffocated me in a long embrace.

"'Now *go*,' she cried. '*Go*, quickly.'

"I went.

"And I knew. I knew.

"And the poison that my Thérèse had taken was one that simply tortured her to death. She must have died in horrible agony, alone, there.

"I *think* that is the worst thing I have ever done. I hope so."

Paladino broke the silence that followed de Nullepart's confession.

"You undoubtedly qualify for membership of the Dirty Dogs' Club," said he.

THE PACIFIST

The fourth story in Part II, "Dirty Dogs of War", of Rough Shooting *(1938) is a short tale of what happened to a man who refused to defend himself or his wife. "The Pacifist" has not been republished until now.*

"Well, Gusbert, have you any ambitions?   Any claims, rather?"

"Claims all right," growled Gusbert, a man who would have shone as a Colonel of Royal Engineers, and who had shone as a very desperate fighter.

He wore the *Médaille Militaire* and the *Croix de Guerre* beside his service medals.

"Star turn in any Dirty Dogs' Club," he said.

"Good," smiled Paladino. "Go to it."

"I am here because I am a pacifist."

"Oh, yeah?"

"Or rather because I was.   And for the same reason I committed the foul deed that haunts me. Left a woman to death and torture. Yes, failed the woman whom I loved utterly; and who loved me utterly. Failed her as badly as that. And not altogether because I was a coward, either. It was because I was a crank, a faddist, which is the same thing as saying a crass besotted egoist.

"Yes, I was a pacifist. And by pacifist I don't mean a man who prefers peace to war. Any sane person does that. I don't mean a man who loathes war with all his heart and soul. For any sane person does that also. I mean a man who simply says he won't fight. Won't fight as a soldier or as a civilian. Won't fight anybody for anything. Not only will he in no circumstances fight for his King and country, but will in no circumstances fight at all.

"That was me, the complete pacifist.

"When sane people said, 'Surely there are worse things than war,' I replied that, to me, there were not. There was nothing worse than war.

"When they said, 'Surely there is *something* worth defending',

31

I said, 'Not by fighting.'

"I used the idiotic argument that it is useless to oppose force with force; and that to do so was merely to set evil to fight evil.

"And when I was asked if I would not defend my country against invasion, I said '*No*'; my home against burglarious entry, I said '*No*'; my property against seizure, I said '*No*.'

"And when my own brother said:

"'Wouldn't you defend your wife? 'I said '*No*.'

"You see, I was a logical Christian, or thought I was. I knew that God could defend me, and I believed that He *would*! Actually I thought that God had time to waste on my affairs; and when it was pointed out to me that Heaven helps those who help themselves, especially in the matter of self-defence, I smiled scornfully.

"Well, I suppose that if a man or a country chooses to be so meek that all kicks, insults, robberies, and other injuries are accepted, if not gratefully, at any rate without retaliation or defence; if they like literally to turn the other cheek also; if they like to give employment and encouragement to every bully and robber, I suppose they have a right to do so—though that is arguable.

"But I . . . well . . . my wife . . .

"I used to be a Civil Engineer; and I was in charge of a road that my Government was driving through a very wild and dangerous part of one of its possessions. Not only was my labour-force dangerous—a quarrelsome, violent, treacherous and mutinous horde—but the inhabitants of the surrounding mountains were the biggest robbers and the most murderous raiders on earth.

"And to that place, with my wonderful trust in Heaven's especial care, favour, esteem and admiration for me, and with my beautiful love for my dear fellow-man—I took my wife, my wife, a very glorious woman who thought me a great and fine man; and who believed not only in me but in everything in which I believed . . . Not in the least because she was convinced of its truth, but simply because *I* believed it!

"Yes, I took her there, against the advice, and in the face of the earnest expostulation, of every European official who knew the country and its dangers.

"'No, no,' said I. 'My trust in God is not a matter of lip-service. We are in His hands here just as we were there. And He can and will watch over us, wherever we may be.'

"'Well, trust in God—and keep your powder dry,' said my Chief as we took final farewell of him. 'In fact, trust nobody else *but* God,' he added, 'and don't stir an inch without a revolver, nor sleep without a couple of rifles and plenty of ammunition in your house.'

"'I have neither revolver nor rifles,' I replied.

"'Then,' said this man whom I despised for his narrow irreligious reliance upon self, 'excuse my remarking that if you've any right to commit suicide, you've none to commit murder.'

"'Shooting another man is murder,' said I in my wisdom.

"'I've told you what happened. As to details . . .

"The labour-force struck, demanded impossible wages, and then, undoubtedly encouraged by the fact of my known pacifism, my lack of weapons, my complete defencelessness, these coolies rioted, and began an orgy of loot, rapine, and murder.

"Mind you, properly handled at the beginning, a native Police-Sergeant and half a dozen men could have kept perfect order. A single European with a thick stick and an air of authority could have done it. But for want of one man of sane views, rational outlook, and a proper sense of discipline—nay, of elementary right and wrong—valuable lives were lost, a great work was ruined, thousands of pounds' worth of property was destroyed, and incalculable political harm done throughout the whole district.

"My faithful clerk rushed to my camp at the risk of his own life, warned me, and fled.

"Even he, a native, bade me think of the danger to my wife—even if I would do nothing to defend myself.

"The mob arrived at my tent, yelling and dancing and brandishing weapons, shouting threats and insults. I went out to them, and was insulted and abused for the coward that they thought I was.

"I wasn't a coward—for I quite calmly faced the yelling mob, unarmed—but I was a fool, a crank, a besotted egoist. My wife paid the penalty.

"They merely beat and stoned me and left me for dead—but

my wife—the sweet beautiful woman who adored me . . . They .
. .

"I cannot talk about it; but still, it was she who paid . . . If they had only killed her! . . .

"That is why I am here. That's why I have spent my life, ever since, trying to expiate my . . ."

"That's enough," growled Paladino. "You can join. I'll put you on the Committee, I think."

THE CAD

"The Cad" is the story of a man who insults the woman he was going to propose to, when she tells him that she is in love with another man. "The Cad" was the fifth story in Part II, "Dirty Dogs of War", of Rough Shooting (1938), and has not been reprinted until now.

Next to *le légionnaire* Gusbert sat his *copain*, Richeburg, a quiet well-behaved man. Also a person of education and good breeding.

"Now, Richeburg," said Paladino, "if your good angel mentions your best deed in extenuation, what is the worst with which the Recording Angel will riposte?"

"Well," smiled Richeburg, "I don't know his tastes, fads and fancies. As de Nullepart said, it is so much a matter of opinion."

"Well then, we must fall back on yourself. So get off your conscience what you think the worst one."

"H'm! I suppose the thing one is most ashamed of is really the worst thing one ever did," mused Richeburg.

"Not at all," interrupted Van Demon. "One is generally most ashamed of the episode in which one has played the poorest part, appeared in the worst light."

"You mean vanity plays a big part in the matter?"

"Of course," replied Van Demon. "We aren't ashamed of the wickedest things we've done, nearly as much as we are of the silliest, the ugliest, the most humiliating. It is when one attempts to do something that not only fails, but also recoils on one's own head, that one is ashamed.

"This is not a debate," interrupted Paladino. "Will you kindly wait your turn, Van Demon, and exercise your mind in thinking out the dirtiest trick you ever played. Now, Richeburg, what's the worst thing you ever did?"

"I shouldn't think the poor fellow ever committed a decent crime in his life," sneered Schenko, who disliked Richeburg.

"Don't suppose he ever met you in gaol, anyway, Schenko. Hold your tongue, will you," directed Paladino.

"Well, we've all done some nasty things in our lives," said Richeburg. "Things we'd give anything not to have done. Deeds of which we are bitterly ashamed. But I'm afraid Schenko is right, and I have never sinned in the grand manner. I have never committed a murder, any more than de Nullepart has."

And as he spoke, he threw a cigarette across to his friend.

"But the worst thing I ever did was in connection with a woman. Perfectly, utterly beastly; and I hadn't the excellent excuse that de Nullepart had—no father of whom I went in terror. It was just my own natural poisonous foulness.

"It happened on a yacht, one of those miniature floating palaces that cost a rich man a fortune to buy and an annual fortune to maintain.

"He was an English milord and spent the best part of every summer on this ocean-going yacht of his.

"For one unforgettable month, I sailed in her."

"A steward?" enquired Schenko.

"No. That was not my rating, Schenko. As a matter of fact, I was the owner's guest."

"I see. A rich man's parasite," sneered Schenko.

Paladino rose to his feet, looked up at the cat-walk where a German lad, Sturmer, stood and stared across the clearing at the solid wall of the jungle.

"Schenko, get you up and relieve Sturmer," he said, and the raised corner of his mouth went up a little and the depressed corner of his mouth drew down a little as he narrowed his gaze into Schenko's eyes. Quick. Or you won't live to join the Club."

Schenko glanced round the circle of hard faces, licked his lips and rose to his feet.

"You command here," he said, climbed the little ladder and relieved Sturmer, taking his stand at a *creneau* and staring out into the jungle, so minatory and sinister; resonant with the croak of thousands and thousands of tree-frogs above, and bull-frogs below, the chirping and shrilling of millions of cicadas; fragrant with the scent of frangipani and *ilang ilang*; redolent with the underlying scent of death, dissolution and decay. Sturmer, descending from the cat-walk, seated himself in Schenko's place, extracted a wilted cigarette from his *kepi* and held it to dry over the embers of the fire.

"Another guest was a lovely girl who was not only really and truly beautiful, but extraordinarily unspoiled, kind, friendly and wholly charming.

"To me she was the embodiment, incarnation I mean, of the Fairy-tale Princess of one's dreams. I was brought up on Hans Andersen and the Grimm Brothers, that sort of thing, and to me there were such people as gnomes, trolls, witches, fairies, Prince Charmings, Sleeping Beauties and, particularly, beautiful princesses.

"I had very clearly and definitely in my mind a picture of the sort of princess one encountered in the Hans Andersen and Grimm stories. And curiously enough, this girl might have sat as a model for that picture. And she was a Princess. Not the daughter of a reigning monarch, but of a house of which the head had always borne the title of Prince. When I say always, I mean for many centuries.

"Well, in those days I was a sufficiently presentable person, young, not bad-looking, an officer in a very good Cavalry Regiment, and quite an eligible *parti* for a girl with money, whose parents were not looking for money. But otherwise I was hopeless, my finances balancing quite heavily on the debit side.

"I was romantic, fastidious and poetic. And I had a truly high ideal of womanhood. I needs must love the highest when I saw it; and Princess Isabelle was the highest, absolutely the highest and noblest and loveliest specimen of womanhood that I had encountered in a fairly wide experience.

"Rightly to use a generally misused word, she was flawless. She was an exception to the rule we've heard to-night, that beautiful women have no brains; for she was clever, or rather, intelligent, and very widely read; and, though clever, she most certainly had a heart, and it was big and warm; and though she was truly fascinating, she certainly had character—sterling and admirable.

"And she was one of those women who, although essentially sweet, are not insipid; though tender and gentle, are not sentimental and sloppy.

"Well, I've said enough, perhaps, to give you some faint idea of my Fairy-tale Princess, and more than enough to give you the impression that I fell in love with her.

"Fell in love with her! I fell as long and hard as Lucifer fell. Lucifer, Son of the Morning. Nine days he fell—only it was the reverse process—for he travelled from Heaven to the earth, and definitely it was from the earth to Heaven that I went at such speed and velocity.

"Oh, those golden days off the coasts of Spain and France and Italy. Oh, those silver nights when the yacht lay in the bays of Villefranche, Rapallo and Naples. I can never hear those names without seeing her, seeing Heaven. And my idea of Heaven, then, was to sit in a deck-chair beside her, feast my eyes upon her face, and listen to the music of her voice.

"Not only were those the very happiest days of my life, but I am perfectly certain I am speaking the truth when I say that no human being upon this earth was ever happier than I was then. Purest, ineffable, sheer happiness.

"And so kind was she, so friendly, so sweet, that—never lacking in a good conceit of myself—I actually dared to come to the decision that I would ask my Princess Isabelle to prolong my happiness indefinitely, to admit me to that Paradise that she created by her presence; in fact, to marry me.

"I decided that when the moon reached the full, the physical world its peak of glory; the night its apogee of beauty; and when men and women are at their maddest, their happiest, their acme of romanticism, I would tell her what she already knew—that I loved her; would beg her to step down from her pedestal to the level at which I walked.

"And on the night before, we sat once again, side by side, alone, at the stern of the ship, looking over the rail at the twinkling diamond lights of the shore, a lovely scene, a perfect setting for the human jewel that I so coveted.

"That hour was the apex of my happiness; of my life.

"At the end of it, I did the vilest thing that I have ever done, rotten as my life has been since then.

"For, putting her hand on mine, she turned to me, called me by my Christian name, and said:

"'Help me say something terribly difficult, will you? I do so want to do what is best, kindest. I should never forgive myself if I hurt you, gave you any cause to think I had been unworthy of your friendship, kindness . . . for I am so grateful.'

"'Why, Princess!' said I. 'Is there anybody alive who'd dream that you could ever be unkind; do anything hurtful, cruel?'

"'I'd never do so willingly,' she said. 'Especially to you, Michael. Especially to you, my dear.'

"How the blood coursed through my veins. How I could have sung aloud a paean of joy. She had called me 'my dear.' She had said, '*Especially to you, my dear.*'

"I took her hand in both of mine.

"'Something difficult, Isabelle? Difficult to say—to me? What could be a difficult thing for you to say—to me?'

"And I thought of the difficult thing that I had to say to her, to-morrow. The thing that had seemed difficult, rather. It was that no longer, since she had said those words, '*Especially to you, my dear.*'

"'Well, it is a little difficult, Michael, but of course I can say it to you. It is this. Don't like me *too* much.'

"'Isabelle!'

"'Don't . . .' She laughed a little warm laugh and put her other hand on mine. 'Don't fall in love with me, will you?'

"'Because,' she went on, 'I am engaged, you know. We haven't announced it yet, because of my parents. They have . . . other views. But I haven't. I worship him. And I'm going to have my way. Nobody knows—except you, Michael, and I thought I ought to tell you because you seemed to be going to—propose to me.'

"You may not believe me, but I heard no more.

"There was such a surging in my ears.

"The shock was such as one receives from immersion in ice-cold water, or from a blow on the head.

"I was not only mentally stunned but physically hurt. I had a real pain through my heart, and a dreadful empty sick ache in the pit of my stomach. My arms and legs felt weak and I feared that I was going to tremble.

"And then, mean base beastly jealousy and vanity, and pride—no, conceit and self-love—came to the rescue, or rather to my undoing. And in answer to this lovely impulsiveness, this beautiful giving of a confidence, I returned the tremendous and generous compliment with an insult.

"'Really, Princess,' I said, 'it was quite unnecessary to mention the intrigue. I am in no danger of liking you too much, and haven't the faintest intention of "proposing" . . . Did you ever hear of the British Miss Baxter?'

"Gazing at me with a hurt incredulity, with tears gathering in her eyes, the Princess made no reply as she withdrew her hands.

"'The famous Miss Baxter, you know.

> "'*You've heard of the fame of genteel Miss Baxter*
> *Who refused a foine man long before he axed her.*'

"And I rose to my feet and left her.

"That was the filthiest thing I ever did," concluded Richeburg.

Paladino, who himself had been something like a gentleman, eyed him thoughtfully.

"You can join the Club," he said.

THE STRENGTH OF THE WEAK

"The Strength of the Weak" is the story of a weak man who was more of an "artist type" than a soldier. He tries to win his wife back by faking an illness, but she sees through his act and fakes trying to murder him. "The Strength of the Weak" is the sixth story of Part II, "Dirty Dogs of War", in Rough Shooting *(1938), and has not been republished until now.*

"Well, what about you, Sobrieski?" enquired Paladino, the tone of his voice critical. "I suppose you are not going to Hell with us, are you?"

"Oh, I hope so," replied the Pole.

"What? A candidate for the Dirty Dogs' Club?"

"Good Lord, yes. Though a very poor cur."

"More dirt than dog, what?"

The man who called himself John Sobrieski was a queer creature, like so many others who join the French Foreign Legion.

There was a screw loose somewhere; a type that would interest Messrs. Freud and Jung and any other keen alienist. He had won the *Médaille Militaire* for a deed that, in the British Army, would have won him the Victoria Cross. And on the other hand, he would at times throw himself down, burst into tears and weep like a child.

"Listen," he said, with his bitter little laugh. "I'll read you my last letter from . . . home."

If brevity is the soul of wit, the letter had at least that claim to wittiness.

Sobrieski read it aloud.

"My dear Mannikin,

"Four years of your time gone! Only one more. I wonder if they have made a man of you yet. I shall be so interested to see if there is anything real about you when you emerge. I

41

shall be waiting.

"Your wife,
"Wanda.

"What do you think of that?" he asked.

"Sounds as though you might have behaved like a dirty dog to her, eh?" replied Paladino.

"I'll tell you," said Sobrieski.

"My father is a General. Fact, I assure you. You can see for yourself that I am a gentleman. All my people have been soldiers, for centuries, and so, naturally, I was consecrated . . . devoted, destined, doomed, damned, to the army.

"And God above us, how I hated it! *How* I hated it! Every aspect, phase, form, and manifestation of it. The beastly school, the rotten college, the branding uniform, the wretched drill, the foul society, the filthy life.

"I am something of a poet, a real musician, and a good deal of an artist—in every sense and use of that much-abused word. What was there for me in the life of the parade-ground, the barracks, military society and—all that? Why, I had to hide my natural tastes and gifts as my companions would hide—or not trouble to hide—some filthy vice or disease. What would have happened to me if I had been caught writing a poem, playing my violin, or painting a picture? As it was, I was suspect—and lucky to be a General's son.

"I tell you I simply hated the life I had to lead; and didn't know whether my duties or my alleged 'pleasures' were the more boring, distasteful—nay, loathsome.

"Frequently I contemplated suicide. Time after time, I decided that the only thing to do was to take my life; escape from it all.

"Then I met Wanda, the darling, clinging affectionate little Wanda—whose annual love-letter you have just read.

"My faith, that's a hard woman, if ever there was one. But strong, mind you. Strong in mind, body and soul; strong as a man. Wire and whip-cord, steel and whale-bone. But beautiful, really beautiful.

"It was a case of love at first sight with me, and I got it badly, for she *was* my first. Literally, absolutely my first; for I had never seen anything in the slightest degree attractive in the garrison-hacks who pursued my comrades; the beer-hall wenches whom my comrades pursued; the sort of women with whom a young subaltern of means, family and prospects comes into contact in a garrison-town in—well . . . never mind where.

"Wanda was different.

"And I don't think that, really, it was her beauty that attracted me, so much as her strength and directness, her incisive speech, the way she knew her own mind, her absolute serenity. And although she was strong where I was weak, fixed where I was vacillating, certain where I was unsure, she was nevertheless, what shall I say?—womanly, kind, gentle. There was nothing of the irritating cocksure egotist about her, whatever.

"She was sweet and low-voiced and kind, and very very helpful.

"I came to depend on her, and she never failed me.

"I literally fell in love with her, but she came to love me gradually. Pity is akin to love, and definitely she pitied me. The first time I proposed to her, she turned me down; and so gently and kindly, simply because she did not love me.

"Not in that way," she said.

"Nor did she believe that I really loved her. She spoke of it as infatuation, a passing fever of the blood. She even used an expression that hurt me, a word equivalent to the English 'calf-love.'

"I took it badly. It really was a dreadful blow. To be forced to follow a profession that I loathed; to have to forswear all those pursuits that would have made life worth living; and then to be denied by the only woman I had ever loved. It was more than I could bear. Literally, more than I *could* bear.

"I wrote and told her so. Told her that she alone made life worth living, and that without her I could not and would not live. Told her that I should not trouble her again; that she would not see me again; that as soon as I had put my affairs in order, I should—meet with an accident; cleaning my revolver; bathing, where the cold waters of the river ran strongest; or through a not unnatural mistake, when taking a dose of the sleeping draught to which I had such frequent recourse.

"She came that night to my quarters—risking her reputation—and talked to me like a mother. Literally like a mother. An older, wiser, stronger person than I altogether. In point of fact, she is five years younger.

"And although she refused to accept the situation that she was responsible for my life, that my death would be at her door if she refused to marry me, she persuaded me to postpone my intended suicide.

"In the end, I gave her my solemn plighted word that for a year, a whole year, I would think no more about taking my life, in return for her promise that she would remain my friend, my companion, my counsellor, and kind good comrade.

"Tacitly, it was understood that I might again renew my suit; that I might hope.

"Six months later, she married me, and within six months after that I grew, oh, so tired of her.

"There was too much good counsel altogether. I had indeed domesticated the Recording Angel.

"Undeniably she was wiser than I, and I grew to resent the fact. She was stronger than I, and I hated it; she urged me, controlled me, guided me, drove me up to the bit, and I enjoyed it as much as a horse enjoys being whipped and spurred, guided and controlled, and driven up to its bit.

"I tell you I hated it, and there were times when I hated her.

"Only times, mark you. I didn't really hate her. It was her lack of understanding of my artistic temperament that I hated; her assumption that, being irrevocably a soldier, I must be always, everywhere, and in every way soldierly.

"When I complained of how I detested the life I had to lead, I found her unsympathetic. She said that a man, a real man, had something else to do in life besides rhyming jingles, making noises on a fiddle, and dabbing colours on paper or canvas.

"She was one of those women who are filled with what is called a burning patriotism. It was not for myself I had to live, nor for her. It was for my country.

"In the end I left her. She got on my nerves. I told her she could clear out, go back to her people. If she didn't go, I should.

"I did.

"And what did my beautiful Wanda do? Weep? Throw

herself at my feet? Pine away, when I left her?

"Not a bit of it. She wrote me the sort of letter I have just shown you. And went on her way rejoicing.

"Well, perhaps not rejoicing exactly; but by no means broken-hearted. By no means hurt, shamed, grief-stricken. She carried on just as usual. Went everywhere, saw everybody, did everything that she had been accustomed to do.

"*Women!* The aggravating creatures !

"I was furious. I missed her, too. Missed her badly.

"It was not until she had gone that I realized what she had been to me; how she had helped me; smoothed the rough path of my life; stood between me and all sorts of shocks and blows and unpleasantnesses. God! How alone and deserted and—well—unprotected I felt.

"And there she was, enjoying life to the full, while I was steeped in misery.

"Before long, I made up my mind to have my revenge. I decided to wring her heart. And I knew that I could, for latterly she had come to love me. Really to love me. Once she had accepted me, given herself to me, she gave *all*. All her self, her soul, her devotion, her love.

"That was my hold upon her. That was where I could hurt her, punish her; could, as I have said, wring her heart.

"I took to my bed and gave out that I was ill. Made myself ill, too. Beastly ill. Salts and stuff.

"One would have thought I had got the most appalling dysentery that ever attacked a man. The Regimental Doctor thought so, anyway. I whispered to my Orderly that it was Asiatic cholera, and he fled, spreading the news.

"The Regimental Doctor, clever fellow, contrived to keep me alive on milk and soda, the white of egg, and a little boiled rice. Behind his back I added to the diet as I thought fit.

"But I contrived to get beautifully thin, haggard, and pale; a most interesting invalid.

"It was rather hard luck that Wanda went away for a change of air before she heard the sad news. But before long a friend wrote and told her that I was dying, and back she came, post haste. Simply marched in and established herself, and started to nurse me back to life.

"I had an awful job to keep the game up. She was so watchful, stayed with me all day, and slept in the next room with the communicating door open.

"I fell in love with her afresh, the noble, beautiful, wonderful Wanda.

"And then, suddenly, she changed so utterly, so completely, that she positively frightened me. Really frightened me, I mean.

"One night, just as she was about to give me a basin of broth or some such stuff, I saw her drop a white tablet into it! She had her back to me, but there were mirrors in the room.

"She was stirring this broth and tasting it; and then, most distinctly, I saw that she took the tip of her ring-finger away from the palm of her hand, which it had been pressing; and, as she did so, a tablet fell from between her finger and palm.

"She continued to stir the broth, but as I noted, did not taste it.

"'There you are, my dear,' she smiled. 'Drink that up.'

"'Thank you, Wanda,' I said. 'By-and-bye. I don't want it just now.'

"When she went out of the room I tasted the stuff, being careful to swallow none of it. It was bitter.

"I flung it out of the window.

"Imagine my feelings, the turmoil of my mind. This was Wanda, my wife, the woman I worshipped; the woman who had hitherto, I was perfectly certain, loved me.

"Might it not be that this was some valuable curative drug, some medicine that would do me good?

"But if so, why this concealment? Why hold it thus artfully and cleverly concealed in her hand? Why turn her back on me, and drop it in the beef-tea or broth or whatever it was?

"Do you know, my friends, I collapsed completely. My mind seemed to dissolve and I—freely I admit it—dissolved in tears. I wept till I could weep no more.

"This was my Wanda, my other self; she was incarnate truth, goodness, sweetness, fineness, nobility, honour; and she was a murderess, a foul murderess.

"And what murder is so foul as the slow slaying by poison?

"Which would kill me first, the poison or starvation? I was already in a low state from the effects of my self-induced illness, my voluntary starvation; and now I dared touch neither food nor drink. For Wanda waited on me hand and foot, prepared all my meals.

"And one day she went out, leaving her handbag in my room.

"Crawling from my bed, and opening it, my mind filled with dark suspicion and dreadful fear, I found that, as I had half expected, it contained a small bottle of white tablets. And the bottle was openly, clearly, glaringly labelled *Poison*.

"I should have collapsed and fainted, but for the fact that I must replace the bag and get back to my bed ere she returned; and for the fact that in the bag was a letter; a letter in a handwriting that I seemed to know—a letter, the last words of which were—

> "*For ever and for ever,*
>> "*Your lover,*
>>> "*Niki.*

"I hung on to the poor remnants of my strength and sanity long enough to read the letter; a burning love-letter that, sick man as I was, nauseated me yet further.

"When she returned, she brought me tea, and the tea tasted bitter—bitter as death. "I drank it.

"'Give me more, Wanda,' I said. 'Let it be even more bitter. *Drop in two tablets this time—and make an end*.'

"And I burst into tears—again. I was so sick, you see. And then, strange creatures that men are, I put my arms about her neck and kissed her.

"'Wanda,' I whispered, 'I love you so deeply; I worship you so utterly, that I am willing—no, *glad*—to die by your hand. Make an end quickly, Wanda.'

"And kneeling beside my bed, throwing her arms about me, and pressing her lips to mine:

"'Darling,' she whispered. 'Yes, let's make an end.

"'It was only quinine, sweetheart,' she smiled.

"'Wanda, you gave me poison. You . . .'

"'Yes, my darling, like you gave yourself an illness. Didn't you, now? Confess. You have wrung my heart. I've wrung yours . . . I hope. And I hope it will do you good . . . you *humbug*.'

"'Wanda !' I cried in my joy.

"And then that dreadful pain stabbed my heart again.

"'Wanda,' I said, 'who is "Niki"?'

"'My brother Serge, darling,' she replied. 'He wrote the letter to my dictation.'

"'What a trick,' I began.

"'Yes, darling, and what a trick—to search my handbag.'

"'Oh, Wanda,' I cried, and strained her to my heart. 'How could you? Wanda, I forgive you.'

"'Yes, my own sweet—humbug,' she smiled, 'and I'll forgive you—when you've made amends and shown me that . . .'"

Paladino laughed sardonically.

"I see," he said.

"Anyhow, her terms were that I served five years in the French Foreign Legion," concluded Sobrieski, "and here I am, a poor little dirty dog."

"H'm. I don't know," mused Paladino. "After all, a dog *is* a dog, and a nice animal. I'll take the vote without comment."

Sobrieski was elected.

SAYING IT WITH FLOWERS

"Saying It With Flowers" is the shortest of Wren's published stories. It is the confession of a legionnaire whose "dirtiest" deed was that he took credit for the flowers that his rival had provided for the girl they both loved. "Saying It With Flowers" was the seventh story in Part II, "Dirty Dogs of War", of Rough Shooting *(1938) and has not been republished until now.*

"You Pancezys," asked Paladino, turning to the next man, a heavy bear-like creature from somewhere near the Baltic, a guileless, harmless oaf concerning whom one wondered what queer straits of circumstance could have driven him from his labours on some Lithuanian farm. Hunger probably, or some peccadillo, though how he ever came to have heard of the French Foreign Legion or the means of getting to it, was a marvel.

"Yes, I did a dirty trick once. I'm a dirty dog all right," he said, haltingly fumbling for words.

"Over Katusha, it was. And my cousin Karl. We both loved Katusha, and she loved both of us. Liked me as much as she did him, I mean, and him as much as she did me.

"Yes, we were proper rivals, and Katusha as good as said we must settle it between us.

"But I wasn't going to fight Karl. Not because I loved him so, either; but because he was a Strong Man.

"Quite famous he was. Why, he was known from Riga to Tilsit pretty well, and from Dvinsk to Libau. One of those men who lift weights at fairs, break chains, bend crowbars, and carry ponies on their shoulders. You'd have thought Katusha would have chosen him, but—he was stupid. A wonderful figure of a man; but he didn't know what to say to a girl at all. I did.

"Well, Katusha fell ill, and they took her to hospital at Kovno, and Karl and I were in a bad way until she turned the corner, began to get well, and could see one or two friends next Sunday.

"So off went Karl and I to the hospital at Kovno, all dressed

49

up in our Sunday best.

"And Karl, for once in his life, had had an idea. He had bought a lovely bunch of flowers and a fine basket of fruit. I never thought of doing a thing like that. Fancy Karl thinking of it!

"And then, when we got to the big building, Karl went all nervous, all of a tremble. You'd have thought he was going to be hanged in there, instead of seeing his girl.

"'Here, I can't go in there, Anton,' he said. 'Look, you take the flowers to her, and the fruit, and this letter; and tell me what she says. You give her my love, mind.'

"That suited me fine.

"So I put the letter in the pocket of my velvet jacket, took the flowers in one hand and the fruit in the other, and marched into the place, pretending I wasn't scared to death.

"Well, they kept me waiting quite a long time, and then a beautiful lady with a white veil on her head came and said:

"'What do you want?'

"'I want to see Katusha.'

"She said, 'Katusha Who?'

"I said:

"'Why, you know, Katusha from Zapiskis.'

"And then she laughed, and took me into a big room with a lot of beds in it, and there was Katusha sitting up and looking lovely.

"And when she saw the flowers and the fruit, what do you think she said?

"'Oh, Anton, how sweet of you! How kind and thoughtful! You *are* a darling,' and put her hands up towards me and her face and her lips—for me to kiss her.

"And then I did it. The dirtiest trick that ever one man played on another.

"I laid the flowers on the bed, stood the lovely basket of fruit on the little table, and kissed her.

"And she put her arms round my neck. She was so glad to see me, or else the flowers and the fruit, and was nicer to me than ever she had been.

"And by and by she said:

"'Well, that *was* thoughtful of you, Anton. That tells me

something about you that I didn't know.'

"'Well, now you tell me something about you that *I* don't know, Katusha darling,' I said.

"And she blushed and laughed, and knew what I was going to say . . .

"And she took me, comrades—on the strength of poor Karl's fruit and flowers! . . . Wasn't that a dirty trick?"

"Married you, eh?" asked Paladino.

"Yes, Katusha married me."

"That why you are here?"

"Yes. She ran away from me within a year."

"With Karl?"

"No. With Marco."

"Serve you right," commented Paladino severely. "You can join."

NO CORPSE—NO MURDER

"No Corpse—No Murder" is the eighth, and longest, of the stories in Part II, "Dirty Dogs of War", in Rough Shooting *(1938). It is the confession of a man who was almost hanged for a man he did not kill. "No Corpse—No Murder" was reprinted in* Ellery Queen's Mystery Magazine *(January 1944).*

Paladino turned his mocking, iconic glance to *le légionnaire* Sempl, a big thick-set man with heavy, lowering face, and eyed him speculatively.

"Wishing to be complimentary," he said softly, "I imagine that you must be in some difficulty, *mon vieux*. However, take any one of a dozen or so—of the dirtiest."

It seemed that *le légionnaire* Paladino was not an admirer of his comrade.

The man addressed as Sempl eyed Paladino in silence, with a bovine stare.

"He's ruminating," murmured Paladino at length. "The good ox is ruminating."

"Well," growled Sempl, a conversationalist who took two minutes to consider any question addressed to him and ten minutes to see a joke . . . "the worst I ever did."

"You've got the idea," observed Paladino.

"Well . . . I don't know."

"I'm sure you don't. Tell us anything you ever did outside eating, drinking and the usual routine of your hectic and brilliant life."

"Well," growled Sempl again, "I was once very nearly hanged for murder."

"Pity," observed Paladino. "But not an offence."

"And did you commit the murder?" he asked, breaking another stolid silence. Sempl laughed gutturally.

"I'll tell you," he said.

"That's the idea," admitted Paladino again.

"It was like this," began Sempl, after taking a long pull at the litre bottle of red wine that stood on the ground beside him. "I was living near a place called Proszl. All alone. In a charcoal burner's hut. That is to say, it was the hut of a charcoal burner."

"Quite. Quite," murmured Paladino.

"What I mean is that a charcoal burner had built it and lived in it, and had abandoned it. When I first came to Proszl and scouted round, there it stood, empty as a snail's shell; and just what I wanted, as there were no neighbours. Not near-by neighbours, anyhow. So I just went in and took possession. There was a clay fire-place and a good door, with bar and padlock and everything."

"*Appartement meublé*," murmured Paladino. "Furnished house, in fact."

"And there I settled down and looked around for—business."

"Business," murmured Paladino. "High finance? Shipping? Railways? Mines? Factories?" he enquired.

"No . . . no . . ." contradicted Sempl mildly, "wood-cutting, and selling it in Proszl. And just a bit of quiet Border smuggling on dark foggy nights, of which there were plenty during the winter, in that part of the world . . . That and odd-jobs."

"Odd *how* odd-jobs can be, isn't it?" commented Paladino.

"Odd what suspicious swine Police can be, especially near the Border," replied Sempl. "It wasn't very long before they seemed to get suspicious of me."

"Of you?"

"Yes. Half a dozen of them with a *brigadier* came one night and turned my hut upside down while I was out.

"Yes," he continued, "I came back from a little trip across the Border with a bit of tobacco in the turndown of my trousers where they were tucked into my high boots, and some silk stuff round my waist, under my coat, and would you believe it, the fools had lighted the lamp. So all I could do was to wait behind a tree in the darkness, and see who came out. As I say, the Police. And I nearly called out something to them too, as they marched off. Because if the silly fools had only come the night before they'd have made a haul!

"Anyway, next time I was in Proszl and saw the Police *brigadier*, I said:

"'*Sorry I was out the other night. You should have let me know. I'd have been there to welcome you.*'

"'*I'll be here to welcome you, one day soon,*' he said, nodding his head towards the Police Station and eyeing me unpleasantly.

"'*What for?*' I asked indignantly.

"'*For seven years,*' said he, '*and for fun and for smuggling, and for one or two other things.*'

"'*Even policemen have got to live, I suppose, though the good God knows why,*' I told him, and went on my way feeling a bit uncomfortable.

"Smuggling. So they were on to me. 'And one or two other things.' That's what I didn't like. Why couldn't the fellow speak up, like an honest man, and say what he meant? But what's the good of expecting a policeman to be an honest man?

"And that night I sat by my fire and wondered whether one of them had seen me reconnoitring Grandfather Grüntz's place. I haven't told you about Grandfather Grüntz, have I?"

"No," replied Paladino. "Has he anything to do with this interesting story?"

"Well, in a way, yes, because it was for murdering him that they didn't hang me. I mean, for not murdering him they were going to hang me."

"The busy fellows! Were they going to hang you for everybody you hadn't murdered?"

"No, only Grandfather Grüntz, the miser. He lived very much as I did—but not in such a gentlemanly way—in a hut like mine, but not so good, and in an even lonelier part of the forest, farther from Proszl than I was. I had offered to change huts with him once or twice, for that reason, but although his hut leaked badly when it rained and had a muddy floor when it wasn't frozen, he said he preferred his own.

"And I knew why. He had got a box of gold buried under that floor. Must have had. Everybody knew he was rich, and his name was Grüntz the Miser. So he must have been rich."

"Clear proof," observed Paladino. "It explains why he lived in a leaky shed in the mud, too."

"Well, there it was. Just a feeble old man whom you could kill with one hand, living in a hut with a rotten door that you could open with one hand, for all its bolts and bars. No dogs, no weapons, and no neighbours for miles. In fact, I was his nearest neighbour."

"And you mean to tell us you didn't murder him?" enquired Paladino. "I am disappointed in you, Sempl."

"You wait," grinned the Pole.

"I am," sighed the Italian.

"Well, how many times I went and watched that old devil through a chink between the logs of his rotten hut when he had covered up the window-hole, I couldn't tell you. But I never saw him handling money. He just sat about and scratched himself, or did a bit of cooking; or cobbled himself a coat, and now and again brought out a bottle of something—vodka or barley-wine or plum-gin. Even there he was a miser, for he allowed himself just one egg-cup full of whatever it was. Never more. And when I knocked at his door he'd whisk the bottle back behind the pile of sacks and rags which was his bed, before he'd open the door. And then, when I'd sniff and say:

"'*Something smells good!*' old Grüntz would say, "'*Yeth. It'th mithe.*'

"Mice! There wasn't enough in the place to keep a mouse healthy. Not of food and drink, I mean, but there must have been gold enough to keep all Proszl healthy, if all the tales were true.

"And there were tales enough, for the silly old beggar used to wander through the streets of Proszl three or four times a week, with a sack of rubbish on his back, that he tried to sell: rusty keys, insides of old clocks, a cup and saucer that didn't match, hats and boots that people had thrown away. That sort of thing. And although his stock wasn't worth ten kopeks, he'd buy things that took his eye: an old chair, a chest, a pair of brass candlesticks, sometimes even an old picture or a grandfather clock. And he'd find the money too. Haggle all day and give a quarter of what the thing was worth, but he'd find the money.

"And then, off he'd go through the forest with a damn great piece of furniture on his back, carrying it off to the capital, or some nobleman's house; and come back next day without it.

"Yes, but not without ten times as much in his old leather purse as he had given for it. So of course he had money, and of course it was in the ground under that hut. Where else would it be? There was nowhere else."

"One has heard of Banks," observed Paladino.

"Banks! Old Grandfather Grüntz? That dirty old bundle of rags, with hair a foot long and a beard two feet long and his toes sticking through his boots. Do you suppose they'd have let him cross the threshold of a Bank, even if he had had the courage?"

"Yes," replied Paladino, "if he brought money."

"Well he didn't."

"How did you know?"

"Shadowed him. Followed him from his hut to his journey's end and back, many a time. He never went near any Bank. He went into queer-looking old furniture shops, and now and again round to the back premises of private houses; but he never went near any Bank."

"But you never saw him disposing of money? Digging in his hut or anything of that sort?" enquired Gusbert.

"No."

"Didn't you go in and have a dig there yourself, one time, when you weren't trailing him?" asked Richeburg.

Sempl gave his thick guttural laugh.

"*One* time? Many a time."

"And found nothing?"

"Nothing whatever. There's an aggravating old devil for you."

"Disgraceful," agreed Paladino.

"Well, he got what he deserved, anyhow. It was after the first snowfall of the winter, just a hint that the cold weather was coming, six inches or so; and a woodman going into the forest to get a job done before the snow really fell, went by way of the path that led past old Grüntz's hut. And there he saw a sight that made him turn round and run back to Proszl quicker than he came, straight to the Police Station.

"For the door of old Grüntz's hut was battered in, and the interior was in a frightful state; his only chair smashed to bits; the table overturned; the bedding kicked into the fire; every sign of a terrific fight. And blood.

"Well, the Police weren't long in getting there, and it didn't take them long to discover that although snow had fallen and then stopped, and had fallen again and then stopped, there were foot-prints in the first layer of snow that were not quite obliterated by the second fall. And the foot-prints led from old Grüntz's hut straight to the river. That's the Leiprich, slow and sluggish and, at this time, frozen over with ice about an inch thick.

"Well, when they got there, what did they find but a hole in the ice. A nice convenient-sized hole—to permit of a body being thrust through it. Then that clever *brigadier*—with his theories all ready in advance and fitting his facts to them as they turned up—discovered that anybody with an eye in his head—the sort of eye that sees what its owner wants it to see—could make out foot-prints in the first layer of snow, again not absolutely obliterated by the second fall, that led from the hole in the river-bank straight to my hut."

"And I suppose on the strength of that, they arrested you?" enquired Mertin.

"No. Not then, they didn't, and I can tell you why. Because I wasn't there. What they did do was to break in and make as bad a wreck of my hut as I had made of Grandfather Grüntz's."

"As *you* had made?" remarked Paladino.

Sempl laughed.

"That's what I said. Yes, a pretty mess they made, with their pulling up and tearing down, and breaking open this and smashing that. And what with digging up the floor and going through everything with a fine-tooth comb, it's a wonder they didn't set fire to the place while they were about it, and burn it down. Anyway, one thing they didn't get was me. But what was as bad from my point of view, and almost worse than their getting me—they got my money. Quite a lot. And that must have put the scoundrels in a bit of a—what's the word?"

"A dilemma?" suggested Paladino.

"Yes. That's it. In a bit of a hole. For if they said they found no money, things wouldn't look so bad against me and I might get off. If, on the other hand, they said they found a lot of money; well, they'd have to hand it over. So they split the difference. They kept all the money that was in coin, and produced a lot of greasy notes that weren't worth much, and one big-denomination note for one hundred roubles.

"And why—the artful devils? Because some fool, as some fools do, had gone and written his silly name on the back of it. Ought to be a law against it. People ought to be sent to prison for doing that, and forfeit the money. There it was, plain as your face. *J. Kienkovitz* written on the back in red ink, and you can bet they lost no time in advertising for J. Kienkovitz, and hunting for him in the neighbourhood.

"Well, in the end, they found their J. Kienkovitz, and who do you think he was?"

"Not your long-lost brother? Or the child of the poor girl you . . .?"

"He was a furniture-dealer in Cratzow. One of those scoundrels who buy poor peasants' antique furniture, fake it up, and sell it to the rich bourgeois to put in their brand-new castles. That's who J. Kienkovitz was.

"And what could he remember about this particular note on which he had written his name? Why, he had paid it to old Grüntz the Miser!

"And that wasn't the only trouble with the money they found, either. Some of it had got smears and stains on it. Of course they said it was blood. Then some clever fellow from Police head-quarters at Warsaw, or somewhere, came along and went through his tricks. He found blood between the two snowfalls, if you know what I mean. Any amount of it. And said that somebody, bleeding like a pig, had been carried along the track from the hut to the river; and but for the fall of snow, would have fairly laid a trail of blood.

"Then he actually pretended he could tell them still more about the business, by looking for marks made by people's hands. What do you think of that? Silly, isn't it?"

"What? Identification by finger-prints? Very silly," agreed Paladino.

"Yes. And to earn his cabbage-soup he had to go off to my hut and pretend he found the same hand-marks on things there. Did you ever hear such villainy? Is it likely that my hands were always so dirty that they made a paw-mark on everything I touched—like a damn great bear in the snow?

"And by the time this clever fellow had had his say, and detectives and police had put two and two together and made forty, all that was left for them to do was to find me."

"Lucky for you they didn't, I should say," observed Gusbert.

"Think so, do you?"

"I do. If Grüntz had been murdered, there was a blood-stained track going from his hut to a hole in the ice, and foot-prints going from there to your hut—in which was money identified as having been paid to Grüntz. What with that and the same finger-prints in both huts, I should certainly say it was a good thing for you they didn't catch you."

"Oh, you do, do you? Well, they did catch me. And yet here I am. See? . . . What do you say to that?"

"What do I say? Why, luckier still if, having all that evidence, they caught you and you lived to tell the tale."

"Escaped, I suppose?" asked Panzecys. "You were able to get away from the Proszl police-cell?"

"Wrong again," grinned Sempl. "I'll tell you.

"I was hiding in Cratzow, waiting till I thought it was safe to go to the railway-station and take a ticket for the longest journey I could pay for. Very uncomfortable it was, too. I was up in a loft over some stables; and any time somebody might have shoved a ladder up to the trap-door and come up and found me. It doesn't look well to be found hiding in a loft."

"Not when the Police are looking for you," agreed Paladino.

"No, and there was the little matter of hunger and thirst, too. And during the evening of the second day I was up there, the man who brought the horse in had somebody with him, and they were talking about the murder, and wondering how much I had got away with, as only a few hundred roubles had been found in my hut.

"Still more uncomfortable I was when I knew that they were actually after me. By name too. It was funny, if you know what I mean, to hear those two strangers using my name. People I had never heard of, and who had never heard of me until that day. Must have seen it in the paper. Yes, and on a notice outside the Police Station, I thought. They'd have my name and description posted up outside every Police Station in the country.

"Well, I stuck it as long as I could, and then I made up my mind I'd sooner be hanged than starve any longer and go without a drink any longer. So, on the third night, I dropped down from the trap-door into the stable, climbed out of the window that pushed outwards—and was fastened on the inside, of course—and got down into the lane that ran beside the shop behind which the stables were.

"I knew my way about Cratzow fairly well, and made for the station. I felt I couldn't get away from the place quickly enough. I might have been safer walking, and then again, I might not. One has to eat, and one has to sleep somewhere, and that means one has to go into shops or break into houses; and I thought the quicker I got out of the country, the better, even if the railway-station was a bit of a risk. That's how I figured it out. See?

"Well, I had figured wrong, for I had only got up the steps and across the hall to the ticket-guichet, when I felt a tap on my shoulder, and as I jumped round, there was a damned great policeman grinning in my face.

"'*Evening, Sempl,*' says he. '*Cold, isn't it? Never mind. You just come along o' me and I'll put you where you'll be safe and warm.... Safe, anyway,*' he grinned.

"Not that he said 'Sempl,' of course. I changed my name when I joined the Legion. Took that of another man. You laugh? Well, I didn't laugh then, I tell you. It wouldn't have been so bad if I had had a good blow-out on the way to the station, but there was I with a belly three days empty and a throat three days dry, and a policeman as big as a house, with the flap of his holster open and his hand on the butt of his pistol.

"'*Come with you?*' said I. '*What for?*'

"'*Fun. See the sights. Inside and out. Outside first, inside after. Come on.*'

"And by the time he had got me out into the street again, there seemed to be half a dozen of them.

"Yes, I was for it all right, and no good kicking, though if there had only been the one policeman I'd have tried kicking all right—where it would do most good."

Sempl took another long pull at the wine-bottle, hiccupped loudly, and wiped his walrus moustache with the back of his hand, while his comrades eyed him speculatively.

"Well, you'd say that I was for the long drop, wouldn't you?" he continued. "You would have done, if you had heard the lawyers talk, anyway. They had got it all, chapter and verse; the motive for the crime; method of committing the crime; disposal of the body; and everything else. A sordid, brutal crime, the fellow called it, standing up there in his black gown and white bib, and wagging his finger at me as though old Grüntz had been *his* grandfather.

"There was one chap who seemed to have been paid to say what could be said on my account, and I came to the conclusion that they couldn't have paid him enough, for he hadn't one-tenth as much to say as the dirty pig who was trying to get me hanged. All he could say was that, in the first place, there was no body; in the second place, that the hundred-rouble note, on which J. Kienkovitz had written his silly name, might have been paid to me by old Grüntz in the way of business; and thirdly, that the man who committed the murder might have walked round to my hut just to put suspicion on to me.

"But the other fellow made short work of that.

"'*What?*' said he. '*No body? No you don't generally find the body after you've shoved it through the ice into a river. How many miles away do you suppose the body is by now? If you chuck a body into the river at Proszl, you don't expect to find it in Proszl a month later, do you?*'

"Then he turned to the hundred-rouble note, and asked the Court to look at me.

"'*Look at him,*' he said. '*Do you think that ever did a job of honest work worth a hundred-rouble note in all its life? And if you do, is it likely he ever did a job of work, worth a hundred roubles, for poor old Grand-père Grüntz? Do you think he ever had anything to sell that was worth a hundred roubles—unless he stole it? And if he had anything worth a hundred roubles, do you think Grüntz would have paid a hundred roubles for it? No, nor yet ten. And, anyway, we all know that Grüntz was no receiver of stolen property, and that's the only sort of property that this fellow ever had to dispose of.*

"'*And as for any talk about the murderer going from that sinister hole in the ice straight to the hut of the poor innocent fellow in the dock there, did anyone ever hear such childish nonsense in all his life? And if he did, let him answer me this question. When the wicked murderer had reached this poor innocent fellow's hut, leaving a trail that the police could follow, why did the trail stop there? Funny that the foot-steps should go to the hut and no farther, if they weren't made by the owner and occupant of that hut!*'

"And so it went on."

"And didn't you have a shot at an alibi?" enquired Mertin.

"Alibi? Alibi? What; proof that I was somewhere else, you mean?" asked Sempl.

"That's it."

Sempl laughed.

"No. It would have been quite a job to prove that I had been anywhere else, when footsteps led straight from my hut to Grüntz's, from Grüntz's to the hole in the ice, and from the hole in the ice back to my hut again! The Police swore, what no doubt was true, that there wasn't a mark in the snow for miles other than that nice triangle—my hut to his hut, his hut to the hole, the hole back to my hut—except for those of the woodman who was the first to go from Proszl along the track past Grüntz's hut. And of course, his footprints were as plain as an elephant's, whereas mine were under a couple of inches of snow.

"The judge was a nasty old man, a lot too fond of the sound of his own voice. Gave me a regular lecture; worse than old Double-Chin in the orderly room. Worked himself up into quite a state, saying it was one of the most cold-blooded, brutal, and dastardly murders that he had ever had the pleasure of hanging anybody for. You'd have thought Grüntz was *his* grandfather too. Called him a poor harmless inoffensive interesting old gentleman who was a credit to Proszl, with his great knowledge of furniture and his wonderful skill in spotting a genuine antique, whether in pictures, tapestry, furniture or what not.

"'A respectable and innocent old man who had never done anybody any harm, battered to death in so brutal a fashion that the whole of the inside of his house was wrecked; and then dragged, mangled and bleeding, through the forest; and thrust, while perhaps still alive and suffering, through the ice into the bitterly cold waters of the Leiprich, to be carried along in the darkness beneath the ice until merciful death overtook him.'

"According to the silly old crow on his perch up there, you'd have thought that Grüntz had been killed with a bludgeon, then frozen to death, and after that, drowned, for a change. I laughed, and that made him madder than ever. Fierce as a maggot he was, about what poor harmless innocent old Grüntz had suffered, and the number of deaths he had died.

"And so I was sentenced to be hanged; and, judging by the noise and the people's voices in Court, everybody was saying *'And a good job too!'* including the fellow who had pretended to try to get me off.

"Well, I got another free ride to Cratzow again, where there was every convenience for people who committed murders in the Proszl district; nice stone cells, good strong gallows, and willing hands to work them. And although a man in the condemned cell ought to have every kindness and consideration, I got a lot more consideration than kindness. They spent the time considering how they could annoy me and do me down. Kept me on bread and water. Woke me up at night, every quarter of an hour, to see whether I was still there. I didn't seem a bit popular in Cratzow prison. You'd have thought they had never heard of a murder before, nor had a man in the condemned cell.

"I tell you, I was quite glad when the day came—I lost all count of how time was going—when they marched in, long before dawn, and told me to get up.

"There was the Governor of the gaol, the Chief Warder, three or four turnkeys, a policeman or two, and the lawyer who hadn't done me any good at all, and another one, and the Chaplain; and they made a procession, stuck me at the head of it with the Chaplain in front, and out of the cell we marched, the Chaplain reading the Burial Service as we went along. Fine—burying you alive like that!

"We went down a corridor, turned to the right up some steps, through a door, out into a kind of shed, and there I had my first squint at a gallows. Just a platform like a boxing-ring with a trap-door in the middle. Well, two trap-doors, really, meeting edge to edge, and a lever, like the things in a signal-box, beside the trap-door. Above the trap-door was a great beam with a rope dangling from it and at the end of the rope was a noose.

"When the fellow pulls the lever over, it draws back the bolts that the flaps rest on, and down they drop on their hinges and let you through.

"Well, up goes the Chaplain—up the wooden steps—on to the platform, and does a right-turn and a halt beside the trap-door, being careful not to trust his own weight on it. And I noticed that someone had drawn a half-circle on one side of the crack between the flaps, and the other half on the other side. I had got to stand in that circle, and then my feet just covered the crack. See?

"Well, the turn-key kindly directed me where to stand, and asked me if I'd like to have my eyes bandaged. I said, '*No, of course not. This is the first hanging I have seen, and I might not see another.*'

"'*Quite likely*,' says the Chief Warder, while one of the turn-keys takes up the slack of the rope, puts the noose over my head, settles it comfortably round my neck and draws it fairly tight, arranged so that the noose is just under my right ear.

"'*That'll be all comfortable,*' he says.

"'*Suits me, Brother,*' says I.

"And then the Chaplain, who had measured it out just right, comes to the place where he does a good gabble to finish just as the lever goes—and I go, too.

"But about three words from the end, the Governor's secretary, or some other useful piece of work, rushes into the shed, yelling at the top of his voice.

"I let my attention wander from the interesting proceedings that were going on, and heard him say:

"'*A reprieve! A reprieve!*'

"And it looked as though all the trouble was for nothing.

"Everybody seemed bitterly disappointed; and I must say I felt a bit that way myself, especially as I had no doubt that I should have to go through it all again.

"The turn-key unfastened the rope, took it off my neck and the Chief Warder pulled me ashore, so to speak, off the flaps on to the part of the platform on which he and the Chaplain were standing.

"The Chaplain looked a bit silly.

"'*Does that go for next time, Your Holinesss, or have I got to hear it all again?*'

"'*Let us trust that you have been pardoned*' said he, looking puzzled, but not half as puzzled as I felt.

"So the procession formed up again, and back we went to my cell.

"'*Can I take my hat and go, then?*' said I to the Governor.

"'*You can't,*' says he, and added, '*I'll tell you more about it later,*' with a nasty look that meant:

"'*I'll tell you when you're going to be hanged as soon as I know myself.*'

"No, they didn't like me a bit in Cratzow gaol.

"Well, by-and-by, back the Governor comes, with some of the bounce taken out of him.

"It appeared that telegrams had been sent from the Police at Proszl to the Ministry of Justice at Warsaw, or the Secretary of State for Internal Affairs, or the President of the Rat-Catchers' Society, or somebody; and, whoever it was, had sent a telegram to the Governor of the Cratzow Gaol, and the secretary had opened it just in time. . . . Just think. If his wife had kicked him out of bed five minutes later, I shouldn't be here!"

"A thought to make one shudder," mused Paladino. "And what was it all about?"

"You'd never believe."

"No," agreed Paladino.

"Why! Who do you think had walked into Proszl the day before, and asked who the hell had been making hay in his house? *Grandfather Grüntz!*"

There was a simultaneous movement among the listeners about the camp-fire, as heads turned, chins were raised from the chests on which they were sunken, bodies shifted as, unconsciously, men sat up from the recumbent position in which they had lain upon their elbows or prone upon the ground.

"*What?*" whispered Gusbert. And even Paladino's cold face lost, for a moment, its mocking smile, and ceased to sneer.

"Grandfather Grüntz?"

"Yes. With a sack over his back, all hale and hearty, and no signs of his brutal bludgeoning, his drowning in the river or his being frozen to death, into the Police Station at Proszl marched Grandfather Grüntz, to make complaint that his hut had been broken into!

"Can't you imagine that clever *brigadier's* face, and the faces of those wonderful fellows who had found the foot-prints under the snow, leading from the blood-splashed hut to the broken ice and thence back to my place—from which I had obviously fled?

"I wish I could have been there when old Grüntz walked in.

They must have thought he was a ghost at first. Probably the *brigadier* ducked down behind his desk and crossed himself, until old Grüntz began to curse.

"*Nom de Dieu!* There were some heads scratched that day. Not only in Proszl, either. Why, when the newspapers came out, half the heads in Europe must have been attended to, and not the least puzzled were the kind gentlemen in Cratzow Gaol who had given me such a pleasant fortnight.

"And knowing that the Governor of the gaol couldn't do a thing to me, couldn't lay a finger on me, I told him just what I thought of him and his prison, and during that fortnight I had thought quite a lot.

"But long before I had finished telling him and the Chief Warder and the turn-keys and all the rest of them what I thought of them, they just turned me out. Threw me out of the place. Opened the gates and asked me to go. And by the time I went—with the money they had taken from me safe in my pocket again—there were some red faces in the reception-hall of Cratzow Gaol, believe me."

"And I suppose there were a few in Proszl Police Station too, when you got back there, eh?" grinned Mertin.

"Well, I can't quite say about that," smiled Sempl. "I didn't exactly go straight back to Proszl."

"No?"

"No. I made my way in the opposite direction, and did just what I had been going to do when that policeman pinched me at Cratzow railway station. Got just as far away from that part of the world as my money would take me."

"But why?" asked Gusbert. "Why didn't you go back to Proszl, and make 'em all look silly? It *was* Grüntz, I suppose?"

"Grüntz it was, without a doubt. There was not another Grandpa Grüntz in all Poland—Austrian, German or Russian. No, nor in all Austria, Germany and Russia, either. Grandpa Grüntz had come back all right; and only just in time, too, the old devil. According to the paper I got in Cratzow, he had just mooched in as usual, with a sack over his back, and no doubt with a fine wad of rouble notes in the money-belt he wore against his dirty hide. When they asked him where he had been, he said:

"'*Bithneth.*'

"He had just been on one of his tramps round the villages, looking into peasant's houses for odds and ends of old furniture and such, and had been away longer than usual. Been laid up with a sore foot or belly-ache or something; and nearly got me hanged."

A silence fell on the group about the fire.

"Yes, but what about his wrecked house?" asked Blanke.

"And the pools of blood and the hole in the ice?" said Richeburg.

"And the foot-prints going from your hut to his, and from his hut to the hole in the ice, and from there back to your hut?" asked Nul de Nullepart.

"Ah!" grinned Sempl. "What about it?"

"This is where you produce your qualifications for admission to the Dirty Dogs' Club, I presume?" asked Paladino.

"That's it. I'll tell you."

And again Sempl applied himself to the litre bottle, emptied it, and flung it over his shoulder.

"Open me another, or I won't say a single word," he grinned.

And with a dexterity which betokened practice, Mertin, with the back of the forte of his bayonet, knocked the top off another bottle of wine, filled a *gamelle* and passed it to the current hero of the evening.

"No, I wasn't going back to Proszl," he sniggered. "And for why? I *had* gone that night to old Grüntz's hut, determined to make the old devil cough up. I knew as well as I knew my name—which wasn't Sempl—that he had got *wads* there in that hut, and I was going to find it. What's the good of money to a man like old Grüntz? A rich man, and he dressed in filthiest rags, lived in a hut you wouldn't keep chickens in, never stood himself a square meal, never got drunk in his life. And there was I, with hardly enough to keep body and soul together. That sort of thing isn't right at all. I'm a good Communist, you know.

"Well—what was I saying? When I got round there, the place was dark, and I was just going to put my shoulder to the door when I heard a dry stick crack under somebody's foot, not far away. So I just crept round to the back of the hut, and lay low.

"This would do. This fitted nicely. The old devil would let himself in, light his old tin lamp, scratch himself, blow on his bit of fire, put on his pot of stew, and sit down to count his money while it warmed up. Then he'd hide the money with the rest; and I was going to see him do it, if I stayed there all night. I wasn't going to be such a fool as to shove his old door in until he was in the act of hiding the money. I wanted more than one day's takings. I wanted the lot.

"If he couldn't spend good money I could. I'd show him what money was for.

"Well, by the time I had found a good enough squint-hole— and the old beggar was always plugging them up with clay or bits of rag—I got a regular start. There was someone in there all right. He had lit the lamp; he had blown up the fire, put on the stew-pot, and he was counting his money.

"But it wasn't Grandfather Grüntz.

"No, it was a Jew pedlar, a man I had seen before. More than once. He worked a tremendous round. Took him about a year to cover his beat. I suppose he thought that, by the time he came to a place again, what he had sold there last time was worn out or lost or wanted renewing for some other reason. He was a man who had a good name, and there's no doubt he did a good business. Wonderful, the amount of stuff those chaps can carry.

"And there, beside the bed was his pedlar's box. No doubt he had met old Grüntz, and Grüntz had given him the key of his hut and told him he could use the place. Told him where to hide the key too. Must have done something of the sort, because I had heard him unlock the door.

"And suddenly the big idea came to me!

"There he was. Old Lowenski the Jew pedlar. Nobody knew where he lived and nobody cared. Nobody knew anything about him at all. Nobody had seen him come and, Name of a Name, nobody should see him go. Proszl would be a good long way on his round, and he'd have all the money he had taken between there and his head-quarters, wherever that might be.

"The chance of a lifetime.

"Round I crept to the door, and had a squint through the key-hole; and I didn't care if he heard me come or heard me breathing. If he did, and came and opened the door, so much the better.

"Well, that was an idea. I knocked. He came and opened the door, and I knocked again. On top of his head this time.

"But how the old devil fought, in spite of that. Fought like a wild beast. He grabbed old Grüntz's chair and caught me a frightful crack with it. And whether it was a genuine antique or not, there was a genuine enough club in Lowenski's hand as the chair came to pieces all round my head and shoulders. Lucky for me I had brought my cosh along, for although he was an old man, it would have taken me all my time to get him where I wanted him, with my bare hands. And by the time we had done, there were certainly what the Police call 'signs of a struggle'—if pints of blood and the smashing of everything in the place was anything to go by.

"Then there was the question of the body. As it was snowing, it seemed to me quite a bright idea to take him along to the river where I knew the ice wouldn't be too thick to break, shove him under, and let him continue his travels that way.

"Well, having got his wallet, I started him off, and then—and here's a funny thing—I found I couldn't go back to Grüntz's hut. Simply couldn't. And I'm not what you'd call a chicken, am I?"

"No," admitted Paladino. "You are not what I would call a chicken."

"Still, there it was. Back to that hut I couldn't go. And as I stood there looking at that black hole in the silver ice, I could see the face of that blasted *brigadier*, and hear his voice.

"'*I'll be here to welcome you one day soon—and for one or two other things.*'

"And I decided, there and then, that there were other places as good as Proszl.

"So I made straight for my hut, got my own little packet of savings, and made for Cratzow.

"And you know the rest."

"There's one thing I don't know," observed Paladino, reflectively. "You hadn't taken any money that belonged to Grüntz then?"

"No, not a *kopek*."

"Then what about the hundred-rouble note endorsed by Monsieur J. Kienkovitz?"

"Yes, wasn't that funny? Old Lowenski must have met Grüntz and done a deal. Met him by appointment for all I know, and Grüntz had given Lowenski that note that Kienkovitz had given him. Funny, wasn't it? It was that as much as anything that put that rope round my neck."

"Very funny," agreed Paladino. "In fact, you are a very funny man, Sempl."

"Yes. Am I elected a member of the Dirty Dogs' Club?"

"A life member," agreed Paladino with his cynical smile.

A VERY DIRTY DOG

"A Very Dirty Dog" is the last of the confessions of "dirty deeds" told in Part II, "Dirty Dogs of War", in Rough Shooting *(1938). It is the story of a young woman, who after a horrendous struggle and sacrifice, finds her lover in the arms of another woman. "A Very Dirty Dog" has not been republished until now.*

Chochinski was a melancholy creature who seemed perpetually to carry about with him the load of a great grief or a great remorse.

It cannot be said that, as a whole, the French Foreign Legion is a riotously cheerful body. The phrase 'merry and bright' does not perhaps describe it quite accurately. There are hectic times, of course, especially on the days declared by France to be National Holidays, great days of rejoicing, such as July the Fourth, or the Legion's own great *fête*, the Day of Camaron, when there is a wild gaiety, alcoholically induced, hectic, noisy and artificial, invariably ending in more or less fatal fighting between battalions or smaller units. But as a rule, the *légionnaire* is a reasonably sober and serious person.

When on Thursday night he goes to the canteen to spend his week's pay of threepence-ha'penny, he drinks to forget, and generally remembers—all that, under the stress of work, he had forgotten.

Paladino eyed Chochinski speculatively.

"Well, Misery," said he. "You ever done anything worth recording? Anything dirty, I mean, that might qualify you for membership of the Dirty Dogs' Club."

Chochinski took another pull at the litre bottle that he was fondling.

"I!" he answered. "I'm the dirtiest dog here. Most of you don't know what it is to be . . ."

"Kindly allow me to judge of that," interrupted Paladino. "We are none of us really the best judges of our own villainy."

"You shall judge, and the decision won't give even you much

trouble," was the reply.

"A girl in it, I suppose," sneered Paladino. "There generally is when a man wants either to whitewash himself or to give himself another coat of pitch. Well, did she go out in the snow with the baby done up in her shawl—as usual!

"Snow! " mused Chochinski. "Snow, did you say? Wonder if you know anything about snow. About real deadly cold. Literally deadly.

"Like most truly terrible and really dramatic stories, it's a short one," he continued.

"Lisa was very lovely. I'm not going to pretend that she was the loveliest woman that ever lived, or the loveliest woman alive, but I venture to say that no one here ever saw a lovelier; whether French, Spanish, Italian, Greek, Dutch, English, Scandinavian, Swiss, Austrian, Russian or any other. The whole lot of you put together never saw a lovelier and probably never one as lovely."

"Well, let's leave it at that. We've only till dawn, you know," interrupted Paladino in his incisive and superior manner.

"Well, I, such as you see me, was the man whom Lisa loved."

"Probably you weren't quite as awful a creature as you are now," said Pancezys. "You've deteriorated a lot, even in my time, Chochinski."

"Thank you," replied Chochinski. "It's nice to know that there was room for deterioration."

"One for you, Pancezys," laughed Paladino. "Who asked you to butt in?"

"Yes," continued Chochinski. "Whether so much different as all that or whether such as you see me, it was I whom Lisa loved. Now, one has heard of your hot-blooded women who'll die for love, or see that somebody else dies for love, if he doesn't do the right thing in the right way at the right time. One has heard of your hot-tempered Spanish women, Italian women, French women, any Latin women, in fact; but not one of the whole tribe or race or sub-division or whatever you call 'em, of Latin women, ever loved more deeply and truly and madly than Lisa did. She almost frightened me, at times, although I was her lover and had made love to her in the first place, roused her love as it had never been roused before, and she had loved no one else. Not to say loved. You would wonder that a girl so extraordinarily angelic-looking, so pink and white and pure, could possibly love as she did.

"If a great artist were painting qualities personified, if you know what I mean, such as Love, Faith, Truth, Purity, Maternity—or a Venus, a Juno, a Ceres, that sort of thing—I'm quite sure he would never have thought of taking Lisa for his model to sit for a personification of Love. She looked too simple, inexperienced, child-like, naive, ignorant. She could very well have posed for a typical *jeune fille*, unawakened, entirely uninterested in love and human relationships; the sort of girl they paint stroking a dove. You know the kind of thing."

"Take it for granted," interrupted Paladino.

"Well, there it was. A more innocent, inexperienced child of a girl never was than Lisa until I fell in love with her and made her fall in love with me; because, you know, love is very largely a matter of propinquity.

"Very like war, too, if it comes to that, with its stratagems, pursuits, sieges, capitulation, and binding treaty whereby the vanquished swears perpetual fealty to the conqueror."

"This story is very interesting indeed, to those who find it so," growled Sempl. "Very interesting indeed," and he yawned loudly.

Paladino turned towards him.

"Seeking sorrow?" he asked softly.

Sempl did not reply.

"Because I give you my solemn promise that you'll find it, if you interrupt again," Paladino continued.

"Well," went on Chochinski, "to cut a long story short and make a dull one possibly a little interesting, Lisa fell in love with me so utterly and deeply and desperately, that nothing else mattered. When I was with her, the sun shone and life was lovely. When I was not, the sky was grey and cloudy, and life a long apprehension. And you can take it from me that it wasn't my fault when I wasn't with her. I was a guide, and had to go away from time to time, whenever I got a job. I was hardly in a financial position to say to some English milord who wanted to climb our famous peak:

"'Oh, I can't be bothered with you. I'm in love.'

"Love may laugh at locksmiths but it cannot giggle for very

long at shopkeepers, landlords and the tax collector.

"Our respective mountain villages were only a couple of miles apart as the eagle flies, but unfortunately I was not an eagle. I had to climb down, and then climb up again, and the two miles were nearer ten by the time I had walked them. And very rough going indeed. Also one had partly to wade, and partly jump the stepping-stones of a torrent of ice-water between the two mountains; and according to the time of year, this water from the melting snows varied from a trickling brook to a rushing torrent that carried pine-trees along.

"If I had to guide a fat tourist down my mountain, across that torrent and up Lisa's mountain, I should have earned good money for the extremely difficult and rather dangerous trip.

"Oh yes, it was dangerous enough, especially when you came to the edge of a little precipice which might only be thirty feet in height, but was covered an inch thick with a film of the slipperiest kind of ice. Also when you trusted to a great unsteady boulder, wondering whether it would be for the very last time.

"No, although it was my profession to take that kind of risk, I never really enjoyed the scramble down my hill or the climb up Lisa's. Still, it varied from rather dangerous to extremely dangerous, and for the greater part of the year it was only 'rather.'

"Now, having told you that Lisa loved me passionately, madly, desperately, I must tell you that her parents didn't— neither her father nor her mother. Her mother objected to me on personal grounds. Her father objected to my income and position in life. He had got great ideas for his only daughter, his only child. One of them was to marry her to a town man; a man who lived in a good brick house, close to fine shops, with trams passing his door, and everything else that goes to make a gentleman. He had been to Rotzberg himself once, and had never forgotten the wonders and marvels of that tenth-rate place. I think he imagined Heaven in terms of Rotzberg.

"And of course the idea was not beyond reason. A good many quite well-to-do tourists came our way, and often a young and impressionable student who carried a fine roll of notes, would ask questions that showed he was wealthy, such as '*Where is the nearest telegraph office?*'; the sort of person who, after a night on a goose-feather bed with another one over him, and a couple of plain meals of bread and cheese and milk, and perhaps some coffee, gave his host what he considered adequate payment, and what was about ten times the amount the latter would have made out, if asked for a bill.

"Yes, old Lintz soon learned enough to judge his man, and when asked what was owing, to reply:

"'*Oh, it's nothing, nothing,*' or '*Well, just what Your Honour pleases,*' an answer which put the tourist on his mettle and old Lintz on the tourist's metal, handsomely.

"Yes, and undoubtedly more than one, and more than a dozen, of them stayed on a bit longer when they had seen Lisa, and could spare the time. Also, before long, as the tourist traffic grew, old Lintz took jolly good care that they did see Lisa, for he sent her to wait on them, and it was surprising what a number could find time to linger.

"So you can imagine that when it came to a choice between me—who made just enough for bread and cheese and an occasional schnapps, vodka, or beer—and some urbane and polished townsman with plenty of money, it didn't take Lintz long to choose. But neither did it Lisa. And when I grew jealous and pretended to do so, she'd laugh.

"'My dear,' she would say, 'do you think I'd look twice at some fat creature who can only walk up a mountain-side one step at a time, or get himself roped to a few others like him, in a place where you and I would walk along singing? I hate them. And I'm ashamed of father, trying to show me off before them. Fall in love! Why, I told a fat German who pawed me, that if he touched me again I'd pour the boiling coffee over his head.'

"Still, I did get jealous. My soul turned sour when I thought of her being offered for sale—for that is what it came to—by old Lintz. I grew bitter, and what is more, dangerous.

"One day, when the season was over and I could spare the time, and also knew that Lisa and Lintz would be unlikely to have any visitors, I went over, had an unforgettable afternoon of love with Lisa; and then, having been fairly caught by him, faced up to old Lintz and talked to him for his own good—if not for mine and Lisa's. I called him, among other things, a pimp and a pander, a foul and filthy rogue who offered his only child for sale, and other endearing epithets. In point of fact, he wasn't offering Lisa for sale, as I knew perfectly well. But he was offering her for matrimony, and to me that was just as bad.

"Well, he heard me out, and old Lintz had a very irritating and aggravating way of hearing one out. In situations like that, he would say not a solitary word until the other person had finished. Completely finished. And then, having enquired whether they really had done so, Lintz would say his say, brief and to the point.

"'All you say may be perfectly true,' he now observed. 'It may also be perfectly untrue. But listen. If there were not another man alive, Lisa should not marry you. Understand? Now, then, don't come here again, for fear I mistake you for a chamois (or a mad dog) and have an accident with my gun. Also, for the next twelve months at least, Lisa will not leave this house, except in my company. Good evening.'

"And that was the best I could get from Lisa's father, the man whom in all her life, she had never thwarted, defied, or even dreamed of disobeying. And mind you, when that can be said of a daughter, the father has stamped himself, his authority, his power and his image, pretty deeply upon the adolescent soul, upon the personality that has been clay to his potter's hand for all those years—about eighteen in this case.

"And so I sat and ground my teeth when I should have been earning something to put between them; ground my teeth and knitted my brows and clenched my fists at the thought of Lisa, across that unbridgeable ravine; thought of her waiting at table, making beds, standing at the door, looking picturesque in the evening, waiting for orders for wine or beer. There, where any wandering lout of a German student, any tripper of some *Bureau de Tourisme*, any wandering artist, any wealthy tourist, could see her as often as he liked, talk to her as much as he liked.

"And here was I who loved her, I whom she loved, forbidden to go near. And mind you, old Lintz was a man of his word, and as good as his word. If he said he'd shoot you on sight, he'd do just that, and explain it away very cleverly afterwards, as an obvious accident.

"Yes, if old Lintz was going to get you, he'd get you, all right.

"Well, I'll tell you things just as they happened and in the order in which they happened, though some of the story I didn't know till afterwards, from the newspapers, the police who came to question me, what old Lintz and his wife said, and what a friend or two of mine told me.

"For a time Lisa put up with it, and was the humble obedient daughter that she had always been.

"Then, as the season grew slacker and there was less to keep her employed, she brooded, thought of nothing else but our cruel lot, began to talk to her mother about it; and at last, gently-obedient and cruelly-repressed girl that she was, she broke loose, had a scene with her mother, and dared to tell her that she had had enough of this oppression, that she had a soul of her own and the right to a life of her own, that she could marry whom she pleased, and that that would be me.

"I think she frightened her mother for once, showed her that there are two sides to an argument, and that even an unmarried girl, a *jeune fille*, might have a mind and a soul of her own. It must have seemed to the worthy woman that a lamb had suddenly been endowed with the spirit of a tiger.

"Anyhow, promptly she sent for her husband and told him what had happened; that their hitherto sane, quiet and obedient daughter had gone mad, raving mad; had said dreadful things, such as that she would marry whom she liked; would marry no one whom she didn't wish to marry; would not be bought and sold like one of the cows.

"And once again, to make it perfectly clear, she repeated that she would not only marry whom she liked, but would marry me, the man whom her father had forbidden to come within range of his gun.

"Old Lintz must have gone mad, literally insane. Probably the only thing that saved him from a fatal apoplectic seizure was the certainty that the poor girl wasn't quite right in her mind, didn't know what she was saying, and would go really mad if she did know.

"Yes, she must be mad. There was no other explanation for the dreadful things that she was saying. Actually defying her father. Her father! Why, it was a kind of blasphemy.

"That evening—as soon as all the work was done, *bien entendu*—she was sent to bed in disgrace, without supper. But it was just as bad the next day. Worse, if possible. She demanded that her parents should hear what she had to say, and realize that they would only have themselves to blame if she did what she threatened to do, and that was nothing less than pack up all she possessed—which would go into a very small receptacle—leave her home for ever and, her lover having made all arrangements, she would go straight to him and be married the same day.

"Only a burst of hearty laughter saved the valuable life of Herr Lintz.

"And how, pray, enquired her mother, would her lover know when she was going? How would he make arrangements for so remarkably sudden a wedding?

"And then, attempting to bluff them, she said she had a means of communication with me, and that she kept me informed of all that was happening; of everything that was said and done.

"And then the seething pot that was the brain of the good and great Herr Lintz boiled over. He saw red, and like any other brainless bull, went *berserk*.

"Rushing at his daughter, shaking his great fist under her nose and threatening to give her a thrashing that she would remember for the rest of her life, he bade her go up to her bedroom immediately. He then instructed Frau Lintz to see her into bed, and then to take away every single stitch of clothing that the girl possessed, from her hat to her shoes and stockings, bring them into their room, lock them in the chest in which he kept his best clothes, money and a few other oddments, lock it again, and bring the key back to him.

"Now then, she could come out of her bedroom just as soon as she liked, by begging the pardon of her outraged father and taking an oath, Bible in hand, that she would never willingly see me again.

"Accustomed to obedience from babyhood and already terrified at her own wickedness in breaking the Fifth Commandment—which her father had bawled at her a dozen times that awful day—she had not the courage to reply to his Fifth Commandment with the verse from St. Paul:

"*Provoke not your children to wrath, but bring them up in the nurture and admonition of the Lord.*'

"Well, he had brought her up in the nurture and admonition of himself, and now he had provoked her to wrath. The worm had turned, or to speak more respectfully of Lisa, the lamb had defended itself and defied its attacker.

"When, next day, her mother went to the room and gave her her choice between bread and water, with imprisonment, and her usual milk or coffee, eggs and bread and honey, with freedom, Lisa replied that if she had to stay in this room till she was white-haired, she would never give her promise to see no more of me. On the contrary, she would marry me at the first opportunity; and that, far from being ashamed of herself as her father expected, she was ashamed of parents who would try to make their daughter marry someone whom she did not love; make her marry to the advancement of their wealth rather than to that of her own happiness.

"And the same the next day, and the next. And after he had humbled, as he thought, her proud spirit, with three days more of bread and water, and little enough of either, the good Herr Lintz himself came to his daughter's bedroom, and said anything that might hitherto have been left unsaid.

"Among other things, he promised that he would, on the morrow, give her the soundest thrashing that ever a wicked, disobedient, deceitful, unfilial, blasphemous daughter had ever received from a righteously incensed and grievously outraged father.

"That night, Lisa did one of the bravest things ever done by man or woman. It doesn't sound much, but if you have the beginnings of an imagination, you can perhaps make a rough guess at what the girl must have suffered before she made up her mind to do it; and, after that, the cruel cruel physical suffering crowned by a mental agony on which, even now, I don't care to dwell.

"Upon hearing her parents go up to bed, she waited until she was certain that they were asleep—and one imagines that they were neither light nor silent sleepers, and that she knew that it would take quite a considerable noise to arouse either of them.

"Getting out of bed and feeling as shaky as even the healthiest person does after lying down for four days, on starvation diet, she went to the window and looked out. How deep was the snow?

About a foot, judging from the present apparent height of a post which she could see by the light of the lamp. It was freezing bitterly, and the north-east wind was blowing, that cruel wind that is just the opposite of the *föhn* wind that thaws the snow and melts the ice.

"And what would be the state of affairs down at the bottom of the ravine? The river would not be frozen, but there would be a treacherous bridge, partly of stepping-stones and snow, partly of snow alone, that would have to be crossed; crossed in the dark.

"Now, consider that state of affairs for a girl properly dressed. To leave a warm bed and a warm house, climb out of a window into a couple of feet of snow and attempt to make, in the darkness, a descent that was not easy in broad daylight; to cross a torrent that was difficult to cross in broad daylight; and to make an ascent on the other side that was even less easy than the descent.

"Again, remember, in darkness, in the middle of the night.

"Now then, what would the same adventure be for a girl who had not a stitch of clothing on her; who had not a pair of slippers, much less a pair of stout nailed boots? Why, it would have been a misery, nay, an impossibility, for the warmly-dressed girl if she had everything but boots. It would have been a cruelty if she had had no gloves. And Lisa had not even stockings, much less boots; not even sleeves, much less gloves. She had, I tell you, nothing. Her damned mother and father would see to that, though not dreaming, we must admit, of her doing anything of such appalling courage.

"Take any of us, with our bits of *ferblanterie*,[4] thinking we are, perhaps, a little bit brave; how many of us hardened ruffians who have lived like wild beasts, would have the physical hardihood, not to mention the courage, to have made such a journey as that, naked, with the thermometer far below zero.

"Well, that's what Lisa did. Somehow—God knows how—she scrambled down the mountain-side; one might almost say the side of a precipice, in darkness, with no faintest sign of a path of any sort. And mind you, with no light, not even a candle. Slipping and sliding, stumbling and falling, at times crawling on

---

[4] *lit. tin-ware. Decorations and medals.*

hands and knees, she partly climbed and partly fell to the bottom of the gorge, and then, having found the river, a thin black line between the banks of snow that rested on treacherous thin ice, she sought for the crossing-stones.

"And time after time, thinking she had found the stepping-stones, she tried to cross where there were no stones at all, got a little way over the snow, and then, as she came towards the middle of the torrent, went through into the icy water. Had the stream been less swift, two or three inches of ice would quickly have formed and the river could have been crossed anywhere.

"At last she either found the stones and crawled across or, having fallen into the water where it was comparatively shallow, made her way to the ice and snow on the other side, and crawled out on to the bank. No one knows, or ever will know, exactly how she got over, because it snowed heavily again that night and all traces were covered.

"And having got across—and she must by then have felt more dead than alive—she began the upward climb, and more on hands and knees than upright, made her way up . . . I had almost said up the side of the cliff. It was a steep mountain-side anyhow, and had she not been a mountain girl, bred and born to scrambling and climbing over rocks in summer and winter, she could never have done what she did.

"She got to the top, and made her way through the trees along what should have been a path, leading to my hut.

"What must her feelings have been when at last, after that nightmare, that bitter cold hell of suffering, she opened my door and stepped into warmth and light.

"And what must have been her feelings when she saw me sitting there in my comfortable old chair by the fireside with Rotzberg Rotha in my lap, my arms about her, hers about my neck.

"Rotha Karlinger, the notorious Rotzberg girl, friend of all the students and anybody else who could pay for her company.

"What must have been her feelings, I say? She could no more return to her home than she could stay there with me, her lover, her betrothed—and Rotha Karlinger.

"I'm glad we shall all die to-night. Glad that I shall, anyway. For though I have lived in Hell since that moment, I haven't the courage to blow out what brains I have. I haven't the courage, and she, that little quiet Lisa, had done as brave a thing as ever man or woman did. Talk of the woman in that American book—what is it, *The Hut of the Uncle Tom*—who crossed a river on the moving cakes of ice—pah!—in broad daylight, fully dressed and shod. Compare that with what Lisa had done in pitch darkness, bare-footed and naked.

"I sprang to my feet and threw Rotha Karlinger from me, and rushed to Lisa, too late. She turned and fled into the darkness, and I, with my eyes blinded by the light, could see nothing. . . ."

Chochinski fell silent and sat motionless, save for a hand that moved as though he had St. Vitus's dance, as though he were spilling sand from it, feeling the texture of a material—or counting thirty pieces of silver.

No one spoke, but all stared at him in contempt, in hatred, in anger, and one or two in pity.

"They found her two days later," he said. "Scratched and torn and cut, she had stumbled on blindly in the darkness, and fallen at last asleep—the sleep of death. Thank God it is a peaceful, some say a pleasant and happy, ending."

"Having tried it, I presume," observed Paladino.

Chochinski smiled feebly.

"I think and hope that that is the worst thing I have ever done, the meanest and basest and most treacherous. Do I qualify for membership of the Club of Dirty Dogs?"

"Handsomely," replied Paladino. "You will probably be elected one of the officers."

Suddenly a Snider boomed and Schenko, looking out through a *creneau*, staggered back and fell from the cat-walk down into the enceinte.

"*Aux armes!*" bawled Paladino, as every man, grabbing his rifle, sprang to meet the rush of Lolos that surged over all four walls, like a wave.

The struggle that followed was long and desperate, ending in a wild *mêlée* in which single *légionnaires* with whirling rifle-butts or darting bayonets fought desperately each against a dozen; dying, man by man, until but one of them was left alive.

I SAW A VISION!

"I Saw a Vision!" is an article about a vision Wren had as a young boy, when a Viking ship comes ashore and abandons a man. The vision might have inspired the next story "Not Seeing But Believing", but the ships are of different types. The article first appeared in the magazine, Prediction *(December 1938). The article was referenced, and a fair amount of it quoted, as a chapter, "When Percival Christopher Wren Saw a Ghost Ship", in the book* Psychic Experiences of Famous People *(1947) by Sylvan Muldoon. The article in* Prediction *included a picture of Wren and a headnote stating that the article was "specially written for Prediction."*

It is my good fortune to enjoy a large number of very remarkable and interesting dreams of great significance to the psychologist. I also experienced a vision once, but only once. Now, a vision must not be confused with a day-dream or any other sort of dream whatever. A dream is the product of the unconscious mind; a day-dream is caused wilfully by the conscious mind; a vision has nothing to do with either, but is external and objective, and is experienced when you are wide awake. You cannot make yourself dream; you can make yourself day-dream; you cannot make yourself see a vision.

And, to me, the vision is one of the most inexplicable of all the curious mental phenomena that puzzle the human intelligence; and this is partly because it is not a purely mental phenomenon, but is also physical. This is obviously so, because, in a vision, one sees with the physical eye and hears with the bodily ear. (Incidentally, I do not know of a case in which the corporeal senses of smell, taste and touch have been involved).

When one reads that Joan of Arc heard voices one knows that she experienced visions, and that the statement that this occurred during day-dreams is erroneous.

Similarly, when the Biblical prophets saw impalpable forms and heard discarnate voices, they were experiencing visions, something entirely different to revelations when angels appeared to them in dreams and made pronouncements. And, once again, the vision is to be carefully distinguished from the hallucination which is the projection of a disordered mind. No, the vision is not something imagined at all, whether by a sane or an insane person, but is something *seen*—hence the name—really seen, although itself not real. Or is it just as real as a bowler hat, though impalpable, imponderable, intangible, inasmuch as it is visible and is within the experience of a very large number of perfectly ordinary common people like myself.

Here is my own and only such personal experience, believe it who will, and explain it who can. It happened when I was a small boy staying at a seaside resort on the east coast, at about seven o'clock on a glorious July morning.

Sleeping and dreaming? I was shrimping, walking along the water's edge, bare-legged, splashing, pushing a net, and as wide awake, as truly aware, and as sharply conscious as ever I have been in my life.

There was no one about at that early hour, and I was just thinking what a sound plan it was thus to prolong the day by getting out before breakfast, when suddenly, looking up from my net and glancing out to sea, I saw the Ship. It was as real as any ship I ever saw; not a phantom ship like the Flying Dutchman, but normal and solid-seeming. It was of about the size of one of those liner's lifeboats optimistically labelled "for the accommodation of 56 persons," but it was of different shape, inasmuch as the high bows formed their own figure-head, crudely dragon-shaped, and the stern was also high.

The sturdy, stumpy mast supported a long yard and a heavy sail, torn, strained and dirty, on which some device had been roughly limned in tar and red paint. Over each gunwale hung a row of shields, whether of wood, or of hide, stretched over metal, I was not sure; for they were dirty, wet and salt-encrusted.

Seated on the thwarts of this boat or ship were four lines of rowers, two men to each oar. Standing up in the stern, and holding a tiller, or perhaps a long and heavy oar resting in a rowlock and serving as a rudder, was the helmsman. Other men, of better sort or superior rank, knelt in the bows, sat in the stern, or stood by the mast.

Heard as Well as Seen

What interests me most, perhaps, about this vision is the fact that it was evident quite as much to the ear as to the eye; for when a man shouted, the heavy sail was let down with a run, and, a little later, at another order, the rowers backed water, the consequent sounds were loud, clear, and precisely those that are heard when any big boat or small yacht is thus handled. The ship grounded gently and audibly in shallow water; and the attention of its occupants was then turned to a man whom hitherto I had not noticed. He half lay on the bottom-boards, half leant against the mast. An enormous man, standing beside the helmsman, pointed at the recumbent one, gave another order, and three or four of the sailors pulling him roughly to his feet, thrust him headlong overboard. There were shouts of laughter as the man, apparently revived by the cold water, slowly rose, staggered ashore, and collapsed, close to where I stood, at the water's edge.

A seaman in the bows, picking up a pole or boat-hook, then thrust the boat off, the rowers plied their long oars, the helmsman put the tiller over, the thick heavy sail was hoisted, and the long-ship made out to sea. It did not vanish like the morning mist or disappear as does the figment of a dream when the sleeper awakes. It "proceeded," as they say in the Navy. Simply sailed away. The man left behind was lying in the posture of the Dying Gladiator, and I realised that he was either badly wounded or mortally sick.

The Message

As I stood—not frightened, bemused or amazed, but accepting the whole impossible affair as the right and proper sort of thing to happen to a small boy, just after dawn on a lovely morning by that magic sea—the man raised himself on his elbow and looked straight at me. I can see his face now, most distinctly; burnt, weather-beaten, lined and wrinkled beside the eyes, his big moustache and beard fair; his hair long and unkempt, fairer still where it protruded from beneath a rusty iron head-piece like a skull-cap, unadorned by the tall white wings one sees in Viking

85

pictures; the face and head, save for the long locks, such as one may see any day on the quay of a Devon fishing village. As I gazed enthralled, he spoke to me and—this is amazing—I understood what he said. His words were :

"Fight well, and you'll win in the end"; and I never heard or understood words more clearly.

As he said them, his eyes closed and his head sank down upon his arms.

Filled with pity, the deepest sympathy, and some alarm—not at these supernatural and fantastic happenings, but at the sight of a man dying, as I knew this sailor to be—I sprang forward with outstretched hands to raise his head from the water . . . and he was not there. Quickly I looked where the ship should have been tacking towards the horizon, but the ship had disappeared as well.

This is an accurate account of a true vision—as distinct from a day-dream or a hallucination. I saw and heard with two of the actual bodily senses, and can give an eyewitness account of this real event—because an eye-witness I was.

What is the Solution?

The explanation? It is folly and a waste of time to try to explain the inexplicable. As to speculation—did my unconscious mind produce from its store of tribal history a memory of this incident and cause the physical retina to behold what was in the mind's eye? Did the time and the place (and the anniversary perhaps) cause the unconscious mind to perform one of its incomprehensible gambols? Or did the time machine slip a cog and—but this brings us to the fourth-dimensional sphere and the time to stop.

Anyway, I have seen a vision, with no imagination about it; for I should have imagined something wholly different from that poor, bedraggled and battered waif of the ocean, with its crew of rough wolfish-looking men in stained homespun leather, and sheepskin, their accoutrements rusty, without panache—all quite unlike the pictures. I should have imagined something pretty, from a picture-book. What I saw was real.

NOT SEEING BUT BELIEVING

"Not Seeing But Believing" is the story of three friends who, after an encounter with a faquir, go fishing and two of the men dive overboard to avoid a ghostly Portuguese galleon. "Not Seeing But Believing" was originally published in The Passing Show *(January 28, 1939) under the title, "The Uncanny Scots." It was the second story in Part I, "Queer", of* Odd—But Even So *(1941).*

Really to appreciate this story, one should have known Alexander Anderson Elliott, one of the most level-headed, sane and sensible men I ever knew. Indeed, practical and unimaginative to a degree, this Lowland Scot, who was sparing of encomium, used "sensible" as his highest term of praise.

Manager of the Mahimari branch of the Rangoon and Shanghai Banking Corporation, he would allude to his most valued and admired customer as a sensible man. A lover and keen student of literature, he would refer to the wife of the Commissioner, a kindred spirit and fellow-worshipper of Burns, as a sensible woman. I once heard him speak of his valued Goanese butler, who had stood behind his chair for a quarter of a century, as a sensible boy.

As he would himself have said, there were no frills about Alexander Anderson Elliott, no high-falutin', no nonsense. Apart from his somewhat dour and Calvinistic religious faith, he believed in what he saw, in what he knew, and in what could be proven. A dependable, admirable, likeable man, slow but very sure; a lover of truth for its own sake, because facts are facts—and there is no getting away from them, ye ken.

While far from saying all he meant, he invariably meant all he said, and that, as a rule, was little.

Sometimes, when I met him at the weekly meeting of the Mahimari Literary Society of which he was a pillar and an ornament, I was reminded of a quotation, I believe from Robert Louis Stevenson's "Weir of Hermiston" in which he refers to the Elliott clan as the 'clay-cauld Elliotts.' For this particular Elliott was, apparently and externally at least, clay-cauld; dour, unemotional, unimaginative, and, save on one or two matters, unenthusiastic.

Incidentally, it was typical and symptomatic of the man, that he had no use for Robert Louis Stevenson whatsoever. Give him Sir Walter Scott. Scott, the whole of Scott and nothing but Scott, rather than any of Robert Louis Stevenson, a weak and windy imitator of the Wizard of the North.

Keep carefully this picture of Alexander Anderson Elliott in your mind when you consider the account that he gave me concerning the deaths of Alistair Lennox Gordon and Angus McIlraith. For he alone saw them die; his tale of their deaths is the sole evidence of how they, in the full flush of their manhood, met their astounding end.

Now, as is plain from their names, Alistair Lennox Gordon and Angus McIlraith were brither-Scots of Elliott, but two men less like Alexander Anderson Elliott it would be impossible to find. They were red Celts and mere Highland men. He was a black Lowlander—and, in their opinion, little better than a Sassenach.

Alistair Lennox Gordon, keen soldier and adjutant of the Second Battalion of a fine and famous Highland Regiment, was, as is by no means so unusual among soldiers as is supposed, a poet, an artist, and such a dreamer as only a really practical man can be. He read metaphysics, wrote verse, and studied as deeply as is possible to a European, the science or art, the theory or religion—or whatever it may be—of *Yoga*.

He was not of that unfortunately large proportion of Britons, and particularly of British soldiers, who do but encamp in the East, albeit for a lifetime, whose life is in the East but not of it, and who pride themselves on creating a cantonment, a bungalow, a garden, a Club, to be a "corner of a foreign field that is for ever England."

Alistair Lennox Gordon considered the East, its philosophies, religions, ethics, standards and viewpoints to be more interesting than those of the West. Not necessarily better or preferable, but more interesting; and if India is the White Man's land of regrets, one of Gordon's regrets was that a White Man can penetrate so short a distance beneath its surface, can know so little of the infinitely varied, interesting and mysterious Indian life which seethes around him.

That such a man should have much in common with Alexander Anderson Elliott seems improbable; and yet they were good friends, possibly by reason of the attraction of contrasts, probably because both came from the right side of the Border, if from different sides of the Grampians.

Angus McIlraith, Civil Surgeon of Mahimari, although bred and born on the heather by the banks of a lonely loch, and within sound of the far northern sea, had traits in common with Elliott, inasmuch as he was by nature something of a cynic, a little of a sceptic, and a scientist trained in research of facts and origins, rather than fancies and theories; of physics rather than metaphysics.

Nevertheless, his mentality, spirit and personality, were more attuned to the tempo of those of the soldier, Alistair Lennox Gordon, than to those of the banker, Alexander Anderson Elliott. For in spite of his acquired cynicism, his trained scepticism, his inherited incisive and practical mind, he was gifted with the blessing, or the curse, of second-sight.

The fact annoyed him intensely, because its phenomena were inexplicable, unscientific; almost, to such a man, something of which to be ashamed, something disreputable.

On the other hand, Alistair Lennox Gordon, having discovered that Angus McIlraith was second-sighted, was not only intrigued and deeply interested, but actually envious. And it annoyed him that when questioned on this subject, McIlraith was apt to turn dour and dumb.

On that amazing day when Angus McIlraith walked into Alistair Lennox Gordon's room and said, "Ginger Stewart's dead!" the former felt that he had given himself away as the miserable unscientific dilettante that he thus admitted himself to be. Superstitious auld spey-wife. Charlatan. Seer. Warlock.

"Damned 'Old Moore,' aren't I?" he growled. "Blethering, havering fortune-teller! Nevertheless, poor Ginger's gone. Fell down the *khud*. Broke his neck."

And in due course, the news had come through from near Chaubattia. Stalking *goural*, Stewart had foolishly crossed a tract of slippery shale that sloped towards a precipice. In doing so, he had started a miniature avalanche, gone with it over the edge, and fallen a thousand feet. It had been a fortnight before the news had reached Mahimari—a fortnight after Angus McIlraith had announced, it to Gordon.

And before Alistair Lennox Gordon had finished questioning McIlraith about his gift and power of second-sight, the latter heartily wished that he had never admitted his knowledge of Stewart's death, and by so doing confessed the disgraceful secret of his irregular and unscientific mentality.

But the fact remained, deplore it or even deny it as he might. The keen scientist, physician, surgeon, and research worker, had an intelligence—however brilliant, razor-edged and diamond-hard—that was apt, and able, to wander in the uncharted mists and bemusing fogs of an unknown, if not unknowable, hinterland of the mind where the normal and the abnormal, the natural and the supernatural, mingle in a mysterious and affrighting confusion.

So the two Highlanders liked each other very well, and tholed the Lowlander, also very well—for was he not a fisherman, a true disciple of Izaak Walton who, but for some inexplicable error of Providence, would have been a Scot, and have fished the Dee, Don, Spey, Tweed, Forth and Tay, instead of the miserable River Dove, and have written poems about great trout and noble salmon; epics of The Compleat Angler, who fished with worms for tiddlers, and yet was so truly possessed of the root of the matter, so great a lover of the noble sport.

Now had Izaak Walton but been Alexander Anderson Elliott, there were the Compleat Angler indeed! For to Elliott, both these ardent fishermen doffed their blue bonnets. So great was he that he could afford to be small. So great a master of rod and reel, so fine an expert of the fly that he was not ashamed to fish with a piece of string, a lump of lead and a hook baited with carrion. In other words, Alexander Anderson Elliott was, *faute de mieux*, a keen saltwater fisherman; and since there were no monsters to be caught with rod and line after a half-day's battle, he was content, rather than not fish at all, to dangle a string in his hand, from the side of a row-boat.

It wasn't sport. He didn't call it fishing. But it was catching edible fish, and might perhaps, in broad-minded tolerance, be called a sort of fishing—fishing for the pot, you understand, in a place where food was neither succulent nor varied.

So, almost every Sunday of their lives, the three Scots put out to sea in a small boat, baited their hooks, let them down into the ten-fathom depths of the tropical sea that washes the shore of Mahimari, and patiently waited to see what good luck would send them.

They reminded me of the Three Wise Men of Gotham, who went to sea in a bowl, for, like them, had the bowl been stronger, my tale had been longer. Or, at any rate, theirs would.

One morning, as was their wont, these three friends set forth at dawn for their daily ride, that liver-shaking, lung-expanding, circulation-improving morning ride which is so valuable and enjoyable a feature of those parts of the East in which it is available.

It is good to rise before dawn; to drink tea and eat fruit; to pull on rat-catcher riding-kit; to find the horse at the door, palm his soft nose, stroke his sleek neck, mount and ride forth to see the rising of the sun; to take an hour's hard exercise; to return, get bathed and dressed and ready for breakfast; and so to the day's work.

As he passed the Club, Elliott would pull up and wait for McIlraith, who lived there, unless the doctor already awaited him at the end of the drive; and the two, riding past the end of the British Infantry lines, would, in their turn await, or find waiting, Captain Lennox Gordon, at the gate of his bungalow compound.

The three would then trot off, canter down the Ladies' Mile, and, from its end, gallop into the desert. For, on three sides, Mahimari is surrounded by the desert like a sea; and on the other, is bounded by a sea like the desert, a sea on which no sail is ever seen, much less the distant smoke of any steamer. Small boats, a few, there are, and on the weekly use of one of them the three had an inalienable lien.

"Hullo! Look who has come to visit us," said Gordon, as they reined in to breathe their horses at the end of the sharp gallop to the sea, and pointed with his switch to where a *sanyasi, saddhu, bairagi, faquir,* or other brand of professional Holy Man sat, cross-legged, facing the sunrise, contemplating Nirvana, and doubtless acquiring merit.

A curious phenomenon in that vast expanse of sand and sea, for as Lennox Gordon observed, he was simply that, and nothing more.

As a rule, such a *faquir* sits beneath a tree, or has, if not four walls and a roof, four posts and a thatch; there are one or more stones, larger or smaller, painted red, as a sign and a token of the presence and the favour of a god; some form, however crude and sketchy, of a shelter or a shrine.

But here was no sort of shelter, no kind of shrine, no signs of the beginnings of either. Simply a man, ash-smeared and almost naked, sitting utterly detached, disorientated; his sole impedimenta a yard-long iron rod to the end of which a ring was jointed, and a small brass *lotah*, a drinking-cup for which in that desert place there was no water.

"D'you mind if I go and have a *bukh* with him?" said Alistair Lennox Gordon, who never missed a chance of conversation, be it but a few words, with any *sanyasi* or *faquir* whom he might encounter, though well aware that a great percentage of them were sturdy rogues, fraudulent beggars and arrant impostors, too lazy to work and too cunning to starve while ignorant and credulous villagers could be terrified and exploited. For he was also aware that a minority of these people were not only genuinely Holy Men, but philosophers and theologians, metaphysicians and students of the occult; men from whom he had much to learn, and at whose feet he was not ashamed to sit.

He would be able to tell, almost with a glance at his caste-marks, and certainly after a few words, whether this man were one of those for whom he was always seeking; or whether, as was more likely, he was a *bhang*-sodden brute, one of the vast horde of pestilent parasites that prey upon the hard-working poverty-stricken peasantry of this benighted land.

"We'll all come," replied Angus McIlraith; and, dismounting to stretch their legs, slacken their horses' girths and give them a rest, the three men, dropping the reins over the horses' heads, strolled over to where the *faquir*, ignoring them, stared steadily out to sea.

The horses, not only trained to stand, but untempted by a

single blade of grass or the sight of any green living thing, stood with drooping heads and whisking tails, and perchance also contemplated an equine Nirvana, even as they acquired merit.

"Good morning," said Gordon to the *faquir*, paying him the compliment of assuming that he was an educated man who could talk English. "You are a stranger here, aren't you?"

"I am a stranger everywhere," replied the man coldly.

"I thought I hadn't seen you before," continued Gordon pleasantly. "Are you going to make a long stay?"

"I am like the wind which bloweth whither it listeth. Why do you ask?"

"Because I should have liked to have visited you occasionally, and had a talk."

"About what?"

"Oh, our respective attitudes to life; our philosophies, and such matters as what it is that drives you to move as freely as the wind, and me to remain in one place, almost like the tree that is but waved by the wind."

"I shall be gone to-morrow. Even had I been remaining, I doubt whether we have any common mental ground on which to meet."

"Oh, I think all intelligent men have that, Swami-ji."

"Yes, intelligent men . . . Do you happen to be a policeman?"

"I think we may as well continue our ride," observed McIlraith, turning his somewhat disapproving gaze from the *faquir* to Gordon.

"No, I am not a policeman," replied the latter, without answering McIlraith.

"What are you, then, besides being a 'Sahib'?" replied the *faquir*, a wealth of contempt in his voice as he uttered the last word.

"Like yourself, a student, a seeker."

"After what?"

"The truth."

"I won't plagiarize Pilate," sneered the *faquir*, "but it would be interesting to know what you mean by the word."

"A difficult word to define," agreed Gordon patiently, adding with a smile as he turned to go, "Volumes have been written about it."

"And no two in agreement," observed the *faquir*. "What you seek is not Truth, but Power, the craze and the curse of the Occidental. To you, *yoga* means some new power, and that either physical or mental—but never spiritual."

"*Yoga* interests me deeply. I had hoped . . ." began Gordon, turning back.

"Hoped . . . ? Hoped to see tricks? Hoped to learn how to do them?"

"Come along, Gordon," said McIlraith, tapping his boot irritably. "Why waste time with a fellow who . . ."

"Oh, your time shan't be wasted, Sahib," interrupted the *faquir*. "Doubtless you are another of the seekers after Power."

"I have the power to . . ." began McIlraith.

The *faquir's* long thin arm shot out, and a skinny forefinger pointed straight at McIlraith's face.

"You have the power to—what? To have me persecuted by your hireling police? To strike me with your whip? To make me what you'd call a present of the toe of your boot? I'll give you a better power than that. I'll give you the power to see the invisible . . . *You*—with your feeble gift of second-sight; a gift which you can neither use nor understand. I'll give you a two-edged gift of power."

"And you too," he added, turning and pointing at Gordon.

"Well, I'm damned!" observed McIlraith, marvelling at the man's accusation. For how should this ash-smeared mendicant, his long and filthy hair matted with cow-dung into a mass, his whole life and conduct, a negation, a denial, a renunciation of his human humanity, know anything about Angus McIlraith and his gift of second-sight? And who had thought for a moment of touching him with a riding-whip or a boot? A nasty-tempered beggar . . .

"To you too, the same gift," continued the *faquir*, still pointing at Gordon, "A seeker, you shall find. Find yourself endowed with the power to use the power with which you are endowed—though you know it not. You too shall have the two-edged gift of seeing the invisible."

"That'll be interesting," replied Gordon. "I'm sorry we could not have had a few pleasant talks together. Good-morning."

And followed by McIlraith, Gordon walked away to where

the patient horses drowsed, since they could not browse.

For a few seconds, Elliott maintained his silent noncommittal stare at this queer daft loon, the feckless wandering ne'er-do-well—proud owner of precisely nothing.

"And you?" sneered the *faquir*, meeting Elliott's slightly bovine stare. "Do you seek power?"

"No," replied Elliott with a quiet seriousness that was not wholly mock solemnity.

"Nor to give your life to the search for Truth?"

"No."

"Nor to ask a gift?"

"No."

And Elliott shook his head, his sagacious face considering and judgmatical.

"No, thank ye . . . And good-day to ye," he said.

"And as good a to-morrow—to you—as may be," answered the *faquir*, while Elliott turned his back upon him.

The three men rode home discussing *faquirs* in general, and this one in particular.

"An impudent fraudulent humbug," said McIlraith. "Probably a rascally seditionist, too."

"A thoroughly dislikeable person, anyway," said Gordon. "A nasty piece of work, on the whole. And as you say, a humbug and a fraud."

But Elliott held his peace, for the practical, unimaginative and sensible man was slightly uncomfortable, though to have saved his life, he could have given no reason that would account for the fact:

But it is a fact, however. I know—for he told me so himself. He also told me what follows, and I wish I could tell it as he did. But I cannot, and I will make no attempt to do so.

This is what he said, and, as always, he spoke the truth.

He, Gordon, and McIlraith went fishing next day.

As usual, they drove out to where the aged salt-encrusted amphibious fisherman, Baghoo, kept the boats, and they set forth in the fourteen-foot broad-beamed dinghy which, by means of its pocket-handkerchief lateen sail and its rudder consisting of a long stick which ended in a circular disc of wood, slowly but surely made its way to the six-fathom feeding-ground whereon they caught their fish—a curious assortment, varying from strange globular spiny creatures of unattractive aspect to what were, to all intents and purposes, excellent bass.

As usual, they had no boatman, for good reasons—of space, odour and uselessness. They had their tin of bait prepared by Baghoo, their excellent lunch provided by the Club, their pipes or cheroots, and their admirable intention to enjoy their sport, and call it fishing. . . .

Toward evening, when Elliott was thinking that after his next catch he would suggest that someone else raise the anchor, a biggish stone attached to a coir cord, he was suddenly aware that Gordon, having made a curious sound of a swiftly indrawn breath, was staring across McIlraith's shoulder, his eyes almost starting from a face whose expression was one of utter incredulity.

He was sitting in the stern-sheets, Elliott on the centre thwart, and McIlraith in the bows.

Turning to see what Gordon was staring at, and expecting to see at least a sea-serpent or some equally amazing portent, he saw precisely nothing at all save McIlraith who, unaccountably, had dropped his line, risen to his feet, and, motionless as a statue, was apparently staring, in astounded incredulity, in the same direction.

Although his back was to Elliott, Elliott had no doubt whatever in his mind that this was what McIlraith was doing.

Glancing back at Gordon, he saw that he was now not only astonished and amazed but frightened. Quite obviously frightened.

"What's wrong with ye, man? What's the matter?" he asked.

"It's a . . . It's a . . ." stammered Gordon, and he also, rose to his feet, pointing, with trembling fingers. Two standing up ,in the boat were quite enough for safety, and Elliott forbore to follow their example, but turning round, also stared, bewildered.

What the devil were they gaping at?

Slowly, and reluctantly, McIlraith turned his head, and though far from leaving it white, the blood had receded from his sunburnt face.

"Do ye see it, Gordon?" he whispered, and even as he spoke it was only too obvious to him that Gordon saw it.

"It's a . . . It's a . . . whispered Gordon.

"A Portuguese galleon," said McIlraith. "Gun-ports . . . soldiers . . . They are in armour. They . . ."

"Look out, man," shouted Gordon. "It'll run us down. *Look out!*"

And without another word, he dived over the side of the boat.

Elliott seized both bulwarks in an endeavour to trim and steady the little craft, as it rocked violently. McIlraith, even as he staggered, threw his hands above his head and leapt straight up, his action, the movements of his hands and body, those of a man who springs up to catch at something above his head at a bow-sprit, chains, a hanging anchor, for example.

"*Jump*, Elliott," he cried, as he sprang.

A second later, he too was in the water, his feet missing the boat as he fell, his hands failing to catch and seize the bow-sprit or chains—which were not there.

The daft fools. What a length to carry a leg-pull; and what a marvellous piece of concerted acting.

But neither of these men belonged to the abominable order of pests called practical jokers. They were serious, sober, and sensible men. Then why the devil were they swimming for dear life and in opposite directions, fully clothed, with their shoes on—and in a sea in which sharks were not uncommon?

"Hi! You fool! Where are you going? What d'you think you are doing?" shouted Elliott to Gordon, whom he knew to be an indifferent swimmer. Not that McIlraith was much of a performer in the water, either.

Well, here were fine doings for sensible men, and for a sensible man to have to witness. Paltry and contemptible, and . . .

Where the devil was Gordon?

Raising the little sail as swiftly as he could, holding its hairy coir cord in one hand and taking the steering oar in the other, Elliott strove to bring the nose of the boat in the direction of the spot where Gordon was . . . had been . . . was not.

Then, standing erect and putting forth all his great strength, Elliott strove to drive the boat along, as does the native paddler in his dug-out canoe.

No sign of Gordon.

Gordon was gone.

And McIlraith?

Nowhere.

Yes, thank God. There he was, still swimming—as though he thought he could swim to the shore, miles away.

No sign of Gordon. What had he better do? Put the boat about and follow McIlraith, or dive overboard and, swimming under water, search for Gordon's body ?

No, to be quite sensible, better a live McIlraith than a dead Gordon—or he'd have dived at once, on the hundred to one chance.

"I'm coming, McIlraith. Hold on," he bawled at the top of his voice, as he put the boat about and thanked God for the evening breeze that had sprung up, bellying the sail, and carrying the boat on a true course, much more quickly than he could have driven it, using the steering oar as a paddle.

"McIlraith!" he shouted.

Why couldn't the fool swim toward him instead of away?

"McIlraith!"

And as though in yet more obstinate refusal, McIlraith sank beneath the smooth water. Just threw up his hands, and sank like a stone.

While the light lasted, Elliott cruised about the fishing-ground, and only when the sun had set and the brief twilight departed, did he return to the shore, Baghoo's cooking fire and oil *butti* his beacon. . . .

"But what happened?" I asked stupidly, when he told me precisely what had happened.

"They were fey," he said. "They saw a ship bearing down upon us. Aye, with all sails set and a bone in her teeth, I doubt not. And yon ship was a Portuguese galleon, manned by such men as captured Muscat and Mombasa, founded Goa, and . . ."

The dour, unemotional and sensible man stopped, and appeared to swallow a lump in his throat.

"Aye, they saw it as clear as you see me. It was running us down. About to crush us like snails under a steam-roller . . . Gordon shouted a warning, and jumped for his life. McIlraith sprang, and jumped for the bow-sprit or up into the chains of that ancient Portuguese galleon—that was, not there. Not visibly there . . ."

"And you saw absolutely nothing?"

"There was nothing to see," replied Elliott.

MRS. NORLEIGH'S NIGHT OUT

"Mrs. Norleigh's Night Out" is the story of a downtrodden housewife who one night desires to go see a movie. Her overbearing husband "allows" her to go to a lecture on slavery, where Mrs. Norleigh has a night out she will not forget. Besides being an entertaining story on some of the social evils of English life, this story is interesting for providing insight into Wren's opinions about slavery, and the sometimes overlooked plight of the common poor in England. Wren wrote similar stories in "Bobball Again, and a Study in Contrasts" (see volume one of The Collected Short Stories*), and in the novel* Two Feet From Heaven *(1940). "Mrs. Norleigh's Night Out" was first published in* Illustrated incorporating Passing Show & Weekly Illustrated *(March 4, 1939) and was reprinted in* The Australian Women's Weekly *(September 16, 1939). Its first book publication was as the fifth story in Part II, "Quaint", of* Odd—But Even So *(1941).*

This is a very immoral story.

Mrs. Norleigh heard the sound of her husband's key in the lock of the front door, and, almost subconsciously, left the drawing-room and went upstairs to her bedroom.

If there were a time in the day when Mr. Norleigh was worse than at others, it was at this time in the evening, between his arrival from office and sitting down to dinner. If he spoke to her at all before dinner, he would say something hurtful; and he had quite a gift for making remarks that were unkind, cutting, or positively cruel.

At dinner he would say nothing whatever, and though the complete silence was apt to be a little difficult and trying, owing to the sense of strain, this habit made the meal-time a period of relative peacefulness.

After dinner, his remarks, happily few and far between, were apt to be sarcastic; and, though not actually wounding, were neither easy to answer nor to leave unanswered, for usually he would press for a reply.

Usually this latter would be the subject either for heavy and unfriendly banter, or else for bitter sneers or angry snarls.

Seated in her favourite armchair, where she had spent so many hours of mental suffering, she heard the dinner-going; and promptly rose to her feet.

Doing her best to conquer her ridiculous trembling and bring her wretched nerves under control, she slowly descended the stairs and entered the drawing room.

Mr. Norleigh, a glass of sherry in one hand, a cigarette in the other, did not look up as she entered.

"Good evening, William," she said brightly, and accompanied the greeting with the best smile that she could achieve.

Mr. Norleigh made no reply. Perhaps he did not think it was a particularly good evening.

"Have you had a good day, dear?"

Whether Mr. Norleigh's day had been good or otherwise remained undisclosed. Finishing his glass of sherry he poured himself another; and, taking his cigarette-case from his pocket, lit a fresh one from the stub of the one which he had finished.

This he threw into the empty fireplace where it lodged upon the walnut foot of the fire-screen which Mrs. Norleigh, as a child, had watched her mother embroider. Should she remove it? Better not, perhaps. It might look like a criticism of William's habits in the matter of cigar and cigarette stubs, which were, indeed, deplorable.

"Oh, I beg your pardon, dear," she said instead, and, taking an onyx ash-tray from a little table, put it on a stool beside his chair.

Mr. Norleigh, who apparently had not yet seen her, shook half an inch of cigarette ash on to the white roses which, in a silver bowl, stood fortunately within reach.

Silence that could be felt held the drawing-room. Even in rolling her handkerchief into a ball between the moist palms of her hands, Mrs. Norleigh made no sound.

Mr. Norleigh finished his second glass of sherry.

Dare she remind him that it must be ten minutes since Walson had rung the dinner-gong? The soup would be getting cold, and Cook would be getting hot. If there were much more delay she would be furious. She would let the sun go down upon her wrath and rise upon it again in the morning; and Mrs. Norleigh would have a bad time at the ten o'clock interview when Cook arranged the meals for the day.

Mr. Norleigh dropped the butt of his second cigarette into the flower bowl where it hissed loudly, perhaps in reprobation.

"I think the gong has gone, dear," said Mrs. Norleigh.

Mr. Norleigh replied only with a long and loud yawn, an answer of which the exact meaning was not clear to his wife, who, indeed, had never claimed to be intelligent.

Beside Mr. Norleigh's chair stood a small piece of furniture which Mrs. Norleigh disliked intensely, or, to be more accurate, a piece of furniture to the presence of which, in her drawing-room, she had the strongest objection. It was an invention of the Devil, or some other devil, intended to hold newspapers or magazines; conceivably even music. The four papers to which Mr. Norleigh subscribed had to be placed, as they arrived, in the upper portion of this receptacle and removed at night. In the lower part were the paper-backed books and magazines which he affected, the whole an eyesore and an offence to the æsthetic mistress of the house—to use a humorous *façon de parler*—for even Ethel, the very large black evil-faced and evil-living cat, with whom Mr. Norleigh appeared to be entirely *d'accord* was undeniably more mistress of that house than was Mrs. Norleigh. Only once had she summoned courage to protest against the newspaper-and-magazine holder, with its ephemeral papers, and its permanent disarray of tattered magazines, and paper-backs, and to suggest that the study was perhaps a better place for it.

Mr. Norleigh had said nothing against the suggestion, and had said it for several days; but he had given her a look that was even more eloquent than his silence.

He now dropped a tired hand upon the newspaper-rack which stood against his chair, took up the evening paper and turned to the financial columns.

Mrs. Norleigh repressed a sigh, for she had known for many years that such sounds were unacceptable. A sigh may express annoyance, weariness, regret, resignation, boredom, all of which are, or may be, forms of insolence. As her husband had pointed out to her, if she had anything to say she had better say it, display the courage of her convictions in speech, and not the coward's lack of them in gusty and disgusting noises.

The door opened and Walson appeared.

"The gong has gone, Madame," she observed in a tone of strong reproof and with even more than her usual severity of manner.

"Oh, has it?" replied Mrs. Norleigh brightly, and with a certain air of gratitude for a piece of useful and interesting information.

This she passed on to her husband.

"The gong *has* gone, dear," she smiled.

William closed his paper and, turning to the back page, began an intensive study of the cricket news.

Walson closed the door and began a rehearsal of the speech in which she proposed to Give Notice.

Through the service hatch in the dining-room wall she informed Cook that the Old Swine was sitting like a graven image, and she'd like to give him a piece of her mind.

Cook, less refined, intimated her preference for the donation of a thick ear.

"If it wasn't for 'Er, I'd walk out on 'im," said Cook. "And if 'e 'as the nerve to say this bloomin' chicken's overdone, I'll tell 'im sumpthink."

"Tell 'im the old 'en was a spring chicken when you started cooking it," suggested Walson, whose imagination was more active than Cook's.

"If I was 'Er I'd get 'im sumpthink from the chimist," asserted Cook darkly.

"Ole 'Erbert's got some weed-killer," observed Walson non-committally.

"*Elephant*-killer," grunted Cook.

And though the ejaculation sounded immeasurably cryptic, its meaning appeared clear to Walson.

In the drawing-room Mrs. Norleigh forbore to scream, and possessed her soul in a patience beyond praise—or beneath contempt.

Suddenly Mr. Norleigh rose to his feet, walked out of the drawing-room closing the door behind him, crossed the wide hall into the dining-room, and seated himself at the head of the table.

Mrs. Norleigh with wisdom and agility made a good second.

It could not be said that the soup was sufficiently cold to be called iced *consommé*, nor could a person regardful of the truth call it warm; but presumably it was of a temperature agreeable to Mr. Norleigh, as he refrained from comment upon the matter.

Mrs. Norleigh herself did not greatly care for tepid soup. In point of fact, food was of even less interest than usual to her this evening as something far more important occupied her mind. On the other hand, the subject might perhaps be referred to as one of food for the mind. She was desperately anxious to see a film of *Katherine of Aragon* at the Imperial Palace Cinema.

She somehow felt that, so far as an obscure and commonplace individual could do so, she might have something in common with Katherine; and that it would be particularly interesting to see how she managed Henry the Eighth.

It was not the sort of film to which William would be likely to go, and it was the last night on which it would be shown. There had been no opportunity during the week, as William had been at home each evening, and to-night he was going out. If she left the house after he did, and returned before him, there could be no objection surely? Nevertheless, it would be as well to give no indication of the fact that she was keenly desirous to go.

William did not believe in encouraging dissipation.

Walson exchanged the soup-plates for clean ones, and, from the service-hatch carried a dish on which reposed a piece missing from the person of some sizable salmon.

Of this Mr. Norleigh accepted the major portion, and his wife a part of what remained. On the subject of the fish Mr. Norleigh had no comment to offer.

Having removed the fish-plates, Walson brought the chicken from the hatch where it had mysteriously materialized, and placed it before her master.

Coldly she watched him carve it, and more coldly noted that, as usual, he placed most of its pectoral protuberance upon his own plate and certain less favoured portions upon that of his wife. . . .

"Oh, William," said Mrs. Norleigh, having artfully waited until he had consumed his first glass of claret. "I see that *Katherine of Aragon* is on at the Imperial."

William accepted this piece of information in silence.

"I've been hoping it would come here," she continued. "I do so want to see it."

This observation also appeared undeserving of comment.

"I thought perhaps I might go this evening, as you'll be out."

Mrs. Norleigh's thought may have been long but her husband's silence was longer.

"Do you mind if I go, dear?"

In some cases silence is held to give consent. Mrs. Norleigh was unable to feel that this was one of them.

"Er—may I go, William?" she asked.

Her deep desire to see the film may be taken as the measure of her courage, and must be accepted as her excuse for such persistent importunity.

Mr. Norleigh refilled his glass and held it up to the light.

"I should so love to," said his foolish wife, and, without commenting upon her statement, William again drank appreciatively of the excellent claret.

Upon the wine he did comment, but only to the extent of loudly smacking his lips and this was his sole contribution to the dinner-table conversation.

As she rose to return to the drawing-room, Mrs. Norleigh, silly woman, screwed up her courage to the point of deliberately and definitely calling her husband's attention to her insignificant self.

"William!" she said, and again "William! . . ."

William cracked a walnut-shell and gave its contents his close attention.

"William!"

William helped himself to salt.

Mrs. Norleigh knew by long experience that three times of asking was the limit to which she could go without incurring really serious trouble.

But this evening she was, for some reason, feeling rather brave. Although she knew well that there was a difference between courage and rash folly, she felt an unwonted impulse to be guilty of the latter error. It may have been that the Call of the Wild was penetrating even to the innermost arcana of the most respectable suburb of Storborough. It may have been that her fancied affinity with Katherine of Aragon was stronger than she knew; or again, it may have been that her Fate was upon her and, though she knew it not, her hour had come.

Controlling her voice, and speaking as naturally and calmly as she might, she carried the high virtues of courage across the line that divides it from the vice of rashness.

"William, I think I'll go to the Pictures this even—as you'll be out."

William's long upper lip seemed to grow longer, his tight wide mouth to grow tighter and wider. Then, as anxiously his wife watched it, his face was briefly contorted by a spasm which, as well she knew, represented something in the nature of a smile. Not a smile of pleasure, of amusement, of approval or humour, but merely a change of expression, a fleeting wintry change, wholly muscular, in no way connected with the eyes and scarcely with the lips.

As his face suffered this slight contortion, William put his hand into his pocket, withdrew an envelope and took from it two pink cards.

One of these he threw across the table in the general direction of his wife and then, like the Delphic Oracle, at last he spoke.

"Want a night out, eh? Go to that, then."

Mrs. Norleigh picked up the pink card and, glancing at it, discovered that it would infallibly admit her to a Meeting; that the Bishop's wife would be in the Chair; that she would address the Meeting, and introduce to it a Speaker who would thereupon deliver a Lecture, and that the subject of the Lecture would be Slavery.

To hunger greatly for bread and to be given a stone must induce feelings very similar to those then experienced by Mrs. Norleigh.

The great cavernous interior of the Imperial Palace; dark, mystical and romantic; with the deep diapasoned music of the noble organ rolling in thunderous beauty about her; that wonderful place which she could visit so rarely, and where for a couple of hours she could be herself; escape from the life that was a living death and long-drawn stultification; where she could not only lose herself but find herself; lose her body and find her soul . . . *escape* . . . Escape to beauty, joy, romance. . . . Be thrall to enchantment.

To ask for that and be given the Hall, the bare and beastly Hall, smelling of unspecified dust, unaccountable gas-fumes, varnished pitch-pine, humanity and clothes, particularly mackintoshes. The Hall, with its glare of unshaded lights, its bare and ugly walls, its stark platform; the Hall into which Romance could never enter, and would fall down dead if it did.

The Bishop's wife in the Chair. Mrs. Norleigh had never really hated anybody. Had she done so, it is a regrettable fact that she would have hated the Bishop's wife. Mrs. Witheringwell-Betherby whom, rightly or wrongly, she regarded as an overbearing, interfering woman, pompous, dictatorial and snobbish.

Mrs. Norleigh had been at school with her at Doedene when she was plain Molly Dunkleby, chilblained, red-nosed and pimply, and had disliked her as a girl for many of the same traits and attributes that made her unpopular as a woman. Not that she had been dictatorial, overbearing and self-important as a schoolgirl but, on the contrary, self-distrustful, shy, stupid, and a thorough little sycophant.

And inasmuch as the Bishop's wife nowadays affected to forget that she had ever before in her life seen Mrs. Norleigh, why should she sit at the woman's feet and grace her triumph when she took the chair at the Hall and rode her hobby.

Mrs. Witheringwell-Betherby instead of Katherine of Aragon! St. Peter's Hall instead of the Imperial Palace!

However, Mrs. Norleigh was inured to disappointment and, far too wise and well trained to provoke her husband to wrath by pointless protest, merely blamed herself for her stupidity in wanting to see *Katherine of Aragon*. Blessed is he who expecteth little. More blessed she if she expected nothing, for thus only would she be in the happy position of getting exactly what she expected.

Leaving Mr. Norleigh to his desired solitude for the better enjoyment of his port, walnuts and cigar, Mrs. Norleigh turned to the drawing-room, there to await his good pleasure and her coffee.

Eight o'clock. Had he gone in to dinner punctually it would now be only seven-thirty, and there would still have been time for her to go to . . . Why on earth couldn't she have had the sense to say nothing at all about *Katherine of Aragon*, and the courage simply to have gone without permission? No, she had once or twice done something without his leave, and it had been once or twice too often. He would be certain to know—and it wasn't worth it. Nothing was worth anything. Why did she go on with it, year after year? Habit. One could get used to anything. But how long could one bear it? How long, oh Lord, how long? Was she a greater coward and a bigger fool than most other women, or was William more powerful than other men, more coldly determined and immovable, more relentless and forceful? She had no friends. She didn't know a single woman to whom she could talk on such a subject, but she was quite sure that most women either managed their husbands or had husbands who required no managing.

How wonderful to have a husband who is himself a friend; who is actually kind and understanding.

Of course she was a fool and a weakling, or she'd never have married William Norleigh. But her parents had seemed so delighted when he had proposed, and had so taken it for granted that she would be only too thankful to marry a man of such good character and good position. They had simply refused to listen to her when, instead of jumping for joy, she had merely behaved as an obedient daughter and, while acquiescing, had admitted that she didn't love William. Mother had said that love came after marriage; and presumably Mother knew. In fact, from earliest childhood, Mother Knows Best had been the final and sufficient answer to any kind of mild protest against parental authority. She had never been allowed to have a mind of her own; and now she had no soul or body, either, that she could call her own. Fool; coward; weakling. . . .

Mother! Not up to the day of her death, could Mother even begin to understand how a girl could be anything but happy who was mistress of such a house as William's; who was married to a man with such an income as William's; and who shared such a position in Storborough as was William's.

And of course it was true that there were millions of women in England who had not enough money to spend, enough clothes to wear, even enough food to eat; whereas she had a beautiful house, adequate clothing, sufficient food, and, if she had no money to spend, William bought anything that was really necessary.

A quarter past eight. William and coffee.

As she handed him the cup, she again experienced that curious surge of almost rebellious, almost courageous feeling.

"William, I'd rather . . . I'd really very much rather go to . . ." she began, wondering at her temerity.

"Don't be late," interrupted William. "And pay attention. I shall be interested to hear what this fellow Jones has to say. Starts at eight-thirty, doesn't it?"

Mrs. Norleigh went upstairs and got ready. Opening the drawing-room door as she came down again, she looked in.

"Good night, William, if I shouldn't see you again this evening," she said.

William apparently didn't hear her; other twitterings being also audible through the open french windows.

For one wild moment, Mrs. Norleigh paused at the garden gate. If she turned to the left she would be going in the direction of the Imperial Palace, of *Katherine of Aragon*, and of escape, anodyne, brief happiness. If she turned to the right, she would be going to St. Peter's Hall, Mrs. Witheringwell-Betherby, and a lecture on Slavery by a man of the not unfamiliar name of Jones.

Not unfamiliar? No, there had been Tiny. He had been called Tiny Jones since he was a baby, an enormous baby that had grown into a huge man well over six feet in height. Now if this—what was it—she glanced at the card in her hand—this Colonel David Vivian-Jones had been Tiny. . .

It was Tiny.

There, sitting on the platform beside Mrs. Witheringwell-Betherby's brother, Canon Dunkleby, was Tiny Jones, looking exactly as Tiny Jones would have looked twenty years after the date on which she had last seen him. Which, in point of fact, is not remarkable.

At first, Mrs. Norleigh did not believe the evidence of her own eyes. Thinking of Tiny—her mind full of memories of the days when Tiny used to lift her up by her hair-plaits, used to let her come and watch him fish, used to take her to dances, used to let her worship the ground he trod on, so long as she didn't get in the way of his tread—this had made her see Tiny in the man on the platform sitting at the lecturer's table.

Of course it wasn't Tiny, and it was amazing that she should have a difficulty in breathing, and that her heart should be endeavouring to escape from her body, and that her hand should be shaking. That man up there with Tiny's face was Colonel David Vivian-Jones.

It was true that Tiny had sometimes been known as "D. V." for a change. Her brother in his very last letter from the Front had said that "D. V. and weather permitting—he was going to have a spot of Paris leave."

Yes, although she had forgotten the fact, the real Tiny's name was D. V. Jones, but he wasn't that Colonel David Vivian-Jones up there on the platform. Couldn't be. The last thing that she had heard about Tiny was that he had got into Mecca and out again safely, years and years ago. She hadn't seen him since she had married. Nor had he written to her. She had always called him Tiny, thought of him as Tiny, and heard of him as Tiny, except when people used the "D. V." nickname.

It was useless any longer to refuse to believe it. There he was. Tiny Jones. D. V. Jones. Colonel David Vivian-Jones. Why had they called him Vivian-Jones on the pink card? Tiny had never called himself that. Just the sort of fool thing that Molly Dunkleby would do. Silly snob. Fancy her roping him in for this Slavery stunt of hers. She was always writing to the papers about Slavery and speaking about it on platforms, and getting up bazaars and jumble-sales to raise funds for its suppression. She had got slaves on the brain. Coloured ones, of course. They must be black or brown or yellow. She wouldn't be interested in white ones; in any silly amateur ones in sweat-shops, factories, or coal-mines; in those East End tailors' slaves who worked about twenty hours a day for a penny an hour; or in any other kind of European industrial-system slaves.

And of course White Slavery wasn't—well—wasn't the sort of thing Mrs. Witheringwell-Betherby would know about, or wish to know about. Not nice. But give her an Abyssinian slave-raid, a Red Sea slave-*dhow*, an Arab slave-market, or anything of that sort, and she'd be happy for hours.

Without disclosing the sources of her information she Knew For a Fact that slaves were exported in thousands and thousands from Africa to Arabia and Persia; that slaves were freely bought and sold in hundreds of secret slave markets; that the cities of the Sahara, Soudan, Morocco, Arabia and Persia were simply Full of Slaves. And that apart from the hideous slaughtering slave-raids, with rapine, fire, murder, and every brutality under the sun, apart from them, it was a Fact that every peaceful and harmless-seeming caravan that traversed the trade routes of Africa carried little children, decoyed from their homes or sold by their abominable parents, to be taken to the secret marts of mysterious towns to be auctioned in the market-place like so many sheep and goats and cattle.

And what was the Present Government doing about it? Nothing. What was the Navy doing about it? Nothing.

As she sat eyeing the ever-increasing audience, happy in the knowledge that, like all her Slavery Meetings, this one was going to be well attended, she was aware that the lecturer, whom she had met for the first time in Town, a month ago, at no less a dinner-table than that of the Lord Mayor of London, was endeavouring to direct the attention of her brother, Canon Dunkleby, to a member of the audience.

Curious that he who spent most of his life out of England and whose home was at the other side of Wales, should know anyone in Storborough.

"No," Colonel David Vivian-Jones was whispering to Canon Dunkleby, "Not '*the fat white woman whom nobody loves, and who had come to the meeting in new white gloves.*' I mean the one in the fifth—no, the sixth—row, dressed in the black suit with a smart little hat . . ."

"Afraid I don't know her," murmured the Canon, who, for some obscure reason, resented the Colonel's implication that he should know by sight and name every woman in Storborough.

But Colonel David Vivian-Jones knew her. He knew her perfectly well, though it was quite obvious that it couldn't be she. Still, how amazingly like little Rubbish she was. Little Rubbish of whom he had been so fond, and who had been so sound a pal. What was her name? . . . Robina Malet, of course. It had been old Malet who had been responsible for his going into the army. He had spent three parts of his time, when not at school, in the Malets' house; and the old General had so taken it for granted that he'd go into the army that he had just naturally gone.

Yes, Malet. She couldn't have been christened "Rubbish," of course, but that was what he had always called her. What was her Christian name? . . . Robbie; that was it. Short for Robina. But that couldn't be she. Nevertheless, it was exactly what Robbie Malet must look like now. Not that she'd changed so very much. Didn't look too happy. She had been such a cheery smiling girl, and this was a woman who had been up against it; been put through it. More like a Dolores than a Robbie. A woman of sorrows and acquainted with grief. Not a miserable face but etherialized and . . .

This wouldn't do. He had got to give a Lecture or something, and that silly hippopotamus was getting to her feet to introduce him. What a fool he had been to let her rope him in for as miserable a week-end as ever he had spent. The dear Bishop's holy house at Storborough. He had had a better time in the wicked old White Monk's unholy house at Timbuctoo. That old bird was *real*. A very real person. And so was his fat and jolly black wife, not to mention the baker's-dozen or so of children.

But what an amazing thing, if Fate had brought him to Storborough just to confront him with young Rubbish again; young Robbie Malet. Of course it wasn't she; it was her double—twenty years on. Why, young Robbie must be a woman of about thirty-eight now. Well, that was a woman of about thirty-eight, and a devilish pretty one, too. It couldn't be Robbie.

But it was.

She was smiling at him, exactly as she used to do. . . .

"Ladies and gentlemen," Mrs. Witheringwell-Betherby's clear voice, loud and important, broke the thread of his thoughts.

Having introduced Colonel Vivian-Jones as she called him, to the Meeting, in a speech of considerable length on the subject of Slavery, Mrs. Witheringwell-Betherby sat down and left the lecturer to add to it anything that might have been left unsaid.

Colonel Jones rose to his feet and spoke easily, well, his manner attractive and his matter interesting.

But to the minds of some of his audience, who knew their Mrs. Witheringwell-Betherby, it soon occurred that the extremely eloquent address that the lecturer was giving must be proving something of a disappointment to the Bishop's wife.

He began well enough by describing his own personal

experiences of slave-markets, and telling his audience how he had visited one of the best known of them all, that of the Holy City of Mecca itself. There, disguised as an Arab, he had walked about the slave-market from one department to another, pricing the slaves, learning all he could about them from their respective owners, and bargaining for them in the role of a prospective purchaser.

So far so good. This was admirable, excellent. Mrs. Witheringwell-Betherby was pleased and proud to think that she had actually produced, for the benefit of the serious-minded philanthropic and Christian inhabitants of Storborough, a real live investigator who had attended an actual slave-market, handled real slaves, and seen and heard them bought and sold.

But unfortunately, the speaker, while most strongly condemning any and every form of slavery, went on to say that his pity was by no means exclusively reserved for these African people who were, on the whole, well and kindly treated and cherished by their owners as any other capitalist cherishes his capital.

A great number of such Negro servants had known no other condition of life than that of slavery, having been slaves from early childhood; and had, as slaves, lived an easier, less precarious, and generally better life than they would have done in the poverty-stricken disease-ridden villages from which they had been sold in time of famine.

An obviously careful, unbiased and open-minded-observer of social phenomena, this widely experienced explorer admitted that slavery as practised in the East, open, naked and unashamed, was not as black an evil as was sometimes supposed; that the slave in the Arab household was just about as happy as any of the paid servants, the members of the family, or the employer himself. And that if a sudden decree of manumission were promulgated and enforced, no one would regard it with greater consternation than the slaves themselves. He informed his deeply-interested hearers that in any country in which slavery is a part of the social system, there is, nowadays, no such thing as cruelty to slaves. Apart from the fact that they are of great value, they have their legal rights; and ill-treatment of a slave would be punished by Law in the same way as the ill-treatment of a horse, cow, dog, or other domestic animal would be punished in England.

They were regarded, he said, somewhat in the light of children—lesser children, of course—but still childlike dependants for whose welfare the owner was responsible. And with a wry smile, the lecturer informed his audience that it was only in England that there existed, so far as he knew, a Society for the Prevention of Cruelty to Children.

Slaves in all Mussulman countries could and would and did complain to the nearest *Kadi* if he or she had a grievance; and if the *Kadi* found the slave-owner guilty of real cruelty, he could and would punish him and free the slave. Not that anything that the lecturer said was for one moment to be taken as a plea in defence of a vile and abominable institution, the deprivation of any man of his freedom by any other man.

But what roused his wrath, what was the real object of his burning indignation and obvious anger, was the foul and villainous form of slavery practised in those countries where legal Slavery was unknown, where it was abhorrent to the public conscience, and was as illegal as murder.

And at this point in his speech, the speaker lashed bitterly, with a sharp and eloquent tongue, the generations of Britons who, stirred up by Wilberforce, gave freely of their time, their knowledge and their money, to obtain the manumission of other people's slaves—provided they were black—and themselves permitted, encouraged and enforced a far worse form of slavery because it was personally profitable. On the Sabbath they shed tears of pity for their black brother of the distant cotton-plantations and sugar-cane fields; and, on weekdays, drove infant children into their factories and mines to work under the worst possible conditions, from early morning until late evening.

And from the days when child-labour was the veriest and vilest child-slavery; when tiny children, half-starved and half-frozen, were made to climb up into sooty chimneys, to emerge more than half-suffocated and half-dead, the lecturer turned to the present day, and spoke of the various forms of slavery practised and prevalent at the very moment at which he was speaking. . . .

It seemed to Mrs. Norleigh that he spoke directly to her. It was almost as though he and she were alone in that bleakly utilitarian ugly Hall into which "Romance could never enter, and would fall down dead if it did." This glorious Hall of Wonder, joy and delight, into which Romance had entered clad in shining golden armour, and which would live as long as she did. For, time after time, he had looked straight at her, had held her eye for long seconds, and, though his tongue spoke of world economics, his eyes told her that he recognized her, remembered her; that if he and she really were alone . . .

Oh, thank God, thank God, that she had not gone to the Imperial Palace and seen *Katherine of Aragon*! And thank even William that he had sent her to St. Peter's Hall, there to see the hero of her childhood, of her whole life.

How wonderfully he spoke, and how nobly. She would always remember, as long as she lived, the words that he was saying now.

"That is the true slavery, the slavery that is all about us in this England of ours to-day. The slavery that even now would justify thousands of women in singing *The Song of the Shirt*, shop girls, factory girls, yes, and mothers of families whose endless work begins when they wake and finishes when they lie down late at night, almost too weary for sleep. That is the real slavery, the slavery of the aged charwoman, bent, decrepit and twisted with pain; of the widows, or the wives of workless men, with many mouths to feed; the land-workers crippled with rheumatism, who have never had a spare penny in all their lives; the sweated slum-dwellers who do incredibly low-paid work in their one wretched family room; the women who, even to-day, might long to be a slave *de jure* as well as *de facto*, and cry—

> "*O! to be a slave along with the barbarous Turk*
> *Where woman has never a soul to save,*
> *If this is Christian work. . . .*

"And if there be one of you here who has an urge to do something useful, something good, something fine, let him make his endeavour in the direction of improving the lot and condition of someone whose life is spent in some form of slavery. If any of us could ameliorate the lot of one child, one woman, one man, whose life is dominated and whose liberty is restricted and curtailed by another man, so that he or she is suffering slavery, whether economic or physical, that one amongst us would not have lived in vain . . ."

And amidst the tumult of the most enthusiastic applause ever heard in that hall, the lecturer sat down.

Mrs. Witheringwell-Betherby rose while yet the hand-clapping was at its height, stilled the tumult by raising an imperious hand, and said, somewhat more coldly than usual, what she was wont to say upon such occasions.

Canon Dunkleby proposed a vote of thanks, and the members of the audience slowly, and as though reluctantly, dispersed.

Mrs. Norleigh sat spellbound, entranced, uplifted, infinitely more deeply thralled to enchantment than ever at the Imperial Palace. Only as he left the platform did she come back to earth, realize where and who and what she was.

But also she realized that she was something other than what she had been an hour or so ago; realized that he had not only cast a spell upon her but had broken another spell, an evil one which had bound her for so long, bound her since he had gone out of her life and William had come into it.

She had come into, the Hall a coward, a weakling and a fool. She would go out of it a woman set free, a woman who henceforth would shape her destiny rather than suffer it. And her first bold step along the path of escape, the path to freedom, would be to go to him, speak to him, claim him as her oldest and dearest friend.

Why shouldn't she have a friend? Why? Surely it was as he had said—a case of "*O! to be a slave along with the barbarous Turk,*" if this were a right and proper state of affairs in a Christian country, that a woman dare not have a friend. For whether or not she had a soul to save, she hadn't a soul to call her own, if she had not, and dared not have, a single friend.

Tiny had given her back her soul; he had saved her soul alive. She would possess it henceforth. Thanks to him she had found herself—and now she would find him, and thank him.

As she stood near the private door which gave access to the green room, ante-room, cloak-room, or whatever they called it, behind the platform, the Bishop's wife and her brother came out. Mrs. Witheringwell-Betherby, glancing at her with no look of recognition, entered her big car, followed by the Canon.

Could he have gone? Her heart sank and her throat constricted at the thought that she had missed him. She had expected that he would come out with Mrs. Witheringwell-Betherby and Canon Dunkleby, and had screwed her courage up to the tremendous height of intending to speak to him, to claim acquaintanceship with him, even in their presence.

Surely he would not have . . .

The door opened again and Colonel David Vivian-Jones came out.

"Rubbish! It *is* you."

"*Tiny!* It *is* you!"

He took both her hands.

"Rubbish! To think of finding *you*. . . . I mean meeting *you*, at Storborough. . . . What are you doing here?"

"I am a slave," she replied.

"Are you? Along with a barbarous Englishman?"

"Yes. He . . ."

"And I'm something of a professional saver-of-slaves nowadays, Rubbish! Are you unhappy?"

"Desperately."

"Does he love you?"

"He hates me."

"Rubbish, I have never actually saved a slave."

And Mrs. Norleigh, while his eyes held hers and seemed not only to gaze into them but through them, into her enslaved but struggling soul, uttered shamefully incredible words, words the sound of which shocked and shamed her as she uttered them.

"Here's your opportunity, Tiny," she said.

"Right," impulsively replied Colonel David Vivian-Jones, ever a man of action. "My car is round the corner, and I'm going straight to London. Coming, Rubbish? Out of the house of bondage and the state of slavery?"

"To London, Tiny?"

"To the world's end, Rubbish. For I love you with all my heart and soul and strength—as I have always done . . ."

Colonel Jones kissed Mrs. Norleigh on the lips. Then, taking her arm, he led her to the car.

And she never saw William again.

CAFARD

"Cafard" is the story of how Captain Le Sage handles his cafard stricken Sergeant Major. The story is probably based on a similar account given in the Foreign Legion memoir, Life in the Legion, *by Frederic Martyn.[5] The earliest known publication of "Cafard" was in the Australian newspaper,* The Barrier Miner *(August 4, 1939). The first book publication of "Cafard" was as the seventh story of Part II, "Quaint", in* Odd—But Even So *(1941).*

"No," said Captain Le Sage said. "Sergeant-Major Brille is not what you think him at all. I have known him since he was a *bleu,* and I can tell you quite authoritatively that he is not mad. He is not a maniac; he is not a drunkard; nor is he brutal; and definitely he is not insubordinate."

"Perhaps you'd tell me what he is, then, *mon Capitaine,*" smiled Lieutenant André Tabouille.

"Well, he's a *crévard* of Oriental diseases, a man who has had every form of fever and illness to which the flesh is heir. To my certain knowledge, in Tonkin, Madagascar and Le Sud, he has had cholera, typhoid, dysentery, hook-worm, dengue, blackwater-fever—and more kinds of assorted malaria than old *Médecin-Major* Parme has ever heard of. And I'll tell you another thing, my lad. I have known him carry on, in command of a post, with a temperature that was never below a hundred, usually over a hundred and two, and sometimes a hundred and four. He's done things, when he ought to have been on a stretcher, that would have been highly creditable to men in the pink of condition. He's a *crévard,* and half his time he's a crock and a cripple; he's a grumbler, a grouser and a surly old dog. He's also a hero."

"He's behaving very funnily just now," observed the young officer.

"So'd you be, if you had had his medical history, not to mention his experiences in half a hundred tropical hells. . . . In what way is he behaving queerly?"

---

[5] Martyn, Frederic. *Life in the Legion.* London, G. Bell, 1911. p. 260-262

"Well, his manner is . . ."

"Don't you worry about his manner, *or* his manners. If ever you are in a tight place, with the odds a hundred to one against you, you pray to have Sergeant-Major Brille there with you. What was wrong with his, manner?"

"Well, as you said just now, surly. Almost insolent. All but insubordinate. If one were not choosing words carefully, one might even say threatening."

"H'm. You must have put his back up."

"Well, I'd like to put it down again. After all, one's an officer . . ."

"And he is a magnificent soldier of blameless, record and unique experience. I've known him for more years than you have weeks. Possibly he has got a touch of *cafard*."

"Well, it's a pretty bad example to other ranks; and if one cannot depend on one's Sergeant-Major . . ."

"Well, you can depend on him. There's no more dependable man in the Battalion, nor in the whole Legion. Nevertheless, since you've made a complaint against him, I'll have him on the mat."

"Damned young fool," growled Captain Le Sage, as Lieutenant Tabouille saluted and left the tent. "I'd sooner have old Brille than him and his twin brother too, and half a dozen more like 'em."

"*Ordonnance!*" he shouted, and his orderly stepped smartly into the tent and saluted. "Tell Sergeant-Major Brille I should like a word with him."

A few minutes later that *sous-officier* stood at the door of Captain Le Sage's tent glaring balefully at the officer who sat on his little wood-and-canvas chair behind the rough camp-table.

Looking up from his papers, Captain Le Sage studied the lined, tanned face of the man before him, that of a professional soldier of some fifty years of age; hard-bitten, grizzled and lean; a face expressive rather of determination, strength and discipline than of thought and intelligence.

He looked ill; his face flushed, his brow furrowed and corrugated by a heavy frown, as though he were suffering both mentally and physically. The officer noticed that regularly his mouth twitched and that his hands were trembling.

Hiding all trace of friendliness, liking, or sympathy, Captain Le Sage spoke sharply.

"I have had a complaint against you, and have sent for you to warn you that I must not have another—unless you are tired of the rank you occupy."

The *sous-officier's* frown deepened and his face darkened.

"Complaint? Against me? From whom?"

"Silence. I will invite your questions when I want them. Don't you presume upon your length of service, your rank, your decorations nor anything else. You are a Sergeant-Major. Behave as one to your superiors as well as to those below you in rank. Do you understand me?"

"No."

"Are you addressing me?"

"Yes."

H'm. Young Tabouille was right, damn him. Poor old Brille was definitely difficult. But that only meant that something had upset the old chap, something gone wrong with him. Some little detail of routine out of order. Quite probably the whole trouble was due to his exalted, even excessive, sense of duty. A proper old red-tape-worm as well as a fine old soldier.

"I should be sorry to put you through a recruit's course of military manners, saluting, recognition of officer's rank-badges, smartness combined with deference, conduct toward superiors, and so forth, Sergeant-Major Brille."

The non-commissioned officer's fists clenched and his eyes blazed with anger.

"I hope it won't be necessary," continued Le Sage quietly. "If it should be, I shall most certainly do it. Listen carefully. You've been reported to me for conduct prejudicial to good discipline, and . . ."

"I? Conduct prejudicial . . ."

"Silence. You've been reported to me for conduct prejudicial to good discipline, inasmuch as you have adopted a surly, insolent, and insubordinate manner toward your superior officer and . . ."

"It's a lie!"

It was almost a cry; a shout of defiance, as well as of denial.

Captain Le Sage, in no wise offended or indignant, was

perturbed.

Was it possible that poor old Brille, after all these years of service, all these brave deeds and exhibitions of determination, endurance and all military virtues, was about to do what not a few old Legion non-commissioned officers have done? Was he going insane?

As his heart softened with sympathy, understanding, and regret, his face and voice hardened with assumed anger.

"And what of your manner now, to me, your Captain? What is this but insolence and insubordination? It is a fortunate thing for you, my friend, that we are alone, and that I cannot personally accuse you of 'conduct prejudicial to good discipline, inasmuch as you are setting an example of insubordinate manner to men of your Section.' Very fortunate. I should have had no alternative but to have you reduced in rank, perhaps *to* the ranks. As it is, consider yourself under arrest. Go at once to your tent, and remain there until I send for you. Dismiss."

With a venomous glare at his Captain, the Sergeant-Major wheeled about and marched swiftly from the tent.

Captain Le Sage gazed at the retreating figure of the old soldier. Should he call him back and really treat him to the rough side of his tongue for going off like that, without saluting?

No. He had given him a pretty severe telling-off, and had put him under arrest. He'd send for him again when he had had time to cool off, and talk to him as man to man, for his soul's sake, and, what was more important, for his career's sake.

He had never known him to drink to excess, and he did not think he was drinking now. Perhaps he had had some bad news from home, if he had got a home. Perhaps Tabouille had been riding him; a cocksure young man who was quite liable to think that a young officer showed his mettle if he rough-rode a Sergeant-Major in front of his men. Where a strong officer would give the non-commissioned man every support, and then speak to him tactfully and privately if necessary, a weak one would bluster, show off, and use his superior rank to humiliate a *sous-officier* whom he knew to be in the right when he himself was wrong, knew to be a better, as well as a more experienced, soldier than he himself was. That was probably it. And a Company Sergeant-Major has a very great deal of responsibility and work. Quite enough for any man to do, even in depôt or *poste*, but a very great deal more when the Company is on the march.

Discipline must be maintained, of course. Discipline, which is the life-blood of the army, the very air which it breathes, and without which it must decay and rot and die, must be rigid as a rifle-barrel; but a good officer can temper justice with mercy, apply the rod of Discipline with the utmost rigour, and afterwards supply the balm that soothes the cuts and bruises of its ruthless iron rod.

Poor old Brille. . . .

Hullo, what was this?

A sound of running feet. Greffier, Kramm, Wicking, rushing swiftly toward his tent. A shout from the leading man, Greffier:

"*Look out, sir! Look out!* Sergeant-Major's loading his revolver, and shouting that he's going to shoot you dead."

Captain Le Sage took his cigarette-case from the side pocket of his tunic.

"Don't run about this camp like a mad dog," he said quietly. "Don't shout. And don't address me without halting, coming to attention, and saluting."

"But, *mon Capitaine* . . ." cried Kramm.

"Silence. Dismiss. Go away. Do you hear me?"

"But, sir . . ."

"Here! Do you want a taste of *crapaudine* or something unpleasant? *Rompez!*"

Captain Le Sage rose to his feet, took his *kepi* and cane, and went from his tent, followed by the men who had rushed to warn him—this presumably having appealed to them as a more desirable course of action than assaulting and seizing the Sergeant-Major, a terrible breach of discipline, particularly terrible when the Sergeant-Major, trembling with rage, was fumblingly loading his revolver.

Tapping his riding-boot with his cane, Captain Le Sage walked in the direction of the Sergeant-Major's tent. As he approached it, Sergeant-Major Brille dashed out, saw Captain Le Sage and levelled the revolver straight at his breast, and at less than six paces range.

The Sergeant-Major was a crack revolver shot, and the hand

that had trembled was now steady.

"Oh, by the way, Sergeant-Major," said Captain Le Sage, speaking precisely as he always did when addressing him, "I have just heard that you are going to shoot me."

Would that hammer never fall? . . . Would he have the ghost of a chance if he sprang at the man? . . . No. The slightest movement would be plain simple suicide.

"I don't think it should be done out here—not where your action might be seen by your subordinates. You would be the first to admit that it is prejudicial to discipline for a Company Sergeant-Major to shoot his Captain. In public, I mean; before the men. And there are several approaching now. (*Stand back, Greffier, you damned fool. Don't move!*) When that has to be done, it should be done decently, privately and without setting a bad example. Isn't that so? Come, come now, Sergeant-Major Brille. Isn't that so? You are a very senior non-commissioned officer and should know. Of course you do. Well then—come along to my tent. That's the proper place for it to be done. Follow me."

And Captain Le Sage turned his back upon the man who was taking aim at his heart. As the target over his foresight moved, a look of annoyance crossed the Sergeant-Major's face, the sort of look it would have worn at the rifle-range when, just as he was about to press the trigger of his rifle and win another cup, a fly settled on the backsight across which he was concentrating on the foresight and the bull's-eye.

He lowered his revolver and mechanically, almost subconsciously, followed the man whose orders he had obeyed ten thousand times.

"*Go away*—you gaping, goggling mules," growled Le Sage *sotto voce* as he passed the men who had warned him, and others who had been attracted to the spot by the unusual sight of a non-commissioned officer presenting his revolver at the breast of the Commandant.

Strolling on, Captain Le Sage reached his tent, stood aside and, with the manner of one who assumes that whatever he suggests will be done as a matter of course, motioned the Sergeant-Major to enter before him.

"Sit down, Brille," he said, indicating his own chair and

seating himself on the bed.

The Sergeant-Major obeyed, and sat staring dully at the revolver in his hand.

This latter was again shaking, the fingers twitching.

"That'll go off in a moment if you are not careful," said Captain Le Sage. "Open the breach."

The Sergeant-Major obeyed.

"May as well draw the cartridges. . . . But here, let me do it," he added. "Your fingers are all thumbs to-day. . . . That's better. Now I'll tell you what I want you to do. Lie down on my bed here."

"*Mon Capitaine*, I . . ."

"Come on, Brille. Come and lie down, and we'll have a mug of good coffee each. Come on now. Take off your tunic and your boots."

With fumbling fingers, the non-commissioned officer rose and clumsily removed his tunic.

Seating himself on a chair he tried to untie his bootlaces.

"I can't. I'm . . ."

"Come on, I'll help you."

And with cool but swift and accurate movements Captain Le Sage unfastened the man's *brodequins* and drew them off.

"Now then, on to the bed with you," he said.

The Sergeant-Major obeyed, lay down on the bed, buried his face in the pillow and burst into tears.

Drawing up his chair beside the bed, Captain Le Sage patted the heaving shoulders of the *cafard*-stricken old soldier.

"There, there, *mon vieux*," he said. "I know all about it. You nearly shot me to-day—and it's not so long since I nearly shot myself! Fact. I know all about it. . . . Now you are not to get off that bed until I order you to do so. Understand?"

Sergeant-Major Brille, man of iron, feared as well as respected by every soldier in the Company, turned his head, raised his face from the pillow, seized his Captain's hand and pressed it to his lips.

To all who are rightly disgusted at such exhibitions of heroics and emotionalism, it will be learned with regret that this story is absolutely true.

CALLED

"Called" is an effective ghost story of what happens to an abusive husband who eventually poisons his wife. After the wife's death, all of the servants in his household keep coming to him saying that they hear the "Nai-Mem", his wife, calling to them. "Called" was the first story in Part I, "Queer", in Odd—But Even So *(1941).* An audio presentation of the story has appeared in Classic Ghost Stories Volume II *(1993, 46.5 minutes),* 19 Classic Short Stories *(1996), and* Classic Ghost Stories *(2001).*

Lesthwaite was not really popular at Sinburi, though he had his friends, of course; or, if not friends, acquaintances, followers. Young men, new to Siam, were quite apt to follow him for a time, as he was always very nice to them, always ready to listen to their troubles, to give good advice, accept their drinks, win their money and sell them ponies. In fact, to one of them he had sold the same animal twice, first as a very shaggy Shan pony, not only hairy at the heel but hairy all over, and a month later, when it had been "stolen," he sold it to him again, beautifully clipped, swept and garnished, and looking twice the horse it used to be. That was why it cost twice as much, the second time.

And among the older men he had such companions as any good fellow has, any man who plays polo well; shoots well; eats, drinks and talks well; plays billiards and poker more than well, and is ready to bet with anyone, at any time, on anything. He was a man very well known throughout the length and breadth of Siam, and yet not exactly popular.

Everyone agreed that Mrs. Lesthwaite was too good for her husband.

John Lesthwaite quite agreed but expressed it slightly differently. She was too good altogether. If she hadn't been quite so good, she would have been a great deal better. As a wife, that is to say, for although she never dreamed of reproaching him, she was a living reproach to him, and no dream about it.

When he returned from the Club a couple of hours late for

dinner, and in a condition that he would describe as slightly sozzled, there were no recriminations. That was the annoying part of it. Had she pointed out to him that, after waiting in a condition of annoyance and irritation for a couple of hours, hunger had turned into sick faintness; that the dinner was spoilt; that it was hopeless to try to keep Ching Li up to the mark if he never knew when he would be called upon to serve a dinner that he had cooked; that she loathed dining within an hour of bed-time; he would have had excuse and reason for voluble and angry reply. He would have told her that women who nagged ought to be muzzled, that a scold needs a scold's bridle, that a wife with a grievance ought to be put out of her misery. He would have shouted her down, shown her who was master, told her he would be as late as he liked and a jolly sight later. He would have had a grievance of his own, and he would have aired it, too. Hot air, and plenty of it.

But what can you do with a woman who never says a word; who gives you nothing to go on, and simply won't be the other party to a row? No, it takes two to make a quarrel, and when one knows that one is in the wrong, it is rather deflating to have no more useful knowledge than that to stiffen one's backbone and feed one's wrath.

Nor if, in a slightly alcoholic gush of sudden *bonhomie* and affection, he packed the car full of others like unto himself, and rolled up at the bungalow with half a dozen extra for dinner, did she utter one word of complaint that a simple little dinner for two should be turned into a dinner-party for eight at a minute's notice. Not a word. It seemed that nothing could ever provoke the placid woman to wrath; not the use of a new clean curtain-end or a silk cushion for the wiping of dusty boots or an oily gun-barrel; not the scarring and searing, with smouldering cigarette-ends of the polished surface of a cherished piece of furniture brought out from Home; not the throwing of stinking cigar-butts into the pretty flower bowls; not the opening and reading of her letters whenever they fell into his hands, though this was a thing she hated almost beyond bearing. It was not that he wasn't perfectly welcome to read every letter she received; not that she had any epistolary secret whatsoever; but she did like to feel that her Home mail was hers, that a letter addressed to her was something private and personal, and that she might at least be allowed to open them herself.

Certainly it was very childish and foolish of her—as she freely admitted—to feel annoyed, hurt, disappointed, in some way cheated, when she found her packet of letters from Home all ripped open and lying scattered just where he had dropped them beside his chair.

Of course, there are silly people to whom the act of opening a Christmas or birthday parcel gives almost as much pleasure as do the contents themselves. And Marie Lesthwaite must have been one of those idiots, for an opened and crumpled envelope and a letter of which the sheets were in the wrong order, was something, not exactly spoilt, but definitely damaged. She had once tried to make her husband understand this queer idiosyncrasy, and the effort had been neither well received nor ever repeated.

"*Oho!*" said Lesthwaite. "Secrets, eh? 'Fraid I might stumble on something. Well, well, well! So that's it, is it? Still waters, eh! What? Like to open the envelopes yourself? Don't talk such damned nonsense. You don't want me to read your letters, and there's some good reason for it."

So thereafter, no reproach, no complaint.

A very foolish woman, one perceives—unless one likes the view that she was a very wise one, realizing that the greatest of all human blessings is Peace, and the worthiest of all human efforts the striving for Peace.

Lest the unfortunate Marie be thought an even sillier woman than she really was, it should be stated that she accepted none of her husband's unkindnesses, his thoughtlessness, his inconsiderate habits, his more objectionable acts and ways, without protest. Once and for all, she told him that she disliked or hated or detested this, that, or the other; but only once—so that when he annoyed, disappointed, irritated, angered, frustrated or hurt her, he knew quite well that he was doing so. He knew, for example, that she loathed being called Maria, with the accent on the second syllable, and by no other name than Maria did he ever address her.

It is probably impossible for people more fortunately situated, to estimate the difficulty with which such a man as John

Lesthwaite bore the yoke of matrimony with so tiresome a woman. A man righteously angered might as well stand and address an impassioned harangue to his horse as to a woman who accepted it in meek silence, or at any rate in silence; for this unfortunate fellow had a strong and abiding suspicion that his wife was not really meek. Not a bit of it. She was certainly no fool; undeniably she was a woman of spirit, she could deal with a recalcitrant servant as well and firmly as he himself could do, and in the give and take of social intercourse at the Club she could hold her own. In his own idiom, she took nothing from anybody. From anybody but himself, that is to say. But from him she took anything, stood anything, bore anything and everything. And it was most damnably annoying. How a good row would have cleared the air. How easily he could have shouted her down, put her in the wrong, routed and defeated her completely. But you cannot defeat an enemy who won't fight. And you cannot make an enemy of a person who won't be inimical.

How successfully he could have defended himself every time. But you can't defend yourself unless you are attacked. And attack him she would not. She wouldn't even remonstrate when he did something to which any other woman would have objected; when he repeated what he knew to be an offence; when he did something which, reasonably or unreasonably from his point of view, she had asked him not to do.

Thinking it over as he sat on the verandah drinking *stengah* after *stengah,* smoking cigar after cigar, he wondered how on earth he had ever come to fall in love with Marie Bardsley, a bread-and-butter-Vicarage-Miss if ever there was one.

Perhaps that had been the secret of it, though. Contrast. She had caught him on the rebound, after his affair with the Black Spider. Gad, if poor little Webber had only died a month earlier and he himself had married the Spider, she would have made the fur fly all right when he came home drunk from the Club, came home two or three hours late for dinner, came to bed drunk, and woke her up at four in the morning.

Rows! He would have had all the rows he wanted. She would have been delivered of a mouthful, and himself endowed with an earful, whenever he annoyed her. Not only that, she would have given him something to talk about, too. By the time she had ticked him off for his peccadilloes and he had returned the compliment with regard to hers, he would have had no cause for complaint on the score of a humdrum life and dullness in the home.

Funny! It had been precisely the other way about with the Webbers. Webber had been all for peace, and she all for the breaking of it. He against her had been Peace-at-any-price *versus* War-at-any-price. Poor little beggar . . .

A dangerous woman, really. Poisonous. No wonder they called her the Black Spider, and, when he died, said that she had eaten him.

Still, John Hector Montague Lesthwaite was rather a different proposition from little Jimmy Webber. Yes, if the Black Spider and John Hector Montague Lesthwaite had made a match of it, she'd have *met* her match. But he had gone on leave, and, although far from bored with the affair with the Black Spider, had met Marie, and just gone all sloppy and sentimental. Something good and noble in him must have been touched by her simplicity. Simplicity, ignorance, sweetness, purity . . . Hell! . . . Another little drink wouldn't do us any harm.

§2

If such a thing were possible, Marie Lesthwaite grew even quieter, more placid, more undisturbably peaceful, as her health failed.

At first, the symptoms of her illness were only an increasing lassitude, listlessness, and general physical weakness, as her body inevitably attuned itself to the condition of her mind. Attacks of dengue fever, increasing in frequency and severity, did nothing to improve matters, nor did her husband's attitude of—

"Come along, Born-Tired. For God's sake, pull yourself together. . . . Get on anybody's nerves. . . . Like a death's head at dinner last night. Spoilt the party completely. If you can't improve on last night's effort as a hostess, you had better not show up at all when people come to dinner. Dunno what has come over you. Can't think what's the matter with you, nowadays. *I* don't know what's wrong with you. And I doubt if you do, either."

But there, for once, John Lesthwaite was wrong. She knew quite well what was wrong. Life itself. That was all. Infinite weariness, boredom, disappointment, frustration. Had she been conversant with the jargon, she might have referred to the damming up of the *libido,* the sapping of the *élan vital.* As it was, she merely wondered if it were possible literally to be bored to death, to be genuinely tired of life and by life.

Then came insomnia and the nightly pacing of the big bare bedroom, while her hearty husband snored undisturbed.

It was the lady doctor, head of the American Medical Mission, who first raised the question of Mrs. Lesthwaite's health. Bluntly, she told John Lesthwaite that it was high time he called in a doctor to have a look at his wife, and that whether it were she herself or another, whom he called in, was neither here nor there. In fact, what she would suggest was that he take his wife down to Bangkok and get the best possible opinion. . . .

And what about his suggesting that she should mind her own business?

Well, wasn't it a doctor's business to do precisely what she was doing? Isn't it anyone's business to help a friend in need?

"Oh, and you think your friend, my wife, is in need of your help, do you?" sneered John Lesthwaite.

"As a doctor, yes. Very definitely."

"Well, I'm sure I hope you'll come and see her and do your very best for her—when I call you in."

But Dr. Amelia Depew called in without being called in, and gave Mrs. Lesthwaite, whom she liked, admired and pitied, a piece of her robust mind; talked to her for her good; and gave her sound advice, medical and other. Also some little white tablets, with strict injunctions never to take more than one at a time, never more than one in twenty-four hours, and never more than three in a week.

"They'll make you sleep, my dear. Guarantee you three good nights a week, anyhow. And that'll help you along tremendously. And now then, one more thing before I scram—I'm going to London in February, on my way back to America. Come with me."

"Oh, but my husband . . ."

"Not talking about him, Marie. We're talking about you.

Think it over."

Marie Lesthwaite thought it over, did her utmost to brace herself against the crushing disappointment that she knew would follow her suggesting the matter to her husband; broached the subject; and listened in a resigned silence to all he had to say about damned meddlesome interfering busybodies who have the infernal cheek to butt in where they are not wanted, and try to arrange other people's lives for them.

And steadily, Marie Lesthwaite's health grew worse; and soon after Dr. Amelia Depew's departure, she was obviously very ill.

And what could have been more annoying than this illness to so hospitably-minded and socially-inclined a person as John Lesthwaite, saddled with a wife who, far from being a social asset and helper at her best, was now an obstacle, a hindrance and a nuisance. It was altogether too bad; intolerable. The climate of Sinburi was no worse for her than for him; no worse than for other women who were merry and bright, played their game of bridge, enjoyed their cocktails and cigarettes, rode and danced and picnicked. If other women could play golf, tennis—some of them, squash, even—surely she could, at any rate, get about the house and do her duty as a wife and hostess?

§3

One night, he returned from the Club in an evil temper, after a long and somewhat disastrous session at stud poker. An infernal dark-horse of a fellow, a bird of passage visiting the American Consul, had taught John Lesthwaite that he was not the best poker player in Siam—a very expensive lesson. Also, his liver was out of order. Must have eaten something. It couldn't be what he had drunk, of course, because he could put away short drinks till the cows came home. Hadn't he been doing it for years, and had anyone ever seen him the worse for liquor?

Entering the bedroom, switching on the bedside lamp, yawning loudly, he disturbed his wife who, with a quiet "Hullo! That you, John?" turned over.

As he sat on the side of his bed, winding up his watch as was his wont, he noticed beneath the bed-side-lamp a little cardboard box which he had not seen before.

What was this? Some other damned doctor interfering behind his back?

Picking up the box, he saw a number of white tablets. Almost guiltily he started as his wife's bed creaked. She turned again and sat up.

"What's this muck?" he growled.

"Give me one, John, will you? I hadn't meant to take any again this week, but I know I shan't sleep to-night, and I've such a crashing headache. I've been nearly blind with it, all day. . . . One in a glass of lime-juice."

And lying back on her pillow she pressed her hands to her face, covering her eyes.

Removing the tumbler from the *nam tohn* (the porous water-container on which it rested) John Lesthwaite poured out a glass of the lime-juice which always stood, at night, on the table between their beds.

Into this he shook a tablet from the box. Another fell. Perhaps his hand trembled, for a third and a fourth and a fifth followed.

Removing the little net from the sugar-basin on the tray, he put in a teaspoonful of sugar and patiently stirred the contents of the glass.

"There you are, Born-Tired," he said.

Marie Lesthwaite took her hands from her face, raised herself into a sitting position, and took the glass.

"Thank you, John," she said. And drank.

"Bitter," she added, speaking her own life's sufficient epitaph, as she lay back upon the pillow.

*   *   *   *   *   *   *

Old Dr. Jackson, who had really retired years before, was sympathetically kind and helpful. Poor lady. Poor, poor dear. And poor John Lesthwaite. What a tragedy. Her heart must have been very, very tired.

Everybody else was also most kind and sympathetic.

It was generally agreed that John Lesthwaite bore himself very well, kept a stiff upper lip, and refrained from any obvious indulgence in self-pity and unmanly grief.

§4

Well, well! Happy days again. Bachelor Hall. No restraints and the sky the limit. Wonderful parties. Great doings.

Not a shadow of regret. Not a twinge of remorse. The poor creature had not been happy. Got no fun from life; was altogether too blooming good for this world—and well out of it.

And doubtless old Jackson was right. Dammit, he was a doctor and ought to know. Weak heart. Tired. Malaria and dengue fever do affect one's heart. Yes, died of heart trouble. Probably those tablets were just doctor's eyewash. You took one and thought it would send you to sleep; and it did. Just as well that nobody knew anything about them, perhaps. There was one thing, they never would now, for he had chucked them into the river and burnt the box.

Who had given them to her? Why, that interfering frumpish old freak, Amelia Depew. Just as well that she had left Siam.

Well, well! All's well that ends well. A month ago to-day.

"*Nai?*"

The house-boy, Ai Soon, appeared on the verandah, where John Lesthwaite was enjoying his post-prandial cigar, alone for once.

"Well . . . ?"

"The *Nai-Mem*[6] called."

"What the devil *are* you talking about, you. . ."

The house-boy stared foolishly, as well he might.

What was biting the lunatic? Damned idiot.

John Lesthwaite rose to his feet.

"*Nai-Mem dy riark*,"[7] faltered the man.

"You thought you heard your mistress call! . . . And she has been dead a month!"

"*Kit lao, Nai*,"[8]

"Thought! I'll give you something to think about!"

The Siamese butler, cringing before his angry master, backed

---

[6] *The Mistress.*

[7] *The Mistress called.*

[8] *I thought so, Master.*

away, turned, and hurried from the verandah.

John Lesthwaite sat down again, more annoyed and angry than the incident seemed to warrant.

Thought he heard his mistress call! The fool. Lazy scoundrel had been lying asleep. Something had awakened him suddenly and, as they all do, he had thought it must have been a call from the front of the house.

And yet the half-wit had never done it before. Never done it with regard to the Master, anyway. Perhaps that was only because there was no mistake about it when John Lesthwaite called! . . . Yes, probably she used to call in that silly feeble voice of hers, and the servants could never be sure whether she had called or the canary had coughed. Well, not to say canary, for one didn't keep them in Siam, but perhaps the kitten had mewed.

"*Nai!*"

"Well?"

The Number Two boy stepped out from the drawing-room on to the verandah.

"The *Nai* called."

"No," roared Lesthwaite. "The *Nai* didn't call."

He rose to his feet, amazed to find that he was actually trembling. It must be with rage, of course.

"And what's more," he growled, "you know that I didn't call. What's this? Some game? Do you mean to tell me you thought that I . . . ?"

"No, *Nai*," interrupted the man. "I thought the *Nai-Mem* called."

"*What?* You thought . . ."

Lesthwaite strode toward the servant.

The man stood his ground.

"*Karrap!*"[9] he said. "I heard the *Nai-Mem* call," he added.

"But, you besotted idiot, you damned half-wit, you cursed croaking mud-fish, you know perfectly well that the *Nai-Mem* is . . ."

"*Karrap!*" repeated the boy stolidly. "*Nai-Mem ty lao.*[10]

---

[9] *Any form of respectful assent or acknowledgment.*

[10] *The Mistress is dead.*

Nevertheless, she called."

" But you blithering son of a sow, how on earth could . . ."

"*Karrap!*" repeated the man for the third time. "It is indeed as the *Nai* says, but a *Nai-Mem* called."

"But there is no *Nai-Mem* in the house, as you know perfectly well."

"It is as the *Nai* pleases. It is as he says. There is no *Nai-Mem* in the house."

"Well then . . ."

"Nevertheless, the voice of a *Nai-Mem* called 'Ai Kheo'."

"Oh, a voice called your name, did it? Well, I'll tell you what voice that was. It was opium, that's what it was."

"*Nai*, I do not drink the black smoke. I am not an opium-fiend."

"Never smoked opium in your life, eh?"

"Once, *Nai*," replied the man simply. "I did not like it."

"Well, I'll tell you what you do like then, if you don't like opium. And that is *nam-fai*—brandy. Tasted that once, and didn't like it, eh? And that's why you hear voices. You touch my brandy again, and . . ."

"*Nai*, I do not drink brandy."

"Well, get to Hell out of this, and when I call you, you come."

"And every time I don't call you, don't come, as quickly as you can, see?" he added, in an effort to bring the whole ridiculous business to its proper ridiculous level.

The man silently disappeared.

John Lesthwaite threw away the cold butt of his cigar, took another from the box and lighted it.

Why was his hand shaking? These confounded fuddle-headed fools, half awake and half asleep. Or were the swine ganging up on him to get a bit of their own back . . .

No, it was he who was being half-witted now. As if Siamese servants would think up a trick like that. It wasn't as though they were Chinese. But no, even they would never have the wit and cunning to plan such a way of frightening him as that.

Frightening him? What on earth was he talking about? Why should he be frightened?

John Lesthwaite poured himself a half-tumbler of whisky and diluted it with soda-water and restraint. . . . Ah, that was better.

135

"Well, what do you want?" he growled, as the grim face of the bullet-headed *durwan*[11] appeared as the man came up the steps leading from the lattice-work enclosed verandah down to the garden.

"The *Nai-Mem* is calling," the stolid ex-soldier replied. "Keeps on calling and nobody answers . . . These lazy house-servants!"

In spite of the fact that he had just emptied his tumbler, John Lesthwaite's mouth seemed a little dry, his tongue inclined to be a trifle stiff, his throat constricted.

"*What?*" he said, and this time the question was almost whispered.

"I said the *Nai-Mem* is calling," replied the Gurkha.

"But Manjit Gurung, don't talk such damned nonsense."

And now the master's voice was almost gentle, almost pleading.

"You know perfectly well that the *Nai-Mem* is . . ."

"Yes, yes. I know. Of course I know," interrupted the Gurkha. "I didn't say your *Nai-Mem,* though it sounded like her voice. I mean the *Nai-Mem* who is in the bungalow now."

"But there isn't one, Manjit Gurung. I am quite alone here. There is no *Nai-Mem* in the bungalow."

"Well, that's funny. One called. That is why I came up. I went and spoke to Ai Soon but he said, '*Yes, yes, all right. I can hear as well as you can, but the Nai was angry about it.*' Then I met Ai Kheo coming away from the house, and I said, '*Can't you hear the Nai-Mem calling, you fool?*' and he said '*Yes, I heard her twice,*' and that when he went to answer, the Nai had abused him."

John Lesthwaite sat upright in his long low chair and glanced from the hard Mongolian face of Manjit Gurung to the empty tumbler.

No, he mustn't try to replenish that until he felt better, had got his nerves under control. His hand would shake so badly that . . .

But good Heavens above! What on earth was the matter with him? What infernal incredible childish idiocy was this? Was John Hector Montague Lesthwaite actually . . . ?

---

[11] *Watch-man; door-keeper.*

"What did the *Nai-Mem* call?" he whispered.

"Well, I don't know. Usual thing. Just '*Boy!*' No, she called Ai Kheo by name, the last time. Yes, I remember. That was why I went to look for him.

"But Manjit Gurung, you knew that the *Nai-Mem* . . ."

His voice was almost pleading again.

"Well, other *Nai-Mems* come here, don't they, *Nai*? Lots of times. I thought there was one here now, and . . ."

The man stopped and stared curiously at his master. His slant eyes narrowed.

"No," he said slowly. "That isn't right, really. It was your *Nai-Mem's* voice. As a matter of fact, I forgot for the moment that she is . . ."

"Well, don't forget any more. And don't imagine things. You were asleep and . . ."

"What, walking?" muttered the old soldier, as he turned away. "There are *bhūts* about this place," he growled, in his native Gurmukhi of Nepaul.

As the clip-clop of the man's sandals died away into the night, John Lesthwaite turned to the bottle. Of course his hands weren't shaking. Not so much as to prevent his pouring himself another drink, anyway.

Ah, that was better. Now then. To get this straight. Or rather, to get to the bottom of this nonsense.

While it was a case of Siamese servants telling the same story, it could very well be a story, in other words a damned lie. But a Gurkha wouldn't join in with them. No Gurkha would, especially Manjit Gurung. He despised Siamese too much, especially house-servants; and anyway, he was too stupid, and probably too simple, to take a hand in a game of that sort. Besides, why should he? He and ex-rifleman Manjit Gurung were on excellent terms. Quite friends, so far as a *durwan* and his master could be called that.

No, it was utterly absurd. The Gurkha was a straightforward, simple, honest sort of chap, one of the smiling, cheerful, merry-and-bright sort, in spite of his somewhat grim and cruel-looking face. Given cause, he might be a bit over-handy with his *kukri*,[12]

---

[12] *National weapon, a heavy chopping-knife.*

no doubt. Violence perhaps—but not trickery of this sort; not entering into rascally plots and plans with a gang of lying servants. He was a bemedalled and decorated soldier, not a plate-licker.

No, his entrance into the business made things bad, took away all chance of writing it off as a pack of lies faked up by a gang of swindling swine who . . .

No, that wouldn't do for an explanation now that Manjit Gurung was in it. The man had heard a woman calling, or honestly thought he had. Therefore, there was no sense in refusing to believe that the house-boys had. There must be some other explanation. . . . A bird? Some of these Oriental birds certainly had funny cries. Some rare specimen might have flown near the house and uttered a cry that sounded like 'Boy,' and one that sounded like 'Ai Kheo.'

No, that wouldn't do. The Number Two boy said the voice had called him by name, and Manjit Gurung said he had heard the voice calling that same name. Could some woman have come into the garden and called? No, most certainly no Siamese or Chinese woman would call '*Boy*'; nor would any native woman shout a man's name round the house like that. Besides, if Ai Kheo's wife were calling to him, Manjit Gurung would know her voice. It was quite impossible that he would mistake it for that of a *Nai-Mem.*

But the whole thing was preposterous. Talk about much ado about nothing!

Rising briskly to his feet, John Lesthwaite shook himself—or shuddered—strode down the verandah, and out into the brilliantly moonlit garden.

Full moon. Yes, it had been full moon the night she died.

Had anybody else heard the voice beside those three? He would make enquiries to-morrow; ask whether my body else in the compound had heard the voice. If Manjit Gurung and the two house-boys had heard it, presumably others had. There were always people about, round the servants' quarters.

As he passed the door of the kitchen, a small detached building connected with the main building by a covered way, the cook appeared at the door.

"*Nai!*"

"Well?"

Merciful Heaven! If the fellow said that he too . . .

"The *Nai-Mem* is calling."

It was the master who recoiled from the servant this time, and who glanced around as though for something upon which to sit down.

He tried to moisten his lips. He must say something. Something.

"Ching Li, you know that the *Nai-Mem* is dead," he expostulated, and in his voice there was a clear note of appeal.

"Yes," agreed the cook simply.

"Well, then . . ."

"A *Nai-Mem* called," he added as his master stared at him, his face pale in the moonlight, his eyes staring widely, his clean-shaven mouth twitching.

"Whom did she call?"

"The Number One boy."

"Do you mean she called him by name?"

"First she called 'Boy,' and then again 'Boy!' and the third time she called '*Ai Soon!*'"

"But it couldn't have been the *Nai-Mem,*" expostulated Lesthwaite.

"No."

"It must have been someone else."

"Yes," agreed Ching Li with his Chinese smile. "Calling with her voice."

John Lesthwaite made his way back to the house. He had a little difficulty with the steps that led up from the garden to the verandah. They seemed unusually steep and high, and he was very glad to reach his chair. Two Siamese, a Gurkha and a Chinese, all saying the same thing.

And that thing the truth.

It was useless and foolish to deny it. Those four had not put their heads together and concocted a tale. Those four separately and independently had all heard the voice.

Why had *he* not heard it? That was the impossible thing, the terrible thing. For impossible it was.

Supposing he himself now called sufficiently loudly for Ching Li in the kitchen, Manjit Gurung in the garden, Ai Soon in the drawing-room and Ai Kheo in the back verandah to hear him—how could he himself or anybody else, seated here in the verandah fail to do so?

John Hector Montague Lesthwaite felt cold in spite of the humid warmth of the night.

Why could they hear her and he could not? Was it because that in life he had so shut her out from his own mind, and so cut her off from all personal mental and spiritual contact, that now it was impossible for him to . . .

Nonsense. He would be saying next that because he never listened to her when she was alive, he could not hear her when she was dead. As if anyone could hear the dead.

But the servants. They had heard her. Perhaps he himself would hear her, next time. He must listen. He must listen hard. Carefully. He must always be listening. He must try to hear her. He must not sleep. He must listen day and night.

But why should he? Did he wish to hear the voice of his dead wife, the voice of the woman whom he had . . . ?

No, no. He had not. He had not done *that*. It was her heart. She had died of a tired heart. Doctor Jackson had said so himself.

What was that? . . . What was that?
Ai Kheo? Had he come again to tell him that again she was . . . No. Good Lord! It was day-light. It was morning.

§5

Sinburi opinion began to change about John Lesthwaite. He wasn't taking his sad loss so well, after all. For a month he had seemed to bear the blow as a man should, with courage and self-control, with dignity and reticence. But it had not lasted. Behind that facade of defiance of Fate, recklessness, occasionally of forced gaiety, the real edifice had been crumbling.

He was taking to drink.

His best friend, if he had had one, could never have called him abstemious, nor his worst enemy a drunkard. But the friend would have to admit that he was a drunkard now. Drunk in the Club bar every night, and always the last to leave. Seemed positively afraid to go home. One could understand that, perhaps, in the circumstances; but on the other hand, could one? He had never seemed as fond of his wife as all that. If no one had ever called him a drunkard, still less would anybody ever have called him a family man; uxorious.

Well, well, one never knew. Fancy Lesthwaite going to pieces like this, with grief . . .

§6

John Lesthwaite sat alone on his verandah neither drunk nor sober. Not sober by reason of any restraint with the whisky since sunset; and not drunk—because, nowadays, it was impossible to get drunk. Drinking since sunset . . . Sunset to moonrise . . . And to-night the moon would be at the full. If one of those servants came and told him that the *Nai-Mem* was calling, he'd shoot him. He would. He'd shoot him dead. He'd go and get his revolver. His fine, fat, heavy, old, army revolver, and lay it on the table beside the bottle.

But not one of them would dare.

Yes, beside the bottle. The bottle and the revolver. They ought to fortify a man. If one of those servants came and said . . .

No, they wouldn't dare. Not one of the house-boys or the cook would dare. But that damned Gurkha would, and enjoy doing it.

Well, if he did, he'd shoot him too—if he could hold the revolver steady enough. Yes, he'd sit here all night, as he had done that night a month ago. Sit all night, and if one of them came, and . . .

But suppose he heard it himself . . . God forbid! But wouldn't that be better than not hearing it, when everybody else did? Better than having that awful feeling that she had cut him off. Cut herself off from him. Better than the feeling that even these wretched servants, Siamese, Chinese, Gurkha, were worthier than . . .

Rubbish.

An hour dragged by. No sign of Ai Soon or the Number Two boy. Nothing from Manjit Gurung.

Should he stroll out and see if the cook had got anything to say about the voice of the *Nai-Mem* calling?

No. Put ideas into his head.

Another hour, and no interruption of his peace, not even by the Gurkha.

Peace. As if he would ever know such a thing as peace again or . . .

What was this? What was this? It was a plot. They were in league.

With a start that knocked the glass from its place beside his hand, he sat upright in his chair.

Ai Soon, Ai Kheo, Ching Li, Manjit Gurung the Gurkha, coming up the steps. And what was that little crowd on the lawn at the bottom? The whole gang of the rest of them—the second *durwan,* the gardener, pony-boy, chauffeur, even the washer-man, the dog-boy and . . .

What was this? What did they want? What had they heard?

"*Nai!*"

John Lesthwaite stared, dry-mouthed, at Ai Soon, his Number One boy.

"*Nai,*" said Ai Soon, the spokesman of the group that stood in respectful silence with crossed hands and bowed heads, all save the Gurkha who stood at attention. "*Nai!* The *Nai-Mem* is calling. We have all come because we have all heard the *Nai-Mem* calling."

John Lesthwaite tried to speak, tried to advance upon the silent band who stood there before him as though with the courage of fear, fear of something beside which his wrath was as nothing. But no muscle of his body moved, save those of his lips from which no sound came.

A tense and terrible silence.

Suddenly John Lesthwaite dropped rather than sat down in his chair. His head fell back and his eyes closed.

Was this a stroke? A heart attack? His liquor getting back at him at last? Was he dying? Would he see her and would she . . .?

When he again opened his eyes he was alone.

Well! What a thing to do! Fancy John Hector Montague Lesthwaite *fainting*! Liver, that was it. Couldn't be the whisky. Who had ever seen him the worse for liquor?

And he emptied into his glass the remainder of the contents of the bottle that he had opened that evening, and drank it neat.

Ah, that was better.

What was it he had been going to do?

Yes, those damned servants. He'd teach them who was master here. Ganging up on him like that. The swine. The ungrateful swine. He'd teach them to disobey his definite and emphatic order not to come telling him a pack of lies.

"*Boy!*" he roared at the top of his powerful voice. Yes, he'd show them.

"Boy!" he bawled again.

Oh? They could hear imaginary voices and couldn't hear that, couldn't they? Wouldn't come, wouldn't they? By gad! They'd be sorry if he went to them instead.

"*Ai Soon!*" he roared.

"*Ai Kheo!*"

Rising to his feet he seized the empty bottle by the neck. He'd brain the . . .

No, no, this wouldn't do. He must pull himself together. Beneath his dignity to go searching for his own house-boys. He'd send Manjit Gurung to fetch them.

"*Durwan!*" he bawled. And again,

"*Ho! Manjit! Ma peh!*"[13]

What? The Gurkha too. By God! That put the lid on it. He had had enough. Now he'd show them something.

Striding through the drawing-room to the back verandah, where one of them must be, he was amazed to find the place empty.

Bawling "*Boy!*" out into the darkness, at the top of his voice, he turned and rushed up the back stairs . . . Nobody in the bedrooms . . .

From open windows and verandahs he shouted with the full strength of his lungs. The night resounded with his roars.

"*Boy! . . . Boy! . . . Boy!*"

Down the front stairs, through the dining-room, out again to the back verandah. The house was deserted.

Snatching up a riding-whip, he ran out into the garden. With

---

[13] *Come here.*

his own hand he'd thrash the first one he met, Siamese, Chinese or Gurkha, cringing house-boy or fighting soldier. He'd show them who was master.

Around the house like a madman he rushed, and then across the back compound to the stables.

Scarcely could he believe the evidence of his senses. Not a syce or stable-boy; no gardener; no chauffeur; no washer-man; not even a dog-boy, not even a servant's servant or hanger-on; not a soul about the place.

Well, the cook. He'd have to bear the brunt of it, then. The cook should have come when he heard the *Nai* bawling.

To the cook-house he ran, kicked upon the door and found the place empty.

And then the truth dawned upon him. They had gone. They had deserted him, vanished as though the place were a plague-stricken charnel-house; as though he, their master, were a leper. They had gone. The rats had left the sinking ship.

As frightened now as he was angry, he made one more despairing effort.

Striding swiftly across to the front of the house, he filled his lungs with air, and as though bawling at a marching battalion, roared at the top of his voice for his staunch Gurkha watchman.

"*Manjit! Manjit!*"

The old soldier wouldn't go. He wouldn't desert his master. He wouldn't stand in with a gang of scullions. He was a man.

Again he shouted. And again. And only the distant echo replied.

Silence. Utter silence. Even the pi-dogs, usually so clamorous at full moon, were silent.

If only he could hear the sound of drumming from one of the Wats.[14]

This silence . . . This dreadful silence . . . And at any moment she might call. He might see her.

One more despairing cry he raised with all his strength. And then, turning on his heel, John Lesthwaite walked slowly up the steps into the verandah and picked up the heavy revolver.

---

[14] *Temples.*

BRUISED HEAD AND TAINTED HEEL

"Bruised Head and Tainted Heel" is the interesting story of a snake seeking, and obtaining, revenge on the man who killed the snake's mate. The story also contains some of Wren's thoughts on the occult and the power of Indian yogis. "Bruised Head and Tainted Heel" was originally published as the third story in Part I, "Queer", of Odd—But Even So *(1941).*

"The Deputy-Commissioner speaking . . ."

Is there anything in this *yoga* business?

Of course there is. A very great deal indeed. *Yoga* is a religion, a science, and a philosophy, and a genuine *yogi* is a learned man. A highly interesting one, too, if only for the fact that his knowledge is so different from our own.

Have they occult powers?

There is a very great deal of nonsense talked about *yoga* and about *yogis.* The genuine *yogi* doesn't claim to be a magician or to have supernatural power. As a matter of fact, he doesn't claim anything at all, except the right to be left alone, to contemplate in peace.

Why then does one hear and read such extraordinary stories about their supernatural powers and miraculous doings— apparently well-authenticated stories?

One is apt to forget what a great part coincidence plays in life. We all of us know of coincidences so remarkable as to be incredible; and it is of course a commonplace that fiction simply dare not use the long arm of coincidence one half so frequently, so aptly, as Fate does. There can be no doubt that coincidence has had a lot to do with the miracles-of-*yoga* myth.

Then, of course, there is clairvoyance. A very large number of *yogis* are clairvoyant, and have powers of that sort that would astonish anyone to whom they cared to exhibit them. But the same is true of any number of auld spey-wives in Scotland, not to mention palmists, fortune-tellers. and crystal-gazers—in Bond Street.

I could tell you of a case within my own personal knowledge of a *yogi* getting undesired and undeserved credit for miracle-mongering when there was nothing of the sort in it at all. He may or may not have been clairvoyant, but the alleged supernatural result was due entirely to natural causes.

At least I think so. I think so. Certainly the amazing affair is capable of rational explanation, and I always accept that kind of solution, where possible. I am not a hide-bound scoffer at things called occult and supernatural, but at the same time, I am not gullible, and as I say, I always prefer the straight-forward, simple and scientific solution, if it will work. And it does, in this case.

But not in every case?

Probably it would, if one could find it; though I admit there are cases where it is extremely difficult, if not impossible, to do so. But as a rule, you can find a—what shall I say—rational . . . physical . . . natural . . . explanation. That's the word, natural, as opposed to supernatural; normal, as opposed to supernormal.

I'll tell you about Tulsiram Jaganath and Captain Brackleigh; and it's a good example of the sort of incident that gives rise to these *yogi*-miracle yarns.

I knew this Captain Brackleigh very well; and the *swami, saddhu, sanyasi, yogi,* what you will, a holy man named Tulsiram Jaganath, I knew as well as a European can know an Indian, a Western materialist know an Eastern mystic. Never the twain shall meet, indeed; but I liked him very much, and I'm quite sure he liked me; and we used to have long and most amicable conversations.

With his whimsical humorous smile, he used sometimes to call me his *chela*,[15] and in point of fact, I always addressed him as *Guru-ji*.[16] If a blameless life qualifies a man for sainthood, he was a saint. He was a very learned man in our own acceptance of the word, and he was a *yogi* who admittedly had advanced unusually far along the Excellent Way of *yoga*. I am not personally competent to pass judgment on that, of course, but I know he was visited by eminent exponents of the *yogi* cult from all parts of India. Itinerant Lamas wandered down from Tibetan

---

[15] *Disciple.*

[16] *Honoured Teacher.*

lamaseries to talk with, him. *Yogis* came from their Himalayan caves and jungle fastnesses. Learned pundits walked all the way from Kashmir to consult him. Holy *saddhus* made pilgrimages from Benares, from Puri, from Hurdwar; learned priests travelled from Ceylon; seekers of the Truth came from temples in every part of India. Learned professors came from the great Hindu universities. Hindus who, in Calcutta, Bombay, Madras, Allahabad, Lahore and other teeming cities, dressed and lived much as you and I do, sat cross-legged upon the ground, clad in nothing but a loin-cloth and talked with him throughout much of the day and most of the night.

But I should think that the fact that he sat almost without food, shelter, and clothing, from year's end to year's end, on the same spot, and was practically worshipped by the villagers for a hundred square miles round, was the real miracle.

Yes, that was his miracle; the only miracle he ever performed, no doubt.

About Brackleigh. He was a good chap, and I used to stay with him when I went on tour. We hadn't much in common, but we had been at school together. He was an excellent fellow in his way, sterling; a very good type of officer, but although he got on excellently with his sepoys and liked them very well indeed, especially Punjabis, he disliked Indians in general, and positively hated those of the *babu* type. All educated Indians, as a matter of fact, were anathema to him.

He used to annoy me very greatly by the way he talked about them; as though, because an Indian was educated, he must therefore be not only disloyal and seditious, but bumptious and offensive as well as dishonest and generally worthless—which of course is not only wholly false but utterly absurd. It is as puerile as believing that every European official is oppressive, inimical, harsh and contemptuous.

It was a subject which I tried to avoid when enjoying his hospitality, for there was a danger that difference might breed acrimony and that argument and dispute might degenerate into quarrel. He was almost rabidly intolerant of the type that he disliked; and he refused to admit my contention that, while—like every other class of Indian and European—this particular class contained highly objectionable specimens, it nevertheless consisted largely of estimable and admirable people, and included some who were of the salt of the earth.

Now, among educated Indians, the type that he disliked most of all, indeed, hated and loathed and detested most of all, was the *swami* type, the *saddhu* and the *sanyasi*. He lumped them all together as *faquirs*, and was wont to observe that that was a damned good name for them, for they were "fakes" from start to finish; humbugs, swindlers and rogues; parasites upon the people; loafing wasters who, under the guise of religion, were worthless criminals, if only to the extent of obtaining goods under false pretences—in other words, terrifying ignorant villagers in to giving them whatever they wanted.

What was it, he would ask, but extortion by menace, when they pretended to have supernatural powers, and threatened, with terrible retribution and the wrath of the gods, those who refused their demands.

And it was useless for me to object that, although the wandering beggars, of India are an economic curse and a burden to be equalled only by the locust, there were genuine Holy Men among them, wandering or cave-dwelling scholars; men of profound learning, Christ-like teachers and exemplars, anchorites who had renounced not only the world but every earthly pleasure and profit that it contains.

Of course there were sturdy rogues and criminal beggars, I would admit, but equally certainly, there were men of the highest and noblest type, worthy to rank not only with the best of the friars of the Golden Age of Religion in Europe, but with such saints and apostles of humility and selflessness as Francis of Assisi, Ignatius Loyola, and Paul of Tarsus.

But he would have none of it. They were all tarred with the same brush, and the only differences among them were their varying degrees of worthlessness.

One can understand the antipathy of that sort of man toward the ash-smeared *faquir*, of course; the contempt and instinctive hatred of the man whose gods are personal cleanliness, exercise, sport, games, activity, and what he considers usefulness; the dislike of such a man for him who represents the negation and antithesis of all these ideals.

To Brackleigh and his type, contemplation is nothing but

vacant-minded laziness; the occupation, or lack of occupation, of a bone-idle useless waster; and the suggestion that Being is more important than Doing is just plain nonsense and an excuse for the avoidance of any and every sort of useful doing.

They were work shy. That was what was the matter with them, said Brackleigh in his wisdom. Lazy, idle, and good-for-nothing. What was the good of them? What sort of a place would the world be if everyone thought as they pretend to think, and did as they actually do. And of course it was useless to point out to him that one might say the same of soldiers, and ask him what sort of world it would be if every man was a soldier and did nothing in peace-time but practise the arts of destruction—and in war-time apply them.

The reply would merely be a snort of disgust and a remark to the effect that soldiers are necessary, and soldiering an honourable profession. You couldn't say that "fakirs" are necessary—or any good at all. And he had yet to learn that squatting under a tree and doing damn-all is an honourable profession.

Well, that's the sort of chap Brackleigh was, and in acting as he did with regard to Tulsiram Jaganath he ran true to form.

And another pet aversion Brackleigh had. Snakes. An utterly unconquerable repulsion, loathing, hatred, and fear. He'd be as cool and plucky as anybody else in dealing with a snake, of course, but he abhorred the very thought of them. Quite an obsession; and he'd kill a harmless snake quite as readily as he would a deadly poisonous one.

And Brackleigh was under the delusion, so commonly held, that snakes like biting people, the silly belief that they just do it because "it is their nature *to*."

Many well-educated men and women simply connect the thought of snakes with that of biting, as they associate wasps with stinging.

Most people do, of course, but quite erroneously. A snake doesn't *want* to bite you, nor as a matter of fact, does a wasp want to sting you. If one settled on you and you kept perfectly still, it wouldn't sting you. And a snake only bites in self-defence, or what he thinks is self-defence, when he is cornered or frightened. Snakes are quite as much afraid of men as men are of snakes.

Much more so, I should say. If a snake sees or hears a man approaching, his one idea is to get away as fast as he can. That thousands of people are killed by snakes, every year, in India, I know; but, in about ninety per cent, of the cases, what happens is that the man treads on the sleeping snake, and it instantly lashes out and strikes because it supposes it is being attacked by. an enemy, just as you or I would do.

What about the hamadryad, the king-cobra? Isn't it a fact that it actually goes out of its way to attack people and chases them like a wild boar or a buffalo or a rhinoceros does?

Ah! That's the one exception, the exception that proves the rule; but there again, I very much doubt whether the king-cobra is aggressive for the sake of aggression, and bites for the fun of biting.

I should say that whenever a person has been wantonly attacked or chased by one, it was because the snake had got a nest of young ones near, and was defending them, as it thought. I doubt whether the male hamadryad would ever do it; and I doubt if the female would, if there were no eggs or young near-by. They are jolly good mothers, and their aggressiveness is just on a par with that of the tigress with cubs. Why, some of the most timid of birds will put up a fight against an intruder threatening its young; and it is my own personal opinion that the hamadryad has got its name for aggressive ferocity, simply because it is a more courageous mother than any other snake.

Anyway, whether I am right or wrong, hamadryads apart, snakes don't want to bite, and only do so in self-defence.

And that was another point on which Brackleigh and I differed. In point of fact, he held the opposite view so strongly that we only differed on the subject once. I told him he was quite welcome to his opinion that nothing gives a snake greater pleasure than to bite you, and that it spends its life thinking out ways and means of doing so. Quite useless for me to point out to him that one often goes months, indeed years, in India, without seeing a snake—simply because they keep out of the way: and that when the native carries a lamp in his hand at night, he is safe from snakes, because they see him coming and promptly clear off.

No, to him snakes were things to be killed on sight, and the more the better. . . .

Well, Tulsiram Jaganath, being so diametrically different from Brackleigh in almost every conceivable way, differed from him in this too. He thought precisely the opposite—that snakes are extremely interesting creatures; in no wise dangerous unless rendered so; no more malicious and murderous than human beings; and that when they were so, it was for the similar human reasons—fear and self-preservation.

In point of fact, and with incontrovertible reason, Tulsiram, was wont to point out that no snake ever yet killed for reasons of religious bigotry, false patriotism, robbery, greed, envy or any of the other base motives for which human beings commit murder.

And he was very practically justified of his belief in the genuine pacificism of the unmolested unfrightened snake, for a very fine pair actually shared his bed and board, in a manner of speaking.

A quaint manner of speaking?

Yes. Reasonable though, for Tulsiram Jaganath sat beneath a tree, and the snakes live under it, down in among the roots below the ground; and not only did they raise no more objection to Tulsiram Jaganath's presence beneath the tree than he did to theirs, but, on the contrary, one or other, of them usually came out at sunset when Tulsiram Jaganath had his frugal daily meal, and shared it with him.

Yes—to the extent of a saucer of milk. I don't say that every evening of his life, with the utmost regularity, he put out the snakes' saucer of milk as the housewife does the cat's; but I do say that whenever a native from one of the nearby villages brought him a *chattie* of milk and poured it into Tulsiram's *lotah*, he'd be asked to pour some into the little clay saucer for the snakes—and the villagers brought him milk, fruit, rice and *chupatties* whenever they came to visit him and beg his advice, help or blessing. So the snakes got their milk on most evenings of the week.

And this, of course, would be quite in order from the villager's point of view. They would completely understand that the Holy Man would feed his "Brahmins"—in this case, his sacred snakes. Nor would it enter any villager's head that there would be the slightest danger to the Holy Man. Of course, the snakes, the servants of Kali, would never harm him, the servant and beloved of Kali and all the other gods.

You are wondering how I know? Why, I used to spend hours in talking with Tulsiram Jaganath; and not only as one educated man to another, but, on many subjects, as an ignorant man to a learned one. And more than once, approaching his retreat, I have seen a shadow glide away, cross the patch of beaten earth on which he sat, and disappear among the tree-roots.

The first time this happened, I said, as I came within speaking distance,

"I say, *Guru-ji*, did you see that? Wasn't it a snake? It has gone down one of those holes there among the tree-roots."

And smiling, he pointed to the earthenware bowl.

"Yes. You've disturbed his evening meal."

And then he told me how, almost invariably, generally one at a time, they came out at sunset and drank the milk that he had set aside for them.

"And there is no danger?" I asked.

"To whom? . . . Danger doesn't enter here," he smiled. "The snakes are in no danger from me, and I am in none from them. They know I won't hurt them, and I know equally surely that they will not hurt me."

"But at first, the very first time that you saw them, or they saw you?"

"Well, I have been here longer than they have; so I am not an intruder on their domain. The first time I saw one of them I just kept perfectly still, and he passed close by me, and disappeared among the tree-roots. They soon got into the habit of going in and out, and not taking any more notice of me than they did of the rocks, the bushes, the stocks and stones. . . . We got accustomed to each other. . . . When I felt that they realized that I was not an enemy, I got into the habit of saying good-evening politely, and of going on with what I was doing. If I was contemplating, I remained motionless. If I was preparing my meal or eating, I continued to do so.

"One evening, I put a saucer of warm fresh milk on their doorstep and it was accepted in the spirit in which it was given, that of peace and amity, kindliness and friendship. And after a while, I began moving the saucer farther and farther, from their doorstep until it was on my own, so to speak. And they raised no objection. They came and drank as readily and freely within a yard of me as they did within a yard of the entrance to their own home. . . ."

Well, after that, I used to try to catch them at it, and on several occasions I managed to get a glimpse of one of the snakes—quite big chaps they were—sitting there within a yard of Tulsiram.

But it always cleared off when I came. Invariably.

I asked Tulsiram how long it would take to persuade the snake that I too was harmless; well-disposed; friendly, in fact; if not actually affectionate.

Tulsiram said that was a very difficult question to answer. Certainly I would have to go and live there with him; probably for quite a long time; and possibly the experiment would never succeed at all.

Why? Because in spite of my conscious mind adopting an attitude of friendliness, my unconscious mind would be filled with an instinctive spirit of antagonism, he said. Though I should outwardly and intentionally say, "I should like to be friendly, and tame you," nevertheless I should inwardly and unintentionally say, "I loathe you: I fear you; and I should like to kill you." And well-read on that subject as on every other, Tulsiram quoted from the Bible. "What said the Lord God of Israel that the seed of Eve should do to the seed of the Serpent? *'It shall bruise thy head and thou shalt bruise his heel.'*"

"Isn't it born and bred in the mind and spirit of the Christian," he continued, "the result of centuries of teaching, that the fall of man was due to the Serpent? Subconsciously, at any rate, the Christian regards the serpent as the symbol and embodiment of Evil; Satan incarnate; the form chosen by the Devil himself for his physical manifestation on earth—from the time of his first appearance in the Garden of Eden. Man must bruise the Serpent's head, and it will bruise man's heel in return.

"It may seem far-fetched to the Western mind, but I believe that that subconscious antipathy not only persists and exists in the human mind, but that this fact is actually realized by the snake.

"And supposing I am wrong, and doubtless I am wrong even more often than I suppose, there still remains another and simpler reason for the antipathy. I believe that a snake knows the difference between Indians and Europeans. I know that a mongoose does. When I was at Oxford, my tutor had a pet mongoose. He was a rather well-known member of the University—the mongoose, I mean. And while it was a little shy with my tutor's English pupils and other visitors to his study, it behaved in an entirely different manner when an Indian student came into the room. It used to welcome me with quite extravagant manifestations of joy, and so it did the one or two other Indians who used to go there. It was really most marked, and the phenomenon interested my tutor greatly. There was no shadow of doubt that the mongoose knew an Indian from an Englishman the moment he entered the room where it was, nor that it was most delighted to see him. A fellow exile, I suppose, and yet it is as likely as not that the mongoose had been born in captivity.

"Anyway, whether the little chap was of British birth or only a British subject, he invariably exhibited the most marked preference for Indians. I used to wish I could take him home with me to my rooms. He would have been quite a companion. Much more so to me than he was to my tutor, I'm sure, though he and the mongoose got on very well together. I could have made a real friend of him.

"Yes, what I have done with this pair of snakes might have been far more difficult, if not impossible, if I had been a European; and I think my snakes would regard you as something far more potentially dangerous than I.

"Instinct or experience? I don't know. But I am quite sure that the European, with his thick boots and leggings, his riding-whip, his gun, is recognized by the snake as a terrible danger, probably the greatest danger of all.

"No, I'm afraid it would take my snakes a very long time to accept you, even on my introduction and guarantee. . . ."

Anyway, I personally never had the interesting experience of actually sitting and watching Tulsiram's snakes behave like domestic animals, accepting the presence of man as natural and desirable—eating out of his hand almost.

It would have been very interesting, though. Very, very interesting.

Well, there it was; and the *yogi* Tulsiram Jaganath was known to be a friend and familiar of poisonous snakes, the villagers' greatest danger. And that alone, you know, is enough to start the miracle yarns and supernatural-power stories. But there was nothing more miraculous or supernatural about it than taming by kindness; and Tulsiram and his snakes were only one degree more remarkable than Auntie Tabitha and her robins, who come and eat out of her hand on a cold winter morning.

Nor was what followed a miracle, nor anything more than coincidence, if it weren't something even simpler—just natural consequence—though it is possible there was a slight element of clairvoyance in it, for one has to admit that Tulsiram Jaganath did forewarn Brackleigh; did, in a sense, prophesy what would happen.

But I could prophesy that I shall play bridge with Wainwright, Macintosh and Winterton to-night, and no doubt I shall . . .

Now, unfortunately, I told Brackleigh about Tulsiram and his snakes, not only as something interesting, but as a sort of little testimonial to the man's character and power—perfectly normal power—to do by kindness what few people would have the patience and courage, not to mention the knowledge, wisdom and understanding, to do. But it only seemed to confirm Brackleigh in his low opinion of "fakirs" as he called all holy men, *swamis*, *sanyasis*, *bhairagis*, *saddhus* and *faquirs*.

"Sort of thing he would do," he grunted, "muck about with snakes. If he is as learned and clever a bird as you think, it's a pity he hasn't got something better to do. I could show the Holy Blighter something better to do—with a snake, anyway. . . . I will, too."

And so it came to pass. The gods of Ind were listening.

But one mustn't talk like that, of course, to a circle of fellows like you, in a Christian British Club. Let us say it was Written on his Forehead—if that is any better. Anyhow, within a day or two of our conversation, Brackleigh came riding home past what he called Tulsiram Jaganath's "pitch" in the jungle; whether intentionally or not, I don't know. Neither I nor you know whether the gods had willed it so, whether it was written on his forehead, whether it was just blind chance, or whether, the slave of his temperament as we all are, Brackleigh did what he intended to do.

Anyhow, as Fate would have it—curious how one uses that phrase, whatever one's views on the subject of free will—Brackleigh, riding along the wide grassy jungle path, came suddenly on Tulsiram, sitting in the usual attitude and on the usual spot, talking to a big snake that was lying coiled a few feet from him, its head raised, its eyes watching the man intently.

Here was Brackleigh's chance. To him a snake was a snake; and the only harmless snake was a dead one. It was his simple duty as a sensible man to kill the brute, and doubtless his simple pleasure to show the lazy brute of a Holy Man the proper way to treat a snake. . . . Tame! . . . He'd *tame* it, once and for all. . . .

Setting spurs to his horse, Brackleigh dashed forward, and, as the snake uncoiled and glided toward its hole, he leant over and struck at its head with his heavy hunting-crop. Had he not been riding his favourite polo-pony; had he been carrying a light switch instead of his malacca horn-handled hunting-crop; had he not been the crack polo-player that he was, this might have been a very different story. But Fate had willed it . . . there I go again—*Fate*.

As it happened, the blow took the snake across the neck, just behind the head, and it lay writhing and coiling. Probably dead already. Doubtless he had really killed it, and its twitchings and squirmings were only reflex action, but it wasn't dead enough for Brackleigh.

Jumping from his pony, he put one foot on the still-moving reptile and stamped on its head with the heel of the other.

"Well, Mister Fakir," he said, when the snake's head was pulped to his satisfaction, "aren't you going to thank me for saving your life?"

"It wasn't in any danger, thank you, Captain Brackleigh," replied Tulsiram Jaganath, "and I quite sincerely hope yours is not."

"What do you mean? Snake's dead enough, isn't he?" laughed Brackleigh.

"Yes, quite dead. But his wife isn't," smiled Tulsiram.

"Oh, married, was he? Well, his wife's a widow now, all

right. May see her, too, if I'm lucky."

"If you do, I hope you *will* be lucky, Captain Brackleigh."

"What? How?"

"I hope you'll see her first. See her before she sees you, I mean."

Without reply, Brackleigh turned and strode off to catch and mount the temperamental and nervous pony that he was breaking in for polo. But here again, we come up against the gods of Ind, or the hand of Fate, or that blind chance that rules our lives, or whatever else you like to call it. Instead of standing, as his charger or hunter would have done, the half-trained pony had trotted away and was cropping the grass a hundred yards from the scene of the execution; and, as Brackleigh approached, it raised its head, shook it in plain negation, and trotted off again.

This annoyed Brackleigh intensely, partly because he had to walk in his riding-boots, and partly because, as an experienced and skilful horse-master, his soul was outraged by such conduct on the part of a beast that he had taken into his stables and was proposing to turn from a hundred-rupee tat into a thousand-rupee polo pony. Serve the brute right if he sold it back into the bazaar. If it didn't soon mind its manners, it would find itself pulling a native *tonga*, instead of gracing famous polo-grounds.

But neither threats nor appeals to its better nature affected the ungrateful beast, and in the end Brackleigh had to follow it home on foot.

After dinner that evening, he gave me his version, of what had happened; and, the following morning, Tulsiram Jaganath gave me his—and the accounts agreed as to facts. But you can imagine—or can you?—the difference between the point of view of the two men with regard to these same facts. What to Brackleigh had been a righteous deed, the act of a public benefactor, had, to Tulsiram Jaganath, been a wanton and brutal murder.

Brackleigh had rid the world of a dangerous and damnable reptile. Tulsiram Jaganath had seen a harmless and innocent animal slaughtered. He had, as he put it, seen his friend killed before his eyes, struck dead before he had had time even to try to save it.

"Innocent? Harmless?" I expostulated.

"Yes, perfectly innocent of any evil desire or intention, and perfectly harmless until harmed. The snake was armed with poison-fangs but that didn't make it harmful any more than your being armed with a revolver makes you harmful, Deputy Commissioner Sahib," he said. "If you were attacked by a murderous thug, you'd use your revolver; but the fact that you possess one doesn't make you a harmful and dangerous and murderous man.

"Still, there it is. My friend is dead and his bereaved companion is not only inconsolable but angry—very angry and vengeful indeed. . . . How inevitably like begets like," he mused. "Naturally, of course. Men beget men, birds beget birds, violence begets violence—and vengeance begets vengeance."

"You mean that the other snake would avenge its companion's death, if it had the opportunity?" I asked.

"Undoubtedly. Snakes are like—I won't say like Christians, Deputy Commissioner Sahib, in that respect. . . .

"I gave a word of advice and warning to Captain Brackleigh," he added. "You might repeat it as from yourself."

"A word of warning? . . . About the other snake?" I said.

"Yes. Captain Brackleigh said he might see the other one, if he was lucky; and I told him I hoped that, in that event, he would be lucky; lucky enough to see it first," replied Tulsiram.

"Well, if he rode this way again and did see the other one, he wouldn't be in much danger, would he?"

"No, he'd be safe enough. . . . But it might not be here that he saw it. And he might not see it . . . in time."

At dinner that evening I mentioned that I had been talking to Tulsiram Jaganath and told Brackleigh exactly what had been said.

He laughed and observed that since that was how the fellow felt about it, he'd make a point of putting an end to any danger that he himself might be in, by putting an end to the other snake as well.

And in his slightly cynical, somewhat sceptical, and rather jeering manner, he observed that presumably that would put an end to this terrible danger, inasmuch as not even a humbugging wind-bag like Tulsiram Jaganath would pretend that snakes had any vendetta gangs, murder clubs, secret societies, or any kind of a snakes' *mafia*, the Black Hand among the black snakes.

I said that I hadn't imagined that Tulsiram Jaganath, or anybody else, supposed anything of the kind; and repeated what Tulsiram had told me, that in the case of certain snakes— hamadryads undoubtedly, cobras probably, and several other kinds possibly—it was an established fact that the survivor would, if it could, kill the slayer of its mate, and that the same thing applied to the mother snake and her young.

Brackleigh laughed the idea to scorn.

"My dear chap," said he, "you talk as though a snake had got the intelligence and mentality of an elephant. The Serpent Never Forgets, what? Nonsense. I dare say it is just possible that among the very best snakes, one would come to the rescue of the other if it saw it attacked. Just possible, though I doubt it. Much more likely to flee for its life. . . . Do you honestly think that if both the faker's snakes had been lying there, the male would have come for me when I swiped the female, or *vice versa*?"

"I don't know what snake it was, but I do believe there are snakes that would do just that," I replied, "precisely as a tiger or tigress would come for you, if you were attacking its mate. As to whether the survivor of a pair of snakes would attempt to track down and kill the slayer of its mate or its young, I don't know; but, inasmuch as Tulsiram Jaganath assures me that this does happen, I am strongly inclined to accept his statement."

"Why?"

"Because he knows far more about the animals among whom he lives than any European naturalist can know; and because he speaks the truth."

Again Brackleigh laughed.

"Do you mean to say you'd believe anything that fakir told you?"

"I mean to say that when that learned *yogi* makes a statement, I know that he believes it. Yes, if he told me *any*thing was so, I should know that he believed it to be so."

"And they've made you a Ruler and Judge over us, eh?" jeered Brackleigh. "And you are supposed to be able to weigh evidence, sift the grain from the chaff, what? I expect he's pulling your leg half the time, if the truth were known."

"Very likely, very likely, Brackleigh," said I. "But for what my opinion is worth, I believe that Tulsiram's warning was genuine, disinterested, and by no means negligible. I honestly believe that that snake's companion would go for you and do its damnedest to kill you, if it knew that it was you who killed the other."

"Pursue me with the utmost rigour of the law, eh?" smiled Brackleigh. "The sacred and immutable law of the snakes as expounded by Tulsiram Jaganath. You are a knowing old bird, Mowbray. If ever a man deals with hard facts and stark realities, it is a senior Indian Civilian, surely. Yet here you are, dealing in superstitious tripe about the Serpent's Vengeance and the Gypsy's Warning and all that."

And as he poured himself a glass of port, he sang with soulful expression and tuneful sweetness,

> *'Trust him not, that dark-eyed stranger*
> *Gently pleading at thy feet.'*

but spoilt the performance by a particularly vicious growl of "Rats!" in conclusion.

§2

That night I was suddenly awakened from a deep sleep by a sound that, for the moment, affected my nerves and my heart, though I was in excellent health and not in the least given to nerve storms or heart palpitations.

It was a cry of agony, fear and horror. Shocking . . . heartrending . . . indescribably terrifying.

As I have said, it affected me mentally and physically, and as I pulled myself together and jumped out of bed, I realized that I had broken into a cold sweat, in spite of the fact that it was a hot night.

Sub-consciously or half-consciously, I knew, not only that something had happened to Brackleigh, but I knew what it was.

Snatching up the electric flash-lamp that I always kept beside my bed, I switched it on, and dashed out into the verandah and into Brackleigh's bedroom which was next but one to mine, his sitting-room being between the two.

"*Look out!*" he cried, as I entered the room, flashed my torch on the bed, and saw a sight that shocked me anew, and gave me understanding of those expressions we use so glibly about our blood running cold and our hair standing on end.

For on the bed was Brackleigh, half-lying, half-reclining, his hands gripping the neck of a big snake that lashed and writhed, coiling and uncoiling about his arms and head.

For a second I was completely immobilized, frozen stiff with fear as the thought flashed through my mind that I could neither shoot with Brackleigh's revolver nor strike with his sword that hung upon the wall, without hitting him. And the revolver wouldn't be loaded and the sword would be blunt.

In the infinitesimal fraction of a second that it took to realize what was happening, and that nothing could be done with sword and revolver, I thought of the Laocoon statue, as the snake, thick as a woman's arm and apparently eight to ten feet in length, coiled and writhed and lashed.

Before I could move, Brackleigh gave the measure of his courage and displayed the mettle of the pastures in which he had been bred.

"Look out!" he panted again. "Mind yourself . . . I'm done . . . Bitten in the face . . . I'll hold it as long as I can. Clear out. . . .

And as he spoke, I was shamed. Laying down the torch on the bedside table where its light fell on Brackleigh and the snake, I joined in the struggle. I seized the snake too, my hands touching Brackleigh's.

"I've got it," I cried. "Leave go. I'll carry it out and chuck it down the well."

"You couldn't," gasped Brackleigh.

"I could chuck it over the verandah. You leave go," I cried.

But I knew I couldn't throw that lashing whirling ferocity of strength, that dynamo incarnate, which coiled itself now about my arms, now about Brackleigh's, now about my neck with suffocating constriction, now joining our heads with a living rope, coiling and—thank God—uncoiling, as it lashed and struggled.

"Leave go, you fool!" groaned Brackleigh. "No need for both of us to be bitten. Leave go. I'm weakening."

With all my strength I gripped the cold scaly neck and body that, grip and crush as I might, I could scarcely hold, scarcely prevent from writhing through my hands.

"Razor! . . . table," panted Brackleigh suddenly.

Of course, if I let go and dashed to the table, and he could hold for another few seconds, I should have a chance to kill the reptile with the razor, and then do what could be done for my dying friend. And if his strength failed and the snake escaped his grasp, I must take my chance of being bitten too. Quite possibly, it would streak like lightning for the open door.

It was the best thing to do. The only thing, if Brackleigh were to be given a chance.

But could not Brackleigh get the razor while I held the snake's neck?

"Leave go," I said. "I'll pull it off you. You get the razor. I can hold it."

"Get it yourself—*quick*!" was the reply. I'm done, anyhow. I can hold it while you get the razor . . ."

Well, the swifter the better. Yes—I must snatch the razor and kill the snake. . . .

As I released my grip, the snake lashed the more violently, whirled and flung its body, winding like a coiling spring, about Brackleigh's arms and head.

Seizing the torch I turned it toward the dressing-table where lay Brackleigh's simple toilet outfit; brushes, a comb, a pair of razors and a strop.

Seizing one of the ivory-handled razors, I replaced the light in position.

"Quick," whispered Brackleigh, as the snake appeared to redouble its efforts and to bury its imprisoned head in the coils and convolutions of its writhing body.

Grabbing with my left hand and bearing down with my left fore-arm and elbow upon the snake and on Brackleigh's arm and chest, I slashed, and with unutterable thankfulness and savage joy, felt the steel bite and grit and grind as I drew it across the squirming body, near the head.

To and fro I sawed. Brackleigh drew a sudden breath as I cut him. There was a mess of blood, reptile and human, and the wild lashing, coiling and writhing slackened, grew quieter and ceased. I had cut the snake in halves near its head and between Brackleigh's hands.

Sick, sweating and trembling, I tore its body from about his arms and neck and flung it to the ground.

"Where?" I gasped.

"Face," he whispered, and put his hand up to where two blue-black punctures showed at the angle of his jaw. "Woke up suddenly . . . something on, the bed. As I went to sit up, it struck and I grabbed it with my hands. . . . Let a yell, didn't I?" He grinned ruefully.

"Permanganate?" I asked. Surely, like most people in India, he kept some handy.

"Left-hand drawer in washhand-stand table in the bathroom. Cardboard box."

"Shan't be a second."

Snatching up the electric lamp I rushed into the bathroom, found the box of permanganate crystals, returned, and replaced the lamp where the light shone directly on Brackleigh's face.

"I'm going to cut," said I, getting the other razor.

"Go to it," whispered Brackleigh.

There was no time to think of such refinements as sterilization, but presumably the permanganate would see to that.

Turning his head to one side and pressing firmly, I made four parallel slashes close together across the bite, arid again four more at right angles to these. I then shook a little pile of permanganate crystals onto the wound and ground them in hard with the heel of my palm. But while I did so, two terrible truths assailed my mind. In the first place, that a tourniquet is essential between the bite and the heart—and you cannot apply a tourniquet about a man's neck. In the second place, that it was in any case too late.

Had he been bitten in the hand or foot there would, perhaps, have been a chance, by reason of the distance of the wound from the heart. As it was, the bite was too close to the heart for there to be any hope. I doubted whether the most skilled physician, standing ready and getting to work within a second of the impact of the poisoned fangs, could have done any good, in view of the fact that it was impossible to apply a tourniquet.

Might he have sucked out the poison? Possibly. Just possibly. I don't know. I had thought of that and—well, I don't wish to sound heroic, for I only did what any other man would have done—I tried that before I cut. Sucked with all my strength, sucked and spat, sucked and spat, until I thought that the sooner I cut the better.

Well, I don't want to dwell on horrors, both for your sake and my own, so I will merely say it was no good; that in spite of all I could do, Brackleigh collapsed and died.

I shouted for the servants, of course, directly I had done all I could and had a moment to spare, and got hot-water bottles and brandy, and sent the syce galloping for the doctor—a medical missionary who lived miles away.

He arrived at dawn and Brackleigh was buried that evening.

§3

It was with mixed feelings that I rode out next day to interview Tulsiram Jaganath. At one moment I seethed with anger, my reason overwhelmed by a raging flood of wrath. At another, I was able to view the matter calmly and coolly, in the light of the simple knowledge that Brackleigh had, like thousands of other people, been bitten by a poisonous snake and died of the bite.

Why should I behave precisely as the ignorant and stupid villagers would undoubtedly do, and implicate Tulsiram Jaganath? Why should I, consciously or subconsciously, connect him with Brackleigh's death, at all? And if I did, why should it be in an accusatory manner, as though he were in some way guilty of Brackleigh's death? Why should I feel an inclination to sit in judgment on Tulsiram Jaganath? Why blame him in any way?

On the contrary, so far as he had any connection with the affair at all, hadn't he clearly and definitely warned Brackleigh? Summed up judicially and impartially, did it not amount to this, that Brackleigh had killed a poisonous snake, had indeed gone out of his way to attack and kill a poisonous snake—and had himself been killed by its mate?

Of course it did, unless indeed, there were no grounds for the assumption that the snake that had killed him was the mate of the shake that he had killed. What proof was there that there was any connection between the two? In spite of what one had heard about snakes avenging their mates and their young, was it not a hasty and unwarrantable conclusion that there was any connection between the snake that Brackleigh had killed, at a spot between three and four miles from his house, and the one that made its way on to his bed and struck him when he disturbed it?

That was the rational attitude to take, surely.

It is a well-known phenomenon that not only will a snake, in certain conditions, bask and sun itself, but will coil up to sleep upon any warm surface. Many a wretched villager, sleeping on the ground, has wakened to find a snake lying either against him or coiled-up on his body.

The one certainly fatal thing to do in such a case is to move, frightening the snake, and causing it to strike in self-defence. Undoubtedly that was the explanation of poor Brackleigh's death.

The snake had come into the house as snakes do, possibly in search of food, shelter or warmth. Food? Yes, snakes follow frogs into bathrooms and rats into store-rooms, dining-rooms, and up among the rafters, in the dark mysterious space between the ceiling-cloth and the roof. This snake had come into the house, had happened to enter Brackleigh's room—it might just as well have entered mine—and, perhaps attracted by the radiated warmth of Brackleigh's body, or again by chance, had climbed up on to the bed.

It may have coiled up and settled down, long before Brackleigh woke. It may have been right on his chest and its weight may have awakened him. On the; other hand, some instinct, or more likely the snake's own movement, may have awakened him immediately. He moved, sat up and the snake struck—a type of tragedy as old as India.

But again anger would blaze up in me as I thought of that fine brave man cut off in his prime by that loathsome reptile. And foolishly and irrationally, I would connect Tulsiram Jaganath with the terrible affair, as though he could have had anything to do with it. And then I would remonstrate with myself for being idiotically childish. Surely my mind was not unhinged by the awful experience? Surely my intelligence had not sunk so low that I was entertaining such ridiculous superstitions as those connected with the phenomenon known as 'sendings'? No, firmly, certainly, decisively, I did not believe in 'sendings'; did not, for one moment, believe that any practitioner of black magic or occult science could send a *poltergeist,* an evil spirit, much more a real poisonous snake, to destroy his enemy. Besides, if I did wallow in such a swamp of crass credulity as to think such things possible, I knew perfectly well that Tulsiram Jaganath was not a practitioner of black magic, if there were such a thing as black magic. If he were a student or indeed a master of what is known as the 'occult,' it was only occult to the person whose learning was purely of the ordinary and accepted kind.

And another, thing that I knew as well as I knew my own name, was that Tulsiram Jaganath was a guiltless man, incapable of wrong-doing. He was as incapable of committing the sin of murder as he was of the power of sending a snake to do his errands. Both utterly absurd and ridiculous. . . . And there he sat beneath his tree, calm, serene and inscrutable as ever.

As a rule, Tulsiram waited to be addressed. On this occasion, he spoke first.

"I am truly sorry, Mowbray Sahib," he said as I approached. "I am deeply grieved, and would have done anything in my power to have prevented it."

"You know what has happened?" I asked.

"Yes. And I had a terrible premonition that it would happen. I warned him and I could do no more."

I stared at him in silence, my anger, rage, resentment, ebbing beneath the steady gaze of his calm clear eyes.

How should I frame the question that I wished to ask, the question as to the snake that had killed Brackleigh, the snake that I myself had killed? How I hoped that the fatal snake had *not* been the mate of the one that Brackleigh had killed, here, within a yard of where I sat. . . . I was really surprised at the strength and earnestness with which I hoped that Tulsiram would be able to assure me that this was the case; that one of the pair still survived and was living among the roots of the tree; that he had seen it there last night, perhaps again this very morning.

I was also ashamed of myself, once more, that I should be so anxious to be reassured on the point, anxious to learn that it was a case of what is known, as accidental death—as if any death is accidental—and that some other snake, some different kind of snake, had casually entered the bungalow and had happened to find its way to Brackleigh's room.

I suppose it was subconscious, for in my conscious mind, I was perfectly certain, of course, that Tulsiram could have had no lot nor part in the affair.

But he answered my question before I asked it.

"Apart from the fact that poor Brackleigh Sahib brought about his own death by killing the snake here," he continued, "his pony was chiefly responsible for what happened. . . . It was the instrument."

"*What?* How?"

"It trotted off; ran away; and Brackleigh Sahib had to walk home. And having in his anger stamped upon the snake's head, he laid a trail straight from here to his bungalow and to his bedside, where doubtless he sat down to pull off his boots Yes, it was my other snake that killed him—and that you yourself killed . . . Violence begets violence and vengeance begets vengeance."

No—there was no miracle, nothing supernatural, nothing occult, about the killing of poor Brackleigh, and it was Nature, not *yoga*, that was responsible.

WHITE ANTS

"White Ants" is the second longest story of all of Wren's short stories: only "E Tenebris" (in volume three of The Collected Short Stories*) is longer. "White Ants" (termites) is, ostensibly, the story of a small Indian village where the head of an unknown (at least to the village) person appears, and where the "bunnia" frames an enemy for murder. "White Ants" is also Wren's most strongly worded short story on the merits of the British in India, and on the demerits of the local Indian leaders. Wren was always a strong imperialist and it is in this story that this inclination really shows. "White Ants" first appeared as the fourth story in Part I, "Queer", of* Odd—But Even So *(1941). The story was also reprinted as a sixteen page individual "chapbook" type of volume in the "Polybook" series published by Vallancey Press in January 1945.*

Mr. Mohandas Lala Misra, B.A., LL.B., pleader[17] and politician, looked round upon the sea of faces upturned toward him, as he stood on the platform erected in the Janwar-bagh, the Public Gardens in which the public meetings of Bharatavad were held.

The vast majority of the faces were those of youths, College students and High School boys who, at any rate until they had completed their education, might perhaps have found better occupation for their leisure time than in listening to Mr. Misra and his fellow-agitators whose spirited addresses had led not a few of such young men to a shameful death upon the gallows for cold-blooded and cowardly murder.

From the point of view of Mr. Misra, it was a good game, paying and safe, for it brought him to the notice of the disinterested patriots who will soon be the rulers of India; and, in the way in which he played it, he ran no risk of punishment from the guardians of the *Pax Britannica* which still, after a fashion, holds good, and guarantees a measure of order and quiet between periods of communal warfare.

---

[17] *Native barrister.*

He was a small man and a fat; the upper half of his face expressive of great intelligence, force and mental power, the lower half indicative of grossness, greed and weakness.

To a physiognomist, there was interest and amazing contradiction between the domed forehead, intellectual brow, the fine clear piercing eyes, the prominent shapely and dominant nose above the facial equator, and the loose blubber lips, receding triplicated chin, and flabby jowls below it.

To the wrongly-educated, overworked and over-examined youths, hapless scholastic heirs of Macaulay's colossal and devastating error, this fluent orator, speaking the clever language of double meaning and of double edge, of political parable and cunning metaphor, the sound of his silver tongue was not only *vox populi Indica* but *vox Dei Indica* as well.

Mr. Mohandas Lala Misra looked around upon that sea of pathetic hero-worshipping faces—their pathos, alas, infinite as his heroism was infinitesimal—and smiled. With a meaning leer which was nod and wink combined to such an audience, he said:

"A previous speaker spoke of White Goats, and of the boundless joy of Kali when in her temple a white goat is sacrificed, and the merit immeasurable of him who offers such a sacrifice at her shrine . . . White Goats. . . . And yet the goat is a harmless and a useful animal, supplying good milk which is both food and drink. Nevertheless, at one moment I am inclined to accept the simile, for terrible destruction can be wrought in the green countryside by a herd of goats. At another moment, it strikes me as inappropriate, for it is these same White Goats who are the milkers. Is not Mother India milked dry by their ruthless, their alien, their foul and filthy, hands? . . .

"Another speaker spoke of the White Monkeys. At one moment, I incline to accept the term, for are they not as mischievous and destructive as monkeys, as devoid of mind and brain and soul as monkeys? Are not they sub-human as monkeys, as far below us, mentally and spiritually, as the long-tailed *bander-lōg* themselves? Yet, at another moment, I remember that in this dear land of Ind, this country of our holy Mother India, the monkey is a sacred animal. What sort of compliment is it to Hanuman, the monkey-god, that we should call these foreign creatures 'monkeys'? If the monkeys that live their harmless and innocent lives in the jungle do a little mischief to the *ryots'* crops; if those that live about the courtyards of the holy temples of sacred Kashi[18] itself, occasionally steal a handful of rice, a plantain or a mango from a pilgrim's dinner—what of it? They are children of the Gods. Their presence is not pollution. Their feet do not befoul our holy soil. They do not set their heels upon broken heads and bruised hearts of a trembling outraged and expropriated people. They are our brothers . . ."

("You are right there, old son!" smiled to himself a swarthy gaunt-faced Englishman who, in the dress of an Indian *maistri*, sat vacant-eyed and open-mouthed, listening with the utmost interest to this average specimen of the intensive extra-scholastic education of the large student population of the somewhat excitable city of Bharatavad.)

"Now it is my aim and object," continued Mr. Misra, "to be constructive as well as destructive. . . . Oh yes, let construction follow destruction—in due course."

And here again came the leering smile that was wink and nod as well.

"In due course, I say; for not only must destruction come first, but it must be very, very thorough. We must destroy, uproot, cast out, slay and kill and burn and wipe from the very face of the earth, this beloved and sacred earth of ours, before we begin to construct."

And the orator paused, and in the taut tense silence that followed his words he ran his practised eye over those hundreds of rapt faces.

"But what was I saying? Construction after destruction? Yes, and the construction, or selection of a name, to replace those that I rejected. And I put forward a constructive idea. If I like not the names White Goats and White Monkeys, what of this other?

"*White Ants!* . . .

"For that is what they are. Let us think of them as that. White Ants. Do we not know, to our cost, the lakhs and crores' worth of rupees of damage done annually in India by those destructive insects that devour and destroy property—clothing,

---

[18] *Benares.*

food, books, documents, and the very houses in which we dwell? Their very name spells injury, damage, ruin. And how cunningly they work! In secret, in darkness, beneath a protective covering, insidiously they work their evil will. Who sees the work of the white ant? No one. Who sees the result of their work? Everyone. In the trail of ruin and destruction that they leave behind them we see the result.

"Your white ants, the insects, build between themselves and the light of day a screen, a covering under which they do their dreadful work. Who has, not seen the signs of their dreadful presence in great patches and long tracts of brown earth-like crust upon wooden box and trunk and chest, wooden beam and pillar, on wall and rafter?

"And your White Ants, two-legged, apparently human, build their covering or facade of justice, of government of the people for the people behind which to work in secret. Hiding their real work of destruction, their labours of ruin and degradation, they conceal themselves beneath their protective crust of talk and show of education, sanitation, municipal and local self-government, their road and bridge building, hospital building, their making of railways and canals, their irrigation works.

"And underneath it all? Subtly they are slaying the Soul of a People, as secretly, but as surely and terribly, as the white ant insects destroy material things.

"So sacrifice your White Goats to Kali with pistol and with bomb; decimate your troops of White Monkeys with the shot-gun that drives them from the holy fields; but when the time comes, and that time is not far off, set your heel upon the White Ants and slay them in their thousands."

An oratorical pause. Another electrical silence, tight and tingling as that before the burst of a storm.

"And meanwhile . . . *meanwhile*, I say . . ." concluded Mr. Misra in a voice impressive and low, which carried nevertheless to the furthermost corner of the Janwar-bagh, "rest assured that there are those who are unceasingly, irresistibly at work tunnelling beneath the White Ant-heap itself; and they whose work will one day—and again I say that day is not far distant— bring it crashing down in irreparable ruin, in utter and final death and destruction upon its dreadful denizens."

As he concluded and sat down, a great cry rent the air, a shout that was heard far beyond the confines of the Janwar-bagh of Bharatavad.

§2

There is a village in Western India, of which the real name is as old as the hills, its origin lost in the mists of antiquity. Its name, painted on its railway station board, printed on the Indian Survey maps, and written in the files and annals of the Collector's *kutcherry* at the headquarters-station of the District, has remained unchanged in spelling or pronunciation for a thousand years and a thousand more. But to-day, it has a second name, an *alias*, and is known throughout the District, an area of hundreds of square miles, as The Virtuous Village. It is quite possible that no European, official or other, not even the District Superintendent of Police, the Forest Officer, the Executive Engineer in charge of roads and bridges, the Civil Surgeon in charge of public Hygiene and Sanitation, not even the Deputy Commissioner Sahib himself, has ever heard the name by which sweet Chinchgaum, loveliest village of the Plains, is now known. But every Indian in the District has not only heard it, but uses it, and knows how the village came to be re-named.

At first, its new name, which means The Virtuous Village, was uttered with a wry smile, a mocking intonation, or a knowing glance, and the stranger who first heard it might have been excused for supposing that the speaker was sarcastic, the term ironical. For, undeniably, Chinchgaum had, for a time, an unsavoury reputation, a fact which was rather the misfortune than the fault of the simple villagers, the name being due rather to the character and conduct of its headman than to the general way of life and level of thought of its inhabitants.

India produces annually its very adequate crop of crimes; and when the Indian errs and strays, he often errs very thoroughly and strays quite a long way. But nevertheless, speaking generally, there is no more industrious, frugal, and innocent a community anywhere, than that of the average Indian village. Slow to wrath, the peasant's rage when aroused is terrible and his crimes of violence apt to be very violent indeed; but they are usually, indeed mainly, committed under a burning sense of some injustice or in a spirit of vengeance for some real or fancied wrong. Apart from being too simple and innocent for most kinds of crime, he is far too busy; too tired, at the end of the long day's struggle, to wrest from an unfruitful soil and against the unfriendly forces of nature, the wherewithal to pay his debts to the village *sowcar* and to win, perchance, a meagre and miserable living in addition.

But there are black-sheep in every flock. It is said that the blackest of them go into the police—which is of course a cruel and infamous slander—and that the remainder are employed by the police as *agents provocateurs*, spies, stool-pigeons and professional witnesses.

And it seems that Chinchgaum, in the dark days just previous to its being known, as The Virtuous Village, was afflicted with an undue proportion of black-sheep, and that Chinchgaum was the more unfortunate in that one or two of the black-avised were men of substance and position, whose good conduct should have been an admirable pattern and a good example. How can a village hope to keep its good name if the *lambardar* or headman himself is a rogue, and the *kotwal*, or policeman, a rascal?

And how shall simple villagers save themselves from corruption by these locally important and influential authorities?

§3

The following statement is admittedly gruesome, but it is absolutely true, and is set forth in the records of the High Court of the capital of a certain native State.

One Dhondu, a dacoit, having been captured red-handed in the act of robbery not only with violence but with murder, was duly tried and sentenced to be hanged. Possibly, the good Christian custom of hanging had not long been introduced into this State; or again, possibly, the executioner was not as skilful and experienced as he professed to be. But for whatever reason, a drop was allowed which was too long in proportion to the weight of the condemned man, and what should have been a hanging causing death by the fracture and severance of the cervical vertebra, became a decapitation.

In accordance with custom, the body of the murderer was handed over to his relatives, that it might be taken back to his native place and duly cremated with proper ritual, at the appointed burning-*ghat*.

Now, as it happened, and as is perhaps natural, the members of the family of this murderous thug were not so particularly anxious to identify themselves with him as to make the long journey from their village to the Assize town, to appear in person in the role of the pestilent bandit's brethren, or to do more than the barest duty demanded of them by religion and their caste customs.

According to these last, the most binding laws of Hindoo life, they must, however, send for the body that in orthodox style it might be disposed of.

And this they did. They sent a bullock-cart in charge of two low-caste or casteless knaves, with instructions that, having received the corpse, they should, driving night and day and sparing not the oxen, return with it as quickly as possible, and deliver it at the burning-*ghat* by the river-bank.

Nothing loath, the two village outcasts accepted the commission and, on both the outward and the return journey, expended a portion of their hire in the purchase of toddy, the fermented juice of the palm-tree, which is the wine of the country, an extremely cheap, fairly potent, alcoholic drink, made by fermentation of the juice tapped from the toddy-palm somewhat as rubber latex "milk" is tapped from the rubber tree.

At Palegaon, a village a few miles from Chinchgaum, they made their evening halt, found the toddy-seller's liquor particularly good, sat over-long, made over-merry, and, by the time they resumed their journey, were definitely under the influence of alcohol. Later, the toddy-seller remembered the abandon, the fine free careless rapture, with which they flung themselves upon their bullock-cart and drove off. Not only drove off but fell off, first the one and then the other, the Providence that watches over drunken men seeing to it that the one who was seated upon the shaft endeavouring to twist the bullocks' tails, fell between the wheels and was uninjured, save by the other who, laughing inordinately, fell upon him from the open back of the cart, as he lay upon the road.

Rising and supporting each other as they steered their devious course in pursuit of their cart, they again scrambled into, or on to it, and proceeded, by slow degrees, from helpless laughter to unhelpful recrimination. This being their condition, it is perhaps not wholly surprising that the patient bullocks, being driven off the road and on to the road; on to bunds and into ditches; being guided and misguided hither and thither; and being urged to such headlong flight as *byle-ghari* bullocks can achieve, the cart was grievously bumped and shaken, as it lurched, swerved and crashed over ridge and ditch, across all obstacles and over stony and uneven ground.

From time to time it departed so perilously from the horizontal that it bade fair to overturn.

Now the village bullock-cart of India is open at the end, having no back-board, the better to facilitate the accommodation of great lengths of sugar-cane, of bamboo and of bales of cotton, mounds of maize, of stacks of other field produce, and to permit of general overloading.

It is not surprising therefore that as the bullocks, returning to the road, dragged the cart up a steep incline down which it never should have gone, it should have shed its grim and gruesome burden. Many times this had threatened, and many times one of the drunkards had clumsily prevented it.

And now the inevitable had come to pass.

However, apparently no great harm was done; and without much effort, though with great argument and much laughter, the body was restored to its place on the straw-strewn bottom of the cart.

The body—but not the head.

This, unnoticed by the cheerful sinners, had rolled from the shroud or other integument of the dead, and lay abandoned in the ditch beside the road that led to Chinchgaum village.

Having restored the corpse to the cart, its custodians went on their way rejoicing.

As to whether his relatives ever knew that the body of Dhondu arrived headless, there is no record. It is possible that it was handed over to the official ghouls of the burning-*ghat* and consigned to the flames unwashed, unhonoured and unsung, and burnt in its winding-sheet without investigation. It is also possible, and indeed probable, that the sobered wassailers, discovering a certain shrinkage or shortage in the goods that they delivered, bribed the recipients to overlook the matter and to give them due receipt therefore—E. & O. E. as it were.

What is important, and what had far-reaching effects upon Chinchgaum village and certain of its inhabitants, is the fact that there, affronting the daylight when the sun rose next morning, lay, by the wayside, the severed head of an unknown man.

§4

Ramrao Luxman, headman of the village of Chinchgaum, was by any standards, a bad man. Motiram Atmaran, the *kotwal*, was a worse one; while Pandurang Vishnu Marwari, the *bunnia*[19] was easily the worst of the three.

It should be clearly stated that such a condition of affairs is most unusual, the headman and the village-policeman being usually very favourable specimens of a very decent community; and the *bunnia* as good a man as a greedy, grasping, usurious money-lender can be expected to be.

In ninety-nine villages out of a hundred, these three men set an excellent example to the others, the *lambardar* representing the Law, the *kotwal* guarding it, and the *bunnia* keeping it. Naturally, the good *bunnia* keeps it with might and main, for it is only with the help and protection of the Law that he exists. In the Golden Age that is coming, when the grip of the Law relaxes, the *bunnia* will soon become a scarce relic of the dark ages that have gone; for his throat will be cut, his account-books burnt and all the villagers' debts will, like himself, be liquidated.

It is more than probable that in the case of Chinchgaum, the *lambardar* and the *kotwal* had been led astray and corrupted by the *bunnia*, for they were perfectly ordinary men, with intelligence no higher than the somewhat low level of the Indian villager, whereas the *bunnia* was even more astute, cunning and clever than most of his kind, which is saying a good deal. It

---

[19] *Money-lender and shop keeper.*

should be understood that the village *bunnia* or *sowcar* is the power behind the throne, the mighty power behind the mud throne of the village headman. For the majority of the villagers are completely in his toils; he is their evil Providence; to him they owe all the money which they have not got; and into his hands will fall their land, their goods and their chattels, if they fail to keep up payment of the interest on their debt to him, a debt usually so heavy that the villager's whole income between birth and death would not be sufficient to pay it.

Not that the *bunnia* wants him to pay it, of course. He, good man, is content with the interest at about a thousand per cent per annum, and *per* all the *annums* of the debtor's life, and those of his son and his grandson.

All being well—and under the strong arm and even-handed justice of British Law all is well—the debt incurred by the villager's great-great-grandfather to the *bunnia's* great-great-grandfather will continue paying, its interest to the great-great-grandson, and unto the third and fourth generation of his seed for ever—or rather until British Law and Justice end.

In nineteen hundred and twenty-five it was computed that, on an average, a debt of one hundred rupees incurred by a villager in the year eighteen-seventy-five, had paid six thousand by the year nineteen-twenty-five, and was still owing and paying, of course, which would appear to be quite good business—for the *bunnia*.

The simple villager regards the wily *bunnia* as a necessary evil, yea, a hundred times necessary and ten thousand times evil, and his attitude toward him is generally that of the one who wrote, "Oh, *Sowcar-ji*, my protector and preserver, my father and mother, my king and my god and my what-not, give me but another week, and at the end of that time, I will either pay you my interest or come and kill you," a letter for which the illiterate writer was very properly apprehended and punished, in spite of his plea that that was not what he had dictated to the person who wrote it for him.

No, it cannot be said that the average villager regards with affection the man in whose cold shadow he dwells, by whose permission he lives and works and, in theory, owns his land; and by whose greed and cunning he is so often kept in poverty, anxiety and fear. Like most other usurers, the *bunnia* has many enemies, usually as harmless as the weak are to the strong, the poor debtor to the rich creditor.

Pandurang Vishnu Marwari, the *bunnia* of Chinchgaum, had as many enemies as most, and more than some, since he enjoyed the greater gift for making foes than for gaining friends. And among his foes was one who was by no means harmless, Rao Bahadur Rama Narayan. Though a private individual, this man was a very important member of Chinchgaum society, being a *zemindar*[20] in a small way, and a reasonably wealthy man. As such, he had no financial dealings with Pandurang Vishnu Marwari, owed him not a penny, and treated him with scant respect. An old soldier who had risen to the rank of Subedar-Major, he was a great admirer and staunch adherent of British rule, though where itinerant agitators and wandering Congress-wallahs complained loudly and bitterly of its cruel strength, Subedar-Major Rama Narayan found fault only with its foolish weakness, the manifest weakness that allowed, such people to disturb its peace, to blacken its name, and to sow the seeds of strife and anarchy among its subjects.

A believer in discipline, because he had known it and seen its virtues and its value, he disliked and despised the undisciplined and the noisy, the upstart and the subversive, those who spoke evil of dignitaries and who would lead fools to the defiance and breaking of the Law.

Whenever the Collector Sahib, the Forest Officer, the Public Works Department Engineer, the Civil Surgeon or, perhaps best of all, the Army Recruiting Officer, came on tour, he always put on his uniform, paid a formal call and his best respects, tendered an invitation to shoot over his land and a request to permit him to give a dinner-party and nautch; and he grumbled heartily at the times, rapidly degenerating, when the rule of the *babu*, the lawyer, the agitator and the Congress-wallah was taking the place of that of the Sirkar.

A blunt-spoken man, he was as different from Pandurang Vishnu Marwari as is a lion from a snake. And more than once the lion had trodden upon the snake and passed on, ere the reptile had had time to strike at a vital spot.

---

[20] *Land-owner.*

But it was biding its time.

Not only was Pandurang Vishnu Marwari biding his time, but he was spending an undue proportion of it in thinking of ways and means to strike effectively and fatally; considering opportunities and the best means of making one, should Fate provide none that was satisfactory.

It goes without saying that what could be done by a campaign of calumny was most thoroughly done; but when a wealthy, successful and firmly-seated *sowcar* sets his ruthless, and gifted mind to the discomfiture of the enemy, he aims at something much more comprehensive, spectacular and rewarding than mere vilification, poison-pen work, and slander.

Once or twice, Pandurang had thought that his enemy's impetuous rashness and hasty temper had betrayed him into his hands, but results had been small, punishment slight, and the thirst for vengeance less slaked than increased. There had been the time when veiled insolence, insufficiently unveiled, had caused the old soldier to raise his riding-whip as though to strike the fat money-lender whose sneer was almost a jeer, but the blow had not fallen, and in spite of the ability and eloquence of Pandurang's tame lawyer, the Subedar-Major had only been bound over to keep the peace. It had, of course, been a pleasure to drag him into Court, a great pleasure to hear him censured, but how immeasurably less than the pleasure that he hoped and intended one day to enjoy the utter humiliation and ruin, yea, the complete destruction of the proud and contemptuous old soldier.

Almost he had succeeded in striking a really useful blow at the landowner's pride, when he had laid some excellent plans for getting his son into trouble, his beloved and only son, whom he hoped some day to see riding at the head of a troop of his own old Lancer Regiment. But the young man had proved unexpectedly wary, and although poor, had refused not only the tempting advance, but even more: tempting advances of the specially imported Daughter of Delight, better known in a certain bazaar of the distant city of Daulatpur than in the quiet streets of such villages as Chinchgaum.

There was also the little matter of the boundary stone. It is written "Accursed be he who removeth his neighbour's boundary-stone." And it had not been very difficult for Pandurang Vishnu

Marwari to procure a couple of sturdy rogues to remove by night a certain boundary stone in such a way that it was fairly obvious, even to the disinterested, that the *zemindar*, Subedar-Major Rama Narayan, had, with amazing wickedness, arrogance and *zulm*,[21] enlarged his own broad and fertile lands at the expense of those of his very much poorer neighbour, the *lambardar*. That made quite a bit of trouble for the *zemindar*; not only legal trouble but social, for the conscience of the village community had been outraged. What a horse-thief was among the pioneers of the West who lived by and on their horses, so, or even worse, is the land-thief among India's hundreds of millions of agriculturists to whom their land is their life.

Nor had it done the *zemindar*, that truculent and overbearing old villain, any good when something quite deleterious found its way into the well whence came the water for the domestic uses of his big farmhouse.

Still, whatever small success Pandurang Vishnu Marwari had scored against Subedar-Major Rama Narayan, they had been but as *hors d'œuvres* to the meal of vengeance to which some day he would sit down.

Like all his tribe he could wait. Waiting was his chief business, patience his one virtue, though viciously applied.

Everything comes to him who waits, and in time there came to him the friendship of Mr. Mohandas Lala Misra, B.A., LL.B., the Unjust Judge.

Now the Unjust Judge has been known in the East from Biblical times, and in the West from tribal times; and neither East nor West has ever claimed, or had, a monopoly. There are those who say that the unjust variety of Judge, like other growths, flourishes more luxuriantly under the Oriental sun. Be this as it may, there is no denying that the reputation of the Indian judiciary stands high; nor that, as a body, it can compare with the Bench and Bar of most other countries. That there are corrupt and unjust Judges in India nobody denies, nor that they are as able and competent in corruption as they are in Law. And such are the exceptions that prove the rule, and rulings, of the rest.

Competent observers there are who declare that more corrupt

---

[21] *Oppression, tyranny.*

and unjust Judges are to be found in the Native States than in British India. This is possible because the general attitude toward bribery and corruption is perhaps more old-fashioned, more tolerant, in those conservative enclaves of the vast Dependency.

In the native State of Khairapipla, for example, there were competent observers who, speaking with utmost feeling and innermost knowledge, said that Mr. Justice Mohandas Lala Misra was a mass of injustice and corruption; but these were litigants who had failed to attain their ends (which may or may not have coincided with the ends of Justice) in his very well-known, if not very popular, court.

Others there were, speaking with equal knowledge and experience, who said that Mr. Mohandas Lala Misra was the right sort of judge, the sort of judge who was wanted; broad-minded; amenable; and not only most competent and experienced in the application of the Law, but of the strictest personal honour, a man whose word was his bond and who, when he had taken your bond, for whatever the amount might be, kept his word. Far, far removed was he from the class of judicial scoundrel who would take your money and give the verdict to your opponent. Such men were a disgrace to the Bench, and should be removed from it. A man who took a bribe from both sides, and gave the verdict to the one who gave the higher bribe, was a pest, a pariah; iniquitous, unreliable and unworthy. How was a litigant to know where he stood, save that he stood in the presence of a rogue, if he were compelled to bid in the dark, as it were?

It was bad enough in the case of bidding for a Public Works Department contract or some such business in British India, where it was impossible to tell what your competitors were offering. You might over-reach yourself and lose the contract by asking too much, but you didn't lose anything but the opportunity. But with a dishonest judge, you lost your money too, and there was no redress. If you said you had given him a thousand rupees and that he had then decided the case against you, you'd be a fool, a God-forsaken half-witted owl. Because if you could prove you had done it, you could get a severe gaol sentence for the corruption of Justice; and if you couldn't prove it, you could get a still heavier punishment for slandering a Judge of the Maharajah's High Court of Justice.

So, said these good people, let us be thankful for a judge not only broad-minded, tolerant and understanding, but honest and honourable, who gave value for money and accepted nothing for nothing. O Upright Judge! What an ornament to the State.

Among those who took this view of Mr. Justice Mohandas Lala Misra was his old friend Pandurang Vishnu Marwari, the *bunnia* of Chinchgaum; for while an ornament of the Bharatavad Bar, before his elevation to the Bench as a Judge of Khairapipla State, Mr. Misra had been Pandurang's lawyer, and had proved himself a magnificent advocate, whether defending or prosecuting on behalf of the *bunnia*.

Never once had Pandurang Vishnu Marwari lost his case when prosecuting a defaulting villager, whose last struggles always failed to keep him in possession of the poor tract of land that had been his and his forefathers' for a thousand years. Never once had he lost his case when prosecuting some rascally slanderer, such as Subedar-Major Rama Narayan, who had publicly denounced him as a blood-sucking usurious rogue and thief. Never once had Mr. Misra failed on the less frequent occasions when Pandurang Vishnu Marwari had been defendant against some lying villain who alleged falsification of documents or denial of the receipt of payments. And that, mark you, in British Courts of Justice, before the utterly incorruptible and narrow-minded men who administered even-handed justice in strictest accordance with the evidence adduced.

Mr. Mohandas Lala Misra and Pandurang Vishnu Marwari understood each other. Mr. Misra understood both the law and the profits. When a pleader, he had understood the handling of witnesses as well as of judges; and now as a judge, he understood the handling of witnesses as well as of lawyers.

Quite naturally then, into the astute mind of Pandurang Vishnu Marwari, a mind ever active and alert, ever plotting and scheming, leapt the thought of Mr. Justice Mohandas Lala Misra in the same minute that he heard the strange, the almost incredible, story of the severed head.

From the depths of his unconscious mind, there rose into his conscious mind the name, of this true friend Mohandas Lala Misra, coupled with the name, as they say in after-dinner speeches, of his true enemy, Rama Narayan. Association of ideas, association by contrast. Now why?

Could it be because, on more than one occasion, when plotting the downfall of the man he hated as perhaps only a Hindu can hate, he had toyed with the idea of trying the old, old Indian trick of the Planted Corpse—a piece of conjuring as widely known as the Rope Trick, as the Boy in the Basket, and as the Miraculous Mango trick, but far, far easier of performance?

To be quite honest, the rope trick is impossible; a myth. The boy in the basket is improbable, and usually a clumsy fraud. The, miraculous mango is fairly easy for a competent juggler, but usually obvious. Like the disappearing-boy trick the appearing-corpse is known from end to end of the sub-continent; but, unlike the former, it is not only possible, but in many cases extremely probable. Moreover, it is easy. Its performance needs no conjurer or juggler. All that is required is the corpse.

Given that essential stage property, all that is needed is a brace of sturdy rogues at a rupee a head, and a cloud of witnesses at four annas[22] a day.

An ancient conjuring trick, old as India itself, and one that has undoubtedly caused the death of thousands of innocent men—even in British India where the Police are very clever; the Law inclined to err in favour of the accused; and the Judge rightly determined not only to regard him as innocent until indubitably proved guilty, but anxious to give him every benefit of every possible doubt. But pitted against the Law, its servants and its administrators, are the keenest and subtlest of brains, the most conscienceless of brazen perjurers and a numerous and flourishing class of citizens whose trade, calling, or profession is that of professional witness.

And so, full many a time and oft, had Pandurang Vishnu Marwari pondered the best way, the safe and easy way, that is to say, of gaining possession of a corpse.

When one says a corpse, one does not refer, of course, to the sort of cadaver that might perhaps be dug up in a Mohammedan grave-yard; or that of a villager well known to have died in his bed, or rather on his *charpoy*, of recognizable disease and in the

---

[22] *Anna equals one penny.*

presence of his sorrowing relatives. That sort of body is no good for the purpose of corpse-planting. To carry conviction—he conviction for murder of the wrongfully accused person, that is to say—the corpse must be fresh, obviously murdered, and discovered in circumstances completely incriminating to the victim of the plot.

Now and again, the wandering *faquir* is painfully constrained to play the role of corpse; but although such a man is an absolute stranger and can be "put upon the list, for he never will be missed" you've got to find your murderers, hire them and keep their mouths shut, and whatever may be the case in big cities, it is very far from easy to hire bravos of this type in an Indian Village.

Nor would any man so wise as the average *bunnia* put himself in the power of people so conscienceless as to do murder for hire, run the risk of perpetual blackmail, and endanger his happiness and his life.

No, the planted corpse trick, as has been said, is easy, but only when you have the suitable corpse.

And Pandurang Vishnu Marwari realized and admitted the fact, albeit most regretfully; for, properly handled, there is no better method of using the Law to do your own dirty work, a game at the playing of which the *bunnia* is a past master.

Small wonder is it then that Pandurang Vishnu Marwari literally sat up and, with veiled eyes and inscrutable face, took particular notice of what the fellow was babbling, when Arjun Gopaldas came running down the village street, and almost before he could recover breath, began telling him, the tale of a ghastly discovery.

"The head," he panted. "The head of a man, lying in the ditch, half a *kos* down the road."

Pandurang Vishnu Marwari eyed Arjun Gopaldas—a babbler, a weakling and a fool, who eked out the barest of livings on what remained to him after paying monthly the interest on the relatively tremendous debt that, like every other Indian cursed with girl children, he had incurred upon the occasion of his daughter's wedding.

"*Chup raho!* Quiet!" growled Pandurang Vishnu Marwari, as a thought, half-seen and unconsidered, flashed through his mind.

He glanced left and right.

No one was in sight save a man who, squatting on his haunches, cleaned his teeth with the chewed end of a twig from the *neem* tree, washed his mouth, and cleared his throat with uttermost abandon.

"Sit down," said the *bunnia*.

And with a salaam, the panting runner squatted on his heels.

"A head, do you say? The head of a man?"

Gopaldas nodded vigorously.

"But where is the body?"

Gopaldas shook his head with equal vigour.

With pursed lips and narrowed eyes, Pandurang Vishnu Marwari stroked his chin.

"One has heard of a headless corpse," he murmured. "Corpseless heads would seem to be more rare. . . . Why did you not bring me the ten rupees yesterday?"

Gopaldas found his voice.

"*Sowcar-ji* . . . Great Banker . . . Master . . . You are my father and my mother. It was like this . . ."

"I'm sure it was. How do you know there wasn't any body?"

"Master, there was none in sight."

"Your sight, blind owl. Is this all a *banao*? Is it your good pleasure to make a mock of me and . . ."

The man broke into loud and fervent protestations.

"Quiet, you fool," growled Pandurang again. "You shall prove that you are not lying. Go to your house and get a sheet, a piece of cloth, an old sari, a sack, anything. Take it, wrap the head in it, and bring it here."

"But . . . but . . ." faltered Gopaldas. "They gave orders that it was not to be touched; that I was to . . ."

"Who gave orders?" whispered Pandurang, and the stare of his narrowed eyes appeared to hypnotize the other as do those of a snake some small animal that is within striking distance of its fangs.

"The *lambardar* and the *kotwal*," he faltered.

"Oh? You told them all about it, did you?" enquired Pandurang Vishnu Marwari. And from the icy tone of his quiet voice, Gopaldas gathered that he had made some foolish error, fatal and irreparable.

"A pity," murmured Pandurang. "A pity . . . Have you that

ten rupees ready?"

Gopaldas, bending further on his haunches abased himself and with his right hand literally cast dust upon his head.

"Presence; Protector of the Poor," he said, without thought of irony, "I will . . ."

"Whom else have you told?"

"No one . . . No one . . . I met them walking as I ran back to the village."

"Where are they now?"

"There. By the head. They sent me to bid Bagu come with a cloth and a basket."

"And you have not told him?"

"I was on my way when I beheld the light of the countenance of the Presence and . . ."

"So you've said not a word to a soul, save to the *lambardar* and the *kotwal*?"

"To none, to none, Master."

Pandurang rose to his feet.

"Come with me," he said.

And leaving his entirely worthy and completely adequate young son, a boy of fourteen; in charge of the shop, he set off in the direction whence Arjun Gopaldas had come running.

Only once, on the way, did he speak to the man who followed respectfully behind him.

"Do you think anyone else had seen it before you did?"

"No. Oh no. Most certainly not," he assured the *bunnia*, and by reason of the fact that he felt that this was what that gentleman would prefer to hear, gave such evidence as was possible in support of his statement that he was undoubtedly the original and sole discoverer of the remarkable trove.

"It was I who found it. I was there first," he babbled. "You see, I was out very early. I was out of the village before anyone, and I met nobody on the way. Nor, when I saw this head, was there anybody in sight, up the road or down the road or anywhere about. There is nobody about even yet, as Your Honour sees. No, no, you may be quite sure that no eyes but mine have beheld it, except those of the *lambardar* and the *kotwal*."

And within a few minutes of passing the last house of Chinchgaum, Pandurang saw in the distance a couple of men standing by the side of the road.

As he drew nearer, these proved indeed to be the *lambardar* and the *kotwal*, and the first words that were spoken were uttered by himself.

"Has anyone else seen it?"

The *lambardar* and the *kotwal* eyed him in some surprise.

"Arjun Gopaldas. He came and told me and I fetched the *kotwal*," replied the *lambardar*.

"Yes. I mean has anyone passed while you've been here, or did you tell anyone else before you came?"

"No. No one."

"Then not a living soul save us four knows anything about this," observed Pandurang, and he pointed to the ghastly relic of the once active and powerful young bandit. "Ah! Well now, this *budmash* Arjun has been trying to deceive us. He pretends he found it here, but he didn't."

"But, Protector of the Poor, I did, I did," protested Arjun Gopaldas, and again gabbled his story, the veracious account of how, setting forth before dawn intending to walk to Tuledala before the sun grew hot, he had seen the hideous thing, and without touching it, had turned in his tracks, had turned back to notify the village constable and the headman.

"Cease lying," growled Pandurang as the man fell silent. "You didn't find it here at all. You placed it here yourself."

"Presence! Protector of the Poor! I . . ."

"Silence. You found it. Unless you murdered the man to whom this head belongs, you found the head and brought it here to shield the real murderer. He bribed you to do it. Silence, I say. Either you are the murderer yourself or you are taking part in a rascally *banao*[23] to protect the murderer . . . Are you a murderer?"

The wretched Arjun Gopaldas, beneath the concentrated glare of the eyes of the three men, who were the most powerful and important figures in the narrow orbit of his life, sank upon his knees and raised his hands as though in prayer to the stony-faced inquisitor.

"Master, I am not a murderer. Why should I slay this man?

---

[23] *Frame-up.*

How should I do . . ."

"Ah! Then it is as I thought. You 'found' the head and brought it here. Here, where it can bear no witness against the murderer. You were paid to do so."

"Presence, I . . ."

"And I'll tell you where you 'found' it, and that is in a field close to the house of Subedar-Major Rama Narayan. I believe you when you say you are not a murderer, but never will I believe—nor will the police," he said with a most sinister intonation—"no, they'll never swallow the yarn that you did not find the head close to the *zemindar's* house and bring it here, away in the open country, by the side of the road which is nobody's property."

The mouth of the miserable Arjun Gopaldas fell open as his somewhat slow brain grasped the significance and import of what the *bunnia* was saying.

On the face of the *lambardar,* a silent witness of this interesting little scene, dawned a slow unpleasant smile.

The *kotwal,* glancing from face to face, saw it, and immediately thereafter comprehended its meaning, cause and reason.

Of course. The wily *bunnia* had got something up his sleeve; something good. Something good for himself and, on the other hand, something pretty bad for Subedar-Major Rama Narayan, his implacable enemy. Very interesting. And possibly very profitable to others as well—others who helped the good *bunnia* in his little scheme.

Anyhow, this was one of those moments when a sensible man uses his eyes and his ears and gives his tongue a rest. Let the *bunnia* do the talking. He was good at it, and invariably talked to some purpose. . . .

But where could the body be? Had anybody on this earth, policeman or common person, ever heard of such a thing as a head that had mislaid its body? The opposite state of affairs was common enough, and every policeman had either known, or heard, of cases in which a headless body had been discovered, the murderer or murderers having taken the precaution to remove that which is not only the easiest but the infallible means of identification. If the body hasn't got a face, it is difficult to tell to whom it belongs; and the simplest way of removing a face is to remove the head to which it is invariably attached. All simple and comprehensible enough, but this was a new game—removing the body from the head.

The *lambardar* put the *kotwal's* thought into words.

"But the body? Where's that?"

"Yes, where is it?" asked the *bunnia*, turning to the bewildered and terrified Arjun Gopaldas.

"Presence, what do I know?"

"Did you help Subedar-Major Rama Narayan bury it?"

"No, no. I tell you I . . ."

"Did you see him bury it?"

"No, no. I . . ."

"Oh, you didn't actually see him bury it. H'm . . . Did you help him cart it off his land in the opposite direction from this?"

"No, no. I . . ."

"You didn't. You brought the head one way while he had the body taken in another, eh? How did he kill the man?"

"Protector of the Poor, I know nothing. I . . ."

"Well, you had better know something before the District Superintendent of Police and his men get you. No good telling the Police Inspector you know nothing. No good spinning a yarn to the Police *havildar* about setting out for a walk to Tuledala and finding this by the roadside. We can tell him a different tale from that."

"Better confess, Arjun," said the *lambardar*, stirring the now prostrate man with his toe. "The Superintendent will hand you over to the Inspector, and the Inspector will hand you over to the *havildar*, and the *havildar* will hand you over to the *naik* and he will send for those good men whose speciality is getting the truth out of liars. . . . Ever had red pepper in your eyes? . . . Better tell the truth to us now and save trouble for everybody—especially yourself."

The *lambardar* had taken his line and as, across the grovelling form of Arjun Gopaldas, his eye caught that of the *bunnia*, complete understanding was signalled between the two gentlemen who, with one accord, turned and glanced at the *kotwal*.

"It must have been he whom you and I saw passing through

the village late last night carrying a bundle," said the *lambardar* to the *kotwal*.

"Doubtless," agreed the *kotwal*, thinking quickly as to where he might have been at a time describable as "late last night."

"Was it I who said to you, or you who said to me, as the light from that *butti* on the platform under the *neem* tree fell upon the prowling night-bird, '*Isn't that Arjun Gopaldas? I wonder what he has got there*'?"

"I think it was you who said it," replied the *kotwal*.

"Probably. Probably. My sight is very good. And it was you who said, '*It sounds like his foot-step*'."

"Doubtless. Doubtless," agreed the *kotwal*. "My hearing is very good."

"Yes, and if you remember, I made the remark, '*I'm afraid he is up to no good.*' Others must have seen him, of course," observed the *lambardar*.

"I did," said the *bunnia*, apparently emerging suddenly from a brown study. "It comes back to me now. Yes. Yes. I made much the same remark to my little son. Assuredly he will remember it. Of course he will, for he too remarked that Arjun Gopaldas was carrying a bundle, which seemed a little strange and unusual, not to say suspicious."

"Oh, you saw him too?" said the *lambardar*.

"Yes, he came out of the shadow of that mango-tree, and the moonlight fell on his face. . . . One or two other people must have met him. . . . Must have done. Yes. I'm sure they did," mused the *bunnia*, running over in his mind the names of a likely quartette or half-dozen whose powers of observation were as good as those of the *lambardar* and the *kotwal*, and to whom four annas, not to mention the favourable notice and good word of the village authorities, would be acceptable.

"It's no good, Arjun Gopaldas," he added.

"Not a bit of good," agreed the *lambardar*.

"Not the very slightest," confirmed the *kotwal*.

And in the mind of the unfortunate Arjun Gopaldas remained no shadow of doubt that it was indeed no good. No good for him to protest and to deny. No earthly good for him to asseverate upon oath that his tale was true, that he really had found this dreadful head lying on this very spot. Useless. Hopeless. If the *lambardar* and the *kotwal* and the *bunnia* had made up their minds that he had brought it here—well, that was that. Facts are stubborn things, and the manufacture of the facts lay in the hands of these three all-powerful City Fathers; these important and responsible men, the word of one of whom was far more powerful than the babblings of Arjun Gopaldas. When the words of all three in agreement were set against his, who would listen to him, much less believe his obviously untruthful twaddle?

"Listen, you, and for the sake of your family, do your best to keep out of gaol," advised the *bunnia*.

"Yes; and to avoid being tortured by the Police," warned the *lambardar*.

"And to cheat the gallows," added the *kotwal*.

Such instantly became the perfervid desire and unshakable determination of Arjun Gopaldas.

"Help me! Advise me! Tell me . . . tell me what to do, Protectors of the Poor," he wept.

"Well, the first thing to do is to take that back again," replied the *bunnia*, pointing to the grinning head.

"Yes, and put it where you found it," added the *lambardar*.

"Beside the body," suggested the *kotwal*. "Unless, of course, Rama Narayan took the body away and threw it in the river, or buried it in the ground, or burnt it, or something," observed the *bunnia*.

"You say you didn't actually see the body disposed of, don't you?" enquired the *lambardar*.

"What a silly thing to say," remarked the *kotwal*. "Is it likely he wouldn't have watched to see what Rama Narayan did with the body before he brought the head away!"

Arjun Gopaldas wept yet more freely.

"Now, are you going to speak the truth?" enquired the *bunnia*.

"Oh, yes, yes, yes," jibbered Arjun. "Every word of it. The whole truth. The absolute truth."

"Oh, you are, are you?" interrupted the *bunnia*. And somehow the tone of his voice did not quite give his hearers the impression that that was precisely what was desired.

Arjun Gopaldas looked up at the *bunnia*, of whom he had lived in terror for more years than he could remember, the terror of the hopeless debtor for the merciless and implacable creditor.

"He had better speak the truth," said the *lambardar*.

"I feel sure he is going to speak the truth," prophesied the *kotwal*.

"And in order that he may make not the slightest mistake in repeating it to other people, I will myself tell him the truth," promised the *bunnia* menacingly.

"We will all three tell him the truth, for he is a stupid and forgetful man," he added.

"Look you, Arjun Gopaldas," he continued softly. "Last night, as you were returning home from the shop of the toddy-seller at Palegaon, walking without sound in the deep dust, beneath the wayside banyan trees, on the road that runs through the fields of the *zemindar*, Rama Narayan, you were astonished to see him standing beside that well-known *tonga* of his, digging a hole in the soft ploughed earth. You were so amazed that you thought it must have been a trick of the moonlight, or possibly of the toddy you had got in your belly. Anyway, the toddy gave you the courage to go out from the shadow of the trees and walk in the direction of the *tonga*. As you approached it, the man—and it was as you had thought, the *zemindar* himself—rushed at you, brandishing a spade as though he were going to kill you with it. As you threw up your arms to protect your head and beg for mercy, he said, as though to himself, '*No, no! . . . Not another . . . One body is enough.*' And as he spoke, his demeanour changed. He lowered his spade and asked whether you wanted to earn twenty rupees and his protection for as long as you lived; and you replied that assuredly you did. Then he said, '*Well, look. I have something here which you must hide; get rid of; destroy. You must take it far away and bury it in the ground or throw it down a well. Or burn it. Yes, that would be best. Burn it and bury the ashes deeply in the earth, so that not even the teeth may ever be found.*' And you said, '*The teeth, Zemindar-ji? . . . Why, what is it?*' and he said that it was the head of an animal, and gave a nasty kind of laugh.

"Well, naturally, you were at once rather suspicious. It was strange that the *zemindar* should want you to take the head of an animal to some distant place a very long way from Chinchgaum, and there either throw it down a well, or burn it.

"However, being afraid of the *zemindar*, who is a very violent and dangerous man, you of course agreed, and he, going to the *tonga*, brought out a bundle and gave it to you. And you at once set off as quickly as you could toward Tuledale. But having passed through Chinchgaum, where at least four people saw you, we three and my son—and we noticed that you were carrying a bundle—and again on for about half a *kos*, you suddenly thought you'd stop and see what it was you were carrying; whether it really was the head of an animal; and, if so, what kind of an animal. And when you undid the wrapping, you were horrified to discover that it was the head of a man. You were struck dumb."

"Yes, deaf, dumb, blind and silly," put in the *lambardar*.

"Not only horrified but frightened to death," added the *kotwal*.

"And when you had recovered your senses," continued the *bunnia*, "what did you do?"

The badly-scared and very puzzled and unhappy Arjun, anxious to learn what he had then done, raised his beseeching eyes to those of the *bunnia*.

"You very sensibly turned about and ran as fast as you could, back to the place where you had been entrusted with this horrible and shameful commission, and given this ghastly burden. Afraid of that notorious *budmash* and oppressor, Subedar-Major Rama Narayan, you might be; but far, far more were you afraid of outraged Justice, the Law within the reach of whose long arm you stood. You felt the cold shadow of the gallows fall upon you; the dreadful feeling of the hangman's rope about your neck. You felt you were being strangled, didn't you?"

Rapidly Arjun nodded his head, as, unconsciously, he raised his hand to that threatened throat.

"Back to Chinchgaum, through the now silent street you hastened, clutching that terrible—er—bundle beneath your garment, hoping and praying that you would not meet the upright watchful *lambardar*, the honest *kotwal*, or anybody else who might ask you where you were going in such a hurry, and what it was that you were taking there with such effort at concealment. But you met no one as you went through the village.

"Hurrying on in the direction of Palegaon, you, came to the place, as nearly as you could tell, where the *zemindar* had given you the head and bidden you dispose of it for him. You could be fairly sure of the exact spot because it was within sight of his house. But did you find the *zemindar* there? No. He had disappeared; he and his *tonga* and the headless trunk of the murdered man. At first, you thought of marching boldly up to his house and bidding his servants give him the bundle that you were carrying; but your courage failed you. Assuredly the *zemindar* would kill you, not only for having failed him, but by reason of your knowledge of his guilt.

"And suddenly, you felt that the one thing you must do, and do immediately, was to get rid of the terrible thing. . . . Supposing you were found with it! You'd not only be suspected, but accused, of murder; not only accused of it, but almost certainly hanged for it. So you just dropped it, then and there, in the darkness among the roots of one of the banyan trees. Understand?"

Arjun Gopaldas understood quite clearly.

"Remember?"

Arjun Gopaldas remembered distinctly.

"Good! Now then, put the head in that basket, cover it with leaves, make your way round the village—well out of sight—go out on to the Chinchgaum-Palegaon road, as near to the *zemindar's* house as you can without being seen, and hide it away, in under the roots of a banyan tree. . . . By the way, if you should see my little boy somewhere about, don't be surprised that he should be out so early in the morning, nor take any notice of him whatever. No, not even if he should seem to be watching you, and to be taking note of the spot where you are concealing something."

The mouth of Arjun Gopaldas opened nearly as widely as his eyes. The side way smile again flickered about the mouth of the *lambardar* as once more he stroked his chin. The *kotwal*, as slowly he nodded his head, emitted a strange brief sound which might have been a laugh.

"And," continued the *bunnia*, "don't be alarmed if my little boy should discover what you hid, and should very naturally and properly do his duty, and hasten away to inform his father, who would of course inform the authorities; nor be alarmed if the authorities, the *kotwal* and the *lambardar* come and question you. You have nothing to be afraid of; nothing of which to be ashamed. There is no blood on your hands, and no burden on your Conscience. Do your civic duty, give them every assistance, make fullest confession. . . . No, no, you fool, I don't mean confession of your guilt, but admission of your *knowledge*. You have no guilt, but you have information, knowledge, and you must withhold from the authorities no facts that may assist them in bringing the murderer to justice. It is your plain duty, as a good citizen, to assist the Law. Understand?"

Sadly Arjun Gopaldas again nodded his head.

"Changing the subject," continued the *bunnia*, "did I give you a receipt for the ten rupees you brought me last night? I don't believe I did."

Arjun Gopaldas did not believe it either; but a great light shone, not so much upon, as from, his swiftly changing countenance of which the expression completely altered.

"Now, lest you make any mistake when you give the authorities every assistance in your power, just tell us again what happened."

The three gentlemen listened attentively to the remarkable story which Arjun told with what was, from their point of view, commendable accuracy.

"That's right. That's absolutely right," approved the *bunnia*. "There is one thing you've forgotten to repeat. You told us that the *zemindar* gave you a five-rupee note in advance, I think? You were to have the remaining fifteen when he saw you again, weren't you? . . . Yes. . . . Well, has it slipped your memory that there was a great smear of purple ink on that five-rupee note— purple ink, that I alone in this village use?"

"No, no, I haven't forgotten. I remember it well. It was the first thing I noticed," babbled Arjun Gopaldas, whose weary brain asked only to be allowed to follow the line of least resistance, to bid the tongue utter whatever words the ears might convey to that minimum of grey matter, for repetition.

"Yes, being very scrupulous and particular in such matters," continued the *bunnia*, "I remember wondering whether that smear of violet ink spoilt the note so badly that I should withdraw it from circulation; pay it into my bank. My little boy will remember my speaking of it. But he said just what I myself was thinking, that, although the smudged blot took something from the beauty of the note, it took nothing from its value; and we both laughed merrily when he offered me four rupees twelve annas for it. He's a sharp little chap. Well, that five-rupee note went direct from me to Subedar-Major Rama Narayan, who is my landlord. There again, as it happens, I have a witness to the truth of what I am saying—were one needed—for my dear son again laughed-merrily when I said I would put it in with old Rama Narayan's rent-money; and the little chap actually said:

"*Drop another blot on it, Father, and I'll smudge it.*'

"But I didn't do that, of course. I put it with the rest of the money—and I have his receipt. Dated yesterday. . . . And what happens last night? He gives you that very same five-rupee note to which I and my son can swear.

"And listen, *lambardar-ji* and *kotwal-ji*," the *bunnia* proceeded. "And you listen too, Arjun Gopaldas. Without seeing that note again, I can tell you exactly what the violet ink-mark on it is like. A big blot evidently fell upon the front of it, about an inch to the left of the centre. Then somebody's sleeve, or a piece of paper, or something of the sort, smeared it right across from left to right but downwards in the direction of the right-hand corner. Then it was blotted with dust from the sand-box in the usual way, and the sand was rubbed off; and I call you three to bear witness that I described the note to you, although it had been in Rama Narayan's possession and the possession of Arjun Gopaldas for forty-eight hours since I last saw it."

The *lambardar* and the *kotwal* nodded their abundant willingness to testify, while their honest countenances showed the admiration and approval that irradiated their minds.

Arjun Gopaldas shook his head sharply from side to side until, realizing that this was evidently the wrong gesture, nodded it vigorously.

At the mention of the return of the phantom five rupees, his earnest face had again been lit up; for, with the ten rupees rent, for the payment of which a receipt apparently, if miraculously, lay awaiting him at the *bunnia's* house, it undoubtedly made fifteen. And this was a good round sum of money which, since the very skies to-day appeared to be raining gold, might yet increase and further enrich a poor but honest man, puzzled but earnestly desirous of doing what was right—in the eyes of his proprietor, the *bunnia* Pandurang Vishnu Marwari.

"Now then," concluded that gentleman in a voice which Arjun knew only too well, "get that head back to where I have told you that you found it; and then go and notify the *kotwal* and *lambardar* in the proper manner. And no more of your vile tricks, and wicked lies about finding it on the Palegaon-Chinchgaum road . . ."

An hour later, and still quite early in the morning, the *kotwal* of Chinchgaum visited the *lambardar*, accompanied by one Arjun Gopaldas who had made a ghastly discovery on the lands of the *zemindar* Subedar-Major Rama Narayan, and not far from his house.

"I will go at once," said the *lambardar*. "Better bring one or two responsible witnesses. . . . Yes, the *bunnia*, Pandurang Vishnu Marwari and the rest of the *panchayat*,[24] if we can get them. I believe Lilaram Tukharam is ill."

The *lambardar* and *kotwal* found that the leading citizen and prominent member of the panchayat, the *bunnia* Pandurang Vishnu Marwari, was in bed; but on being informed by his son that important, indeed urgent and tragic, business was toward, he came down from his bedroom at once.

And in the presence of Ramrao Luxman the *lambardar*, Motiram Atmaran the *kotwal*, Pandurang Vishnu Marwari the *bunnia* and two other City Fathers (who were really village grandfathers if not great-grandfathers) whom he had led to the spot, Arjun Gopaldas revealed the dreadful Thing, the hideous evidence of murder most foul, brutish and beastly; and, having shown it to them in the place where the murderer must have hidden it beneath the roots of the banyan tree, he made full and clear statement of his finding of it. . . .

Promptly the *kotwal* did his duty, notified the Police *havildar* at the Tuledala *thana*[25] and the Law was set in motion.

What more natural than that the *lambardar* and the *kotwal* should talk over the terrible business with that prominent and active member of the village *panchayat*, the *bunnia* Pandurang

---

[24] *Council of five village elders.*
[25] *Police Station.*

Vishnu Marwari, and discuss it in all its bearings?

It was a long discussion. And it had lots of bearings.

By the time it was finished, things looked black for the man near whose house the head had been found; the man in whose possession it had been seen by a witness; the man who had actually given that witness five rupees and promised him fifteen more to take it far away from Chinchgaum and destroy it beyond recognition; the man who had given an indubitably identifiable five-rupee note as a bribe to the fortunately unbribable witness; the man who was notorious for violent truculence, and who had been, not long previous to the murder, bound over to keep the peace.

There is small wonder that after careful investigation of the matter by the Police, the *zemindar* Rama Narayan was arrested, charged with murder, refused bail and committed for trial.

§5

Nor, in the Khairapipla Court, presided over by Mr. Justice Mohandas Lala Misra, did the case at any time look otherwise than black against the accused. Of course, he produced witnesses to testify that he never left his house upon the night of his alleged encounter with Arjun Gopaldas.

Prosecuting Counsel soon made short work of those hirelings, all, as he pointed out, relatives, dependants or employees of the prisoner. And in any case, there were quite as many, in fact a good many more, witnesses who had seen him abroad that night. One man, a wandering *faquir*, had met him on the Chinchgaum-Palegaon road and had noticed that he was carrying an axe. He had distinctly seen the moonlight shine on the blade. He knew him by his square-shouldered upright carriage, and his big moustache.

No, there was no possibility of the *faquir's* being mistaken. He had sat begging by the roadside close to the prisoner's house and had received alms from. him.

Then there was quite a little band of people, gypsies who, with a couple of bullock-carts, had passed through Chinchgaum on their way from Tuledala to Palegaon that night. Yes, they

always travelled at night, when there was a moon. They had all
noticed a man, whom they identified as the prisoner, talking to
another, a much smaller man.

What sort of a man? Oh, he looked a bit of a *budmash*,[26] and
obviously a *gharib admi*[27]: Yes, the big man, the prisoner, was
threatening him. No, they didn't hear what you'd call sounds of a
quarrel. The small man wasn't back-answering, so to speak; he
wasn't defiant. He appeared rather to be begging for mercy.

Did they see any blow struck, or hear any cry?

No. Nothing more than that. They didn't stop. They just
passed by; but one or two of them had commented on the
incident. . . .

And so it went on, the evidence piling up against the accused
to overwhelming height; a mass of evidence against which the
poor subterfuges, concoctions and inventions of the obviously
interested and naturally untruthful members of his family,
retinue, and employees, were but as a handful of dust.

Nor did Counsel for the Defence really seem to be surpassing
himself in his efforts to save his client. Perhaps in the face of the
five-rupee note produced by Arjun Gopaldas; the blood-stained
axe found by the little boy who was the son of the village *bunnia*,
and a witness of admirable lucidity; and the plain straightforward
account told by the man whom the accused had endeavoured to
make an accessory after the fact, the defending pleader felt it was
hopeless.

Possibly a quiet talk that he had had with a gentleman who
was in no wise concerned with the case, of course (a worthy
citizen of Chinchgaum, a *bunnia* who wished to make a nice
subscription to any charity in which the good pleader might be
interested), had helped him to come to that conclusion; or
possibly, again, the attitude of the Judge, in whose favourable
regard the pleader particularly desired to stand, may have helped
him to make the decision that any hope of proving his client's
innocence was a forlorn one.

Certainly the summing-up of the Judge (whose old friend
Pandurang Vishnu Marwari had naturally paid him a most

---

[26] *Rascal.*
[27] *Poor creature.*

delightful visit when he came to Khairapipla) left no doubt whatsoever in the mind of any impartial listener—left no possible shadow of doubt—that the accused *zemindar*, Subedar-Major Rama Narayan, had committed a murder, had disposed of the body, and unsuccessfully endeavoured to get rid of the head. Murder will out; and in this instance the murderer's own clumsy attempt at concealment of the most dangerous and damning piece of evidence had led to its exposure.

That the identity of the dead man remained undiscoverable; that no shadow of motive for the commission of a murder by the *zemindar* could be adduced; that the witnesses who swore that the *zemindar* had never left his house that night, were, to say the least of it, as reliable arid reputable as those who swore that they had seen him outside it; that he had a not only blameless but most honourable record of service as a soldier; that several people of high standing, irreproachable reputation and public position, testified to the excellence of his character; that no tracks in any way corresponding to the wheel-marks of his *tonga* could be found near the spot of his alleged encounter with Arjun Gopaldas—all these facts appeared to carry no weight with His Honour, and were not mentioned in his summing-up.

The evidence of Arjun Gopaldas and the rest; the matter of the inky five-rupee note; that a blood-stained axe had been found near the spot by an innocent child, appeared, on the other hand, to carry absolute conviction to the Judge. He said as much in so many words, and the *zemindar*, Subedar-Major Rama Narayan, was found guilty and sentenced to death by hanging.

Incredulous, but proud and defiant, with firm step and head erect, he was led out of the ancient wood-and-mud-built Court-house by the police who were his gaolers.

Ere the Court could rise, the spectators, in a loud buzz of conversation, swarmed out after him, to look their last upon the man who for so long had been so important a figure in their midst.

Annoyed, Mr. Justice Mohandas Lala Misra rose to his feet. Prosecuting and defending Counsel gathered their papers together. The *bunnia* Pandurang Vishnu Marwari smiled his own peculiar little smile, first at the *lambardar* of Chinchgaum and then at the *kotwal* who had so ably assisted the Law in its findings, and then at the Judge. For a silent moment all waited as His Honour turned to make his way to the door leading to his private room.

"The Court adjourns," cried the Clerk of the Court.

And in response, as suddenly as bursts a clap of thunder, there came a mighty roar, a rending, smashing crash, accompanied by a blinding cloud of dust, as the Court-house of Khairapipla collapsed and fell in upon itself, as did the Temple at Gaza upon the blind Samson who pulled down the pillars that supported it.

But the name of the insignificant blind Samsons that destroyed the wooden pillars of the Court-house of Khairapipla was Legion.

White ants.

Postscriptum. So greatly shocked was Arjun Gopaldas at this most obvious intimation of the anger of the Gods at his little paltering with the truth that, forthwith and unceasingly, he proclaimed the actual facts of the matter, and of his original finding of the trunkless head.

THE PAHWANG

"The Pahwang" is the story of an Englishman in the jungles of Malaysia who falls in love with and marries a Malay girl. Tragically, the young wife is killed by an enormous crocodile, and the husband wants revenge but cannot find the crocodile. Similar to a snake charmer, a pahwang is a crocodile charmer. "The Pahwang" was first published as the fifth story in Part I, "Queer", of Odd—But Even So *(1941).*

As has been remarked, East is East and West is West, and never the twain shall meet. Nevertheless, in defiance of this Law, they do occasionally meet. Perhaps it is because the meeting is in defiance of the Law that it is usually disastrous. Whether it is a Law of God, of man or of Nature, is not stated, but it would appear that all three endorse the rule.

There have been many meetings of East and West, but rarely a fortunate one. That there are some that have been happy, one must be prepared to believe, for every rule has its exceptions.

Of course, the meaning of the word "meeting," in this use, has to be properly understood. It must not be confused with encounter, or professional, sporting, service, or business relationship.

The statement that the twain shall never meet, means that the man or woman of the East cannot meet the woman or man of the West spiritually and mentally so that there is complete fusion, so that the two halves make one complete and perfect whole; that no Eastern woman has her complement among Western men; no Western woman among Eastern men; that no man from the East has his perfect complement among Western women; no man from the West among Eastern women. With exceptions. And I think I encountered a perfect example.

But even in this case the Law did not play fairly, though perhaps one should here use the word Fate instead of Law; and even so, they are but different names for the same Power. . . .

Richard Wheeler was by any standards a good man, and not

only a good man but a good chap, which is different; a good sportsman, which is different again; and he was also a good friend, a good employer, and a good employee. I doubt if he had any enemies, and if anyone at the Club sneered at him—because he wasn't much of an asset to the bar; because he wasn't extraordinarily fond of losing his money at poker; because, the race-course wasn't really his spiritual home; or because he held what they considered narrow views on the subject of pretty little Malay housekeepers—the sneer did him no harm and the sneerer no good. In short, he was a typical man of the West of the better sort, and had no idea of meeting the East save as a most interested friendly observer of its ways, and as an interested and sympathetic student of its history, customs and religion.

To his servants, coolies and other employees he was a just and kindly master; and to those Malays whom he met officially, village headmen, chieftains, officials, and petty Rajahs, he was courteous, pleasant and scrupulous in all his dealings.

But though he knew the language, liked the people and enjoyed the life, it never occurred to him that East and West, Malayan and Briton, could meet—that is to say, coalesce.

Until he fell in love with Amai.

When he did, he laughed to scorn the idiotic fallacy of the tag and amended it to

East is East and West is West, and when the twain shall meet,
The severed halves of a perfect whole shall unite and be complete.

Now this Richard Wheeler was not only a man with a conscience, a solid and self-respecting sort of fellow, but was also exceedingly thorough. I don't know that he ruled his life by wise saws, ancient sayings and modern instances, but he infallibly behaved as though his slogan or motto were—

All, that you do, do with your might, for things done by halves are never done right.

And thus it was in the case of his first, last and only love-affair.

It was quite evident when he was a prominent and respected member of the Spotted Dog, the famous Kuala Lumpur Club, that women did not interest him. Not that he was a misogynist; not that he was rude or even casual in his manner toward any of the wives or daughters of other members; but they simply did not interest him. He did not dance or play any "mixed-doubles" games. He was a man's man; apparently a dyed-in-the-wool bachelor; and his name was never for one moment in any way connected with that of any girl. He once remarked with his dry humour, it must have been that he was born a bachelor; and on my observing that all men began life like that, he commented on the pity of their not preserving the state in which, happily, they were born.

A pity indeed in Richard Wheeler's case.

As most thoughtful people have occasion to remark, we positively do not know our blessings from our curses, our rewards from our punishments; and what happened to Richard Wheeler was the direct result of his successful handling of the Semiot Rubber Estate. He had made it, and made it extraordinarily well; so his Directors sent him to do a similar work at Tembilang, there to carve out of virgin jungle another great and richly-productive rubber estate.

At very far back-of-beyond Tembilang, Richard Wheeler lived a life totally different from that which he had led at Semiot, with its numerous and various social distractions, its facilities for golf and tennis, the infinitely delightful sailing on a sea that was a yachtsman's and fisherman's paradise; its bridge, picnics, amateur dramatics, and the constant and cheerful companionship of congenial men—fellow-planters, officials, visiting travellers and others.

At Tembilang there was none of these delights. There was indeed nothing at all—but work. Absolutely no social intercourse whatsoever, no games nor any other form of exercise than walking about the *tote,* or rather the lush dense jungle that he was to make into a *tote.* When he first met Amai he lacked even a house, and was living in a native hut.

For the first time in all his thirty years, Richard Wheeler knew what is probably the most terrible affliction that Life, so rich in afflictions, has to offer to man—loneliness.

At Tembilang he knew loneliness in all its forms—spiritual, mental and physical; and, albeit a strong man, it was only work that saved him, in the early days before he had been accustomed to the sudden and violent change, the change from a broad and full life with every amenity, amelioration, satisfaction and indeed gaiety, to one of utter isolation and emptiness, a place of spiritual twilight, of mental and physical silence and gloom.

And Fate, as usual, was doing things thoroughly; for, to the deprivation of the desirable, she added a plenitude of the pernicious. For here he encountered for the first time malaria and dysentery. At Semiot, with all the medical resources of civilization at hand, in the shape of excellent doctors, well-stocked chemists' shops and an admirable hospital, he had enjoyed perfect health. Here in Tembilang, where he had nothing, he very quickly contracted the prevalent and pernicious form of malaria, an evil sufficient unto the day and the night, without the addition of amœbic dysentery.

So was the way prepared for the coming of Amai, and conditions could not have been more fortunate for her had she wished to make a conquest of the *Tuan*.

But nothing was further from Amai's thoughts. It was not a case of love at first sight. On the contrary, Amai was as much surprised as interested at the appearance of this strange new creature that so suddenly invaded her little world, the tiny and narrowly circumscribed sphere of her life in the buried jungle village.

So this was a *Tuan*! This was a sample of those strange half-legendary beings of whom she had heard talk between her father and the hunters, and gossip among the women who washed their clothes at the ford. Her cousin Suliman knew all about them, for he was a policeman, had served under a *Tuan* and spoke of them very highly. But what funny hair, what a curiously coloured face, and strange clothes, especially on his head and feet.

Nor, on the occasion of his first seeing her, did Amai herself particularly catch Richard Wheeler's eye. He was not given to noticing native girls; and when, stopping one day in the village street to speak with her father Ibrahim, he saw Amai pass by, it might as well have been her mother—grey-haired, wrinkled, aged and bent, at the advanced age of thirty-nine. . . .

It was not until he had been at Tembilang for more than a year and had come to know and to like Ibrahim very well indeed, that he really saw Amai with the eye of appreciation. Nor probably would this have occurred, but for his sudden desperate illness and the weakness that followed it.

Ibrahim, hunter, sportsman and cheery good fellow, greatly admired the *Tuan* whose coming had brought prosperity to Tembilang and to himself, and he had no desire to see the white man die for want of such care and nursing as Ibrahim's village could provide.

Taking charge of the situation when he discovered that the *Tuan* was at death's door, lying helpless, motionless and speechless (when not delirious), he installed his wife in the *Tuan's* bungalow as cook and nurse, bade Amai give her every assistance, and sent for his father-in-law, Yussuf, an aged gentleman famous both for his knowledge and his power—his knowledge of curative herbs, potions and incantations; his power to combat the machinations of evil spirits and to invoke the help of good ones.

Yussuf came, saw, and prescribed. Day and night he laboured to save the *Tuan's* life, and save the *Tuan's* life he did. Whether because of, or in spite of, his infusions, brews, incantations and mysterious performances, the sickness abated.

By his direction, Richard Wheeler's bed was carried out into the compound. About it a circle was described; within this, three small fires were lighted at the points of a triangle drawn within it; powders were cast upon the fires, and incantations uttered through the smoke. The whole village watched with deep interest, Ibrahim and his wife and daughter with great and proprietary pride. Here was their famous relative adding to his great reputation by averting the curse of malicious devils from their own *Tuan.*

Later, somewhat ungratefully perhaps, Richard Wheeler was apt to ascribe his salvation to old Meenah's nursing, to her sweat-inducing potions, her bathing and cooling, warming and drying; and the following of the treatment that she had learned from her own mother and applied to her own children; and, later, to her chicken broth and cooling fruit-drinks.

But quite possibly Amai had more to do with his recovery than either Yussuf or Meenah, although her sick-room function was but the humble duty of watching the patient. To this she added the pleasing work of fanning him, giving him drink when, racked with pain and parched with thirst, he awoke.

Doubtless it was with a dream Amai that he first fell in love; an Oriental ministering angel; a very lovely vision, desirable, incredible.

Incredible? The really incredible thing was the fact that this tantalizing mirage of female beauty should remain while the miasmic phantasmagoria of fever-nightmare faded.

Out of the horrors of the torturing dreams the one thing beautiful, glimpsed from time to time through mists of suffering, survived, proved to be real, to be a flesh-and-blood Amai.

Thus did Richard Wheeler fall in love with the Malay girl, and in no other circumstances could he have done so. And from kind womanly sympathy and sweet pity grew the girl's love for the strange *Tuan,* and could have grown in no other way.

By the time Richard Wheeler was well enough to write letters, send messages to the nearest, but far distant, outpost of civilization, there was no need to send them. He did not need a doctor, nor the medicine of his Western pharmacopœia. He didn't want to go to a hospital. He wanted Amai.

And he wanted her in Richard Wheeler's way. To have and to hold, for better for worse, for richer for poorer—and for ever. He wanted to marry her. And with all the determination of his slow tenacious mind and powerful will, he set about the overcoming of all obstacles.

East is East and she was a Malay girl? Well, he had come to the East, and it should be his home wherein he would spend the rest of his life in close association with that of this Malay village. What fitter wife for such a man, leading such a life, than Amai?

West is West and he was a man of Western culture, education and tastes? Well, if this applied to the first twenty years of his life, could he not add to it, broaden it, and mellow it with Oriental culture, education and tastes, so that by the time he had lived twenty years in the East he had made the best of both worlds? And by the time he had been married to Amai for twenty years, would they not be as close in sympathy, understanding and tastes as is possible for two human beings?

She was a Mussulmani and he a Christian? What of it? If, by a thousand years of heredity, her god was Allah whose prophet was Mahomet, whereas by the accident of birth and breeding his was God, whose Son was Christ, that need surely be no barrier. Better a girl who had deep and different religious principles than one who had none at all, as was undoubtedly the case with quite a large proportion of the European women of his acquaintance.

She was ignorant and uneducated? So was he. He was deplorably ignorant of Eastern lore and culture, utterly uneducated in Oriental wisdom, knowledge and understanding; and surely the wise and ancient East has as much to teach the new and blatant West as the West has to teach the East, whence come all the religions and philosophies of the world?

They had nothing in common? What unutterable nonsense, bosh and idiocy. They had in common the one thing needful, the all-embracing indispensable—love. What else mattered? Where love was, there also reigned peace and joy, happiness made perfect.

Thus Richard Wheeler, man of fine mind and high ideals, in love for the first time.

The marriage was solemnized according to Islamic rites in Tembilang, and again according to those of the Christian Church at the Mission Station of Taipoh; the first, a terribly noisy, protracted, and public occasion, the other quick, quiet and private—and, to Richard Wheeler, in spite of his resolutely open mind, the more satisfying, binding and irrevocable.

Now was Amai his wife in the sight of all men of the East and of the West. In the persons of himself and Amai the twain had met, and should never be put asunder.

§2

For how long would such a man as Richard Wheeler have been happy with such a woman as Amai, who had all the virtues, accomplishments and graces of the Malayan jungle-village girl and no others?

One can only wonder; but it is an incontrovertible fact that for as long as Amai lived he was, in his own words, as happy as the day was long, happier than ever he had been in his life before, happier than he had supposed it possible for a man to be.

But Amai only lived for eleven weeks from the day when, laughing and telling her it was an old Western custom, he carried her over the threshold of their new house.

Early one morning she kissed him on the lips as usual, in the way in which he had taught her, and went out as had been her custom from early childhood, to bathe in the river where the overhanging trees shaded a deep pool of dark and quiet water.

Here, diving like a kingfisher, merrily disporting herself like a river naiad, revelling in her health and strength, youth, beauty, and the joy of her new great happiness, she suddenly uttered a piercing scream and disappeared before the eyes of Sara, her maid and relative, who stood on the bank holding the garment into which Amai would change when she came out of the water.

This she never did.

The Malays are a brave people, women as well as men, and Sara was worthy of the best traditions of her pirate and dacoit ancestors.

Although she had caught a glimpse of a truly enormous crocodile, she dived into the river, swam beneath the blood-tinged water in the vain and foolish hope of rescuing her mistress. There was nothing that she could do save die for her or with her, and to this end she made her best endeavour. Although a fine swimmer and accustomed to moving under water with open eyes, she saw no more of the tragedy; and, after diving repeatedly in different places, up-stream and down, the thoughts of her distracted mind turned from rescue to revenge, a sentiment never far from the injured Malay heart.

Amai was now beyond human aid. The crocodile must not escape beyond human vengeance—and was not old Yussuf a *pahwang*?

Gasping for breath and fighting off a paroxysm of grief and rage and horror that would render her incoherent, she fled from the river bank, up through the village, shouting the terrible news to Ibrahim as he emerged from his hut, and ran on to the house and straight into the *Tuan's* presence.

When Richard Wheeler understood what she was saying and

grasped the fact that Amai had been taken by a crocodile, he received a blow from which he never recovered. Although he did his best to refuse to believe it as he seized and loaded his rifle, subconsciously he knew that it was true, knew that this terrible physical pain in his heart was a prelude to mental agony that would be unbearable. Grasping his rifle and still questioning the girl, he dashed off in the direction of Amai's bathing-pool.

As he ran through the village he was followed by all who beheld this strange spectacle of the calm and dignified *Tuan* rushing bare-headed, bare-footed, clad only in his pyjama trousers, toward the river.

And soon they realized that he had been afflicted of Allah, that he was mad, and therefore a very proper object for their veneration, regard, and care. Anything that he wanted must be given to him. Any order that he gave must be carried out, and his slightest whim must be humoured.

Quickly it became clear that the one and only thing that the *Tuan* desired was to see the crocodile that had killed Amai. Throughout the first day, while his strength lasted, he repeatedly dived into the pool, swam about beneath the water, returning to the bank to lie panting while he recovered strength.

But as Ibrahim pointed out to him, this was folly. Suppose he saw the crocodile which Sara described as being by far the biggest that she had ever seen, what could he do while he was in the water unarmed? It would merely mean that the brute would take him as it had taken the girl.

No, the sensible thing was to sit and watch. Watch and wait from morning till night, until the crocodile came out on to the river bank, or at least showed its head above the water, as, sooner or later, it was bound to do. Then could the *Tuan* avenge Amai. Meanwhile, Ibrahim would send again for old Yussuf who, unfortunately, had gone off on one of his mysterious expeditions—this time to visit some of the Sakai people from whom he was learning about a new poison.

"And what can Yussuf do?" panted Wheeler, emerging from the pool for the hundredth time.

"*Do?* Yussuf? Why, he's a *pahwang*," replied Ibrahim in evident surprise.

"And what the devil is a *pahwang*?" asked Wheeler.

"Why, a crocodile-charmer, of course."

"What do you mean?"

"He can fascinate them. He calls them. Has the *Tuan* never heard of a *pahwang*?"

"No."

"But the *Tuan* has heard of snake-charmers, surely? Men who can play upon a gourd a tune that causes all snakes who hear it to come forth from their holes and hiding-places and gather round him; and as he plays they sit up as high as they can, and sway to and fro in time to the music. They dance indeed, in the way that a nautch girl dances with her whole body, but without moving her feet."

Richard Wheeler raised himself on his hand and stared Ibrahim in the eyes.

"You mean to tell me that Yussuf could attract a crocodile? Call it? Make it come out of the water? Make it come to his feet, as snake-charmers do snakes?"

"I do."

"Lies," growled Wheeler, and sank back again upon the ground. The good fellow was just talking to comfort him, of course; to humour him; to keep him from diving again into that terrible pool of death, where lurked the Thing that had destroyed Amai, destroyed his happiness, his life.

"I'm a liar, am I?" smiled Ibrahim.

"All men are liars," plagiarized the Malay, after a brief silence. "But at the moment I am speaking the truth. Much as the *Tuan* knows, he does not know everything, if he is ignorant of the powers of a *pahwang*. And old Yussuf is one of the greatest. Ask the Sakai, ask any jungle Malay from here down to the sea and up to the mountains."

"Have you ever seen Yussuf call a crocodile from the water?" asked Wheeler.

"Dozens of times," was the prompt reply. "Why, he calls the sacred crocodile of Bukit Lohor whenever he goes-up there, just to keep his hand in, or his voice, rather."

Wheeler, like everybody else in that part of the country, had heard of the sacred crocodile that dwelt at the mouth of the gorge of Bukit Lohor, where it had been known and respected, in fact worshipped, by several generations of the Bukit Lohor villagers.

Its size and age were proverbial and, unless grossly exaggerated by report, phenomenal.

Doubtless the brute was fed by the villagers at regular intervals and came up out of the water at such times, whether he were called or not. It would be easy enough for an artful old villain like Yussuf to establish a reputation as a crocodile-charmer, by taking up a safe position and there going through some mummery before, and until, the crocodile came out to be fed. That was probably the beginning and the end of the legend of his occult powers as a "fascinator" of crocodiles. . . . And yet nobody denied or doubted that snake-charmers could call forth snakes from the jungle; and the nature and attributes of both classes of reptile must be fairly similar.

"Are there many *pahwangs*?" he asked. "Do you know of others?"

"O-ho!" laughed Ibrahim, whom no tragedy depressed. "Plenty! Well, not to say plenty, but one here and there. I have known several myself."

"And they could all call crocodiles out of the water? Any crocodile?"

"Bless you, yes, *Tuan.* Any good *pahwang* can call a crocodile."

"At any time or place?"

"Surely. Any crocodile that hears the genuine call of a real *pahwang* has got to come."

Of course he must be going mad or he would never accept such nonsense as even possible, much less act upon it. He could scarcely believe his own ears as he heard himself bid Ibrahim spare neither trouble nor money to find Yussuf and bring him as quickly as possible.

"I'll give him anything he wants—all that I have—if he brings this crocodile out to where I can shoot it."

Not until darkness fell did Richard Wheeler return to his house. There he spent the night striding up and down the verandah, walking through the rooms, pausing only to finger things that had belonged to Amai; to pick them up, speak to them, replace them, and then resume his pacing. Her little gold-embroidered heelless shoes with the over-curling toe-points, brought tears to his eyes as he handled them. For some reason, they were more pathetic, more appealing than such other things as her bangles, neck-chains and other ornaments that lay upon her table, her girdle of heavy silver, her saris. As he picked up her needle-work, some fine embroidery in which still stuck the threaded needle as she had left it, he was only saved from a breakdown by a surging rush of red rage that started him again on the swift pacing of the verandah and watching the sky for the first pale streaks that should herald the dawn.

Most of the next day he spent in the water, in spite of Ibrahim's protests. Impossible for him to explain to the Malay that if he could but recover her body and give it Christian burial—or Mussulman burial—he might win the fight against the madness that was overwhelming him.

But what hopeless folly. A huge crocodile. . . .

When he could swim no more, he sat motionless and stared at the water, his rifle across his knees—a strange sight even to Malayan villagers. Tousled, unshorn, naked to the waist, madness blazing from the eyes that watched the water.

Again he spent the night in impatient waiting for the dawn, now sitting for a while in heartbroken grief, now striding up and down the house in seething rage. And again before dawn, he hurried to the river and crept silently as a ghost to where, with the coming of the light, he might see if the crocodile lay on the river bank or floated on the surface of the water.

This day he would spend in perfect silence and stillness, hoping that the reptile might come forth and bask, as sometimes they did, on mud-banks, in gravelly shallows, or with head protruding, by a river's edge.

That afternoon, Ibrahim, followed by Yussuf, cautiously approached the place where Richard Wheeler sat.

"He has come, *Tuan*," he whispered. "All will now be well, and the *Tuan* shall find peace. Be ready."

Bidding the other two remain silent and hidden, Yussuf walked down to the edge of the pool, took up his position some twenty yards from the water's edge, filled his lungs deeply and emitted a long low call. It was a strange and eerie cry, and Wheeler marvelled that so small and aged a man could produce not only so great a volume of sound, but could prolong the note at such inordinate length without pausing to draw breath.

Richard Wheeler found himself trembling violently, shaking from head to foot with so great a rigor that to have held his raised rifle steady would have been an impossibility.

What was this? Chill, malaria, or the fever of uncontrolled excitement?

The call died slowly away. There was a brief silence as Yussuf breathed swiftly and again deeply inhaled. A second time the long mournful insistent cry burst forth, and, to his own amazement, Wheeler felt that he must himself obey it, must rise to his feet and to go where Yussuf called.

He moved, and Ibrahim laid a restraining hand upon him while the long note prevailed, urgent, insistent, ineluctably demanding.

As for a second time it died down and ceased, completest silence reigned throughout the jungle.

A third time Yussuf lifted up his voice and uttered the strange cry, authoritative, irresistible and yet appealing.

That was it, decided Wheeler. It was an appeal; yet uttered with irresistible power; an appeal that was also a command which could not be disobeyed. And suddenly the surface of the water broke, a black nob appeared, a snout protruded, a great and terrible head rose clear of the water and Ibrahim's powerful hand closed on Wheeler's wrist.

"*Timsah!*" he whispered. "By Allah, it is the holy one. It is the sacred crocodile of Bukit Lohor."

The *pahwang's* cry grew louder, waxed and increased in intensity and power and demand. . . . The crocodile was swimming slowly, steadily, directly toward Yussuf.

As it reached the edge of the pool and raised its head and shoulders, the crocodile uttered an answering cry, a terrible bellowing roar as though simultaneously an angry lion and a wounded bison gave voice together.

Then only did the *pahwang* move.

Extending both his arms toward the crocodile, he made a waving motion with his hands, crossing and recrossing them, with the palms outward; and then, raising and lowering his hands, he made an imperious beckoning motion, the downward beckoning signal of the East.

As in obedience, the crocodile crawled up on to the bank,

clear of the water.

"Wait, *Tuan*," said Ibrahim, as, with shaking hand, Richard Wheeler moved to raise his rifle. "The *pahwang* will bring him to where you cannot miss, for they are hard to kill, even with the *biladi* rifles of the *Tuans*."

The *pahwang* now stood with both arms extended laterally, his head bent forward, the steady hypnotic gaze of his eyes concentrated upon those of the crocodile.

Slowly he brought his hands together and downward, so that they rested upon his knees. The crocodile moved forward.

The *pahwang* repeated the movement, and again the crocodile moved nearer, crawled slowly onward, until it came to rest not a yard from the man's feet.

With both hands extended as though to touch either side of the reptile's head, the *pahwang* paced slowly backward, insistently beckoning as he did so, with swiftly fluttering fingers that turned inward to touch his palms. As he moved, the crocodile followed. And, while Richard Wheeler stared fascinated, incredulous, the *pahwang* stepping backward, passed not six feet from the spot whereon he sat.

"Ready, *Tuan*! Ready!" whispered Ibrahim, as the *pahwang* again halted. There, apparently mesmerized, helpless, motionless, lay the enormous crocodile, broadside toward Richard Wheeler, and not six feet from the muzzle of his rifle.

With a tremendous mental and physical effort, he conquered his trembling, took steady aim at a spot just behind the huge fore-arm, and fired.

With a convulsive leap, surprising in so huge a carcase, the crocodile responded to the impact of the heavy bullet that, striking below the almost impenetrable back-armour, pierced the soft side behind the shoulder, and shattered the reptile's heart. As the body quivered into stillness, Richard Wheeler fired the second barrel of his express rifle at the creature's eye, and again a violent convulsive tremor and twitching ended in stillness.

The ancient and sacred crocodile of Bukit Lohor lay dead.

Leaping to his feet and roaring with laughter, Ibrahim smote Yussuf upon the shoulder.

"That is how a *pahwang* works, *Tuan*," he cried, "and our Yussuf is the greatest of all *pahwangs*. . . . I promised him that you would give him two dollars."

"He may have all the money that is in my house," replied Richard Wheeler. "And this rifle. You will find it here by the pool to-morrow morning."

"All the money and the rifle, *Tuan*?" gasped Ibrahim.

"Yes. And you may have the rest. All that is in my house."

That night, Richard Wheeler bathed, shaved and arrayed himself with care, and at moon-rise, taking Amai's shoes in his pocket and his rifle in his hand, went down to the bathing-pool.

On the edge of the steep bank where the water of the pool flows on as a swift river, he stood on the extreme verge with his back to the water, placed the butt of his rifle upon the ground, and bending over, pressed the trigger with his thumb.

East is East and West is West and there is danger whenever the twain shall meet.

ORDEAL BY WATER

"Ordeal by Water" is the story of a Sikh who falls in love with a Malay girl who is also the desire of a black panther "leopard-man" in a village in Malaysia. The Sikh eventually has a fight, in a lake, with a black panther. "Ordeal by Water" was previously published as the sixth story in Part I, "Queer", of Odd—But Even So *(1941).*

Of course, everyone in the amphibious village of Tambu knew that Ibrahim was a leopard-man. Nay more, Ahmit, who was a professional hunter when he wasn't doing just a little work at the tin-mines or at the dacoity—as in less happy lands a professional poacher might do a little work at the harvesting or pilchard-fishing—knew more. Not only was Ibrahim a leopard-man, but he was a bad specimen of the very worst form of leopard-man, a black-panther man. When asked by the other villagers how he knew, Ahmit laughed contemptuously at their stupidity, and pointed out that Ibrahim was too like one in his human manifestation for there to be any doubt about that. Wasn't he darker than other people, just as a black panther is darker than other leopards?

And in addition to the fact that his eyes were green and that he could see in the dark as ordinary leopard-men can, wasn't he more savage, more swift and silent and dangerous than other leopard-men, just as the black panther is more savage, swift, silent, and dangerous than other leopards?

But these weren't the only things. By no means the only things. And what was more, by no means the most important and convincing.

Ahmit knew something. He could tell a tale about Ibrahim if he chose to do so. And he went about the village looking important, and firmly refusing to disclose this intriguing piece of scandal concerning Ibrahim, a man feared and detested by everybody, and by no one so much as by Menah. In point of fact, Ahmit, a man of high courage, as are all Malays of his class, did not greatly care to talk about Ibrahim.

217

He wasn't really afraid of him, but he would rather have had trouble with any other man in the village than Ibrahim; and, while he would deny indignantly that he feared him, he admitted to himself that he was uncomfortable in his presence, didn't like meeting him on lonely jungle paths, and would have stretched his honour as far as possible in the matter of avoiding a quarrel with him.

Because, after all, it wasn't fair. A man's a man, and of no man on this earth was Ahmit afraid. But a leopard-man is a leopard-man, and anybody save a blazing fool is careful how he offends a leopard-man. And when that leopard-man is a black-panther man, well . . . !

So Ahmit kept his knowledge to himself until the Great *Tuan* sent Umrao Singh the Sikh to take up his official duties in that part of the world, chief of his duties being to keep an eye upon people like Ahmit himself, when pursuing one of his seasonal occupations such as dacoity, or when extending hospitality to Chinese gentlemen, missing from the distant tin-mines at the very time when the money-chest containing the mine-coolies' weekly wages was also missing.

Now, professional differences aside, Ahmit liked and admired Umrao Singh, a man after his heart, a man who could run like the wind, wrestle like the devil, and use his *chukra* with amazing skill.

This *chukra* fascinated Ahmit, who, until its uses were displayed to him by Umrao Singh, would never have imagined that a quoit could be a most deadly weapon of offence. But in Umrao Singh's practised hands, the quoit became a death-dealing missile, infinitely more alarming than a *kris*. Incidentally, it is quite possible that Umrao Singh considered a wavy-bladed *kris* to be a much uglier weapon than the *chukra*. For that, after all, is only a small flattened ring of steel of some twelve inches in diameter, its outer edge as sharp as a razor, the inner edge quite blunt. Nothing more than a little thin steel hoop. Nevertheless, when Umrao Singh threw it with the action of quoit-pitching, but with all his strength, and with a terrific spin on it, it went through the air with the speed and force of an arrow, and it struck not only with great violence but with the cutting action of a circular saw.

Without the spinning action it would have inflicted a very nasty gash. With the spinning action, it was about seven times more destructive, dangerous and deadly. As a buzz-saw slices through a log, so the spinning quoit sheers through flesh and bone. To the Gurkha his *kukri*, to the Malay his *kris*.

That evening, after a long discussion on the interesting subject of opium, to the use of which drug both were addicted, Ahmit raised the subject of the character and conduct, personality and powers of the black-avised and sinister Ibrahim.

"See that man?" said he, pointing, as Ibrahim slunk furtively along in the shadows of the village street.

Umrao Singh, in his fingers a pellet of opium which he was about to eat--for he held the smoking of opium to be an abuse of a wonderful health-promoting and fever-preventing drug— looked down from the rickety verandah of Ahmit's house on which they were sitting.

"Yes. What about him?"

"He's a leopard-man."

"*Wah, wah!*" replied the Sikh. "I have heard of such people. We have tiger-men in India."

"And I'll tell you another thing about him, and you must make a note of it, and act accordingly when the time comes. He's going to murder me."

"Oh? Why?"

"Do you notice how he walks?"

"Yes. Left foot turned in a trifle. Gives him a slight limp."

"Well, I did that for him."

"How?"

"Shot him."

"Well then, it looks as though it was *you* who tried to murder *him*. No wonder he intends to get you. You've no right to go about shooting people, you know, Ahmit, just because you don't like them."

"Ah, but it wasn't as Ibrahim the Man that I shot him. It was as the Black Panther."

"What do you mean?"

"Well, surely you've heard of the Black Panther that haunts these parts."

"I did hear something about it. Some silly fool told me not to ride my bicycle down the jungle path after dark because of a black panther or some such nonsense."

"Well, he gave you good advice. He was warning you against *the* Black Panther."

Silence . . .

"One moonlight night I was out with my gun," observed Ahmit.

"What for?"

"Oh, pigeon-shooting."

"What, at night time? With a rifle?"

"That's it," grinned Ahmit. "And just as I was coming to the end of the village there, I saw something move on a branch of that banyan tree. It's the big branch that points straight toward this hut. The moonlight was full on it; and, standing quite still and staring hard, I saw it was the Black Panther, and that it had turned its head and was looking at me. I raised my gun and fired. And as I did so, it dropped down from the tree.

"Well, I thought I was done for, because its moving had disturbed my aim, and any man with an unloaded gun ten yards from any black panther is in an unhealthy position.

"But instead of springing at me as an ordinary panther would have done, it slunk between the roots of the banyan, and disappeared. It may have bounded off on the other side, keeping the great trunk of the tree between itself and me; or it may just have got well into the middle of that great cluster of roots and branches and turned back into Ibrahim the leopard-man."

"How do you know it wasn't frightened off by the bang of your gun? You must have missed it."

"Well, I didn't miss it. And I'll tell you how I know. Ibrahim didn't come out of his hut next morning, and when Suliman looked in, because he thought he heard someone groaning, he found that Ibrahim was lying on his mat, up in the corner, and that he was wounded. He had been shot in the foot.

"Then I knew that what everybody had suspected was absolutely proved. Ibrahim was the Black Panther. And I had shot him."

The Sikh grunted non-committally.

"And do you know why he was lying along the branch of that banyan staring at my hut?"

"Waiting for you?"

"No. For Menah my sister. That's what he was waiting for."

"Why was he doing that?"

"Because he wants her."

"Well, why should he wait up in the tree as a black panther?"

"To spring on her and carry her off when she came out in the morning to go down to the river. Drag her away into the jungle. Then turn himself back into Ibrahim, and frighten her to death. She'd be so frightened that she'd do anything he ordered; and she'd never dare to say a word about it, either. She'd know that at any moment he could turn himself into a black panther and tear her to pieces. She has always had a childish dislike of being torn to pieces by a leopard or a tiger."

"*Has* she now?"

"A sort of fear, I mean."

"And Ibrahim still wants Menah, does he?"

"Oh yes. . . . As we have no parents, he asked me for her hand, you know. Made a very good offer, too. But Menah said she'd kill herself the very same day that I turned her over to him. Women are like that, you know—faddy."

The two men fell silent, and while Ahmit prepared the sizzling pill for his opium pipe, the big Sikh chewed his uncooked one.

Ahmit finished his pipe in three deep luxurious inhalations of the black smoke.

"So if you find me down there one morning, clawed to death, you'll know. I have been murdered," said Ahmit. "And you'll know who the murderer is, and you must see that he is hanged."

"You can't arrest a black panther, try it for murder and hang it, you know," observed the Sikh.

"No, that's where you've got to be smart. These wizards that have the power to turn themselves into animals can only do it between sunset and sunrise. He can turn himself back into a man whenever he likes, but it is only at night that he can turn himself into a leopard, so you'll have to arrest Ibrahim in the daytime."

"H'm," mused the Sikh. "I don't know about arresting Ibrahim in the daytime because a leopard had killed you in the night."

"No, it's all very difficult, really, isn't it?" sighed Ahmit.

"And if I just shot Ibrahim now, when he comes back, you'd arrest me as a murderer, I suppose."

"Have to. What you want to do is to shoot him while he's a panther."

"That's what I want to do, but he's not going to give me a second chance."

"Suppose you killed him as a panther, would he be dead as Ibrahim?" asked the Sikh.

"Oh yes. If I shot that panther through the brain, I should really be shooting Ibrahim through the brain, and he'd be dead."

"What? Would there be the dead body of a man lying where you had shot a black panther?"

"No, the black panther would be there all right, just where I shot him."

"And where would Ibrahim be?"

"There. That would be Ibrahim; and Ibrahim, as a man, would never be seen again."

"Oh, I understand. Yes. That's very interesting."

"But if, on the other hand, you only wound the black panther, you also wound Ibrahim," mused Umrao Singh.

"Yes, of course. The black panther is Ibrahim. Don't you see, when I shot the black panther that night, I must have hit it in the foot, just as it rose up and dropped from the branch.

"In the morning, what did we find?" continued Ahmit. "Ibrahim had been shot in the foot. He had changed back into a man and hobbled into his hut."

"Suppose he couldn't have walked?" asked the Sikh, who had a certain contempt for these jungle superstitions, but was uncomfortably aware that he by no means rejected them; not whole-heartedly and with amusement, as his white Superintendent of Police would do.

"Then he'd have lain there until somebody came along—and he'd have told some lie about a dacoit having shot him and run away."

"Well," rumbled the Sikh, after the somewhat slow and cumbrous machinery of his very good brain had creaked and revolved, "what you had better do is to lay for the Black Panther and shoot it dead. That, according to you, will put an end to Ibrahim, and certainly won't put you in any danger of the Law of the *Tuans*. . . . They don't understand why there are times when killings are right, proper, and desirable. They just make a hard and fast law that you must not kill; and if you break it, you are killed yourself.

"That doesn't apply to black panthers though," he added, as he stroked his fine curling beard which had never known the razor.

"Ibrahim wants Menah, does he?" he asked suddenly.

"Yes, he is going to kill me and then get her; because there will be no one to stop him."

"Won't there?" replied Umrao Singh.

§2

The whole subject of the Black Panther would have faded from Umrao Singh's mind, but for the matter of Ahmit's sister.

Umrao Singh was a Ludhiana Sikh; his faith as much a part of his mind as his blood was of his body; the *Granth* the one and only Truth, "*Khalsa ji ki fateh*" the only slogan and war-cry; uncut hair the only possible kind of hair for a man who would save his soul by True Religion; and an iron bangle the only ornament.

Nevertheless, true and fanatically religious *akhali* though he might be, holder of the tenets of the highest and purest form of Hinduism, whole-hearted despiser of Mussulmans and all other unbelievers, he had fallen in love with an Infidel lass, daughter and sister of Mussulmans and, so far as a woman can have any religion at all, a Mussulman herself.

Had he never left Mother India, had he lived within visiting distance of the Golden Temple of Amritsar, lived in the Punjab, a man of Lahore, Ludhiana or Patiala, or out in the mofussil in any village of the Doab, leading the life of a Sikh among Sikhs, he would never have cast the eye of favour upon an Infidel, and followed after strange women. He would have married a Sikh girl, and been to her a splendid husband, a magnificent father of her sons.

But here, in this jungle hole, this wretched village, where there wasn't so much as a Hindu *bunnia*, let alone a Sikh, things were different. Strictly religious or not, a man is a man; Umrao Singh was very much of a man, and Menah a very beautiful girl.

And about Menah, Umrao Singh thought constantly—thought of little else, in fact, until she became an obsession, a burning and beautiful *idée fixe*.

And this dog, Ibrahim, was making offers for her, was making promises and threats; promises of what he would give her brother Ahmit if he consented, and helped him to attain his chief desire; threats of what he would do to him unless that desire was soon consummated.

"Ibrahim," growled Umrao Singh aloud, as he strolled through the brief twilight along the path toward the village of Tambu, "let that Infidel dog be . . ."

And suddenly, Umrao Singh froze into immobility as though turned to stone, for in the gathering dusk a shadow moved—and then froze into immobilty exactly as he himself had done, crouched, quivered and gathered' itself to spring.

Oh, fool that he had been! Treble fool; offender of the gods; that he should have allowed this to come to pass, that he should have met the Black Panther face to face and he unarmed.

Even as the panther crouched to spring, Umrao Singh's right hand shot up to his turban, and took from its folds the quoit that was always there, the piece of sacred iron that every Sikh must carry.

And almost in the same swift action, he flung it with all his strength at the panther's head as the beast quivered for the spring.

Through the air shot the heavy razor-edged flat ring of iron, spinning like a circular saw as it went. With an audible thud, it struck the panther in the face, the terrific cutting power of its swiftly moving edge—driven forward by its travelling momentum, and driven sideways by its spin—causing the quoit to embed itself deeply, cutting the creature's right eye in halves, and penetrating almost to the brain.

With a tremendous snarl the panther recoiled, rolled, tearing at the ground, and striking at this terrible thing that was blinding it, and Umrao Singh, turning, fled for his life, ran a mile, climbed a tree, and remained in it till dawn. For he knew that there is no more cunning and vengeful beast than the wounded panther, unless it be the *seladang*, which in India they call the buffalo.

By daylight he descended from his tree, boldly strode along

the path to the village—for in daylight there is safety—found his blood-stained *chukra* at the spot where he had defended himself from the panther; and, going to the house of Ahmit, told him of the adventures of the night.

"You threw the steel ring and heard it strike the Black Panther's face?"

"Yes, with that thud which tells that it has struck home."

"And, wounded, it rolled as wounded panthers do, and you fled and climbed a tree. And that was nearly twelve hours ago. . . . Will you come with me and visit the house of Ibrahim?"

"I will," said Umrao Singh.

They found Ibrahim in a bad way and desperately in need of such help as they could give him.

Holding the once white sleeve of an old *baju* across his right eye, as he lay upon his blood-stained mat, he told, between groans, how he had been attacked by gang-robbers, Chinese; how he had put up a desperate fight until slashed across the face with a knife.

Umrao Singh and Ahmit looked at each other across the prostrate man, with raised eyebrows and complete absence of comment; but Umrao Singh nodded his head with a slow and heavy acquiescence.

But however puzzled and perturbed, however closely driven to unwilling belief he might be, here was a badly wounded man who must be helped; and to the best of his somewhat limited ability, Umrao Singh gave First Aid and all other aid that Ibrahim got in that village, where he was most unpopular among compatriots in any case somewhat callous.

And in an incredibly short time, blind in one eye, hideously scarred from the centre of his forehead to the middle of his right cheek, Ibrahim recovered in the amazing way that horribly-wounded and terribly-neglected village jungle-dwellers are apt to do.

A fortnight after receiving the injury he crawled out of his hut and sat about in the sun; and a week or two later, was going about his business, now one-eyed as well as lame, but more sinister than ever.

Meanwhile, Umrao Singh's suit prospered. The village Jessica had found her Lorenzo, and the Sikh Cophetua his beggar maiden. And Ahmit, a broad-minded man (who had had a love-affair of his own with a Siamese girl who was a hell-doomed Infidel of a Buddhist just as Umrao Singh was unfortunately a hell-doomed Infidel of a Hindu) raised no objection. On the contrary.

§3

"I'll sharpen it for you," said Ahmit, taking the quoit from the Sikh. "I'm a wonderful one at putting an edge on blades."

And Umrao Singh thanked him, left the *chukra* in his hands and went about his business, which took him to the next village some seven miles distant.

As he walked along, consciously enjoying the early coolness of the morning, he turned and looked behind him. People often do this and are usually surprised to find that there is some reason for turning round. Sometimes there is no apparent reason, and they wonder why they did it.

But Umrao Singh instantly saw why he had turned. He had heard nothing, smelt nothing, and had had no reason for turning, but there, within fifty yards of him, was the Black Panther, and, a most unusual thing in broad daylight, it was following him. Steadily and purposefully it was coming after him at a quick walk.

Instinctively putting his hand up to his turban, he remembered that his quoit was in Ahmit's house. Swiftly glancing round, he saw no tree that would not be as easy for the panther to climb as for himself.

What should he do?

He was a notable runner, and he turned and ran as he had never run before. If the panther bounded after him at top speed, it would be a short run.

The path turned and ran beside a lake. Into the lake rushed Umrao Singh, flung himself forward as the water deepened, and swam with all his strength toward a small island.

In India, tigers swim across rivers, but he had never heard of panthers doing so.

Glancing back as he turned to swim side-stroke, he saw that this panther was doing so, was swimming with amazing speed, was overtaking him.

As his feet touched bottom, and he scrambled forward, the panther reached him, still swimming, clawed at him and ripped his wet clothing.

Turning about, Umrao Singh, the water up to his waist, flung himself forward upon the panther, seized its head with both his strong hands, and forced it under the water.

And then began a struggle great and grim, Homeric, between an unarmed man and a black panther, a panther that strove to get foothold for a spring, a man that strove to prevent this and to keep the beast's great head under water.

Well was it for Umrao Singh in this terrible hour that he was a trained wrestler, a man whose prowess was known from Sialkot to Ludhiana, from Ambala to Multan; that he was in splendid form and fettle; and that, against his sound common sense and rational experience, he believed that he was fighting with the human devil who coveted and intended to possess the girl whom Umrao Singh loved.

At times, both were under water as the panther dragged him down. At times, Umrao Singh was on his feet, and with mighty grip on both ears of the beast, held its head beneath the surface until its tremendous writhings and struggles threw him off his balance.

And for once, in a fight between unarmed man and powerful savage beast, conditions were in the man's favour. For when he was on his feet, his head was above the water and he could use his great strength to deadly purpose; while the beast, when on its feet, was under water, and was hampered in its power to strike.

One blow from those mighty paws would have disembowelled the man, clawed his face off, torn his chest from his ribs, but, so swift, untiring, and skilful was his wrestling, that the panther had no chance to strike, its struggles being directed to save itself from drowning.

And at last Umrao Singh got his hold, the grip he wanted and the stance. At arm's length, beneath the water, he held both fore-arms of the tiring leopard. His body upon the back of the brute's head and neck, he held it beneath the water; held his own breath as he went under, gulped mightily, as his head emerged, and all the while strained with every nerve and sinew to keep the animal beneath him, to keep it from shaking free, getting to its hind legs, climbing up him, as it were.

Once it could rear itself on end like that, he would be beaten, for no man can stand up to a leopard that fixes its fore-claws into his shoulders and with its hind-claws tears out his entrails while its great fangs sink into his throat.

And as the champion wrestler holds his failing opponent, holds him, tires him, weakens him, even though he has air to breathe, so Umrao Singh held the leopard's fore-paws as in a vice, held its head beneath the water as weakening, drowning, dying, its struggles grew less nearly successful . . . grew less terrible . . . grew feebler . . . died away . . . ceased.

And when at length Umrao Singh, himself exhausted almost to the point of collapse, released his hold, staggered back, and fell to the ground at the edge of the water, the leopard was dead.

When, having recovered breath and some measure of his strength, during which time he had never taken his eyes from where the great beast lay almost entirely submerged, he rose to his feet and dragged it to the water's edge, he found that it was, as he had supposed, the same leopard that he had before encountered.

Its right eye was closed, the fur about it scarred. . . .

It is a coincident and established fact that one Ibrahim, black-avised rogue of Tambu village, lame and one-eyed, disappeared at that time and was never seen again.

Whether there be educated and intelligent people who believe that there are men who can turn themselves into animals or not, there are surely none who believe that an unarmed man can fight and kill a black panther? Nevertheless, should anyone care to verify the fact, he will, on consulting the London press of Tuesday, November 9th, 1937, find the following:

"An Indian in the Malay State of Perak took refuge in a jungle pool from a black panther, which, however, followed him into the water. A terrific struggle followed, but finally the native managed to hold the animal under water long enough to drown it, says a Reuter message from Singapore."

AS IN A GLASS CLEARLY

"As in a Glass Clearly" is a story where the narrator, in a dream, relates the battle known as Wilson's Last Stand, or the Shangani Patrol, which occurred in December 1893 during the First Matabele War.[28] Wren's account of the battle differs slightly in the number of men involved (Wren has 80, while the real number was 37), and in the name of one of the commanders (Wren has Burroughs instead of Borrow). "As in a Glass Clearly" was previously published as the seventh, and last, story in Part I, "Queer", of Odd—But Even So *(1941).*

Since the proper study of mankind is Man, there is surely no department of human study more interesting and, indeed, more important, than that of his dreams, for the psycho-therapists tell us, and undoubtedly rightly, that dreams are cartoons drawn by the unconscious mind and presented to the conscious mind for its enlightenment, information, and guidance.

Unfortunately, it happens nine times out of ten, or more probably, ninety-nine times out of a hundred, that the unconscious mind is a poor cartoonist, or else that the conscious mind is a poor interpreter of the meaning of cartoons; the result being that, far more often than not, our dreams are completely meaningless to us.

To the interested and earnest enquirer, the, psycho-analyst may be of great help, and may be able to explain to the dreamer the true significance of his dream, just as a father can explain the meaning of a newspaper cartoon to his child who wants to know what it is all about. Joseph was the first recorded psycho-therapist, and the Pharaoh who sent for him the first candidate for dream psycho-analysis.

But undeniably, there are exceptions to the rule that dreams are cartoons of esoteric meaning which must be sought with skill and patience; for there is a type of dream, rare but existent, which is a prophecy; and there is another which is a vision, or rather one in which a vision is presented to the mind's eye, while the

---

[28] http://en.wikipedia.org/wiki/Wilson%27s_last_stand

physical eye is closed in darkness.

In the former class of dream, things which have not yet happened are accurately seen in the act of happening; in the latter, still more rare, perhaps, things which are actually happening far away are seen as though the dreamer was present in the flesh, and literally an eye-witness.

It seems to me undeniable that these two classes of rare and remarkable dreams are in a category wholly different from that of the ordinary dream dreamt nightly by countless millions of people, wherein the cartoon, usually uncomprehended if not incomprehensible, is presented by the unconscious mind.

It is concerning one of these extremely uncommon, quite inexplicable and intensely interesting dreams that I wish to tell; one belonging to the class of true visions, the beholding in fullest detail, as though by an eye-witness, of events actually happening in another place.

A point that adds a little further interest to this amazingly interesting dream is the fact that I dreamt it in the daytime. Though it was none the less a genuine dream, there was no question of any sort of clairvoyance, second-sight, or waking-vision about the matter.

I was ill, and had a temperature, whether due to influenza, malaria, or by reason of incapacitating accident, I do not remember. What I do remember, is that I had been awake and in pain, probably severe headache, all night, and that I slept during the day.

I was not in the habit of taking a siesta, and do not suppose that, from year's end to year's end, I slept between daybreak and night, save as in this instance, when suffering from illness or accident. That morning I had taken either quinine or some analgesic, and quite possibly, whether intentionally or unintentionally, some form of narcotic. What I mean is, that the doctor had given me something to allay pain and fever, and perhaps something else to induce sleep.

This is what I dreamt, and I tell it here without embellishment—as without explanation.

Quite suddenly, without any preliminary dream that I can

remember, I was one of a party of mounted men; with them but not of them; able to see everything, myself unseen; to hear everything, myself unable to speak. And this was the only dream-like aspect of this amazing dream; for, save for this degree of unreality, everything was *real*. Many a man, sick, absent-minded or weary, has taken actual part in real events, and seen, heard, known, and remembered, less of them than I did of what happened in this dream.

I was aware that there were twenty-five files of troopers, a man riding out on each flank, a Leader riding ahead, and another man riding behind as a sort of rearguard scout. Exactly where I rode I do not know, for I was riding with all of them. Not only was I there but I was everywhere—with the Leader, with the flanking scouts, with the man who rode in the rear, and with the small main body. I was with each of these fifty-four men. I heard what he said. I saw what he did and, moreover, I knew what he was thinking.

The Leader was brave, cool, resolute—and anxious. His was not the courage that recognizes fear, grapples with it, and overcomes it. It was not the type of courage that enables men, cold with fright, to seem cool; speechless with terror, to appear silent with the strength that avoids the shouting of unnecessary orders. This Leader was brave simply because he did not know what fear was. He had no fear to conquer. But nevertheless he was anxious.

I was aware that the same kind of courage infused the man who was away out on the right flank. Like the Leader, he knew himself to be in gravest peril of imminent death, but he was not afraid. The certainty that his end was at hand interested him more than the knowledge that his breakfast was, but it perturbed him no more. Fear was not a sensation that came within his experience.

On the other hand, the man who was riding away out on the left flank was afraid. His fear was not that he might be slain and perhaps tortured, but that he might show fear. I knew, in the amazing way that one does know things in dreams, that he was visualizing with horror a horrid death. He didn't want to die. He was afraid to die. But far more was he afraid of showing this. And I knew that when the end came, he would make as good a showing as any man of that doomed patrol. And the word "showing" was the *mot juste*. He would be deliberately making a show of that cold unflinching courage that was natural to the others, and I wondered whether he was not therefore a braver man than they who were all so brave.

I was then, or rather simultaneously, aware of the rearguard scout, aware of his personality, psychology and mental attitude. Like the Leader and the first flanking scout, he was utterly unperturbed, was either incapable of fear, or unaware of any cause for it, in spite of the fact that he knew that he, like the others, was in the greatest danger, and that escape from early and violent death was improbable. In that he was not interested. His concern was with his business of scouting, of keeping watch and ward against danger from the rear.

With regard to the rank-and-file of the troopers, there was complete uniformity of courage, and, at the same time, variety.

There was the courage that is an "absolute"; the bravery that is complete, and is shewn by the type of man whose courage is perfect because, for him, fear does not exist. This was displayed—though here, displayed is a misleading term, since there was no display whatever—by the old hands, men so inured to danger that they thought of it no more than of the air they breathed.

The most different variety of courage was that of the youngest men, the kind that might be called the manufactured article, the constructed, the screwed-up courage, which enables its possessors, albeit frightened, to show as calm a front and cool a bearing as those of the others.

These men, whose imaginations were their enemies, men who at heart were afraid, were for the most part relatively inexperienced, some of them boys in their teens. Though afraid, they were as brave as the veterans. Though nervous and perturbed, they were as cool and calm as their elders. Fearing and hating mutilation, torture and death, they wore the air and appearance of those who were above hate and fear.

All were equally brave in their different ways, unless indeed, the young and frightened men were the braver.

Not heroes in bronze, but bronzed heroes in the flesh, the flesh from which their brave spirits were about to part.

One trooper, little more than a boy, probably the youngest of all, interested me particularly, perhaps even more than did the Leader, that heroic man to whose preoccupations was added the burden of responsibility. The boy's name I knew to be Laurence, but in curious dream-fashion, I did not know whether this was his christian or his surname—and I have hitherto been unable to find out.

His beardless face was sensitive as well as strong, fine as well as bold and resolute. To my mind, he was the handsomest man of that half-hundred of handsome men; and splendid as was the general physique, his was among the best. Though scarcely grown to full strength and stature, he looked to be one of the strongest and was among the biggest of them all.

And reading his thoughts, I knew that he was afraid.

He was afraid lest, in the ultimate agony, he might flinch.

Let it not be thought that he had any fear of death. It was of life that he was afraid; life spoilt by knowledge of some failure in the hour that was approaching. He did not want to die; but before all things, he wanted to die well, if die he must. . . . In my dream or vision I knew all this as though I were reading it in a book. . . .

Suddenly the rearguard scout wheeled about, put his rein in the crook of his left elbow and raised his rifle. I have forgotten now (but I knew then) whether it was a Lee-Enfield magazine rifle, or a single-loading Martini Henry. I think the latter.

Riding away from the little column to a small mound, he stood up in his stirrups, shaded his eyes with his hand, and soon satisfied himself as to the nature of the body of men rapidly approaching from the right rear.

Having done so, he wheeled about, and galloped to the Leader.

"Reinforcement," he said, with a sketchy salute. "Officer and twenty-six men."

By his voice and intonation I knew that he was an American.

"Right, Ingram," the Leader smiled. It was like this good scout to report so much in so few words . . . An officer and twenty-six men. That would bring his force to eighty men. Himself and eighty men. And the enemy would be more like eight thousand. A hundred to one, and any number of hundreds more.

The thirteen files of the newcomers galloped up and fell in at the rear of the column, and their officer rode up to the front. He was of the right type to command such men as these. He looked about five-and-twenty, and distinctly I remember his moustache, big and black and curling, the Cavalry moustache of the day.

"Hullo, Burroughs," said the Leader.

"Morning, Major."

And just then I knew, in the curious fashion of dreams, that the Leader's name was Alan or Allen.

"Shangaani's rising very fast," said the officer addressed as Burroughs. "All that rain. We only just got across. . . ."

Suddenly the Leader threw up his hand. The column halted, and at the same time, the two scouts riding out on the flanks, came galloping in. There was no need for them to report "Enemy in sight," the enemy suddenly being only too clearly in sight of the whole column.

From the shelter of donga and spruit and river-bank, from behind kopje and boulder and bush, sprang up the plumed warriors. It was as though the earth itself, sown with the dragon's teeth of Cadmus, produced this swift fearful harvest.

Almost in less time than it takes to tell, a landscape of baked and yellow earth, of sear and greying thorn-bush, of dwarf scrub, acacia, boulder and gravel and sand and sun-baked clay, sterile and dead, came to life, moved and seethed and swarmed and teemed with men, each man a great stalwart warrior, each warrior covered by a mighty shield, and clasping in his left hand a bunch of assegais, while brandishing high above his head his bright-bladed stabbing spear. Thousands and thousands and thousands, whose tread seemed to shake the earth, whose deep-throated roar might well have shaken the hearts and the courage of the bravest men.

At a signal from the Leader, the files clotted into fours, the fours closed up, and as the Leader turned about, he faced a small and compact squadron four men wide and twenty horses deep.

"Form circle," he ordered; and, riding out to left and right, the fours again became files, the files a single line, and in a minute, the oblong block was a circle complete and unbroken, the horses standing head to tail.

"*Prepare to dismount. Dismount.*"

Drill as steady as on parade—this last parade of these disciplined men, some of whom were cavalry soldiers; some, highly-trained mounted-police constables; some, youths who, but recently, were recruits to this little army that had fought Lobengula and his fierce Matabele.

Then, in the same harsh voice, cold and unemotional, came the terrible order, the order that was also the death-warrant of those brave men.

"*Shoot your horses.*"

And, without hesitation, each man drew the heavy revolver from the holster at his belt, put it to his horse's temple, and pulled the trigger.

Some had to fire twice; but, almost as the fusillade ended, every horse but five, those of "Alan", Burroughs, and the three scouts lay dead in a ring, and behind them crouched the men who had ridden them so often and so far. And in more than one pair of those hard eyes there was moisture that collected in the corners.

What had been a squadron of horses bearing armed riders was now a parapet of flesh. The noble beasts that had carried their masters, and that had so often saved them in life, now protected them in death.

Was there incongruity in the thought that those splendid troopers and their fine horses had in their lives been beautiful and in their deaths were not to be divided?

And now, around the two officers and the three scouts, all still mounted, lay a ring of men prepared to receive the attack of hosts innumerable from every point of the compass.

Many of these men's faces were bearded and expressionless. Most wore heavy moustaches that hid their mouths. Some of the faces were hairless and their expression plain to be seen.

The boy Laurence, though able to hide the fear that was in his heart, was totally unable to conceal the misery, the grief, the horror that overwhelmed him; as his faithful friend, his "long-faced chum," as the British trooper calls his horse, lay quivering in death.

His own mouth quivered also. Tears overflowed from his eyes. As he lay awaiting orders, his rifle across the body of his horse, he put his head down upon his arm; and, as I looked away,

I noticed that his shoulders heaved.

The Leader turned to one of the scouts.

"I want you, Burnham," he said, "to ride for it, with Ingram and Gooding. Try to cut your way through. Get back to Major Forbes' column. Tell him how things are—and he will know what to do.

"If there is anything he can do," he added quietly.

And without a word, as though they had been sent with some peace-time despatch from one camp to another, the three men rode out from the little *laager*, put spurs to their horses and charged straight at the oncoming Matabele, sword in the right hand, revolver in the other.

And I knew that, impossible as it seemed, these three men fought their way through the Matabele *impis*, swam the now raging Shangaani River and rode on to where Major Forbes' column was encamped—only to find it the centre of a fierce attack by another huge Matabele army. Unscathed, but with reddened swords and emptied revolvers, they charged headlong through this enormous force, galloped beneath a storm of bullets and assegais, rode into Major Forbes' *laager*, and delivered their message. Offering their lives, the three saved them, for after a day and a half of fighting, the enemy were beaten off—too late. Too late for Major Forbes to send the help for which they had come to ask.

Too late. Even as Burnham, Ingram and Gooding cut their way through the Matabele surrounding, "Alan's" little band, they charged; charged right up to the breast-work of dead horses behind which the troopers lay, flung their assegais, thrust with, their stabbing spears, and fell in dozens, in scores, in hundreds, to add a rampart of dead men to that of the dead horses.

So swift, so accurate, was the fire from the eighty British rifles, that the Matabele recoiled and fled to the cover of the kopjes, the bushes and the dead ground from which they had advanced, giving a breathing-space to the defenders of the *laager*, giving time for their rifles to cool, time for them to take a drink from their water-bottles, time for a glance round to see who was hit, who was alive.

One thing seen by those who glanced inward, was that the Leader and Burroughs had shot their horses in the middle of the ring, forming a last rallying-place and citadel, and adding to the confidence, if that were possible, of their followers.

"*There's no discharge in the war.*"

There was to be no retreat from this fight. There was to be no escape. There was to be no survivor.

Unless help came from without. . . .

The Matabele charged again. Again the rattle of rifle-fire from the *laager* was so rapid and continuous that it was more like that of machine-guns.

Again the massed charging *impis* wavered and broke, as the warriors fell in dozens, in scores, in hundreds, strewing the plain and building the wall; building a rampart of dead bodies, and building a rampart over which the living would charge when the volume of the defenders' fire grew too weak to stop them.

And ever nearer and more boldly crept and crawled, from bush to bush, and from stone to stone, those Matabele warriors who were armed with rifles, with smooth-bore guns, with a variety of weapons ranging from sporting guns, looted from the home of slaughtered settlers, to the ancient muzzle-loading *roers* with which their slain Boer owners had hunted big game.

Poor marksmen, but so large a target, so short a range. . . .

Of the dead within the *laager*, the dead who lay facing the foe, their hands still grasping their rifles, some were transfixed with far-flung assegais, some stabbed to the heart or through the throat with short stabbing spears, some shot through head and breast with soft leaden bullet and slug of every shape and size.

And round the circle, between attacks, went the two officers, collecting bandoliers from the dead, easing the dying, helping the wounded, cheering and enheartening the living.

Nor did they make pretence that help would come; that this was anything but the end; the last stand and glorious death.

And again arose the great and terrifying roar from thousands of bass voices as, with the thunder of the stamp of feet and the clash of spear on shield, the Matabele host again charged the little group. And again the rapid rifle-fire made defiant reply.

Again the dauntless spearmen swarmed up to the rampart of dead men and dead horses, thrusting, stabbing, hurling their assegais at close range. And now some of the survivors, their ammunition expended, met them hand-to-hand with swung gun-butt, white men falling as spears transfixed them, black men as heavy rifles crashed upon their skulls.

Others of the fallen defenders, kneeling or lying, were using their revolvers at point-blank range, their empty rifles useless, dropped from hands too weak to wield them as clubs.

Many yet lay prone behind their horses, shooting as swiftly as they could load and fire, their rifle-ammunition running low. . . .

Was this the end, the last charge that, sweeping across the low barrier, would stamp them flat, annihilate them?

No, once again rifle, revolver, and Heruclean, Homeric hand-to-hand fighting with the rifle-butt drove them back.

And, as once more they retreated, making opportunity for their own riflemen to pick off the survivors, a big bearded trooper rose to his feet and stood swaying, blood pouring down his face, running down his neck and dripping from his beard, down his chest, spreading over his shirt, and his bare forearms.

"Cowards," he shouted in Matabele, "Women! Boys! *Umfanes!*" dropped his empty rifle, raised his empty revolver, staggered forward as though to pursue the retreating enemy, and fell dead.

The Leader stood up in the middle of the circle.

"Close in," he said, and seven men, rising up at his word, joined him and lay down behind the two dead chargers that he and Burroughs had shot.

Across his own horse lay Burroughs, not dead but too weak from loss of blood to do more than feebly fumble with the revolver that he was trying to load.

Hastily, the Leader went round the outer circle, collected what little ammunition was left in bandolier and pouch, and then rejoined the others, as once more the Matabele charged like a pack of wolves upon a wounded stag at bay.

Halting within a few yards of the rifles and revolvers fired with superhuman speed and unerring accuracy, they hurled their assegais in such numbers that they fell like hail upon the little group.

One by one, rifle and revolver fell to earth as its owner received his last and mortal wound. And still a man, resting on one hand, would raise the other and fire his revolver; a man would shake his head as though to clear his brain, wipe his arm across his eyes as though to clear them from the mists of death; and would fire his rifle once again.

And suddenly, with spontaneous rush, the vast horde, as though at word of command, charged in once more, with stabbing-spear and knobkerry raised aloft. With a roar of *"Bulati! Bulati!* Kill! Kill!"* they charged in, that great army— upon one man. One man who, unwounded, rose to his feet and fought, desperately, heroically, clubbed rifle against knobkerry and spear, a rifle which whirled about his head in a circle that, for prolonged seconds, kept his foes at bay; a rifle that rose and fell, crashing like the hammer of Thor upon the head of the man after man who faced him.

It was Laurence. So active, so powerful was he, that his end *was* a fight and not a murder. Alone in the heart of that black mass of savage warriors he kept his footing, he struck, he fought, he killed. Dying, he slew those who slew him.

He need have had no fear of fear. He made as brave an end as ever man made before or since.

When, wounded in a dozen places, he fell to his knees, his head held high, and the spear-points met in his heart, he died happily, consenting to death but conquering agony.

And the Matabele, brave men who honour the brave, forbore to stab his corpse.

"This was a lion," cried an *induna*, as he stood over him. "They were all lions, *abagati*—wizards—rather than men!" And spontaneously, the warriors, crowding in a packed ring about the last of the white *inamasoja*, raised their stabbing spears aloft, point uppermost, in salute to the dead.

In this amazing dream I had seen, as in a vision, and as though an eye-witness, Wilson's Last Stand. Later, I learned that his christian, name was Alan.

MEANING OF DREAMS

"Meaning of Dreams" is taken from an article published in the Australian newspaper, The Central Queensland Herald, *on Thursday, February 9, 1939. In this article, Wren writes about two of his "dreams" in particular detail. One of the dreams is an abridged version of the previous story, "As in a Glass Clearly." The other dream is a "prophetic" dream concerning his father. That particular dream was referenced in an article, "Do Dreams Foretell the Future", published in another Australian newspaper,* The Courier-Mail *(Brisbane), on Friday, December 26, 1952. The version of the article reprinted here contains a reference to the article being published earlier in* The Daily Mail *(London), but that particular version has not been discovered as of July 2012.*

The British Union of Practical Psychologists recently held its annual conference. These gentlemen, most of them, fortunately, are qualified doctors, heal the body through the mind, and concern themselves mainly with that part of the mind known as the unconscious. They are usually referred to as psycho-therapists and psycho-analysts, writes P. C. Wren, author of "Beau Geste," in the "Daily Mail."

As practical healers, they diagnose the condition of the unconscious mind, mainly through its manifestation in dreams. Dreams, they tell us in brief, are cartoons drawn by the unconscious mind for the consideration of the conscious mind. Unfortunately the unconscious mind is not always an accomplished cartoonist, nor the conscious mind a gifted interpreter of cartoons; and that is where the psycho-analyst comes in. He tells the patient the meaning of his dream, and advises him to act in accordance with the advice given him, in that dream, by the unconscious mind.

And undeniably there is a great deal to be said in favour of this branch of the system of healing known as psycho-analysis.

There is undoubtedly a compact and recognisable code and body of dream symbols, and the study of this dream symbolism is a fruitful and rewarding labour. I am what might be called a somewhat gifted dreamer; my dreams being considerable in number and remarkable in content. The majority are cartoons, many of which, thanks to a certain amount of study of the subject, I can read. But others are utterly different and neither come within the cartoon category nor can be forced into it.

For some have been prophetic of things that later happened; some have been pictures, glimpses, or visions of events happening at the same time; and in others, again, I have seen things which I am perfectly certain did happen in the past.

CARTOON DREAMS.

Interesting as are the ordinary cartoon dreams to those who can interpret them as Joseph interpreted the dreams of Pharaoh, the other class of dreams, with which the psycho-analysts do not appear to concern themselves, are infinitely more interesting. They are also quite inexplicable. The following are excellent examples of this class of dream.

First a prophetic dream.

One night when I was at Oxford, having read until a late hour, I rose from my book-laden table and seated myself in a deep armchair in front of the dying fire, and very quickly fell asleep. It was a bad habit into which I had fallen that summer term.

Quite frequently I would sleep in the chair until awakened by the sun, and then, after a bath and change, would breakfast without going to bed at all. On this particular occasion I dreamed that I was walking down the familiar road that led to my home. It was late at night. Near my house a high dog cart passed me, driven at considerable speed; and the voice of a man whom, by the light of the moon, I could see fairly plainly, called out a cheerful good-night.

He was wearing, among other garments, a white bowler hat, and his voice was rich and fruity. I did not know him or anything about him, but I was quite sure he was not a repressed and ascetic person.

When I reached home the door was opened by a maid who looked agitated and frightened, and in the middle of the hall stood my step-mother, who said repeatedly: "You are in time," but made no reply to my questions.

Turning, she led the way upstairs and, entering my father's bedroom, I saw him lying on the bed, apparently dead. There was blood on the pillow and on the sheet. Striding swiftly from the door to the bed I . . . awoke.

It was an amazingly vivid dream, and I was worried. As soon as the post office was opened I telegraphed home, "Is all well?" and received a laconic reply, "As usual."

Now, in describing that dream I have described precisely what happened about a fortnight later, even to the dog-cart and its uplifted, light-hearted driver.

My father had had an almost fatal haemorrhage of the lungs just before I reached the house.

No psycho-analyst can persuade me that this prophetic dream was any sort or kind of "cartoon drawn by the unconscious mind for consideration and interpretation by the conscious mind."

A few months before this experience I dreamed that I was riding across a burnt-up barren country with a party of men dressed as Colonial troopers.

Although their leader interested me, I was particularly attracted to, and concerned with, a youth whose name I knew to be Laurence, though whether this was his christian or his surname I did not know. (I'd give a good deal to be able to find out.)

I knew that all the men of this squadron were anxious; that Laurence was afraid; and his great fear was that—he might show fear.

They trotted along in column of files, with two flankers and a single distant rearguard, until this man galloped up to the leader and announced that a troop of horsemen was overtaking them from the rear.

The squadron halted, the troop joined it, and, as its officer rode up to him, the leader said, "Hullo Burroughs!" and the newcomer replied, "Morning major. The Shangaani's rising very fast. All that rain. We only just got across."

And in my dream I was aware that the leader's name was Allen; though, there again, I was unaware as to whether it was a christian or a surname.

Before any more could be said, the whole plain seemed to come to life, as from the shelter of donga and spruit and river-bank, from behind kopje and boulder and bush, hundreds and hundreds of plumed warriors sprang up.

At a signal from Allen, the column formed single file, and, at an order, the line became a circle. The men dismounted and, at another order, to my dream-horror and dismay, every man shot his horse.

As each horse fell its rider threw himself down behind it and opened fire on the swiftly advancing foe, whom I supposed to be an impi of Zulus.

As the last charge surged over the little rampart of horses and corpses, one man, unhurt, rose to his feet and fought with desperate heroism until he was stabbed to death. It was Laurence.

MAGNIFICENT FIGHT.

Neither I nor anyone else ever saw a more magnificent fight, nor had a more truly realistic dream; but the truly remarkable thing is that, as I afterwards discovered from my newspaper, while I dreamed that dream Wilson was making his famous "Last Stand" against the Matabele.

His Christian name was Alan. I have been unable to discover the fact from records, but I know with the utmost certainty that one of his men bore the surname or christian name of Laurence.

That dream was no cartoon nor, of course, was it "prophetic."

So whenever I have talked with the psycho-analyst, or listened, as I have been privileged to do, to those great scientists Freud and Jung; or when I have read the absorbingly interesting books written by the brilliant alienist who pioneer in the immeasurably vast and strange realm of the subconscious. I have accepted with reservations their definition of a dream as "a cartoon drawn by the unconscious mind for the information and guidance of the conscious mind that in the light of knowledge so imparted it may act for the benefit of the body."

Some are cartoons; others undeniably are not. They are visions.

SIMPLE

"Simple" is the story of the laziest man in town (and maybe all of Central America) and how he earns enough money so he does not need to work or beg again for thirty years. "Simple" was previously published as the first story in Part II, "Quaint", of Odd—But Even So *(1941). It was reprinted in* Ellery Queen's Mystery Magazine *(January 1943) and in* Mystère-Magazine *(January 1949, under the title "Très Simple"), the French version of* Ellery Queen's Mystery Magazine. *In both magazine appearances, the editor invites the reader to solve the mystery before reading Don José's solution by turning the last two paragraphs upside down. "Simple" was also the source of an episode in the 1953 anthology television series, "Rebound", produced by Bing Crosby Enterprises and aired on the ABC and DuMont network. The series was called "Counterpoint" when it was in syndication (1955-1956).*

Central America covers a big area and contains a large and very mixed population varying from hundred-per-cent. Americans and pure-bred Europeans by way of fifty-per-cent. half-bred *mestizos* to equally pure-bred Indians and Negroes.

Among the people of Mexico, Guatemala, Honduras, Salvador and Nicaragua are hard-working men and lazy men, and among the latter are to be found the very laziest in all the world.

It is a rash statement, but a reasonable and a tenable withal, that Señor José Hernandez held the palm, as The Laziest of the Lazy, between the Rio Grande del Norte and the Panama Canal.

Naturally he was almost as poor as he was lazy, but not quite, because, being a *hidalgo* of bluest blood and unmixed descent, he had but to ask and it was given unto him—to the extent of at least ten centavos a time. But even asking involves effort, and, every evening, Señor José was constrained to rise from his comfortable seat in the shady Plaza, stroll along the Avenida Reale and accost such Europeans as he might meet. Only white men, of course; for José Hernandez had his pride, and no *caballero* begs from an Indian or a half-caste, however much better off such people may be than himself. A *caballero* may have no shirt, no socks, only a shoe and a half, and a cotton coat and trousers long unassailed by a Chinese laundry-man, and still remain a *caballero*, a *hidalgo*, and a gentleman, a *Don*.

And to such, any right-thinking and well-behaved European will give a ten-, twenty- or fifty-centavo piece, or even a peso. For his heart will be touched at the sight of quiet and dignified, suffering, provided he has not been "touched" too often.

So, to the extent of walking a few yards and saying a few words, Señor José Hernandez had to work. It was annoying, but when he had collected a few tens, twenties and fifties, he could go to a stall and there take his choice of hot *tamales*, fried bananas, *cuchilladas*, *frijoles*, enticing sweetmeats, admirable rolls and excellent coffee. Thereafter a few cigarettes, pleasantly enriched with just a little *marijuana*, and a glass of *tequila*. And so to bed—on the same bench, his arm-chair by day, his couch by night.

Ours is a strange world, replete with remarkable phenomena. One of these is the fact that José's brother, Don Pedro Hernandez, if not one of the busiest men in all Central America, was undoubtedly, and by far, the most industrious, hard-working, capable and successful men in San Antonio if not the whole State of Sonango.

And, as naturally as completest idleness and unadulterated laziness kept José poor as a man may be and live, so, inevitably, had constant hard work, hard scheming and the ruthless seizing of every opportunity enriched the admirable Pedro.

While one brother sat in his two-piece suit and his piece-and-a-half shoes, the other dwelt in a fine house, rode in a fine car, and enjoyed that universal admiration and respect, regard and honour which are the right and proper due of every wealthy man.

One thing Señor Pedro Hernandez did not enjoy was the sight of his disgraceful and abominable brother seated ragged, unwashed and unshorn, from morning till night on his bench in the Plaza, or making his evening predatory stroll along the Avenida Reale in search of the easy centavo.

José was to Pedro a thorn in the side; a curse and a cross which he bore with ill grace. He was the elephant in his ointment.

Not only was it galling to Pedro's pride that his own brother lived upon the casual and careless charity of Pedro's fellow-citizens, but it was particularly irksome to know that his enemies—and even the rich have enemies—took a mean and despicable pleasure in tossing coppers to his brother as they passed the spot where he sat at the receipt of custom, or when they met him on his evening excursion between the Plaza and the Hotel Grande Imperiale. For there were not a few malicious scoundrels in San Antonio who, laughing aloud, would enter their favourite bar and observe to their friends its *habitués,*

"Just met Pedro Hernandez's begging brother and tipped him a fifty. A bone-idle loafer! But damned, if I don't like him the better of the two."

And another, with a nasty snigger, would observe:

"Inasmuch as Don José Hernandez does nothing whatsoever, he does nothing wrong. Which is more than one can say for the noble Don Pedro."

Kind friends—as kind friends will—always told Pedro all about that sort of talk.

But whether José were more likeable than Pedro or not, it is unfortunately undeniable that José was by far the happier of the two, beyond any possible shadow of doubt.

That such should be the case, is, of course very wrong, undesirable and unmoral.

But such, nevertheless, was the position of affairs when there dawned that epochal day, known thenceforth in San Antonio and the parts adjacent, as Boulder Day.

During the darkness of the early hours of that memorable morning, the Earth, as it so frequently did in the state of Sonango, seemed to stretch in its sleep, to turn over, to yawn (in several places) and to give a comfortable little wriggle ere settling down to dream again.

On this occasion, the comfortable little wriggle dislodged a boulder perched somewhat precariously on the side of the mountain that somewhat dubiously protects San Antonio. It was quite a considerable boulder, being about the size of a well-nourished hippopotamus; rotund, almost spherical, indeed.

Released from its resting-place, and doubtless (unlike José) weary of the spot where it had slumbered for so long, it rolled away merrily, and, positively bounding with glee, and gaining momentum at every leap, careered down the mountain-side, skipped joyously over a shallow *arroyo*, playfully burst through the houses on both sides of a street, and, by them slightly diverted from its course, bowled innocuously as a child's hoop, straight down the centre of the Avenida. At length, with a sigh of satisfaction, it came to rest, none too soon for the safety and welfare of life and property in the town of San Antonio.

But it was definitely unfortunate that the Boulder, which stood higher than a big boy and would have needed the outstretched arms of three men for its encirclement, should have come to rest in the exact spot where, somewhat casually perhaps, the tramlines cross the light railway that runs through San Antonio from Jimenez to Loyopa, and right in the way of the not inconsiderable motor, wagon, *burro* and other traffic that throngs the busy Avenida.

Imagine if you can the consternation of the City Fathers, the anxiety of the worried Mayor, as angrily the wires hummed from up and down the railway, on the subject of the complete blockage of line; as angrily the manager of the San Antonio Light, Power, and Tramway Company assailed him about the blockage of the track; and as leading citizens protested by telephone, telegram and letter, against the inconvenience and annoyance to which they, as merchants and tradesmen, were subjected by the traffic hold-up.

But, as the Mayor pointed out to the Municipality in Council, it was very easy for railway traffic-superintendents to send telegrams, for tramway managers to make telephone calls, for lorry and taxicab proprietors to make personal calls and personal remarks; but, among the few things they forgot to tell him, was how to remove the colossal Boulder!

"Couldn't it be dragged away?" enquired a Municipal Councillor, desirous of offering helpful municipal counsel.

"Oh, undoubtedly, undoubtedly," said the Mayor, "if only we had ten thousand traction engines and the means of harnessing them to it."

"Couldn't one of our leading contractors, such as Señor Pedro Hernandez, construct a sort of platform, on wheels and attach . . ."

"Oh, doubtless, doubtless," smiled the Mayor. "Given a few months, I am perfectly certain he could build 'a sort of platform on wheels' of sufficient strength to bear the immeasurable weight of that gigantic rock. . . . And he having done so, perhaps you yourself would be good enough to push the stone on to it, my dear friend?"

Undeterred by the Mayor's sarcasm, another Councillor made a suggestion.

"What about a crane?" he said. "Are not such contrivances made for the lifting of great weights?"

"True, true," agreed the Mayor. "Brilliant. I shouldn't be in the least surprised to learn that in Pittsburg, U.S.A., or Birmingham, England, there exists a crane that could lift a stone as big as a house and weighing hundreds of tons. But this is San Antonio, Sonango; and I do not at the moment recollect seeing a crane a hundred feet high and a million horse-power strong, in anybody's back-yard."

In silence the Council sat biting its nails, gnawing its knuckles, nibbling its beard, or merely scratching its head.

Then, as was, his place and duty, the Vice-President of the Municipal Council did his bit, and was delivered of a helpful suggestion.

"Dynamite!" he said explosively. The Mayor suppressed a groan, refrained from rudeness, and observed:

"The Señor would suggest blowing the Boulder, San Antonio, and half the State of Sonango to . . . to . . ."

"To hell," murmured a Councillor readily.

"To dust, I was about to say," continued the Mayor. "But doubtless our friend knows his own destination best."

But dynamite, like many other dangerous subjects, has a certain attraction.

"Couldn't we have holes drilled in the Boulder and then let sticks of dynamite be inserted in the holes; and then, not exactly blow it to pieces, but—er—break it up, disintegrate it," suggested a grave and reverend Señor.

"Oh, we could. Undoubtedly we could," replied the Mayor. "Suppose you go and tell the proprietor of the Hotel Imperiale, outside which the Boulder rests, that you propose to do it.

"And ask him if he has any objection to having his windows

blown in, his ceilings brought down, and such of his guests as are not killed, driven insane, or deafened for life," he added.

Other solutions were propounded, each more fantastic than the last, until, through sheer weariness and a laudable desire to prevent a free fight, if not murder, the distracted Mayor dissolved the Council, with nothing accomplished, nothing done to earn a night's repose—or achieve the removal of the Boulder.

One thing he could, and would, and did do; and that was to offer a reward of one thousand pesos to anyone who could make a practicable suggestion for the removal of the colossal stone; and ten thousand pesos to him who should achieve it without further damage to life and property in the city of San Antonio. . . .

Returning that night from his office in the City Hall to his once happy home, weary and worn and sad, dejected and depressed to the lowest depths, he passed the seat in the Plaza on which rested Don José Hernandez.

"Señor!" languidly murmured that gentleman. "You want the Boulder removed. I will remove it for you this very night—at the stated price."

The Mayor was not amused and briefly intimated the fact.

"Nevertheless, Señor," smiled José gently, "if the sun should rise to-morrow upon the spot where the Boulder now rests and find it empty; find the Boulder vanished with the other miasmas and mists of the morning, I shall apply to you for the sum of eleven thousand pesos."

"Yes. And you'll get them!" grunted the Mayor. "And eleven thousand more," he added contemptuously. "Doubtless you propose to eat it."

"The money? Most of it. I shall drink some of it, of course."

"I meant the Boulder," replied the Mayor, added a little blasphemy, and went on his way, not rejoicing.

And in the morning the sun rose as usual upon the town of San Antonio and beheld it as usual, inasmuch as no gigantic boulder lay paralysing the transport activities of the city.

Informed of the fact ere yet he had left his bed, the Mayor could not believe his ears; and five minutes later could not believe the evidence of his eyes.

Slowly, and in a sense reluctantly, he did believe that of the tired-born, languid-bred and lazy-living Señor José Hernandez who, looking if possible more weary than ever, approached him and murmured:

"Would you rather pay the *twenty-two* thousand pesos into the Bank of Mexico in a lump sum, or hand me two pesos daily for the next thirty years?"

The Mayor appeared to swallow something large, and drew a deep breath.

"Name of the Eternal Father!" he stammered. "But . . . But . . . How did . . . you . . . do . . . it?"

"Oh, I induced a number of my friends, simple-minded and hard-working peons, to dig a big hole beside it. It rolled in, and they covered it up."

Since Boulder Day, Don José Hernandez has been spared even the labour of begging.

THE PIOUS WEAKLING

"The Pious Weakling" is the unbelievable story of two Europeans who have been kidnapped by a Chinese bandit. One of the Europeans is a cardsharp and is able to win their freedom by cheating at poker. The other European, an Englishman, is unaware of the cheating until they are almost home. What makes this story so unbelievable is when the Englishman does find out that it was because of the cheating that they were set free, he rides back to the Chinese bandit since he has never cheated in his life before and is not about to start now. In a stereotypical story the Chinese bandit would again let him go free, but Wren was not writing such a clichéd story. "The Pious Weakling" was previously published as the second story in Part II, "Quaint", of Odd—But Even So *(1941).*

The three men who sat on the clay-built *kong* of the Manchurian village contrasted, most strongly each with the others, although two were Europeans and the third was a Chinese bandit-chief.

A *kong* is a huge communal bed, a dais raised two or three feet from the floor, and warmed by mean of an iron pipe that comes from the stove, when it is not, in point of fact, a kind of stove itself. On it, the whole family sleeps, much in the manner in which sardines take their last sleep in their tin box.

The Chinese was a renowned and redoubtable villain; a great lover of little children; a wholesale murderer and torturer; a large-scale thief; a brute; a scourge; and a man of his word. When he said he would burn an unhelpful village and slay every living thing that it contained, he kept his word. When he said he would reward and enrich a friendly village, making gifts to every one of its inhabitants, he kept his promise. When he said he would get his man and kill him, be he mandarin or beggar, Foreign Devil or runaway member of his own band, he did so. When he promised safe-conduct to the emissary of an enemy, be that enemy a rival bandit, a Chinese General, a Japanese official or a local mandarin, the messenger was in no danger.

He was tall, as are many Manchurian peasants, very strongly

built, active and powerful. His face, amazingly wrinkled, was wolfishly cruel; the close-set reddened eyes those of a beast; the mouth straight, strong and hard as those of a fighting fish. And yet some of the wrinkles beside his eyes were those of laughter; and when anything tickled his deplorable and macabre sense of humour, he could chuckle merrily, and upon rare and deserving occasion, roar with hearty laughter.

He was clad in long coat and trousers apparently made from a bed-quilt of stout material, the ends of the trousers being stuffed into high boots of soft Manchurian leather, shapeless, warm and comfortable. On his head was a hat shaped almost exactly like a sailor's sou'-wester, but lined with soft and beautiful fur. The great furred ear-flaps, which could be tied under the chin, now stood out at right angles to his head, increasing the wild-beast suggestion of his face.

Bandoliers, filled with revolver cartridges, crossed each other upon his broad chest and back, themselves supporting crossed belts that girt his middle, while from them, upon his thighs, depended two large, automatic pistols. As he talked, he played with these in a manner visibly disturbing to the Englishman, who watched him fascinated.

The man with whom he talked, sometimes in rapid hissing Chinese of the Southern Manchurian dialect, sometimes in the broken English which he loved to display, was even bigger than the bandit himself. A very well-known member of Tienchang society, he was so cosmopolitan, widely travelled and nationally detached, that the English supposed him to be American because his name Dobroff was not English, while the Americans supposed, him to be English because he talked, like an Englishman, belonged to an English firm, and had an English wife.

Whatever nationality he claimed, however, he had been born of a Russian father and a French mother in Odessa; had drifted about the world and several times around it; and had sojourned for considerable periods in London, Montreal, San Francisco, Seattle, Singapore, Hong Kong, Auckland, Sydney, and Shanghai.

In Tienchang he had settled down and become a *taipan*[29] and an institution; an ornament of the Tienchang Club and an authority on horse-racing, polo, golf, bridge and all other card-games. Particularly poker.

With cards, he was a wizard; and with them but few stalwarts cared to pit their skill and luck against him, particularly again, at poker.

There were nasty-minded people—those, who had played that game with him too long and lost too much—who said, well behind his back and far out of his hearing, that they would not only admit that he was a wizard at poker, but would go a little further and say that he was a conjurer; and not only a conjurer, but a juggler. Moreover, that the wonderful card-tricks that he quite frankly displayed when asked to do so, were far from being the only card-tricks that he knew, and still further from being the only card-tricks that he did display.

Anyway, poker tricks aside, he was a magnificent bridge-player, and the man who drew him as partner was lucky.

There were a great many people who liked him, especially at first, and particularly those who had no business dealings with him, and who were not so foolish as to try to win his money at cards—especially at poker.

And it was of the game of poker that he was speaking with his present self-constituted host Chen Lung, the bloody-minded and brutal leader and autocratic ruler of five hundred savage Hunghutze bandits, cold and cruel killers to a man, who thought no more, in the way of ransom-business, of slicing off an ear or chopping off a finger than of striking a match.

"How can I trust you? You are a Christian, aren't you?" asked Chen Lung.

"How can I trust you? You are a bandit, aren't you?" was the reply.

"Well, you can trust me. Everybody knows that. You know it yourself," said the Chinese.

"Well, so can you trust me. Everyone in Tienchang knows that. How should I be a wealthy merchant if I were not honourable and trustworthy? How do your Chinese merchants become wealthy and prosperous, save by being truthful, reliable,

---

[29] *Rich merchant.*

honourable and trustworthy?"

The Chinese eyed the speaker speculatively.

"We have a proverb, you know—'*Never trust a Japanese and never cheat a Chinese*'," continued Dobroff.

"*Hao!* That is good. That shows that you Foreign Devils have some sense, anyhow . . . Well, if we can come to terms, I'll trust you."

"You said a good thing when you said that," Chen Lung added and grinned with pleasure, displaying sound and strong teeth in which he evidently took no interest.

"We'll trust each other," smiled Dobroff. "British merchant and Chinese—er—merchant."

"What do you offer?" asked Chen Lung.

"A thousand silver dollars each," was the reply.

"What? Two thousand dollars for the pair of you? Go out into the dark night and whistle till Mao Kui comes and wrings your neck."

"Why should the Devil of the Night wring my neck?" asked Dobroff.

"Well. No. Perhaps he wouldn't," grinned Chen Lung. "He'd be more likely to adopt you as his son. Two thousand dollars, after all the trouble you've given me! Half the Japanese army hunting me about. Two thousand heads of *kao liang*, more likely. Talk sense. And in any case, you stand a chance of getting off scot-free if we come to terms and you win the game."

"Well, five thousand, then.

The bandit chief made a vulgar noise.

"And you've just admitted that you are a prosperous merchant of Tienchang! If you can't talk sense, I'll go.

"And I'll send a couple of right ears down to Tienchang to-morrow," he added as he made to rise.

Dobroff thought quickly. Mustn't rouse the man's suspicions by raising the price too quickly.

"Very well, then, ten thousand. Ten thousand silver dollars."

"Each?"

"Talk sense yourself," replied Dobroff bluffly, in the manner of his bluff-spoken and hearty captor. "What do *you* propose?"

"Twenty-five thousand silver dollars each."

"Each?" Dobroff affected to be stricken with faintness.

"And where should I get twenty-five thousand dollars from?" he whispered weakly, when he had recovered breath.

"From the Hong Kong and Shanghai Bank," replied Chen Lung, who was literal and well-informed, having, like Ulysses, known far cities and strange men, some of them quite strange, in Bias Bay, Hong Kong, Shanghai and elsewhere.

"And even if I could raise twenty-five thousand dollars by the sale of all that I have got, where do you suppose my poor young friend here could get so much money? For poor he is."

"From his Company," replied Chen Lung. "They'll ransom him. Very cheap too."

"They'll never do it."

"Won't they? Then he himself will have to pay."

"He can't."

"Oh yes, he can. And if not in dollars, cents and *kash*, then in fingers and toes and ears—and what not."

"That won't do you any good, Chen Lung."

"No. Nor him," replied the bandit.

"You'd sooner have money, wouldn't you?"

"Much."

"Well, take what you can get."

"I'm going to. I'm going to get fifty thousand dollars from you, and you can get his twenty-five thousand from him afterwards."

"He could never pay it, nor raise it."

"That's your trouble."

"Or, look here," added Chen Lung, in the manner of one who wishes to be reasonable, "I don't mind pricing you at forty thousand dollars, and taking a chance on whether I can get ten thousand for him, some time or other."

"Oh, I couldn't do a thing like that. I couldn't leave my friend."

The bandit made a noise which may have been a kind of laugh.

"Do you mean, to say that if I told you that you could go free for your miserable one thousand dollars ransom, each, now, with an escort to take you within sight of Tienchang—on the understanding that I was free to cut your friend's throat as soon as your back was turned—*you wouldn't go*?"

Dobroff eyed the Chinese sharply, attempting the impossible feat of reading his mind, following his real thoughts.

"Er—of course not," he said. "Europeans don't do . . ."

The door of the hut was flung open, and a small squint-eyed man of most unprepossessing appearance, dressed in a wide conical straw hat, crossed bandoliers and blue cotton trousers, appeared on the threshold.

"Soldiers!" he hissed. "Manchukuo devils. Coming through the *kao-liang* from the direction of Tienchang."

"Mounted?" snapped Chen Lung.

"No."

"Hurry up, you," said the leader, climbing from the *kong*. "Be ready to ride in five minutes—or else you will walk."

"What's up?" asked the Englishman.

"Those damned Japanese again," replied Dobroff to his companion in captivity. "That's all they can do, keep us on the move. How do they suppose they can get Chen Lung and the pick of his crowd, without cavalry—and especially with those Manchukuo clodhoppers? Do us a damned sight more harm than good—putting him in a bad temper. If they'd let him sit quiet in one of the villages and carry on negotiations with our people in Tienchang, we might do something."

"What, raise all that ransom?"

"Yes, and then trick him, somehow. The police catch him with it in his pocket before he can clear out. All that these silly swine are doing is to make us move on, every two or three days. And if he once clears right off to his headquarters, that'll probably be the end of us."

"Too far from Tienchang to carry on negotiations, you mean?"

"Of course. He must be fairly near to be able to negotiate with any safety. How could they get coolie messengers to travel all that distance and shove their heads in the lion's den at the end of it? Even supposing they could find it, that is."

"Which I suppose they couldn't?"

"No. It's probably unfindable. Caves in the mountains; or some entrenched stockaded village, surrounded by rivers, swamps and marshes and square miles of *kao-liang*. And if he sent bandit messengers they'd only be beheaded when caught."

"Blast the Japanese!" he added, as he endeavoured to pull on the riding-boots which he had been wearing when the two were captured when hacking across country one Sunday morning.

"Wonder if they really think they are doing any good, or whether it's simply a case of '*mai yo lien,*' just to save face. Every time they've come clumping along in the direction of the village where he has been lying up, Chen Lung has simply butchered every man and woman in it, on the chance that someone had split on him and sent for the Japanese; and also *pour encourager les autres* of any other village he may come to. What's more important, we get a hell of a day's march and as likely as not on foot, till he has put thirty or forty miles between himself and the clod-hoppers. Buck up or you'll . . ."

"Merciful Heavens!" cried the Englishman, suddenly clapping both hands to his ears, as piercing shrieks and screams and blood-curdling groans told their hideous tale of the truth of Dobroff's prophecy. When you enter a Spaniard's house he says that all it contains is yours—and doesn't mean it; when Chen Lung enters a Chinese village he says that all it contains is his—and does mean it. Chen Lung and his men were performing the work of looting and of punishing the villagers, who might or might not have sent word concerning his movements, and of preventing the giving of any further information to the Japanese troops when they should arrive.

This was business combined with pleasure. Pleasure combined with business was the burning down of every building in the place, so that the weary Japanese on arrival should have no shelter whatsoever, and only such food as they themselves brought.

Striding to the rice-paper-paned window, the Englishman thrust his hand through it, looked out, and recoiled shuddering. An almost headless woman, clutching the completely headless body of a baby, lay in front of the next hut, through the door of which clouds of smoke were pouring out.

Again the door was thrown open and a couple of Hunghutzes entered.

"Come on, you," growled one of them, "unless you want to be burned alive," and the other seized the home-made tallow candles burning on the *kong.*

"You foul swine! You filthy murdering brutes!" cried the Englishman, advancing with tethered clutching hands upon the leading bandit. "I'd . . ."

The Chinese raised his clubbed rifle.

"Shut up, you damned fool," growled Dobroff, shouldering the other aside. "I don't want to have to carry you—or your dead body. Get your boots on."

"I can't. My feet are one big sore. Gangrenous, I believe."

"Well, come bare-footed, then, and pray God we get ponies."

A pity the lad hadn't a little more self-control and a lot more—guts.

The man at whom Dobroff glanced somewhat contemptuously was short, thin and fair, his face redeemed from insignificance by a certain austerity and determination about the mouth, and a look of intelligence, if not intellectuality, about the eyes and forehead; on the whole, a refined face, and though sensitive, neither weak nor foolish. Nevertheless, it appeared that Dobroff held no high opinion of John Morlay. If only because he was a teetotaller, a non-smoker, and in other ways a wilful and foolish stoic, denying himself the pleasure of good fun and good times, he was a dull dog. He was a fool, a man who never went near a race-course, never played cards, never laughed at a good story, and probably had never spoken to a sing-sing girl in his life. In fact, a prig, a psalm-smiting hymn-singer and a kill-joy.

Yes, Fate must have been in quite a funny mood when she chose, as a companion in captivity for Serge Dobroff, a young man who was a pillar of the Y.M.C.A., who said his prayers every night, had a pious horror of a good round oath, and had not a single idea, opinion, view or standard in common with him. Very humorous indeed. . . .

Fortunately for the prisoners, a pair of undersized half-starved ponies was available; and, as thankfully he mounted his, Dobroff whimsically observed to the limping bare-footed Morlay that he need have no qualms about taking the one provided for him, since its owner would certainly have no further use for it.

Morlay appeared too broken-spirited to reply, as he glanced to where some emaciated bodies lay in their filthy clothes like rag dolls flung down by pauper children. . . .

By the following midday, Dobroff again congratulated

himself and his fellow-prisoner on their possession of the ponies, for the band had covered some fifty miles before it halted. The wretched village tats had carried their riders well, wonderfully indeed, and Dobroff's in particular, for that stout citizen weighed some sixteen stone.

"By gad! This must be their headquarters," he whispered to Morlay, as, riding out from interminable fields of high *kao-liang* and fording a river, they came upon a big and strongly entrenched village, its high stockaded wall surrounded by deep trenches and lofty look-out posts.

"We shall be for it, if those damned Japanese find the place and attack it," whispered Dobroff.

"Are they likely to?"

"No . . . Even if they found it, they'd soon see that it would take a brigade to capture it."

"And what good would it be to them when they had got in? There'd be nothing here but our two rather unpleasant-looking bodies."

§2

Chen Lung actually laughed as he smote his thigh. He was feeling good, having dined heartily on his favourite dumplings, pork *chiaotzes*, cabbage and a noble dish of *kao-liang*, beans, garlic, and bad eggs. He had also drunk well of rice spirit, and a liquor sold in the Panshan or Yingkow bazaar under the name of brandy. As the identical liquor was also sold as whisky, as gin, and as rum, it must have had varied qualities; but Chen Lung was not drunk, merely merry, and insisted upon being addressed by all and sundry, especially the two Europeans, as *Lao* Chen Lung.
. . .

"That's understood then," he bawled. "A game of poker. No, seven games of poker. Seventy games. We'll play all night. And if I win, you and the other Foreign Devil die at once. I'll shoot you myself, eh? No, I'll give you the slow strangle. If you win, you shall go free, and the very men who have been your guards shall be your escort and take you back to Tienchang, or as near as is safe for them to go," and he roared with laughter.

"Good," smiled Dobroff. "*Lao* Chen Lung, you are a

sportsman. You are a real *Lao* and you ought to be a General. You will be, some day."

The Chinese shook hands with Dobroff, proud of his social aplomb and knowledge of this strange custom of Foreign Devils.

"What is it?" asked Morlay in surprise, his face lighting up with hope.

"It's a game of poker, my son. And our lives the stake."

"And if we win?"

"If I win, you mean. We go free. He sees us safe back to Tienchang."

"And the ransom?"

"He knows it is perfectly hopeless now."

"Why?"

"Two reasons. He has had word from some newspaper-reading spy down in Tienchang that it has been decided that to pay a ransom for us would start a vast and nourishing industry throughout China—European-kidnapping-for-ransom. No. We are the goats. They are going to use us as Awful Warnings, both to Chinese and Europeans; a warning to Europeans not to get kidnapped, and to Chinese that kidnapping doesn't pay. No money in it, and the death penalty if they are captured."

"And what's the other reason?"

"Sheer impossibility of carrying on negotiations without giving away the position of his headquarters here. He doesn't want the Manchukuo General, Li Shek Toon, to know it, nor the Japanese, nor anybody else. And he can't have messengers, negotiators, people of that sort, coming here from Tienchang without its being known. Anyway, he has quite given up all hope and all idea of ransom. He merely mentioned this morning that we weren't worth feeding any longer, so he was going to bump us off. Then I appealed to his sportsmanship. He's a not uncommon type of Chink in that . . . All tremendous gamblers. . . . Tickles his sense of humour to have a game of cards in which he has got nothing to lose except the pleasure of killing us, and we've got our lives and everything else to lose."

"Will he keep his word?"

"If I win? Absolutely.

"So he will if I lose," added Dobroff grimly.

"Well, for Heaven's sake, play your best. And I shall pray my best."

Dobroff eyed his companion.

"We ought to bring it off between us," he laughed.

"Untie us, *Lao* Chen Lung," he continued, turning to the Chinese; and, at a nod from the leader, one of the guard standing up on the *kong* untied the ropes, the other ends of which were fastened to the cords with which the prisoners were ingeniously constrained. Though bound hand and foot, they could walk and could use their hands for raising food to their mouths, for removing their boots, or washing their faces; but the cords, crossed behind their backs and passed in a slip-knot about their necks, rendered any but the smallest movements not only painful but a constant threat of strangulation.

From a vast pocket of his gown-like padded coat, the bandit leader produced two dirty packs of cards wrapped in paper—to Dobroff's surprise and delight European cards, the markings and numbers of which Chen Lung evidently understood. Doubtless he had played with such cards thousands of times in waterfront dives in Shanghai, from Macao to Port Arthur.

"Clear the *kong*," ordered Chen Lung, and, seated crosslegged with a clear space between them, the players began.

Before long, the room was completely filled with Hunghutzes, wild gamblers to a man, and thrilled to the marrow of their bones at the thought of a game between a Foreign Devil and their leader—on which so much hung, on which one of the players hazarded the greatest stake of all.

Soon the paper windows were broken from their frames, the apertures filled with heads, the doorway blocked, the room literally crowded to the roof, as men climbed on to rafters to get a better view of the sport.

§3

By the end of the game, John Morlay was soaked from head to foot with sweat. Illness, exposure, semi-starvation and anxiety had weakened him so that he could scarcely bear the strain, the effort of willing success to his friend, of mental wrestling with the Powers of Darkness, the devils of Doubt and Fear. And when, at last, with a quiet triumphant laugh that was intended to show complete freedom from the slightest anxiety, Dobroff swung his legs over the side of the *kong* and rose to his feet, Morlay fainted.

For his friend had won, and if Chen Lung kept his word, they were safe. . . .

Chen Lung kept his word.

"*Mai yo fah-ze*," he growled.

At dawn, well mounted and accompanied by a heavily-armed escort whose orders were to see them safely to within a few miles of Tienchang, the two rode away.

"Well, Morlay, you are not saying much," smiled Dobroff, some twenty-four hours later, as they left the cultivated fields of *kao-liang* and entered a howling wilderness of tall reeds, followed by their escort.

"No, but I'm thinking a lot. And I'm thanking God from the bottom of my heart," was the reply.

"And me?"

"I thank you too from the bottom of my heart, Dobroff. You were the instrument of God's mercy."

The older man smiled whimsically. Serge Dobroff God's instrument, eh?

"You doubt it?" asked Morlay.

Dobroff laughed.

"You don't really doubt that you were helped?" said Morlay.

Dobroff roared with laughter.

"Doubtless I was," he replied. "Doesn't Heaven help those who help themselves?

"And I helped myself," he added pointedly.

"How d'you mean?"

"Why, my good innocent, I cheated, from beginning to end."

"*Cheated?*"

"A magnificent exhibition, if I may say so, of the conjurer's art."

"You *cheated?* And Chen Lung?" asked Morlay.

"He played as honestly as—a curate playing beggar-my-neighbour with his aunt."

"A perfectly honest straight game without any attempt at cheating?"

"Absolutely."

"And he *could* have cheated?" asked Morlay.

"Have you heard of the Heathen Chinee? *'For ways that are dark and tricks that are vain, the Heathen Chinee is peculiar'*; and there isn't a trickier or a more heathen Chinee alive than the good Chen Lung."

John Morlay drew rein and brought his horse to a standstill.

"I'll say good-bye, Dobroff," he said coldly, and turned his horse about.

"What the devil do you mean? Where are you going?" cried Dobroff in amazement.

"I'm going back."

"What in hell for?"

"To tell Chen Lung that it wasn't a fair game."

"So what?"

"I don't know. But I have never cheated at a game myself and I'm not going to be cheated *for*."

"He'll kill you, you fool."

Morlay struck his horse and rode back along the muddy path through the vast moor of giant reeds.

"Come back, you damned idiot," shouted Dobroff, and Morlay urged his pony into a sharp canter.

Puzzled almost beyond speech, the leader of the escort bade one of his men follow the mad Foreign Devil, while the remainder accompanied Serge Dobroff who was now in a great hurry.

§4

Chen Lung was nursing a very filthy and sore-eyed baby, calling it his little *pou-pei*, tickling it and ludicrously burbling "*Gao-chi, gao-chi, Tickle-tickle*," as he prodded its ribs with a stubbly forefinger.

He stared in amazement, and slowly scratched his head, as Morlay dismounted, advanced and told him why he had returned.

"Ai-ya! Cheated me, did he? . . . And you wouldn't cheat?"

"No."

"You never cheat?" he asked, chewing slowly, spitting skins of pickled melon seeds from his mouth.

"No."

"Do you tell lies?"

"No."

"Tell me the truth now, then. Would it punish the cheating Foreign Devil more if I tortured you to death, or if I sent you back to revile him to his friends, and to make him lose face in Tienchang?"

"I think he would deny that he cheated."

"Then it will hurt him more if I kill you and he knows in his heart that he has caused his friend's death?"

"Yes."

"Then I will give you the slow strangle. We'll ride out to the nearest village and do it there. The news will soon spread—and your friend will hear how you died.

"Perhaps I win so, after all, eh?" he added.

And Chen Lung laughed quite merrily.

A FOOL AND HIS MONEY

"A Fool and His Money" is the entertaining story of the competition between a dour and reticent Scot and a multi-millionaire as to what is more important: money or "man's best friend." "A Fool and His Money" was previously published as the third story in Part II, "Quaint", of Odd—But Even So *(1941).*

It would be a mistake to imagine that Mr. Hiram K. Slocombe was very aggressive about his wealth, although undeniably he was enormously rich, and therefore knew all about the power, the very terrible power, of money.

On that subject he had no illusions whatsoever, unless it were the belief that anything can be bought if you have enough money wherewith to buy it, and that every man has his price.

Clear-sighted, level-headed and fundamentally very decent, he admired independence, provided it were not shown by one of his employees; estimated Yes-men at their true value; and was rather apt to like and approve No-men, provided they did not say "No" to some project and proposal of his own.

On the whole, he did good with his vast wealth, would have done more if he had known how to do it, rarely misapplied any of it, and never intentionally used it to do anything that he realized to be harmful.

A self-made man, he was proud of his creative effort, and was at no great pains to conceal the fact. Nevertheless, it is not for one moment to be supposed that he was a *nouveau riche* rough-neck, an objectionably purse-proud plutocrat, or a vulgarian ostentatious of his wealth.

And at about the time that he had turned the twenty million mark, he accepted the extremely expensive word of his famous and fashionable medical man that he needed a holiday, a rest and a change.

"In fact, if you don't take a rest, your heirs will soon take your change," said his physician.

And thus it was that Mr. Hiram K. Slocombe having "done"

Europe, Egypt, India, Ceylon, Burma, Sumatra, Java and Bali—particularly Bali—came in due course to Narut, and there sojourned a while because he was heartily tired of his holiday and wanted to look into the rubber situation on the spot.

Knowing that rubber was in a very bad way, and that not only rubber-shares but rubber-plantations were going dirt-cheap, he thought he might perhaps buy a few hundred thousand dollars' worth of shares at the price of dirt; and that if plantations were going for an old song, he might listen to that oldest and sweetest of songs, his favourite of all, "Buy at the bottom of the market and sell at the top."

Like most places that are situated in a quiet backwater, well off the beaten track, Narut had one or two "characters," men whom loneliness and monotony had rendered eccentric, or in whom eccentricities, kinks, and queernesses had been unduly developed.

Narut considered Dour Davie to be their prize exhibit; regarded him with pride; and showed him off, so far as was possible, to the somewhat rare visitors who came to their little Paradise; wandering artists and writers, butterfly and orchid hunters, catch-'em-alive-oh collectors for zoos, rubber companies' visiting-agents, explorers, prospectors, film-camera men, and other lunatics.

Such people did not stream through Narut in a ceaseless procession; but hardly a month passed, except in the rainy season, when Narut did not get a visitor of some kind. As many as half a dozen in a good year. Or perhaps a bad year. Like the one in which a well-known author came, exploited their hospitality to the utmost, learned all their secrets, foibles and little scandals, and then went away and pilloried them all practically by name and with careful personal description, in a manner that made both the men and the women of Narut wish he would come again—just once.

In spite of this occasional abuse of its friendliness, Narut warmly welcomed the multi-millionaire, Hiram K. Slocombe, with entirely disinterested hospitality and kindliness. It gave him of its best, showed him all the sport it could, including that of baiting Dour Davie.

Perhaps baiting is not the *mot juste*, for it implies a greater or less element of cruelty in a sport, and of this element there was none. It was merely a matter of getting a rise out of Davie, getting good fun out of him without hurting or annoying him in the least. Quite possibly, in fact, without his being for one moment aware that he was providing fun for the visitor. . . .

There are several types of Scot, one of which is the dour reticent kind, so laconically silent as to give the impression that he finds speech painful; so sparing of words as to appear unfriendly, surly, inhospitable.

Making Davie talk was one of the recognized forms of sport among the favourite games of Narut, and was played according to established rules. The man who could make him say the greatest number of words in a given time was the winner, provided he had not provoked Davie to wrath, had not illegitimately made him drunk by tampering with his liquor, and had not insulted him in such a manner that Davie had no alternative but to utter words of resentment.

Naturally cautious and averse from speech, under the spell of loneliness David Urquhart's economy of words had become parsimony, his quietness taciturnity, and, though admired and liked to the point of popularity, no man ever did less to seek and ensue it.

The soul of hospitality, he issued no invitations and accepted none; fundamentally fond of argument, he initiated no subjects of conversation and contributed to none; yearning for friendship, he made no friend among his acquaintances, and sought none.

Though a generous supporter of all local funds and subscription-lists, he rarely came to the Club, and when he did, answered salutations with nods of the head, and enquiries with "Yes" and "No." Or, to be exact, "Aye," and a short sharp bark of negative sound which might be spelt "Na."

Although many of the amusing stories about this alleged misogynist and misanthrope were true, others floated in his direction and clustered about him, while still more again were pure—or impure—inventions, *non vero* but definitely *ben trovato*.

He was made the hero of every new Aberdonian quip; and members of the Narut Club returning with the latest crop of good stories, would father them, if possible, upon Dour Davie.

One belief which his friends professed to hold was that, to save the use of words, Davie talked to his servants in a kind of deaf-and-dumb language which they completely understood; and another was that he communed with his dog in dog-language which Davie clearly understood.

There's many a true jest spoken in words that are not intended to convey truth—but in the joke about Davie and his dog there was, in point of fact, more truth than joke.

No one had ever seen Davie pat, fondle, scratch, tickle or caress the dog, any more than they had ever heard him speak to it; but, as they were wont to tell the visitor to whom they were showing Davie off as one of the local curiosities, no one had ever seen him without it. It lay by his bed, sat by his chair, stood by his side, or walked at his heel, and went wherever he went; but otherwise it ignored him. Davie, apparently unaware that the dog did these things, ignored it completely.

Mad Micky O'Malley, *doyen* of the European inhabitants of Narut and President of the Club, who never ceased talking save when he ate and slept, and not entirely then, regarded Davie Urquhart, his absolute antithesis, with an almost proprietary feeling; and, in his rôle of chief showman, was wont to put Davie through his motionless paces, and invite the approving attention of visitors to his soundless eloquence.

To this ebullient Irishman, principal planter and authority on the rubber situation, Hiram K. Slocombe brought letters of introduction, and received in return planter-hospitality, than which there is none warmer.

Having given of his best in every other form of hospitality and helpfulness, O'Malley concerned himself with his guest's diversion, and, to that end, introduced first the legend and then the person of Davie Urquhart to the great man's notice.

Now, like the rest of us, Hiram K. Slocombe had his little failings, and one of them was an impatience of opposition and a great dislike of any form of defeat or relegation to second place. While contemptuous, of sycophants and barely tolerant of his Yes-men, he respected an independent indifference to himself, his position and his vast wealth—up to a point. He liked to feel that those who were introduced to him were sensible of the fact that the honour was theirs, that they were meeting, a bigger man than themselves, and that a certain deference was his due.

When Davie Urquhart, on one of his rare visits to the Club, was introduced to the distinguished visitor, he exhibited none of the symptoms that Mr. Hiram. K. Slocombe was wont to observe, and liked to observe, in those who were presented to him. Having heard all about Davie he was prepared to make allowances, and to treat him as a joke; but in point of fact, he did not find him a very good joke. Davie was no more rude to Mr. Hiram K. Slocombe than he was to anybody else, but that isn't saying much in favour of his manners and conduct; and Mr. Hiram K. Slocombe's acute mind entertained a suspicion that Davie, far from going out of his way to be more polite than usual, was also not going out of his way to be more rude.

Mr. Hiram K. Slocombe wouldn't have objected to extra and special rudeness from Davie. He would rather have welcomed it as an unintentional tribute to his importance, and an intentional assertion of Davie's independence.

The slightly strained situation at the bar of the Narut Club and of public opinion that evening, was not improved by mad Micky O'Malley's impish humour which prompted him to suggest that Mr. Hiram K. Slocombe should make Davie an offer for his dog.

Unfortunately Chauncey Vanheusen, a compatriot of Mr. Hiram K. Slocombe, had, at dinner the previous night, betted that gentleman that he would not make Davie speak at the rate of a-word-a-minute during any period that they were in each other's company.

"Not thirty words in half an hour?" the multimillionaire had asked.

"No; nor sixty in a whole hour," Chauncey had replied, and the bet was on.

To the ever-active mind of the financial magnate now came the bright idea of connecting the subject of the dog with that of the bet.

"Gee! That's a real canine dog," he drawled, eyeing Davie's only friend.

"Begob, you're right, sir," agreed O'Malley, as he picked up his fifth pre-prandial stengah. "Do anything but talk English . . .

"Talks Scotch, of course," he added.

"Is that so now? With Mr. Urquhart, I presume. Sort of dog I'd like to take back to the States with me. Do you think Mr. Urquhart would part with him?"

"Well, no doubt he's open to a deal. Especially in these hard times. He sold his pony last month. We'll ask him."

"Davie!" he called.

Urquhart turned from the bar against which he was leaning and eyeing his whisky-and-soda with the absorption of a crystal-gazing clairvoyant.

Slowly he turned and focused the gaze of his close-set queer light-greenish eyes on O'Malley.

"We were just admiring The Hound."

David Urquhart accepted the statement in silence.

"Mr. Slocombe was saying he'd like to take a dog like that back to the States."

Urquhart regarded Mr. Slocombe in silence.

"As a matter of fact, he was hoping you'd let him buy it."

By way of reply, the Scot turned his back to the speaker and applied himself to his whisky.

Chauncey Vanheusen looked at his watch.

"Time three minutes. Score nought," he murmured, and intentionally or otherwise, put Hiram K. Slocombe on his mettle.

"Mr. Urquhart," said the latter, and slowly that apparently unsociable person turned about and looked at the man who had somewhat imperiously called to him.

"I'm sure you won't take offence where none is meant, but I've gotten a great fancy for that dog, and if it should happen that you are, by any chance, thinking of disposing of him, I'd very much like to have him. And since that sounds like a piece of shameless begging, may I offer you fifty dollars—er, I mean ten pounds—for him?"

Urquhart gazed at and through Mr. Hiram K. Slocombe as though he were unaware that that gentleman was speaking.

"No?" continued Slocombe pleasantly. "Well, let's say a hundred dollars. Twenty pounds sterling."

Definitely the queer close-set light-greenish eyes now focused on those of the would be purchaser.

"Not being wise on the market-price of that particular kind of dog, perhaps I am just talking foolishness," smiled Hiram K. Slocombe, as Urquhart looked at him with expressionless face and made no reply.

"What about fifty pounds?" asked Slocombe. "That strikes me as quite a decent offer.

"Unless the dog is a prize-winning World Champion or something," he added.

Urquhart turned back to his whisky, and again Chauncey Vanheusen consulted his watch.

"Second round," murmured he. "Three minutes. No points to Slocombe."

Mr. Hiram K. Slocombe was faintly annoyed. He liked to win his bets, albeit the winning of a five-dollar wager gave him as much satisfaction as the winning of a five thousand one. And this looked like a double defeat, since he had accepted a bet that he would not make this Urquhart guy talk at the rate of a word a minute, and one that he would not succeed in buying his dog.

All the qualities that had raised Mr. Slocombe from the position of a small-town retailer's third son to that of one of America's first ornaments of Big Business, now raised him from his position in the bar of the Narut Club. He was not accustomed to having his offers rejected; still less to having them ignored.

Rising and crossing from his table to the bar, he took Urquhart by the arm, and gently, in friendliest fashion, swung him round.

"I offered you fifty pounds for your dog, Mr. Urquhart, but apparently you didn't hear me. I apologize for mumbling. And for making so poor an offer I'll give you one hundred pounds for the animal."

In words Urquhart made no reply, but with a thin and somewhat contemptuous smile, he slowly shook his head and again turned from Slocombe to the bar.

Mr. Slocombe raised his right hand, not to assault Urquhart as, for a moment, O'Malley sympathetically feared—or hoped— but to smooth the back of his head, an action which, his secretary could have informed the company, indicated that he was aroused and annoyed.

"Well, Mr. Urquhart," he said, still quite pleasantly, "I take it that the sense of your answer was, on the whole, in the negative;

and as you haven't stated in so many words, or so few, that the dog isn't for sale, I can only suppose that the price is not right. So I'll apologize again for having wasted your time, and offer you two hundred and fifty pounds for the beast."

Two or three heads were turned sharply in Mr. Slocombe's direction.

Could it be possible that their ears had deceived them, and that a man, apparently sane and obviously sober, was offering two hundred and fifty pounds for a dog who had never cost more than a guinea in its life?

Pretending that he was enjoying the joke as much as anybody, the millionaire turned and winked at his friends O'Malley and Vanheusen, and then, smiling round at those of the company who were looking at him, he turned back and tapped the Scot upon the obviously cold shoulder.

"I'm giving myself the pleasure, and I'm doing myself the honour, of addressing you, Mr. Urquhart," he said majestically. "Would you have the kindness and courtesy to tell me whether you'll take—er—five hundred pounds for your dog?"

Perhaps unconsciously Mr. Slocombe had raised his voice in giving clear and distinct utterance to his offer. Conversation ceased in his neighbourhood, and silence spread throughout the bar as it was realized that something very unusual was happening. All eyes were turned in the direction of the Club's Distinguished Visitor and its prize Character Exhibit. Evidently O'Malley had started something, was playing a trick again, some game or joke, the essence of which was that the Distinguished Visitor should be led on to bait Dour Davie. O'Malley was a mad devil, but it looked as though it was Slocombe who was equally mad, if their ears didn't deceive them and he was actually offering Davie five hundred pounds for his cur, the animal to which he never spoke, which he never touched, and to which he had not even given a name.

Urquhart again turned round and faced the persistent gentleman who appeared to have taken a fancy to the wee hoond. Was the chatterbox under the impression that he was a humorist? . . . While he was studying the would-be purchaser's face, as though in search of enlightenment on the subject, the millionaire spoke again.

"You didn't exactly jump at the offer, Mr. Urquhart . . .
Well—I'll make it more attractive, for I'd hate you to lose money
through a kindly desire to oblige me. I wouldn't like to exploit
your good nature and trade on your hospitality. No sense in
mixing friendship and business. Listen. I'd like to buy your dog.
I don't know its value, but I'll offer you five thousand dollars—a
thousand pounds sterling for it. And I've got my cheque-book in
my pocket."

Urquhart's long clean-shaven upper lip slowly disappeared
inside the lower one, as he pushed the latter upward and outward
in a characteristic facial gesture of distaste, disapproval, and
denial.

All eyes and some mouths opened more widely.

"Hmph!" grunted Davie.

"Doesn't count," said Chauncey Vanheusen. "It wasn't a
word. Only a noise. Five minutes' play—and no score to
Slocombe."

Dour Davie drank, pushed his glass across to the barman with
a meaning nod, which quite clearly conveyed a sense of the
unspoken words, "The same again, laddie."

The circle of deeply interested listeners closed in about the
protagonists in this queer little drama. Was the big man pulling
Dour Davie's leg; or was Davie leading him on? When a man
makes an offer publicly, and says he's got his cheque-book in his
pocket, presumably he means business. On the other hand, Davie
was a good and canny Scot—and his dog was worth about a
pound, of anybody's money, if anybody was out to buy a dog of
that kind.

Who was fooling whom?

If the multi-millionaire who brought up rubber-estates as
though they were postage stamps was in earnest, was Dour Davie
holding out for a better offer? But a man like Hiram K.
Slocombe couldn't be a fool. And whatever Dour Davie was, he
wasn't a fool, either. If the millionaire was bluffing, as of course
he must be, what would he do if David, called his bluff?

Was Slocombe just teasing Urquhart by pitting his bank-roll
against the Scot's stubbornness?

Who was bluffing whom?

It was a queer business; and a slight feeling of tenseness was becoming apparent. The big man evidently did not quite appreciate Davie's apparently contemptuous refusal to answer him; and Davie didn't look, as though he was enjoying the situation in the slightest. Of course, it wasn't in the very best of good taste, to offer a man a price for his dog; but, damn it all, a joke's a joke, and some people in Davie's position might think a thousand-pound joke a very good one indeed.

Mr. Hiram K. Slocombe scratched the back of his neck with the index finger of his right hand, a trick that his secretary again would have recognized as one indicating that he was still more on his mettle and getting just a little het-up.

"If your answer was in Gaelic, Mr. Urquhart," he said smoothly, "I'll frankly confess I don't understand the language. Now, will you tell me in plain English whether you will accept what I think must be a very adequate offer for your dog—fifteen hundred pounds sterling?"

Several of his hearers gasped.

Mike O'Malley laughed audibly, and Chauncey Vanheusen again consulted his watch in the manner of a time-keeper.

Dour Davie drank, looked down at his dog, seated firmly beside his right foot, and again stared at the face of the over-persuasive candidate for its ownership. It was a long and searching look that probed the eyes of the bidder, a look very much of the kind which that gentleman was himself wont to bestow upon an opponent in a business deal or duel.

In a way, Mr. Slocombe was enjoying himself; but only up to a point. Undoubtedly he liked to be at the centre of things; the observed of all observers; what he had heard described by the English Professor at College as "the cynosure of neighbouring eyes."

To the holding of the stage he was well accustomed; and to the limelight he had no objection. And he was well aware that, right here and right now, he was playing the leading part in a little drama that the audience found mighty interesting; a leading part, but, so far, not exactly a winning part. Up till now he had not succeeded in making this dumb guy utter, nor had he beat him to it in the matter of the dog. Childish as he realized both these goals to be, the fact remained that they were goals which he had backed himself to reach, and had done so in public.

And a goal was a goal; an object that he had set himself to achieve was an object he was *going* to achieve, whether it were making a backwoods planter speak or a big country's Prime Minister speak; or whether it were buying a big fleet of ships or buying a goddam dog.

It would be another tale to be told about him—and he was just as fond of having tales told about himself as Henry Ford was—if he bought the highest-priced dog in the world; gave more for a hound, because he fancied it, than ever man had given before in the whole history of the human race. Damn it, he'd make the prices offered for racing-greyhounds look like chicken food, if this dumb guy held out.

"I see you are thinking it over, Mr. Urquhart," he said, meeting Davie's stare. "Fifteen hundred pounds—seven thousand five hundred dollars—is about in the neighbourhood of your price, eh? . . . No? . . . Well, we won't let a few cents stand between us. In the presence of this distinguished company, I offer you ten thousand dollars—two thousand pounds—for this dog."

In a tense, electrical, and almost painful silence, the members of the Narut Club awaited Dour Davie's reply.

Why on earth didn't he cry "Snap!" call the fellow's bluff, and give him the choice of planking down two thousand golden jimmy o' goblins for the wretched dog, or eat his words and look a fool.

The taut silence was broken, not by David Urquhart but by old Tommy Burroughs who, with a fruity laugh, rumbled:

"Seen the tyke swallow a big diamond, Mr. Slocombe?"

A little perfunctory laughter greeted the joke.

"No, sir; no, sir," smiled Hiram K. Slocombe. "Fact of the matter is, I've just taken a fancy to the hound. Just that and—I'll tell you boys in confidence—I do believe he'd just fit a kennel I've got back home in the States. Kennel been standing empty, eating its head off since poor Carlo died. Died on me and left me flat, Mr. Urquhart."

There was more laughter, nods and chuckles.

"Mr. Urquhart, sir," he continued to the dour unsmiling Davie, "I appeal to you. Will you take two thousand five hundred pounds, and let me call him mine? I'll have my secretary cable home instructions for the kennel to be made over. I'll put in central heating; running h. and c.; air-conditioning. Why, if you like, I'll even have it whitewashed. And I'll send you a photo with What's-its-name sitting at the kennel's front door. Twelve thousand five hundred American dollars, Mr. Urquhart, or two thousand five hundred pounds sterling. Is it a deal?"

Dour Davie's lips parted.

"Sh-h-h!" hissed Mike O'Malley. "He's going to speak."

He was mistaken, however. The lips closed again and Davie slowly but methodically shook his head from side to side.

"Ten-minute chukka, and no goal to the Slocombe side," observed Chauncey Vanheusen.

"No? Not enough? You refuse my bid of two thousand five hundred pounds, eh?" said Hiram K. Slocombe, as Davie once again turned his back and took up his drink. "Well, as I said before, I don't profess to be an authority on dog values, and wouldn't presume to criticize your judgment, but it certainly must be some dog if its price is above two thousand five hundred pounds."

"Oh, definitely above rubies," observed Mike O'Malley. "Full of virtues that don't leap to the eye. Can't weigh virtue against gold."

"What is gold but filthy lucre and dirty dross?" asked Mr. Vanheusen.

"Dirty dross," agreed O'Malley. "And nobody could call What's-its-name a dirty dog," he mused. "Still, it's a fair offer. Quite a fair offer."

"I thought so. I thought so," said Hiram K. Slocombe, smiling at his friends and savouring the joke. "What would your own idea have been, Mr. O'Malley, if you had been making an offer for the dog?"

"Ninepence," replied O'Malley promptly.

"So you weren't so far out, you see," said Vanheusen.

"Well, the bid wasn't an insult to the dog, was it?" laughed Slocombe.

"Mr. Urquhart," he continued as the Scot put down his glass, turned about and moved as though to leave the bar, "I'll ask one more favour of you. Would you kindly consider an offer which will be open for twenty-four hours, of fifteen thousand dollars for the dog? Three thousand pounds. If you'll close the deal at once, I will give you my cheque right now. And if you prefer to think it over and let me know to-morrow, I'll have the cheque ready."

"Thanks," replied Dour Davie. "Guid-nicht, all."

And he walked out of the Club followed by his dog.

"Four words in forty minutes," observed Vanheusen. "That's not a word a minute, Slocombe. As far as I can work it out, it is at the rate of a word to ten minutes. . . . And the dog said still less."

§2

A couple of evenings later, David Urquhart sat in a long chair on his verandah, his whisky on one side of him, his dog on the other.

Silently his bare-footed boy approached and tendered him a letter on a brass tray.

From the table beside him, Urquhart picked up a large, strong, long-bladed knife which was his almost constant companion. He wore it in a sheath at his belt when he was in the jungle, and usually laid it down on this table when he came into the bungalow, for in its time it played many parts, both as tool and weapon.

He now used it as a paper-knife, opened the envelope and read the letter that it contained:—

> "*My dear Mr. Urquhart,*
>
> *I should like to apologise for having bothered you as I did on Tuesday evening at the Club. It was really unpardonable, and I hope you'll forgive me. As I have heard nothing from you, I take it that you do not wish to sell the dog for three thousand pounds. Well now, I'll make you a real offer, and I'll leave this one open again for twenty-four hours. I'll pay you the sum of twenty-five thousand dollars—five thousand pounds sterling—for your dog.*
> >   *Sincerely,*
> >   *Hiram K. Slocombe.*"

Without comment, David Urquhart gave the letter to the dog

to read, and was not surprised to note that the dog gave it no more than a perfunctory glance.

Receiving no reply to this offer, Hiram K. Slocombe behaved a little childishly, even as the biggest of big men sometimes do.

"You were right when you said that guy was nearly as short on manners as he is on speech," he remarked at breakfast, to his friend and host, O'Malley. "Looks like I'll have to hand it to the stiff, and lose two bets."

"Well, perhaps the first one was hardly fair," smiled O'Malley. "It was what I believe you call a cinch. Nobody ever heard Dour Davie talk at the rate of a word a minute. But I admit I'm surprised about the dog. What was your last? Five thousand pounds?"

"I can't believe it, but it's a fact," grinned Slocombe.

"What would you have done if he had called your bluff?"

"What would I have done? Why, paid him the money. Given him the money—and the dog too. I don't want the hound. Wouldn't be seen dead with it. . . . But I'd have liked to put Urquhart where he belongs."

" I think you have," smiled O'Malley. "Or rather, you've left him there."

Hiram K. Slocombe put down his coffee cup and stared hard at his host.

"Tell me," he said, "you think he comes out of it better than I do? You don't think he's just a plain dumb fool to refuse twenty-five thousand dollars for an animal that's worth no more than five dollars to anybody."

"Yes, I think he's a fool," replied O'Malley. "A splendid one. I'd never be such a fool myself. Unfortunately. . . . Are you going to try again?"

"I am. If it's a competition in folly between fools, I'm going to beat him to it. I'm going to offer him ten thousand pounds for the cur. And I'm going to have the cheque ready written, and I'm going to offer it to him."

"Interesting. . . . Amusing. . . . Very," observed O'Malley, lighting a cigarette. "And you'll pay that for the dog if Davie accepts?"

"No, sir. Dog nothing. I'll pay it to show your Mr. Urquhart who is the bigger fool—and who's the better man—when it comes to a show-down."

O'Malley pursed his lips and studied the tip of his cigarette judgmatically.

"Fair enough, eh?" asked Slocombe, sharply, sensing something of criticism, if not disapproval, in O'Malley's attitude.

"Well! . . . Yes. . . . Yes, I suppose so—although ten thousand pounds may be nothing to you, and the dog may be everything to Davie."

"Oh, come, come," expostulated Slocombe. "Every man has his price, and surely every dog has."

"Has every man his price, eh?" asked O'Malley, gazing through half-closed eyes at his guest.

"Every mother's son in the whole wide world, though it may not be a cash one," was the reply.

"Well, I shall be very interested to see what Davie's price is. Or his dog's," smiled O'Malley.

Nor were Micky O'Malley and Chauncey Vanheusen the only people interested in the matter. It would be but slight exaggeration to say that every white man in Narut was intrigued and amused at this remarkable duel between Slocombe and Urquhart. Or, as O'Malley phrased it, between Urquhart's stubbornness and Slocombe's cheque-book, a description to which Chauncey Vanheusen demurred, saying he preferred to view it as a contest between a dour Scot's stubborn independence and his love for his dog on the one hand, and a Big Business man's pride, determination, and cheque-book on the other.

Speculation was rife as to whether Dour Davie would come again to the Club, while Slocombe was in Narut. Some members thought that he would keep away out of sheer dislike of publicity; while others thought he would come to show; that he didn't funk the battle, and for the pleasure of denying and thwarting his persecutor.

The latter, were right. That evening, word went quickly round the Club that Davie was in the bar; and when it was known that O'Malley and Vanheusen had brought Slocombe, men left the billiard-room, tennis-courts, verandahs and purlieus of the Club, and drifted toward its spacious bar-room.

To each of the numerous greetings of "Evening, Davie!"

Urquhart replied with an unsmiling nod.

Once, when asked if he'd have a drink he raised his half-filled glass by way of reply.

Asked again later, he not only nodded but went the length of saying:

"Aye!"

When, seizing a favourable opportunity, Hiram K. Slocombe came up to him and said:

"Good evening, Mr. Urquhart. I was sorry not to get a favourable reply to my note asking if I might buy your dog. It wasn't a case of silence giving consent, I suppose?" Davie tightened his tight lips and shook his head.

"No? Well, I want to tell you something, Mr. Urquhart. I do sincerely regret to seem—uh—persistent, importunate, but I really do want to buy the dog, and I want you to humour me. What's more, I want to make you feel you *want* to humour me. And feel good about it, see? I want to put an end to the annoyance I am causing you.

"With this," he added, producing a cheque from the wallet that he took from his pocket. "My cheque for ten thousand pounds. . . . Shake?"

And Mr. Slocombe extended his hand.

So did Davie, but it was to pick up his glass.

Having drained it he put it down, took out his handkerchief, wiped his lips and made a brief speech.

"Dog not for sale," he said; and, followed by the most valuable dog that ever lived, walked out of the bar-room and the Club.

That night he sat late on his verandah in his favourite long chair, a magazine in one hand, and in the other, the knife with which, from time to time, he cut its leaves.

Toward midnight the dog arose, yawned, stretched itself fore and aft, and looked at its master.

Davie nodded in reply, refraining from remarking that no doubt the dog was right and that it was past bed-time.

Fastening the door of the lattice-work verandah he went along to his bedroom, and five minutes later was reading himself to sleep. His eyes closed.

He opened them, laid down the magazine and the knife,

turned lower the wick of the reading-lamp and, a minute later, was asleep.

He was awakened by a noise, a thud, a crash and a piercing yelp.

In the act of springing up he saw by the brilliant light of the moon and the dull glow of the lamp, that a leopard was in the room, that it was holding the dog down with one foot while looking back over its shoulder, either disturbed by Davie's movement or to see that its line of retreat was clear.

Seizing the dog in its teeth, it turned about, and all that Davie had to do was to lie still and let it go.

With a shout of—

"No, you don't, b'Goad!" Davie snatched up the oil lamp and flung it in the leopard's face as it gathered itself for its spring at the open window through which it had come into the room.

The lamp smashed and went out. Scarcely had it done so ere Davie had seized the knife from where it had lain by the lamp and sprung from his bed. The panther, partly blinded, dropped the dog, shook its head and reared up on its hind legs as Davie leapt and stabbed.

With a terrifying snarl, the panther, clawed at Davie's shoulders and strove to bury its fangs in his throat.

With his left arm pinned across his body, Davie thrust his elbow into the great open mouth, and stabbed again and again at the panther's side.

But a panther's real assault, against a foe that fights erect, is made with the claws of its hind feet.

Crunching the man's arm, embedding the claws of its fore-feet in his shoulders, it flung its weight upon him, and with the terrible talons of its hind feet, clawed and tore and tore.

The dog, painfully dragging itself to its feet, seized one of the immensely powerful hind legs that worked with piston-like speed and power, crunched, held, and hung on.

Beneath the dead weight of the terrible impetus of the attack, Davie, in spite of his great strength and powerful build, was borne back and fell, the panther above him.

As they crashed to the floor, Davie stabbed again, driving the ten-inch blade of the hunting-knife into the side of the panther's neck.

With blood spouting from its mouth, the brute, stabbed through the lungs, stabbed to the heart, stabbed through carotid artery and jugular vein, bit and tore and bit and tore again, until with a choking cough it ceased, lurched, collapsed and fell sideways.

*   *   *   *   *   *   *

The tombstone that Hiram K. Slocombe insisted upon erecting above the spot where David Urquhart and his dog were buried together, is perhaps the finest that covers the grave of any European in the East.

Nor did anyone in Narut take exception to the inscription which he ordered to be carved upon it. This concluded with the words—

"Greater love hath no man than this, that he lay down his life for his friend."

THE PERFECT CRIME

"The Perfect Crime" is the story of a man who commits the perfect murder of the woman he does not want to marry. But is it the perfect murder? "The Perfect Crime" was first published as the fourth story in Part II, "Quaint", of Odd—But Even So *(1941). The story has also appeared as an audio recording in* Classic Tales of Murder *(1992),* Classic Stories of Crime & Murder *(2001),* Classic Tales of Horror, Crime & Murder *(2003?), and* Murder Most Foul *(2007).*

We have it on accepted authority, that of Shakespeare, I believe, or some such writing-fellow, that the sight of means to do ill deeds makes ill deeds done.

I don't know about that, but I suppose it is quite possible that the sight of a loaded pistol might give some person of ill-balanced mind a bright idea of shooting-up his wife or some other individual whom he didn't like. I don't know. But what I do know is that dalliance with the ideas of methods of committing an ill deed may very easily lead to the doing of it. All these detective-stories about very clever murderers, for example. I can quite understand how anybody given to the study of such alleged literature, might find himself given also to the study of how to commit the absolutely undetectable murder or other crime, and then proceeding from the study to the exercise, so to speak; from theory to practice.

Like war. If there were no generals, dictators, kings, and people who study the art of successful war and think out undefeatable strategy and tactics, there would be no army peace-manœuvres and no army war-manœuvres either.

Of course, I don't for one moment pretend that all murders or even the majority of murders are brought about through people becoming interested in the theory of undetectable killing, and then in its practice, but, I do say that there is danger, and very great danger, in the study.

I also know that some murders are the direct outcome of the academic study of the subject, and thinking out a method of committing the perfect murder. And I say it because I know.

I committed one.

It was the perfect crime, the absolutely undetectable murder, and it remains and always will remain, undetected. It is just possible that the truth may come out when my safe is opened after my death, my papers examined, and this document read.

But I doubt it, for I don't propose to lay a trail to the spot where the murder was committed, nor say anything to identify either the victim or the murderer. What I desire to do is to warn people who make the reading of these murder-stories their hobby, anodyne, and way of escape from the realities of life. It is a dangerous practice, and might make any mild-mannered, well-behaved and law-abiding citizen, such as myself, into that most dreadful, degraded and criminal of human beings, a murderer.

Now I freely admit that I heartily disliked Phœbe Wallowes. To me she was wholly antipathetic as a type and as an individual. She got on my nerves, as the saying is. She had never done me any real harm—not the sort of harm or injury for which one can obtain redress in a Court of Law, that is; nor the sort of harm against which one could protest, with angry and righteous expostulation. She merely annoyed me every time she spoke; merely irritated me beyond bearing, by everything she did and she was nothing worse than a terror, a burden, and a curse.

And not only was she a terror in the sense in which one uses the word when one says of a man, woman or child who is a bore, a nuisance, or otherwise objectionable, that he or she is "a perfect terror." No, I lived in genuine terror—that some day, somehow, Phœbe Wallowes would marry me. I am not a weak-willed person of feeble intellect. Quite the contrary. But I have a gaping joint in my armour, and that, curiously enough, in a self-confessed deliberate and cold-blooded murderer of a woman, is—chivalry!

I knew in my bones that if ever occasion arose through which Phœbe Wallowes could make me feel that she had a claim upon me, that I ought to marry her, if only for auld lang syne (or because a bunch of auld lang-toothed maids were coupling our names) I should propose to her. Nay, beg her to marry me as though it were the dearest wish of my heart.

And patiently, skilfully, cunningly, she was—what shall I

say—creating such an atmosphere, establishing such a situation, weaving a web in whose invisible, imponderable but unbreakable meshes I should be inextricably entangled.

Don't mistake me. I don't want to wrong the memory of Phœbe Wallowes, nor exculpate myself. She did not endeavour to trap me. She was incapable of anything so vulgar. Her thoroughly nice mind would have revolted from the thought of evolving some plot and hatching some plan whereby I should be discovered in compromising circumstances—circumstances so compromising that I should be left with the choice of scandal or matrimony, a choice between hopelessly damaging a reputedly innocent maiden's name or irrevocably changing it. She was no man-trap, no vulgar designing gold-digger or husband-hunter. She was a modest and virtuous American woman; a well-educated, right-minded gentlewoman; well educated, well bred, well behaved; a thoroughly good daughter to her aged parents; a good sister to two younger brothers making their way in the world with her help; a good mistress to her employees, cook, maid and gardener; and a good friend and neighbour.

Yes, like everyone else in our small town, I looked upon her and found her good. In every manifestation and capacity, position and situation, save that of wife. For me, that is to say. No one could agree more readily than I that she would be a magnificent wife—for somebody else. And no one, unless it were a fortunate husband, would have been more delighted to view her in the role of wife—to somebody else.

But when I thought of this good, able, worthy, conscientious and accomplished woman as my wife, I hated not only the thought, but her as well.

And slowly, ineluctably, the coils closed and tightened about me. People began inviting us together. It dawned upon me suddenly that I never went to any kind of social function, any gathering or party to which people came by invitation, without meeting her. Not only meeting her, but finding her beside or near me. Not only was I unable to go out to dinner without meeting her, but soon I could not do so without finding that she was my partner.

"Let's see, you'd like to take Miss Wallowes in, wouldn't you?" hostesses began to murmur.

And before long it was a case of—

"You'll take Phœbe in, of course, won't you ? "

Nor am I, unfortunately perhaps, of the type that could deal promptly with such a situation by the help of raised eyebrows, a sideway smile, and a murmur of—

"What, *again*?"

If, at a dance, I ventured to stray from her side and waltz with some girl whom I really did like and who really could dance, there was of course no word or glance of reproach from Phœbe Wallowes. But oh, how I had hurt her, and how well I knew it; and how I raged against the false position into which I had been manœuvred.

No, I withdraw that. Let me say, the false position into which I had drifted; but I will add to it. If not in self-defence, at any rate in explanation I may say—the false position into which I had drifted on the strong current of Phœbe's will-power, determination, and force of character.

No—there was never a reproach, whether uttered or expressed by look and manner, but only a maddening conviction of sin.

Damn it, why shouldn't I dance with Helen Vansittart if I wanted to? What right had Phœbe Wallowes to be hurt because I did so? None whatever. But hurt she was, horribly; and it hurt me horribly to have hurt her, curse her!

I don't suppose that anyone reading this confession will really understand the position unless they knew Phœbe. And me. I am that sort of fool, so sensitive that I blush from head to foot, and break into a cold sweat at the thought of some tiny *gaffe* or *faux pas* I made years ago, or at the memory of some careless, thoughtless and completely accidental word that may have hurt somebody.

And yet I could commit a murder.

A queer thing, human nature.

Not only is man the proper study of mankind, but the most intriguing study, the most puzzling. And one of its most interesting puzzles is that of mutual attraction and repulsion; likings and antipathies. Now though I disliked Phœbe Wallowes the very first time I saw her, it was for no reason that I could put into words.

In appearance she was tall; too tall for my liking; strongly-built; rather more Amazonian in type than any woman needs to look; always just a little untidy, faintly blowsy, though always looking, nevertheless, well, quietly and expensively dressed. She had big—no, let me say, very useful—hands and feet; and ankles and neck thicker than my particular taste demands. I didn't like her hair nor the way in which she did it, and though I liked her features, I didn't like her face. Lest this sound foolishly captious, I might express it by saying that though I could find no fault with any individual feature, I found insurmountable fault with the assembly. (It is generally admitted, I believe, that any assembly is much worse than the members thereof.)

And so far as a woman of birth and breeding, culture and refinement may be, she was gushing. Not a notorious gusher; nothing suggestive of the oil-well or geyser; but just a little, a very little, too voluble, too expansive, and if there is anything I detest in man, woman or beast, it is lack of self-control, particularly lack of reticence in speech and gesture.

As I say, I disliked her from the first, on sight; and if there be such a thing as love at first sight, this was a case of hate at first sight. Personally, I don't agree that there is such a thing as either of these. But I know, and so does everybody else, that there is liking and attraction at first sight, and in the case of Phœbe Wallowes, I know there was dislike and repulsion at first sight; and every time I saw her I disliked her more—until the day dawned when I admitted that I feared her as well, feared her because I knew that not only did she intend to marry me, but that she would inevitably do it.

Why didn't I go away, and escape my threatened fate by ignominious flight?

Because it would have been ignominious. Because it wasn't fair or right or reasonable that I should be driven from my inherited home in which I had been bred and born and which I loved. And because my business, my friends, my interests, my everything, were in my home town, which I loved.

No, let *her* go.

And it was at about the time when I had come to the conclusion that something really must be done about it, and also that there was really nothing to be done about it (inasmuch as I couldn't go and she wouldn't go) that I picked up that well-known thriller "The Murder on the Mat."

It was a dreadful book, really; absolutely beneath contempt as literature, but sufficiently justifying its name of thriller to keep me from thinking of other things, and particularly of that other Thing while I was reading it.

And from "The Murder on the Mat" I went on to "The Murder in the Moat" and "The Murder in the Boat" and "The Murder in the Tote."

Tripe and trash.

I was a little ashamed of my addiction to this vice, in the sort of way that I should have been rather ashamed of addiction to the whisky bottle, the hypodermic syringe, the little white tablet; but secretly I indulged, and, like any other bad habit would have done, it grew upon me. Soon I read with avidity every detective-story and crime-novel on which I could lay hands.

And having been a critical reader from my youth up, I read these sad products of our latter-day civilization critically—not from a literary point of view, God wot, but from that of the amateur detective, and indeed from that of the amateur murderer.

One day I read a rather superior specimen of this class of mental drug, a story called "The Perfect Crime." And as it was set forth, it was in point of fact, the perfect crime, fool-proof and undetectable. Very satisfying.

Satisfying, yes. For suddenly there leapt up from my subconscious mind the hideous thought, or rather realization, that I had, without knowing it, cast Phœbe Wallowes for the role of victim in these murder stories!

The effect of the shock quickly wore off, and before long, without self-deception or subterfuge, I deliberately imagined the Corpse on the Mat, or in the Boat, or the Moat or the Tote, to be that of Phœbe Wallowes. Also I estimated the murderer's worth, merit and ability—as a murderer—and, discounting the supernatural abilities of the amateur detective who is inevitably so very much superior to the best of the highly-trained and widely-experienced professionals, I envisaged myself as the murderer, gauged my chances of evasion, not only of punishment but of detection; and I exercised my mind in discovering the point at which he went wrong, the vital mistake that he made, the weak link in the chain that bound him to success and safety.

I became an amateur of crime; of the greatest crime of all; and if it were not, as I have said, a case of the sight of means to do ill deeds making ill deeds done, it was undeniably a case of dalliance with methods of committing an ill deed leading to the doing of it.

And coincidentally with my increasing interest in this fascinating subject of successful murder, grew my increasing fear and hatred of Phœbe Wallowes. Daily she grew more possessive, more overwhelming, more persuasive; relentlessly probing and prying and interfering; and ever she grew more arch.

Merciful Heavens, how arch that woman could be! And how I shrank and cringed from that terrible finger-shaking, smiling, suggestive archness.

Don't misunderstand my use of the word suggestive. It is a word that has a special and ugly meaning. Nothing could be further from any thought or word or deed of Phœbe's than that sort of suggestiveness; but her archness was suggestive of unutterable profundities of understanding between us. More—it implied that there was an understanding between us. It implied that there was an "understanding" between us in the most matrimonial sense of that word. It was implicatory of collusion, if you know what I mean; and at one and the same time it made my flesh creep and my blood boil, a mixture of abject horror and angry resentment at such an assumption.

And one day, after reading a cheap and silly crime book, written by some boisterous semi-illiterate, in which the murderer had simply shoved his victim over the edge of a cliff, I went for my favourite walk which took me along some bluffs by the river, and suddenly I realized that I was passing the spot where the Perfect Murder could be committed.

Although in a shallow dip, the quiet country road here ran along a steep bank which dropped sheer to the River that ran, strong and deep, below the slightly overhanging edge, to its famous whirlpool.

I stopped, went to the edge, and looked down. The swiftly-rushing water swept past. Not the strongest swimmer on earth, not the most powerful oarsman in the lightest of boats, could have made headway against that stream; could, with his utmost efforts, have remained stationary; could have done anything to prevent being swept to the supposedly bottomless hole, where the water surged and swirled before entering the narrows and rapids that lead to our little local Niagara.

So powerful was the current that, a mile or so farther back from where I was standing, a stranger had once taken his harnessed horse to drink at a tiny shelving pebbly beach where the road ran at river level. Amazing as it may seem to anyone that doesn't know this river, the horse, taking a few paces too far into the water, lost its footing, or was swept from its feet and both horse and cart were engulfed by the whirlpool, and were never seen again.

As I stood and stared at the glassy, flecked and convoluted surface of that dangerous death-trap, the Perfect Crime was conceived in my heart; and all that night I lay awake and pondered it.

I must not take her there, lest we be seen together, as of course we should be. Someone always saw us when we were together, and mentioned the interesting fact

> *With quips and cranks and wanton wiles,*
> *Nods and becks and wreathed smiles,*

and there was more archness, implication and suggestion—of matrimony.

And now my addiction, initiation, my training and experience in crime, albeit theoretical, stood me in good stead—or bad—for, hard upon the heels of the realization that I must not take her there, came the cunning thought that I had but to let fall a reference to the place that had become my favourite haunt, and inevitably I should sooner or later discover that it was hers.

Without doubt I should meet her there; without doubt we should sooner or later stroll past the scene of what was to be my Perfect Crime. Perhaps on the first or second or third, occasion it might happen. Possibly on the first occasion a passer-by might see us, and the deed would have to be postponed. Except on Sundays and Saturday afternoons, the probabilities were that we should be there alone at any time other than evening, when romantic couples, released from their day's toil, occasionally made it their place of pilgrimage.

The very next day, taking tea with those busy-minded busybodies, the Misses Conklin, I encountered Phœbe. The two old gossips were of course aiding and abetting her to the utmost of their power. As inevitably happened, we left the Conklin house together. As we strolled away, she asked me, as usual, what I had been doing with myself since last we met—a question that always irritated me almost beyond bearing, as the time "since last we met" was never more than a couple of days.

"Oh, nothing," I replied. "The usual. What does one do? Business till lunch-time and then a stroll out to the Point. I've seen a couple of the loveliest sunsets from there, this week. I wish I could get the colours on to paper. I must try."

It was enough. Three days later, there she was, watching the sunset from the Point. A few yards of turf separated the bank-edge from the road, a slight hollow made a most comfortable place in which to recline. She was sitting there when I arrived; and, having greeted me with the surprise proper to so remarkable a coincidence as my appearing just there and just then, pointed to the turf beside her.

I sat down. Across the river the steep rock that was the opposite bank rose twenty or thirty feet higher than the one on which we sat. To the left and right the road dipped down to this promontory known as the Point. I realized that we were absolutely alone.

As often as I might do so without appearing restless, and thereby arousing her interest in that phenomenon, I watched the road to left and to right, and when not doing so, I stared at the opposite bank where, silhouetted, was the outline of a dense thicket.

"Isn't it rather wonderful," gushed Phœbe, "to think that we are so near to the busy marts of men, so near the madding crowd, and yet we might be hundreds of miles away from human habitation. So near and yet so far. Quite in a little world of our own, Edgar. Our own little world."

"Yes," agreed I, and strove to keep any hint of grimness from my voice. "We might be hundreds of miles from the nearest human habitation. Quite alone beyond sight and sound of our fellow man."

"Not a soul to see us," murmured Phœbe, her moist lips parting, her moist eyes widening.

I shuddered.

"You are not cold, my dear?"

"I certainly shivered," I replied, and rising to my feet, I found that I was trembling violently.

This I endeavoured to disguise by busily brushing myself down, patting my pockets as though assuring myself as to whether I had cigarette-case and matches. And then, with a great effort of will-power, having conquered my nerves, I pointed with steady hand to the water.

"Look!" I cried. "Look! . . ."

Rising to her feet Phœbe took a few steps that brought her within a yard or so of the edge, and then with a swift glance to left and right to assure myself that we were alone, I stepped behind her and thrust with all my might.

Staggering forward, she threw up her arms, and fell.

Without horror, remorse, or regret I saw her swept away at amazing speed. Her head never appeared. For a second I saw a hand, and then she was gone. A minute later she must have disappeared into the swirling vortex, have been whirled round as she disappeared for ever. The dreadful sucking whirlpool would for ever remain as secret as the grave—the watery grave that it was.

In that moment a tremendous weight was lifted from my mind. A terrific burden fell from me, as the woman whom I hated, loathed, and feared, fell from the point into the rushing water.

Straining my eyes to stare at the opposite bank, I was certain that no one was there. Indeed, I knew that no one could be there. It would be practically impossible to approach the river through the dense trackless undergrowth of that thicket.

Glancing to the-right, I saw that the road was still empty.

Turning to the left, the same reassuring sight met my anxious gaze. An empty road.

Heaving a deep sigh of relief, I dusted my hands one against the other, as though they had been in contact with something that had sullied them; and then, turning about, I came face to face with a man who, seated on the grass some yards from me and above me, regarded me intently.

I'm quite sure that in that second I very nearly died, so great and so terrible was the shock.

I do not use a mere *façon de parler* in saying that my heart stood still.

It did stand still. It stopped so long that, as I say, I thought I should die. My strength left me, and it was all I could do to keep from collapsing upon the ground.

My Perfect Crime, committed within a few feet of a deeply interested onlooker! In that dreadful moment or minute—if it were not an hour or a lifetime—I saw the crowded Court, a severe-faced Judge, a condemned cell, a death-house in which stood the stark and ugly Chair.

My Perfect Murder! I could have laughed aloud, a gust of maniacal mirth.

And then another evil thought—product of the wretched books with which I had debased my mind—a second murder to cover up the first! Many times that had happened in the crime stories that I had studied.

This man must die too.

And that murderous thought was followed by another, a thought of fear and dread and disappointment. It was one thing to thrust an unsuspecting woman over an edge that lay almost at her feet. It was quite another to throw over it a man as big and strong as myself, a man who had just witnessed such a deed, a man forewarned and forearmed, who would fight with all the strength that was in him.

It was as likely that he would throw me over. Likelier still that, grappling on the verge, we should both fall to mutual destruction.

Or supposing that I was the winner in the death struggle, and succeeded in thrusting him over. What of the Perfect Crime then? What of the signs of struggle? What of my return with torn and dishevelled clothing? Perhaps with cut, bruised and damaged hands and face. And what of the chances of some wayfarer coming over the hill to left or right, and, seeing what was happening, rushing to interfere?

How long was it before, trembling and sweating, I moved toward that dreadful figure of doom, seated so calmly there, sitting so coldly in judgment, a human Nemesis, figure of fate and of death.

What was in my mind as I walked toward him, I know not. But I know that I strove to speak and could not. He rose to his feet, and as he did so, picked up the stout staff that lay beside him.

No, not that he might strike me down, but to tap his way across the soundless turf until he reached the hard high road along which, without a word, he proceeded.

In nightmares I hear that perfectly noiseless tapping still.

Pity the Blind!

       *   *   *   *   *   *   *

He sits, patient and still, at the corner of the block, close to my house, holding a tin for the receipt of alms.

Every time I see him, I am reminded of my successful and perfect crime.

§2

To-day, as I passed him, he opened his eyes, looked up, and winked at me—a leering wink of most terrible promise and threat.

He is no more blind than I am.
He knows . . .

Tap. Tap. Tap . . . Up the path to my front door.

TELEPATHY EXTRAORDINARY

"Telepathy Extraordinary" is the story of twin brothers, Alphonse and André Tabouille (André also appeared in the story "Cafard"). The brothers claim that since they are twins they have a telepathic connection with each other. During the Riffian campaign, the brothers are stationed at neighboring posts when Alphonse hears that a lieutenant has been killed at the neighboring post. He then claims to know the details of his brother's death due to the telepathic link that they share. "Telepathy Extraordinary" was first published as the sixth story in Part II, "Quaint", of Odd—But Even So *(1941).*

From their early childhood, the twin brothers Alphonse and André Tabouille exploited their extraordinary likeness, both in ways that were perfectly legitimate and in some in which the legality was less perfect.

In the home, at school and at St. Cyr, they occasionally arranged matters to their mutual satisfaction by impersonating one another. Sometimes they deceived friends in this way, more particularly women friends.

And, apart from particular examples of their turning their remarkable resemblance to good account, there was also the general and continual condition of satisfaction resultant upon the phenomenon. It put them *hors concours*; made them more remarkable and interesting than other young men of equal merit, ability, and attractiveness; gave them an enjoyable distinction.

Yes; it may fairly be said that, in every possible way, they made the most of themselves as twins; not only extracting the utmost usefulness from the physical likeness, but exploring every mental, spiritual, and moral avenue, and exploiting all possibilities discoverable therein.

They assiduously developed a remarkable and exact similarity of tastes, opinions, attitudes, particular preferences and peculiar likes and dislikes. As for their telepathic accord, it would seem that almost they were indeed two minds with but a single thought.

Short of doing anything so vulgar as advertise themselves,

they took good care that none who knew them should fail to know that they were not as other men.

Occasionally some envious creature would make the shameful suggestion that the Tabouille twins deliberately staged little scenes designed to exhibit remarkable instances of their mental and spiritual twinship, and the wonderful telepathy that existed between them when they were parted.

That sort of remark merely displayed the meanness and stupidity of the speaker. There are some who almost always jeer at what they cannot understand; and there are quite a number, it would appear, who completely fail to understand the workings of the wonders of telepathy.

However, facts are stubborn things, and the Tabouille twins provided innumerable proofs in support of their contention that they lived in a state of completest telepathic communication.

Not only would one know intuitively and in his waking hours, when something important or remarkable happened to his brother, as though his brain had received a wireless message, but also each, at night, would dream of the absent brother, see him in a vision, and know exactly what he was doing and what was happening to him. At least, so they said, and no one, even if sufficiently churlish to desire to do so, could disprove it.

In due course, the twins Tabouille were gazetted to a Line Regiment and thence seconded to the Foreign Legion, where it is possible that the somewhat mixed Mess of their Battalion was less interested in them and their phenomena than had been that of their Line Regiment. In piping times of peace and the dull routine of an ordinary garrison-town, even the psychical phenomena of twin-brother members can provide interesting conversation for a bored Mess.

§2

In the Riff campaign, the strong *poste* of Taffrant, held by six companies of the Legion, a key position of the greatest importance, was completely surrounded by a great Riffian army that outnumbered its defenders by a hundred to one. Not only were the Moorish sharp-shooters provided with unlimited ammunition, but their Commander had at his disposal a battery of field-guns served by German artillerymen. Incidentally, it is quite probable that among them was the famous deserter from the French Foreign Legion, Odo Klemens (or Otho Klems).

The nearest French force at Fez el Bali was in a position of equal, if not greater, danger, inasmuch as there was a large number of wounded in the *poste*; a big accumulation of transport-baggage and mules; and the troops were more than over-fatigued, they were utterly exhausted, literally weary almost to death.

Far from being able to afford any relief to the force at Taffrant, surrounded, and in danger of being overwhelmed, Fez el Bali could not in itself hope to hold out for any length of time, if attacked.

What troubled the officers, more than the danger to themselves and their comrades at Taffrant, was the fact that, if Taffrant fell and the victorious Riffian army then swept down upon Fez el Bali, the road to Fez itself, the capital of Morocco, would be open; and if Fez fell, much of Maréchal Lyautey's work would be undone, and the fruits of the Moroccan campaign lost.

As night descended, messages came from Taffrant by signal lamp: "*Send help if you can.*" And when a battalion of the Legion asks for help, it is known that help is badly needed. Nor was Colonel Pompey, commanding the beleaguered force, the man to make such an appeal easily.

After an even more urgent message, "*We are very hard pressed. Can you send help?*" no further signal was received; but, hour after hour, the battle at Taffrant continued with increasing violence.

Suddenly, at three o'clock in the morning, it stopped. An attempt was then made by Fez el Bali to call up Taffrant by signal lamp.

It was made in vain.

The garrison of Fez el Bali was aghast. Was the *poste* blotted out; a battalion of the Legion annihilated; their comrades killed to the last man, and the Riffian harka, even now creeping swiftly and stealthily through the darkness, to achieve a similar victory over the other little force?

Standing beside the anxious Commandant was Lieutenant Alphonse Tabouille. Suddenly, as they stared into the darkness, the garrison of Fez el Bali were overjoyed to see an answering flash. With breathless anxiety, the message was read out:

"Enemy beaten off. Heavy casualties. Officer losses. Four Captains and one Lieutenant killed, and . . ."

"That's my brother," groaned Lieutenant Alphonse Tabouille, reading no further; and in the anguish of his anxiety and grief, he momentarily forgot discipline.

"*Stop!*" he cried, as though the far-distant signaller could hear him. And then to his own Commandant, urgently, angrily:

"*Ask for the Lieutenant's name,*" he cried. "*For God's sake stop them—and call them up yourself. Stop them—and ask for his name. It is my brother. I know it.*"

Naturally no notice was taken of this request; and doubtless the young officer was utterly ashamed of himself before the words were well out of his mouth.

When the long message from the Commandant at Taffrant was concluded and answered by the Officer Commanding Fez el Bali, that kindly gentleman—after a word of reproof to Lieutenant Alphonse Tabouille—allowed the young officer's question to be transmitted.

"*What is the name of the Lieutenant killed?*"

The state of mind of Lieutenant Alphonse Tabouille may be imagined as, weary to death, half dead from lack of sleep, and with nerves frayed beyond endurance, he awaited the reply.

None came. The question was ignored. Doubtless the Commandant had something else to do than to furnish names of dead Lieutenants.

"And so my brother is dead, eh!" was all Tabouille said, as stoically he gave up hope, accepted the blow and lay down to sleep.

In the morning the first person to whom he spoke was Lieutenant Lebœuf, whom he did not like, a sly-looking sarcastic fellow of macabre humour and mordant wit; a probing sceptic, whose attitude to Life, Death and the Vast Forever was one sweet smile of complete agnosticism.

"Hullo!" he said. "I had an amazing dream last night. Really more a vision than a dream. Sort of thing that you and your brother go in for. Must have caught the complaint from you. Most realistic dream I ever had. Thought I had better tell you. I dreamed about your brother."

"Indeed?" observed Lieutenant Alphonse Tabouille coldly, in spite of the fact that he was warmly indignant.

Who the devil was this Lebœuf to dream about André? If any dreaming were to be done about André, he, Alphonse, would do it; and Lebœuf was probably lying, anyway, the incorrigible and impudent *blagueur*.

"Yes," continued Lebœuf, "your wonderful brother. But surely you must know. That marvellous telepathic communication between you has surely . . ."

"I do know, thank you," interrupted Lieutenant Alphonse Tabouille.

"*Mon Dieu!* You saw it too? The sudden rush. The overwhelming wave of savage Riffians, hacking, slashing, stabbing . . . and your brave brother. . . . To think that it was I, and not you, who saw the end. I and not you who saw him fall, and who know all about it!"

Alphonse Tabouille, whose nerves were frayed to rags and tatters by fatigue and anxiety, found difficulty in controlling the curiously savage rage that boiled up in him.

"If that was what you dreamed, it's neither interesting nor significant," he said cuttingly. "Lieutenant André Tabouille died from bullet wounds. In the first place, not only did I know it intuitively the instant that he fell; but in the second place I saw the whole affair in a dream last night, saw him die as clearly as though I had been an actual witness, present on the spot; and in the third place, as I was in the act of waking from that dream, my brother appeared to me, and *not* in a vision. I saw him, himself."

"Saw his astral form, rather," interrupted Lebœuf, speaking in a serious tone of great gravity and unwonted solemnity.

"And he took farewell of me. Of this I do not wish to speak," added Alphonse, turning his head away.

"Of course not. Naturally," replied Lebœuf with deep sympathy. "But it is strange that I should have dreamed a different dream of him."

"Not at all. The truly strange thing would be that you should dream of him at all," replied Alphonse Tabouille contemptuously.

"Well, we shall soon know which of us is right," said Lebœuf as his Sergeant approached and saluted. "In my dream—my vision—I saw him struck down. He cried '*I die that France may live'* . . . The Colonel cried *'But yes! France would surely cease to live if you didn't,'* and Lieutenant André Tabouille closed his eyes. He had been struck on the nose by an onion thrown with frightful force by a huge Chleuch tribesman. I say that thus your brother fell. . . . Excuse these tears. . . ."

"Your good taste is as remarkable as your wit," answered Tabouille crushingly, as he walked away. . . .

Again only a mean-spirited person, such as the sceptic Lebœuf must have been, could have felt that the unfortunate Lieutenant Alphonse Tabouille exploited his bereavement; wore his grief upon his sleeve; and drew the attention of everyone with whom he spoke, to the fact that he had known instantly when his brother was killed; had, in a dream or night-vision, seen him die; had beheld the scene of his death as clearly as though he had been there present; and had, on waking, actually seen his brother himself, or rather the ghost, the spirit, the astral form of his dead brother.

At the hurried bivouac breakfast, he bore himself bravely and well, winning the admiration and respect of his brother officers, all of whom with the possible exception of the miserable Lebœuf, marvelled at this amazing example and conclusive proof of telepathic communication between twin souls; this power of love to conquer death. Even in so hazardous and anxious a position as was theirs, these war-hardened men had time to give a passing thought to the strangely interesting affair, and to note once more that this Tabouille was a remarkable man.

None, save again, perhaps, Lebœuf, entertained for one moment the unworthy thought that Alphonse Tabouille was enjoying the eminence to which his brother's death, or rather the manner of his knowledge of his brother's death, had raised him.

Getting up from the ammunition-box on which he was sitting and from the trestle table at which he had made a brief show of attempting to swallow food, he strode away with head erect and firm step, his face a mask of grief repressed, of courage triumphant over pain.

Evidently the news had spread throughout the little garrison. Doubtless Sergeant Glock, who had come up while Lebœuf and he had been talking, had heard them saying that Lieutenant André Tabouille was dead. He was sure there was sympathy in Adjutant

Besicker's glance as he passed him; and even in that of the iron-visaged Sergeant-Major Russki's voice as he spoke to him. And the tired men, as they glanced up when he passed, or turned toward him from *créneau* and embrasure, had a look of interest and concern.

Why, if one were fanciful, one might toy with the poetic thought that the very foe themselves remained silent out of respect, and refrained from attacking Fez el Bali. Silly and whimsical—but a pleasing fancy. . . .

The Commandant passed, and Lieutenant Alphonse Tabouille sprang smartly to attention and saluted. It was evident that he knew too. One could see it in his kindly eye and the expression of his strong but haggard face.

Lieutenant Alphonse Tabouille liked, admired and respected him the more for the fact that he said nothing. Silent sympathy. It always made the Chief's heart bleed afresh when he lost "one of the family," as he called his officers. Doubtless he refrained from speech for fear that the brave young soldier's lip might almost tremble. . . . Twins. . . .

Seating himself on a sandbag, Alphonse leant back against the wall and closed his heavy eyes in thought.

He was awakened by a headquarters' messenger who stolidly gave him the orders, the first of which was that Fez el Bali was to be evacuated in an hour's time.

Alphonse suppressed a groan.

"No further message signalled from Taffrant, I suppose?" he asked wearily, sadly, bravely, when the orderly had finished.

"From Taffrant, sir?" was the stolid reply. "Yes. One. Just now. But it was only from your brother enquiring whether you were safe."

RENCONTRE

"Rencontre", which means a meeting or encounter in French, is the story of a man who is bored with life in England (after spending most of the last seventeen years out of England), and who sees an advertisement in the "Agony" column of his local newspaper that seems to perfectly fit his qualifications. "Rencontre" was first published as the seventh, and last story in Part II, "Quaint", of Odd—But Even So *(1941).*

To my mind, England is one of the very finest countries in the world from which to depart. On the other hand, it is undoubtedly the finest country in the world to which to return. Fortunately, or unfortunately, I have not very often spent the Spring in England since the days of my youth; the joy of leaving London on a horrible February morning is only excelled by returning to it on a glorious June afternoon.

And this was a February morning of the basest sort; raw, damp, bitterly cold, gloomy and dreary beyond description; one of those days when the rain only ceases that it may give way to hail, sleet or snow; the sort of day of which it is written with knowledge and sympathy,

"And the blasted English drizzle wakes the fever in my bones," or words to that effect.

On this occasion, I had been in England too long; I had come back at the wrong time of year: and I was aware that nothing would become my life in my dear native land like the leaving of it.

And I was bored. I hate to admit it, for it is a shameful thing that any healthy, intelligent person should ever suffer from boredom. But I had seen every play worth seeing, and many that were not. I had been to all the concerts and almost had a surfeit of good music; I had been to all the picture galleries; and worst of all, I had read all the good new books; I had looked into all the interesting shops in the West End, and had entered all those that appealed to me. I had spent weary hours in my club, waiting and hoping to see a face that I knew, and I had even gone the length of scraping acquaintance with strangers.

Ugly as it is, I like that phrase "scraping acquaintance with strangers." It aptly describes the acute and rasping discomfort that I suffer when I first come in contact with new people with a view to cultivating social relationship. I have often been told that it is extremely foolish of me to feel like this toward all my fellows whom I have not the good fortune to know; that I should love my neighbour as myself; that I should turn outward, so to speak, and give freely of myself; and that the world is a mirror in which I shall see reflected the smile or the frown which adorns or mars my own countenance. Doubtless this is so, and my attitude is foolish.

But it is also foolish to stub your toe in the dark, to have influenza, or to have your pocket picked. Who shall change his own nature, escape his temperament or avoid his destiny?

Anyhow, I make friends slowly, painfully almost, and certainly with considerable difficulty. But, I realize that when— in spite of myself, and in spite of my being what I am, and appearing to be what I am not—I really do make a friend—that man or woman is a friend.

I have a few friends of course. I have one somewhere in Morocco, one in Central Asia, one on a leper island not a thousand miles from Madagascar, one in Dartmoor Prison, and another one—a very good one—who is I know not where, but whom I last saw on a trim and discreet little craft of which the cargo might be described as indiscreet.

Great fun, gun-running, rum-running, gauntlet-running for dear life, and very dear cargo.

But at this moment there was no one in all England whom I could really call a friend, and the truth of the matter was, that in spite of my self-sufficiency and self-protective attitude, I was lonely, damned lonely.

It wasn't boredom, it wasn't that at all. It was utter loneliness in the midst of seven million people—my punishment for hating my neighbour as myself. Why, only the day before, in a well-known and fashionable West End bar, I had actually encouraged a "con" man to tell me his artless tale, and to work his incredibly childish trick on me.

It was drearily amusing too to lead him on until the *dénouement*—the mutual act of trust, the exchange of wallets—and then to show him a far better trick; to tell him I knew his face, I knew his name, but didn't know that anyone worked such a stale old line as that, nowadays. Then, having thus "scraped acquaintance," I stood him a drink and kept him in further conversation awhile, endeavouring to impress upon him that he ought to be most heartily ashamed of himself—not for being a professional confidence-trickster of course, but for doing it so badly. And while I favoured him with my opinion that what is worth doing, is worth doing well, he returned evil for good by picking my pocket.

Taking advantage of the entrance of a trio of prosperous-looking sportsmen, I recovered my gold cigarette case and took his silver one. While he turned to do some more scraping of acquaintance, I scribbled on the back of one of my cards, "Very clumsy. You're only fit to earn an honest living," put it in his cigarette case and returned it to his pocket.

And that had whiled away only half an hour of a weary day.

Curiously enough, I have never felt lonely when really alone; never lonely in the desert for example; never when prospecting in the Andes; never when canoeing up a tropical river; and least of all when I had a tiny tropical island all to myself. I suppose one explanation of my present need for human contacts lies in the fact that, for the first time in many years, I had nothing to do; that life, until I had foolishly come to England for this holiday, had been far too full of various forms of activity and occupation for there to be either cause or time for complaint, whether on the score of loneliness or anything else.

Why, even when I was aboard my little ship and did not speak once in a week except to give a terse order to one of my small crew of hand-picked toughs, and did not, for months on end, have a friend with whom I could talk, I did not feel lonely. No. Not in the slightest degree lonely, although my second-in-command, my engineer, and my gang of nautical thugs were no more human and companionable to me than the flying fish which skimmed over the opal sea—for there was plenty of occupation in navigating, managing and defending a little ship "wanted" by the customs officers, coastguards and police of several countries at once.

Yes, undoubtedly, I was suffering from just a trifle of loneliness, and a good deal from lack of occupation, and I was fully prepared to subscribe to the dictum of Samuel Smiles, Dr. Watts or some other noble soul, to the effect that "Nothing is so difficult to do as nothing."

§2

So that the advertisement that caught my eye that morning in the Agony Column of my paper made instant and strong appeal to my restless mind.

I always study the Agony Column of my daily paper, and amusingly occupy myself in imagining the stories that lie behind those queer cryptic messages; in trying to fathom the depths of human gullibility displayed by some of the advertisers and by some of those that appeal for money; and marvelling at the eternal optimism of the utterly unqualified persons who offer themselves for any and every form of employment requiring qualifications of a high order.

On that particular morning, as I settled myself in the comfortable armchair between the cheerful coal fire and the uncleared breakfast-table in the sitting-room of the quiet old-fashioned hotel that confers the cachet of its own impeccable respectability upon those who patronize it, I scanned first the column which is almost my favourite literature.

That enchanting, intriguing Agony Column, and its amazing habitués!

There they were—all on parade. There was the generous philanthropist who would lend me anything, from ten to ten thousand pounds on my note of hand alone, interest very moderate, almost negligible in fact and no security required. How did the poor chap contrive to live in such a greedy, grasping and wicked world?

There was the poor unfortunate lady with the beautiful mink coat, scarcely worn, that had cost eight hundred and fifty pounds, and for which she would take ninety-five—and I paused to wonder whether she had had it re-modelled to suit the changing fashions, for I remembered that the same coat had been for sale by the same lady, on the same terms when I was an innocent youth, earnestly seeking good opportunities of becoming less innocent.

There was the puzzling biblical text without context, which makes one wonder whether it contains "grape-vine" communications, crooks' information for crooks, a secret service message, or whether some pious would-be benefactor of the human race scatters selections from the Word as seed, in the hope that some will fall upon good ground, take root and bring forth fruit a hundredfold.

There was the poor chap out of employment, feeling frightened, and getting desperate, who wanted any job at any price, and was willing to go anywhere and do anything (legal) that the prospective employer might require.

There was one of those pathetic and not uncommon appeals for some erring son or husband to return home in the assurance that he would be forgiven. As, in this particular case the errant William Jennicks had been absent for thirty-two years, I could but feel the appeal was vain, and the forgiveness premature.

There were the usual offers of very special bargains, by pawnbrokers and other shopkeepers pretending to be private persons living at private addresses; the usual requests by the secretaries of hospitals and of well-known—and entirely unknown—Charitable Societies for subscriptions, and the familiar touting by "A Lady of Title," for the daughters of less exalted members of Society, who desired to breathe the rarefied air of the heights which the Lady of Title trod. . . .

And here, by Jove, was something new, and definitely interesting. The sort of pabulum I daily sought, in idly speculative mood.

I read it, and read it again.

Queer, naïf, and rather appealing:—

"Confidential Secretary Wanted. Willing to undertake wide range of other duties including travelling-companion, champion, bodyguard and friend. Complete reliability the great requirement. Ex-officer preferred. Experienced man of the

world, strong, active, courageous, resolute, tough and undauntable. Unimpeachable record and references essential. Excellent terms and conditions for right man. Applicants should be young, unmarried, and without family ties, but be prepared and free to occupy situation for any length of time. Post possibly not without danger. Application by letter only. Photograph essential, return not guaranteed."

Quite a little gem in its way. A museum piece in fact, and worthy of a prominent place in my collection of these curiosities.

Well, well, well! thought I, here's the reverse of the medal. The employer who wants the employee to go anywhere and do anything (legal). No mention of the legal, either. What about it, Nick Rufford? It might be quite amusing; and although the financial situation was for the moment comfortable, I was far too good a citizen of the World to have any objection to being well paid for any pleasures.

Let's have a look at the qualifications again, thought I.

Confidential? Certainly I could fill that part of the bill satisfactorily, for the uncommunicative oyster has nothing on me when it comes to reticence and to tenacity in keeping a secret. Yes, I could be more "confidential" than most people. And when I am paid for doing something, I do it. I like reliable people and I like to be reliable.

Secretary? Well I can read and write, and I felt no doubt as to my ability to deal with the average man's non-technical correspondence, and it sounded as though the actual secretarial duties were the least part of this job.

Travelling companion? As far as the travelling part of it was concerned, I had had a pretty wide experience of every kind of travel, varying from little ships and big ships, windjammers and the lordliest liners, to what poets and other people, who know nothing whatever about them, call "ships of the desert." I had travelled in at least five continents, seven seas, luxury trains, mule trains, and a slave-gang. And as for the companion part of the travelling, it would merely depend upon the kind of man the advertiser wanted. In that capacity, I should have suited Carlyle admirably, for few people can say less in more time than I can. If, on the other hand, he wanted someone to beguile him with bright conversation throughout the day, and sit by his bed and talk him to sleep at night, I can fill that bill too. For though I agree that silence is golden, and far prefer it to speech, I can, when put to it, talk the hind leg off a donkey, or wheedle the cockyolly bird from the twig of the tall green tree.

In point of fact, of course, both silence and speech are valuable in their proper place and time.

I suppose that living for some years among native tribes whose language I did not understand, and again with laconic toughs and thugs, as unsociable as they were unsocial, lessened any inclination I might ever have had in the direction of chattiness.

Anyhow, I wasn't going after the job, and if I were, it was as likely as not that by "companion," the man meant "a good listener." Those people do.

Bodyguard? There I could probably give satisfaction, unless the advertiser wanted what is known in America as a strong-arm-guy. I was not extraordinarily fond of pugilistic rough-housing nowadays, but I could still take care of myself, and of someone else as well at a pinch. There are ways and means, and I could still hope to give every satisfaction.

Champion? What on earth did he mean by that? Someone to stand up for him presumably, or did he want someone to act for him as his Champion does for the King? Champion his cause for him in some way, somewhere or other?

Perhaps he was up against someone or something, and simply needed what he said—a champion; someone to represent him, or to support his cause whatever that might be. It could hardly be a champion boxer, or something in that sense of the word.

Well, I've done a bit of championing in my time, and could do a bit more if I felt like it.

Friend? Depends on what you mean by "friend," thought I. As I have said, I am more than slow at making friends, and I don't much like the phrase. Friends aren't made. They're born, and one meets precious few of these born friends in a whole lifetime. As a rule when one meets with such a man, or woman, one knows it at once.

I don't mean that one becomes a fast friend in five minutes, but one knows that here is someone whose character and personality are congenial, acceptable and attractive.

Nevertheless, one can act as a friend, even in the case of people with whom it would be impossible to be a friend. And did I agree to be hired as a friend, I would be a friend in need.

Reliability? Yes. Full marks. For if there is one man on this earth whom I loathe, detest and despise, it is the untrustworthy, undependable creature, the cur who deserts an ally, a friend, or anyone who has good reason, or any reason, to trust him.

Whatever else an employer found me, he would find me loyal and reliable, for there would be no bribe big enough to induce me to forfeit that particular form of my self-respect. I could cheat, lie, forge, swindle or pick pockets, with less shame than I could deserve a reproach of disloyalty and unreliability to a trust I had accepted.

Ex-officer? That would be the snag if I were answering this intriguing advertisement, since British Army officer was presumably implied, and I have never held commissioned rank in our own army. I have been every other sort of an officer ashore and afloat, varying from captain of my own little ship, to captain of my own little squadron under Villa, the Mexican General bandit, revolutionary and *de facto* President.

Possibly a prospective employer might regard this as an even better qualification than having been a British Army officer, since I could navigate a little ship with good luck and Heaven's help, and both lead and control such a gang of desperadoes as were my merry Men of Mexico.

Probably qualifications which he had never dreamt of demanding or hoped to get—in his bodyguard, champion and friend, who was to go anywhere and do anything in this post that might not be without danger?

Experienced man of the world? Described me to the life. If I'm not that, I'm nothing. In fact if I'm not that, there is no such thing. Experienced man of a good many worlds too, including the Under-World which has always held for me a fatal attraction. Very nearly literally fatal, too, on more than one occasion.

There are nice little under-worlds in Paris, Berlin, Lisbon, Madrid, Marseilles—especially Marseilles—not to mention New York, Chicago, Mexico City and Buenos Aires. Also a very nice one in London. And I know them all.

Yes. One way and another I am quite a citizen of this dear old world, and very much at home in more than one of its many mansions.

Strong? Active? Courageous? So-so! Been pretty strong anyhow, still pretty active and not really timid. My years of rough living, prospecting for gold, years of army service, especially with the Mexican Cavalry, my intensive and prolonged course of physical culture, my travels with a circus when I was thinking of becoming a professional boxer, my hobo-ing and ranch-riding in the States; my sea experience in the little ship business had all helped in these directions. Moreover, I was born lucky, physically speaking, have never had any use for alcohol or tobacco, and always a strong preference for simple food and simple pleasures.

This undoubtedly makes me sound somewhat of a prig, but I can honestly claim a few redeeming vices, and although not a really vicious person, I frequently keep very bad company and almost as frequently find it very good company indeed and quite to my taste. And although I have my own standards, I am almost completely unhampered by moral scruples.

I have a violent temper, a dour vindictiveness against anyone who really annoys and thwarts me, a regrettable lack of religious feeling, and a deplorable tolerance of cheerful sinners. I suppose I acquired this laxity of outlook and intolerable toleration through so often associating perforce, and per preference, with the under-dog, and, by starting out to scratch for myself at the age of sixteen, since when I have lived by my wits, by my nerve, and made a pretty good living too, and, looking back, a marvellously varied one.

Anyhow, I am very free indeed from the good man's inhibitions.

Resolute? Tough and undauntable? The lad wanted plenty for his money, but I've certainly needed resolution and toughness now and again, nor was it for lack of the other thing that I rose from Trooper to Captain in Villa's bandit army, and turned an honest dollar running around against heavily armed coastguard patrol boats, and more heavily armed hi-jackers. Not to mention the gun-running, which is apt to be a very spirited pastime.

Unimpeachable record? That depends entirely upon the

point of view, thought I.

Some of it definitely impeachable before judges of the high courts of justice in a few countries. And yet I could lay my hand upon my heart, and honestly say I had done nothing of which I was ashamed—but that again might not be a testimonial to virtue.

Anyway, I could truthfully say that I had an unimpeachable record for keeping my end up, and depressing that of mine enemy—and I rather gathered that that might be the sort of thing the advertiser wanted.

If he were looking for the wearer of the white flower of a blameless life, I was not interested. Nor was he likely to get the sort of merchant prepared to go anywhere and do anything on a job not without danger, in the role of bodyguard.

Personally I have never met pale Galahads in that line of business.

References . . . H'm . . . References. I could write myself a few of course, and could find one or two useful citizens to impersonate the alleged referees if necessary. It might be a bit difficult to find genuine ones, although they exist.

There's the Captain of the cattle-boat, who promoted me from fo'c'sle hand to bosun. He'd certainly give me a testimonial for my possession of the qualities approved in the Mate's Watch of a hell-ship.

There was the revolutionary Chinese general whose Chief of Staff I was. He would testify that to his unbounded surprise I never robbed nor swindled him, never attempted to double-cross him, and that when things went badly with him, didn't desert him.

There were the officers commanding various irregular units with which I had served, but their testimony was not available. Had it been, it would have borne little witness to my possession of the softer, gentler virtues.

No. I could think of no one to whom I could refer a prospective employer on the subject of my character and conduct.

Young. Not in the first flush of ingenuous youth perhaps. On the other hand, not completely decrepit. Easily pass for—forty, say. Call it thirty-nine, sounds much younger. Definitely young in health, strength, activity, and vigour, but feeling mentally as old as the hills since I lost Diana.

Unmarried and without family ties. Full marks. . . .

Any length of time. I was certainly prepared to go anywhere for the rest of my life, especially if the sun shone in that part of the world and it were not a place in which police had long memories, hard hearts, and incorruptible morals. A place to which I had never been before might suit me best.

Nor could I flatter myself that anyone, especially any woman, would even pretend to shed a tear on being informed—which was a highly improbable event—that I had embarked upon the most dangerous of enterprises.

And as for the possibility of the post being not without danger—well, well, a little danger is a dangerous thing, but life is full of it, what with traffic, insects and microbes.

Still, on the whole it was just as well that I was not under the painful necessity of applying for the post. What with its dangers and unimpeachable references and spotless records.

I sat and smoked my pipe, and pondered awhile and came to a conclusion.

Yes. It would be definitely amusing to answer the advertisement if only to find out what the game was. It would be something to do, and it might lead to something else to do, and possibly to someone attractive with whom to do it.

It would be rather wonderful if it led to one's meeting a chap of the bad-man-of-the-best-sort type, with whom I always get along very nicely. It wasn't likely, but it was possible, and I not only wanted, but rather needed a friend; by which of course I meant a friend, and not merely another acquaintance.

And the doings might be something quite amusing. It might mean a trip to East Africa and a spot of big game shooting or something of that sort. It might be a treasure hunt, one of those exciting little ventures in which you may get a broken neck, a poisoned arrow, a fatal fever, a sad, sad end from thirst and starvation, or a ten years' sentence in the calaboose of the country afflicted by your presence—anything except treasure, in fact.

It might be one of those interesting little jobs of exploration which take you into Thibet, New Guinea, The Grand Chaco, the upper reaches of the Amazon or some other green hell or the country romantically known as the Country of the Wild Wahs.

It might be another job of taking a consignment of guns and ammunition to the spot where they'd do most good to those who most needed them.

It might equally mean a search for the missing heir, the missing papers or the missing link.

Anyhow, I arose and went straight away to the silly little desk in the window, and on a sheet of the hotel notepaper made out my application for an appointment with the advertiser, appended a very brief and optimistic description of my qualifications, and stated that I had been out of England for so long that I could give no references of any value beyond my Club and my Bank.

Thereafter I pursued my uninteresting way, while waiting for better weather, better times and better things, and I had almost forgotten the Case of the Queer Advertisement, when one day, about a fortnight later, I received a letter asking me if I could call at the Audley Hotel, ask at the reception office for Lord X of suite 4, and come up and have a talk with him upon the subject of my application.

§3

The Audley Hotel—if you do not happen to know it— avoiding plush and gilt mirrors on the one hand and imitation marble and chromium fittings on the other, but remaining somewhat consciously faded and expensively shabby, caters for rich people, who, unostentatious and money-conscious, seem rather ashamed of their miserable state of wealth.

I should imagine that it is both the most expensive hotel in London, and the least pretentious, ornamental and publicity-seeking. Far from endeavouring to attract your favourable notice and obtain your patronage, it shuns every form and kind of advertisement, and seeks a privacy which more than justifies its claim to be a private hotel.

When brazenly entering its forbidding portals you present yourself at the window of the gloomy, quiet and apparently deserted reception-office, the perfect gentleman who suddenly materializes there, seems very surprised to see you. He cannot think why you have come, what you want, or who you can be. He does not know you, and obviously does not want to know you.

These were only impressions of course, but undoubtedly the gentleman's manner thawed, and became almost welcoming, when I said I had an appointment with Lord X of suite 4.

There are no bright-faced, bright-buttoned page-boys at the Audley Hotel, but this immaculate gentleman, arrayed as though about to grace a wedding, impressively attended me, by lift and corridor, to a door on which he knocked, and entering said,

"A gentleman to see you, Sir."

Seated in an armchair by the fire was an elderly man—apparently hale, hearty, and healthy.

Also his fine face was very familiar—though I had not seen it for seventeen years and more. We had then quarrelled violently. He was, in fact. . . . Good Lord! What a cosmic jest!

"H'm!" he said, rising and extending his hand. "Willing to join me in a search for yourself, eh? How are you?"

"Pretty fit, thank you. And you, Sir?"

"Oh, shoving along," replied my father. "No younger, you know."

BROKEN GLASS

"Broken Glass" is the previously unpublished story, attributed to Wren, of a man who encounters a mysterious woman on a train. The text has been taken from the photographs of a six page handwritten manuscript graciously provided by Bevis Clarke of Clearwater Books.[30] The provenance of the manuscript is unclear. Bevis Clarke purchased the manuscript "from somebody (not a book-dealer) who picked it up at a 2007 autograph auction. It was part of a batch of signed cards and other ephemera that came from the collection of somebody called Michael Cantor."[31] In a subsequent email, Bevis Clarke stated that the name might have been Michael or Maurice Clarke. The manuscript has several words and phrases that were hard to decipher and have been rendered as [xxx] in the following text.

"For Great Messing?"

"Yes, sir. Forward right along there please"

Reginald Farrer walked up Hoy Platform Victerloo. The train seemed of enormous length; he passed carriage after carriage without finding himself getting any nearer to the already puffing engine.

Suddenly he heard a raucous voice shout out: "All seats—seats please". There was a slamming of doors; bewildered porters rushed to and fro; some one waved a green flag up and down; there was an anxious cry of "Guard, Guard," and Reginald Farrer realised he would have to make an effort to open a carriage door and get in or miss his train and incidently an important engagment at Great Messing. Jumping over a discarded portmaneau and several other pieces of luggage strewn over the platform he leapt at the door of a First Classer and wrenching at the handle until he thought it would really break in his hands he managed to gain a seat as the train, with a blowing of many whistles, streamed slowly out of Victerloo.

---

[30] Clearwater Books, 213b Devonshire Road, Forest Hill, London SE23 3NJ. www.clearwaterbooks.co.uk

[31] email from Bevis Clarke, May 23, 2012.

Already out of breath and temper he was further annoyed by the fact that he plunged into a non-smoker whose sole occupant was the lovely figure of a woman sitting on the far corner seat.

She was gazing out of the window, disconsolately, Farrer thought, as her back was turned towards him. He could not see her face and it was evident that she not taken the slightest notice of him or his sudden, hurried entrance. Surely she must have seen him struggling at the door-handle when the train was slowly steaming out of the station. But though she must have realised she was no longer alone in the compartment she ignored his presence and betrayed no curious feelings nor evinced any sort of interest towards this disturber of her peace.

Extraordinary woman; Reginald Farrer for being tall, good-looking, and well-built he usually commanded attention wherever he went, especially from those of the opposite sex.

Looking her closely up and down (for there is nothing so galling to a man than to be vouchsafed but the completest in difference from the object of one's sole attention) [xxx] Farrer realised that after all she had seen him jump in and probably knew more [xxx] himself than he did.

There was something in her studied indifference; in her calm but aggravating pose, the half-turned shoulder, the carelessly-set fur that hid her chin and neck from sight and the obviously drooping curve of her hat. That suggested to him this fact; that she had seen him and had purposely turned her back. One silk clad ankle with a neat suede shoe to match swayed provokingly up and down held his attention; she had ridiculously small feet. And then her hand; it was lying outstretched, fingers curled carelessly up, on her lap. She was expensively dressed and Reginald Farrer knew he was in the presence of a very clever and dangerously fascinating personality; she made him feel that.

He put his hat in the rack above his head and tossed an illustrated paper on to the opposite seat; then, he drew out his cigarette-case.

He had made up his mind that before long she would be speaking to him and he to her. But how was it to be done? He fidgetted in his seat, crossing and re-crossing his legs. She was still gazing out of her window but now, he caught sight of a delicate pointed chin. She was silently laughing at him—at his obvious impatience. He swore softly under his breath. He had not come into the carriage to be made a fool of and by an unknown woman too, hang it. He pulled at his window-strap and it was on the tip of his tongue to say—"Do you mind it up or down?" when he stopped himself just in time. That, was so pointed and he vowed to open fire subtly on the well trenched enemy.

"Will you forgive me smoking?" No, that was also an apparent remark and Reginald Farrer cursed himself and his lack of brains. Dash it all; what did he care if she was a pretty woman, he was thinking a few moments later; he was going to ignore her very existence and settle down to his illustrated paper.

But still she held his attention and at last he gave up all pretence of reading and merely looked at her instead.

She started to open a bag, still with her back half turned to him; there was the faint, elusive scent of mignonette in the air. She seemed to be trying to find something. Suddenly a small key dropped on to the dusty carriage floor. Quick as lightening she had bent down and picked it up. Reginald Farrer, already half across the carriage felt as though he had received a smack full on his face. Hardly had he recovered himself and regained his seat when they crashed into a tunnel. For one wild minute Farrer dared himself to go over and touch on the arm, the still silent figure of the distant corner-seat; holding his breath he half-rose . . . Then, as if sensing his intentions she moved in her seat. Reginald heard [xxx]; [xxx] a laugh, a low musical laugh strangely familiar to his ears, across the dark intervening space:

"Dreadful isn't it, this sudden plunge into night; but they never will turn on the electric light these days." Dumfounded he fell back on his seat and just managed to murmured an astonished assent before he gave himself up to fervent prayer:

"Oh, give us light" he whispered, but the railway authorities were not answering any prayers that day. He longed for daylight; surely he would see her face now and who she really was? The ice was broken at last and he had not committed himself in any way after all. But the journey through that tunnel seemed interminable, like a bad nightmare. Windows shook, doors rattled, and the whole train seemed to rush and roar into endless darkness for ever and ever.

At last it was getting lighter; he was beginning to make out the walls of the tunnel, the rails. He bent forward to catch the first possible glimpse of her face.

Now sunlight was streaming through the fog-smirched panes once more; they were free of the tunnel at last.

He caught sight of two dancing eyes, two vivid [xxx xxx xxx xxx xxx xxx xxx xxx xxx] laughing mouth, gleaming hair . . .

"Why on earth . . . oh my dear, but . . ."; there was a crash, the splinter and fall of glass and Reginald Farrer woke up.

Dazed and blinded by the glaring midday light he looked round; he was quite alone. On the floor was a small round object, presumably a stone. He stooped to pick it up, stopped, and then hurriedly looked across to the distant window-seat. It was empty. He continued to stare vacantly across mid the wreckage of broken glass.

Available P. C. Wren Titles
from
Riner Publishing Company

The Collected Short Stories

Volume One: ISBN 9780985032609
Volume Two: ISBN 9780985032616
Volume Three: ISBN 9780985032623
Volume Four: ISBN 9780985032630
Volume Five: ISBN 9780985032647

The Collected Novels

Volume One: *The Geste Novels*
    Part A: ISBN 9780985032678
    Part B: ISBN 9780985032685
Volume Two: *The Sinbad Novels*
    Part A: ISBN 9780692639382
    Part B: ISBN 9780692639429
Volume Three: *The Foreign Legion Novels*
    Part A: ISBN 9780999074909
    Part B: ISBN 9780999074916
Volume Four: *The Earlier India Novels*
    Part A: ISBN 9780999074923
    Part B: ISBN 9780999074930
Volume Five: *The Later India Novels*
    Part A: ISBN 9780999074947
    Part B: ISBN 9780999074954

Further information can be found at
rinerpublishing.wordpress.com

14 June 2019

Printed in Great Britain
by Amazon

26553862R00189